In the Dark

MAI JIA

PENGUIN BOOKS

PENGUIN BOOKS

UK | USA | Canada | Ireland | Australia
India | New Zealand | South Africa

Penguin Books is part of the Penguin Random House group of companies
whose addresses can be found at global.penguinrandomhouse.com.

First published in Mandarin 2003
This translation first published 2015
001

Set in 10.68/13.26 pt Minion Pro
Typeset by Jouve (UK), Milton Keynes
Printed in Great Britain by Clays Ltd, St Ives plc

A CIP catalogue record for this book is available from the British Library

ISBN: 978–0–141–39145–8

www.greenpenguin.co.uk

MIX
Paper from
responsible sources
FSC® C018179

Penguin Random House is committed to a
sustainable future for our business, our readers
and our planet. This book is made from Forest
Stewardship Council® certified paper.

Prelude

1.

Maybe one day you suddenly bump into an old friend that you have not seen for decades in the street, or maybe a total stranger suddenly becomes one of your very closest friends, and afterwards your life takes on a whole new direction, changing in unexpected ways. I reckon this is something that happens to everyone sooner or later. It happened to me. In fact, the origins of this book lie in just such an encounter.

2.

My encounter was kind of interesting.

This all happened twelve years ago. In those days I was a young man, not even thirty years of age, and I was doing a very ordinary job at my work unit, whereby when I went on business trips I didn't even get to fly. However, there was this one time when my boss went to Beijing to report to his senior managers. The report we had produced was nicely printed out and when my boss leafed through it he must have decided that I did not need to go in person. But then all of a sudden the senior managers changed their minds about what they wanted a report on and my boss started to panic; he demanded that I fly to Beijing immediately to produce a new report on the spot. That was how I got to fly for the first time in my life. Just as the poet says, 'Availing myself of the possibilities of space', I arrived in Beijing in less than two hours. My boss was only a junior manager so when he came to the airport to pick me up it was not just a matter of politeness; he also wanted me to 'hit the ground running'. However, having just made my way out of the airport and said hello to the boss, two policemen walked across and stood between us. They didn't ask any questions but demanded that I go with them. I asked why, and they said that I would find out when I went with them. They then started to drag me off. My wretched boss was in an even worse state than I was! He asked me what on earth was going on, but how was I to know? I was sure that them taking me away was some sort of mistake. The two policemen asked me my name, and I told them it was Mai Jia. My parents picked this name for me partly because they were not educated and partly out of humility; perhaps they were hoping that I would be a humble person. Mai Jia is a peasant's name, really ordinary and everyday.

To return to my story, when the policemen heard my name they announced that it was indeed me that they wanted. This might seem completely unreasonable but in fact was not so, because someone had pointed me out to them and told them to arrest me. From that point of view they had made no mistake. Actually there were two men who had instructed the police to pick me up, and they had been sitting in the same row as me on the aeroplane. Hearing their private conversation I had realized that they came from the same town as me, and I felt as though I had suddenly arrived back at my far-distant home. Having noticed their familiar accents I started chatting to them. I had no idea that this short conversation would bring disaster down upon me, would bring these two policemen into my life, and would see me being arrested like a criminal.

The police were part of the airport security team and I actually have no idea whether or not they did have the right to arrest me. At the time the issue of jurisdiction did not seem all that important; what was much more crucial was how I was going to get out of this! The policemen took my boss and me into their office. This consisted of an inner and an outer room. The outer office wasn't very big and when the four of us entered, it seemed even smaller. Once we had all sat down the policemen started questioning me: name, work unit, family, political persuasion, social position, and so on and so forth, as if all of a sudden I had become a suspect. Fortunately my boss was present and he kept reiterating that I was not some kind of criminal but a perfectly respectable Party cadre. As a result the interrogation really wasn't too bad.

After that the police changed tack and started to ask me about what I had observed on board the plane. I really had no idea what to say. This was the very first time in my life that I had been on a plane, and my observations had been so many and various, so complex and confused that I did not know where to start. When I asked them what kind of thing they meant, the two policemen started interrogating me with a particular aim in mind; in fact the whole thing boiled down to a single question: What had I heard of the private conversation between the two men from my home town? Just at that moment I realized that the two men I had sat next to were no ordinary passengers and my current predicament had come about because I had overheard – or rather could understand – their discussion. They thought if they jabbered away in their thick regional dialect no one would understand a word they said, and so they had been discussing something secret as if there were no other people around them – in fact walls have ears and everything they said could have been noted down.

No wonder they were so worried.

No wonder this stray sheep had been rounded up.

To tell you the truth, I hadn't heard them say anything special. To begin with they had not been speaking in my regional dialect and I am not the kind of person who is driven to chat to passing strangers, besides which this was the first time I had ever been on a plane and I was really excited until I discovered that there was nothing special about it. Once the plane had actually taken off, I felt that there was nothing to it and just sat there, watching the television with the earphones on. It was only when I took the earphones off that I noticed they had switched to speaking in my regional dialect and once I had heard that, I felt like I had been joined by my family and immediately started chatting to them. I had absolutely no idea what they had been talking about before. I dare say this all sounded as though I was making it up, but I swear that I am telling the truth.

Actually, if you think about it, if I was up to something why would I have told them that we all came from the same place? And another thing, given that I was going to draw attention to myself in this way, why would I wait until they had been speaking for ages and then give myself away? Besides which, given that I introduced myself the moment that I noticed that they were speaking my dialect, is it likely that I would have heard anything important? Although there was no proof one way or the other, my assertion that I hadn't heard what they were talking about won the day. My patient explanations and my boss's praise resulted in the two policemen agreeing to let me go. However, they demanded that I swear that I would never tell anyone under any circumstances about what I had overheard, for it touched on issues of national security. Any failure to do so would have severe consequences. Of course I swore the oath, and that was the end of the matter.

3.

How could that be the end of the matter?

Over the next few days, these events kept twisting through my mind like a snake, to the point where I could feel the hairs on the back of my neck rising. I could not imagine who those two men could be to possess such amazing powers and secrets that I was not allowed to hear even one word of their conversation. I knew something about the world, but this was a facet that I had never come across before, and, truth be told, it was more than a little scary. When I left the policemen's office, the very first thing I did was to take the name cards that the two men had given me out of my pocket and tear them to bits; then I threw them in the bin. The first bin I found at the airport. Given that every bit of information printed on those name cards was wrong, you could say that they were rubbish right from the start. The reason I wanted to get rid of them so quickly was not just because it was pointless to keep them, but because I was hoping that by destroying them, I would also be preventing the two men from causing me any further trouble and the pair of them could go to hell! That was very important to me, because as an ordinary member of the public the last thing you want is to get into trouble with the authorities.

But I had a feeling that they would come and find me.

Sure enough, shortly after I got back from Beijing, they phoned me up (the address and telephone number that I had given them being perfectly genuine) and took turns in explaining themselves, asking about what had happened to me, apologizing and trying to cheer me up. They also very politely asked me if I would like to visit them. They said that their work unit was located not far from the county town, somewhere in the mountains. I had heard tell that there was a large work unit out in the valleys there, very mysterious, and that after they moved in no one from the town had ever been allowed to set foot in those mountains again and the original inhabitants had all been forced to move out. Given the circumstances, no one had a clue who these people could be. There were lots of stories though: some people said they were working on atomic weapons, some said it was a holiday residence for the members of the Central Committee of the CCP, some said the place belonged to the Ministry of National Security, and so on. If someone asks you to come and have a look at a top-secret work unit like that, most people would leap at the chance. However, since I was worried about the whole thing, there was no way that I was going to get involved lightly. It was because I had so many mental reservations that I kept stalling.

On the anniversary of the founding of the People's Republic of China, someone came to my house to find me and said that I was invited to dinner. I asked who it was, and the man said it was the director of his work unit. I asked again who that might be, and he said I would find out when I got there. Given that this was more or less what the police at the airport had said to me, I immediately realized that this must have something to do with the two mysterious men. When I got there, I found that I was right, but there were a number of other people present who also spoke my home dialect, some male and some female, some old and some young – about seven or eight in total. I discovered that this was a kind of reunion for people from my home town and that they had held such an event annually for the last five or six years, the only difference being that this time I had been invited along.

You could say that that was the origin of this book, and that afterwards one thing followed on smoothly from the next.

4.

This book tells the story of Special Unit 701.

Seven is a strange number; it seems to have a black aura about it. Black is not the most beautiful of colours, but it is certainly not vulgar. It can be serious, secretive, brutal, aggressive, independent, mysterious, even mystical. To my knowledge there are many countries in the world whose national security organizations are connected with the number seven; Britain's MI7 in the First World War, the seven main administrations of the Stasi in former East Germany, the seven intelligence agencies that advise the President of France, the seven directorates of the KGB in the former Soviet Union, the Japanese Unit 731, the United States Seventh Fleet, and so on. In China there was Special Unit 701, an intelligence-gathering organization modelled upon the seven directorates of the KGB, which was 'special' both in terms of its organization and its remit. In particular, it had three main divisions:

Intercepts
Cryptography
Covert Operations

The intercepts division was primarily responsible for detecting enemy communications, the cryptography division was in charge of decrypting ciphers, while the covert operations division was of course about undertaking operations in the field – that is, going out and spying upon people. Interception involves listening to unearthly sounds, to noiseless sounds, to secret sounds. Cryptography involves cracking codes, whereby you have to read runes and understand hieroglyphs. In covert operations you set off in disguise to venture into the tiger's den, standing firm against the storm. Within the unit, everyone called the people working on intercepts 'Wind Listeners', while those working in cryptography were called 'Wind Readers', and the spies were called 'Wind Catchers'. When you get right down to it, people who work in intelligence have to have a sense for which way the wind is blowing; it is just that the different divisions go about it in a different way.

Of the two mysterious men from my old home town, one was then the head of Unit 701, and his surname was Qian. To his face people called him Director Qian, but behind his back he was known as the Big Boss. The other man was a very experienced spy from the covert operations division, a man named Lü, who many years before had been part of the Communist Party underground in Nanjing. People called him 'Old Potato', meaning that he had been in the underground. Both had joined the Revolution before the Liberation, and with the passing of the years they were now the only ones of their generation left in Unit 701. Later on I got to know both of these men well, to the point where gradually I was able to become a special visitor to the Unit, and was allowed to wander round the mountain.

It was called Five Fingers Mountain, and from the name you can imagine how it was shaped – like the five fingers of a hand standing up from the plain. In between the peaks there were four valleys. The first valley was the nearest to the county seat, which was maybe only two or three kilometres from the mountain. There was a little village here, the houses clustered along the mountainside. Given that this valley was the broadest, the housing compounds for Unit 701 had been constructed here, together with a hospital, school, shops, restaurants, guest house, playing field and so on. It was a complete little community, and although getting to meet the people there was a bit more complicated than usual, it was not that difficult to be able to come and go. Later on, when I was writing this book, I came to visit quite regularly and would stay at the guest house for days at a time. After a few such visits lots of people recognized me and since I always wore sunglasses (since the age of twenty-three, thanks to a condition that makes my right eye unusually sensitive to sunlight, I have always worn sunglasses when I am out of doors), everyone called me Specs.

The remaining three mountain valleys were much narrower and the difficulties of getting in increased the further you went. I was lucky enough to be able to visit the second valley three times and the third valley twice. The fourth and furthest valley I was never allowed to set foot in. My understanding is that this valley is where the cryptography unit was situated and that was the most security-sensitive area in the whole mountain. The covert operations division was based on the right-hand side of the second valley, with the training centre on the left; the bosses of both work units held the rank of deputy bureau chief. These two work units spread across the valley like a pair of wings, but the left-hand side was clearly much bigger than the right. Usually there were not many people from the covert operations division in residence, since they were all out in the field.

There were also two work units in the second valley: one was the intercepts division and the other the head office of Unit 701. The layout of these two work units was different from that of the covert operations division and the training centre, which had been built face-to-face, in that they had been built in a row – the head office of Unit 701 came first, then the intercepts division. The two work units shared the space between them, where they had put in a soccer pitch, a dining hall, a little clinic and so on.

Since no one now lived on the mountain, it had been left untouched by humans for so many years that the trees were completely overgrown and birds and animals lived there undisturbed. When driving on the single road leading through the valleys it was not uncommon to see birds flying about or animals walking across before they vanished into the wilderness. The road that wound its way through the mountain had a nice tarmacked surface, but it was very narrow with many hairpin bends, really testing the skills of the driver. I was told that there was a tunnel cut right through the mountain, to allow people to get from one work unit to another at top speed. The second time I visited the intercepts division, I asked Director Qian if it would be possible for me to see the tunnel. The old man glared at me and ignored what I had said, as if it were a completely unreasonable request.

Perhaps it was.

To tell you the truth, in my dealings with people at Unit 701, including the Director, I could clearly sense that their attitude to me was somewhat complex: they appeared to be worried about having anything to do with me, but in actual fact they were hoping that I would talk to them. If they had really been too scared to get involved, how could this book ever have been written? It would have been impossible.

Thank God for that hope.

And of course, thank God for the annual 'Declassification Day', that very special occasion.

5

I can tell you that being a special unit, the unique features of Unit 701 were everywhere to be seen, but some of them you probably cannot imagine. One example of this was the annual special day that everyone who worked there called Declassification Day.

The people who worked for Unit 701 placed national security above all other considerations, and the strict secrecy that their profession demanded resulted in them losing even the most basic of personal freedoms: they did not even have the right to send mail. It was only after being thoroughly investigated that a decision would be made as to whether the letter should be delivered to the intended recipient. If you wrote a letter to them, whether or not the person you posted it to would be able to read it would depend entirely on what you had written; if it aroused the slightest suspicion, there was no chance of them being able to look at it. Even if they were lucky enough to be able to get the letter, they would only be allowed to read it once, after that it would be returned to the archives, for the individual concerned had no right to keep it. If you go back twenty years, supposing that you were so fortunate as to receive a letter from one of them (and that possibility was very remote unless you were a close relative) you might have wondered why the letter was always a carbon copy. The fact is that there was nothing to be surprised at in this, because the original of any letter that they sent would have to go to the Party. In the days before photocopying machines, the best way to make multiple copies was to use carbon paper. An even more unimaginable intrusion into their lives was that when they left the unit, they would have to hand over all written material, including such things as private diaries, to be kept by the archives department, until the day when their contents were no longer deemed to compromise national security, at which point they could go back to their original owner.

That day was their Declassification Day.

That day, old secrets finally came out into the open.

Originally there had been no such thing: it started in 1994, three years after I first bumped into the two men from my old home town. That was the year that Director Qian finally retired, and I first got the idea of writing this book. As I am sure you understand, I wrote this book not because I got to know the two men from the plane, but because they held the first ever Declassification Day in the history of Unit 701. Because of that Declassification Day, I had the right to go to the mountain and walk round the valleys, seeing what there was to see. Thanks to Declassification Day people from Unit 701, or rather it would be more correct to say people who were no longer deemed to hold secrets vital to the nation's interests, were allowed to be interviewed by me.

You do not need to be told that without Declassification Day, this book could never have been written.

6.

Who I am isn't important; like I say, the people here all call me Specs. My name is Mai Jia, as I have already told you. I have also mentioned that it is a perfectly normal thing to bump into someone unexpected or to have some unusual experience. In my opinion some of these encounters are a regular part of life, an experience that adds a bit of spice to things; they do not change your life in any meaningful way. Some encounters on the other hand change you root and branch. I am sad to say that my meeting with the two men from my home town belongs to the second kind, and changed me enormously. Writing has now become my greatest pleasure. I am proud of my work but I also suffer for it; writing is everything to me. I don't think this is a good thing, but there is nothing that I can do about it. That is my fate and I cannot change it.

As for this book, I really think that it is not at all bad. Mystery, suspense, sex, unfamiliarity; it describes classic emotions in a contemporary context. You also get to feel something of the bitterness and helplessness that these people felt in the face of their destiny. My only regret is that Director Qian, the biggest supporter of my writing project, died before it went to press. His death made me realize how insubstantial life can be: just like love, it is here today and gone tomorrow. Once it is gone, it is gone – life becomes death, love becomes hatred, the things that you have are the things that you will lose. It is my greatest wish that the publication of this book should allow his soul to rest in peace.

This book is dedicated to Director Qian and all the other members of Unit 701.

Wind Listeners

Thanks to the special permit I received from the Director, not only was I received with courtesy and politeness on my secret mission, but I enjoyed unprecedented support and everybody looked at me with new eyes. Only one thing escaped me and that was ordinary, everyday luck. I may have had a special permit, but that didn't make me lucky.

Blind Abing

I first learnt of Abing's story from Director Qian. It was the first story, in fact, that I ever heard about Unit 701. When I was told the tale, Qian was still the man in charge; still in the service; still a 'man in the know'. He actually related the story to me before official declassification, and even now it is still classified. According to conventional practice, declassification of Unit 701 documents normally takes place about ten years after the agents in question have officially retired. If I were to calculate according to this practice, the story I am about to tell you would probably have to wait until next year before finally coming to light. As a result, I do not know all of the specific details. I must therefore be very careful not to speculate about what happened and most definitely not to engage in flights of fancy. This hasn't got anything to do with being brave or cowardly of course; it's just common sense, really. Those who make mistakes in the face of common sense aren't brave, they're just stupid.

Well, how is it then that Director Qian dared to tell me this very story about Abing before it was declassified? I've thought about that for quite some time. Probably it was because he knew that official declassification was imminent and that Abing's files would be amongst the first batch of released documents (which has turned out to be true). You could perhaps say that Director Qian possessed a certain boldness, a certain foresight. He was audacious. Since at that time he was in charge of everyone else at Unit 701, it is natural that he would usually be the first to know what was going on. But to my mind, this wasn't the main reason for him to tell me this story in advance. To be honest with you, there is perhaps no concrete reason for him to have told me, only possible ones. First, he was the primary person involved in it, the sole authority. Secondly, I suspect that he had misgivings about his

In the Dark

future. When we spoke, he seemed overly preoccupied with the very real possibility that in the very near future, on any given day, he might find himself summarily dismissed from his post. I guess he thought that telling me in advance was his best option. Later, as he expected, he was indeed retired with very little advance notice. On that night then, it must have seemed to be best to telephone me, to speak of the past; perhaps he felt that to sleep would mean to never wake up. I shall relate to you the story that he told me, serving as his medium, as it were; his voice.

What follows is the old man's verbal record . . .

1.

My long-dead parents, my wife, my three daughters and my son-in-law knew nothing of my life as an operative of Unit 701. It was my secret. But first and foremost, it was a national secret. Of course, every country has its secrets, its clandestine organizations, classified weaponry, covert agents, secret . . . there is really no end to the numbers of secrets kept by a nation. It's hard to imagine a country with no secrets. I wonder what such a nation would be like. But perhaps that's just fantasy; such a country cannot exist, just like an iceberg would cease to be without its hidden mass lurking beneath the waves. Indeed, how can things exist independently of what is concealed beneath the surface? Sometimes I think that such secrets are terribly unfair, especially to those closest to the person keeping them. But if things weren't like this, quite possibly the country I call home would have long since disappeared, or at least be under threat. You just have to let this unfairness continue to be unfair.

But having secrets does not mean one is some kind of criminal. Throughout the whole of my secretive life, I've never done anything I am ashamed of. You know my position: I wasn't part of some frightening organization, I was part of a very important information-gathering agency, tasked with listening to the airwaves and decrypting ciphers. This type of agency exists in every country's armed forces; so we can perhaps say that the existence of all these secrets is, in fact, an open secret. The real secrets are those surrounding the location of these agencies, the operatives who staff them, their methods, their frustrations and results – these types of things are what I would not tell you even if you beat me to death. These are the things that are more important than my life.

In Unit 701, people like Abing who intercepted communications across the airwaves are called 'Wind Listeners'. Their ears put food on their plates; they serve as their weapons and their rice bowls; they are also the source of their stories. It goes without saying that to engage in the surveillance profession Unit 701 requires persons of singular auditory abilities. They must be able to hear that which the rest of us cannot, as well as distinguish between minute auditory inflections that pass beyond the notice of common folk. This is why most people hail them as having 'preternaturally good hearing'. Such ears are said to go with the wind. Wherever the wind blows, their ears follow; there is nothing they do not hear, nothing they are unaware of. However, in that one year, in that single moment, all of us Wind Listeners were rendered silent by our enemies, for we all went completely deaf.

This is how it happened. In the spring of that year, the military chatter of X Country that we were responsible for monitoring simply stopped broadcasting for a total of fifty-two hours. Across its entire broadcast range, every radio station, without exception, went silent. In the history of covert radio communications there had been no record of anything like this happening before. If you were to say that this silence came about because of a tactical military need, then this would have to be considered an unprecedented strategy. To tell you the truth, it would be no strategy at all, it would be madness. Think about it: in those fifty-two hours, how many world-altering events could have occurred? In truth, anything could have happened! Our enemy's actions were downright insane.

Yet, despite their lunacy, they were victorious. Over the course of those fifty-two hours, nothing at all happened. That was their first triumph. You could say that was a piece of luck. As for their second victory, it was the amount of energy we expended in trying to find them; they forced us to work incredibly hard. During those fifty-two hours our enemy was able to change everything – their equipment, radio stations, radio times, call signals, all of it. What does this mean? It means that over the course of those fifty-two hours, all of the listening we had carried out for the previous ten years, all the sweat and toil, the accumulated intelligence, the experience, the tricks of the trade we had learnt, the techniques, everything, was wiped clean: we were back to zero. That was how they left us far behind them. In that moment, all of our agents, our technology, our equipment, the whole lot, was useless. In the language of the trade, Unit 701 had been blinded.

Thinking back: in those chaotic years when war could have broken out at any moment, it was completely terrifying.

2.

News of the situation soon reached the upper levels of command, which resulted in a terse response: we do not relish the prospect of war, but we like being beaten by the enemy even less.

The meaning was plain: this situation had to be remedied, and fast.

Yet it would be impossible for Unit 701 to overcome this situation in a short period of time. Perhaps with a view to setting up a future scapegoat, headquarters hastily promoted a former lower-level agent to handle the operation. Of course, this entailed a huge amount of risk, and the amount of intelligence that could be gathered in this way was strictly limited, so it could only be an interim solution. We needed to fix things, but except for getting our intercept agents to scour the airwaves for traces of the enemy stations, we had no other option. In our efforts to quickly identify the enemy frequencies we had lost, Unit 701 was temporarily transformed into a recruitment station with agents scurrying about in all directions, trying to find new talent. We were put under the direct command of Bureau Chief An Zaitian, with Radio Surveillance Chief Wu giving orders. Below these two men were seven other agents. I was the first of those seven, the assistant chief.

With the help of headquarters, we managed to get an additional twenty-eight agents from other branches of the intelligence service to assist in our task. We became a 'special operations group'. Every day, relentlessly, we combed the airwaves in search of the enemy broadcast stations. We redoubled our efforts, but our reward was not forthcoming. Our concern grew, but things only went from bad to worse. In our special operations group, in spite of all those agents being added to our regular staff and despite everyone being hard at work twenty-four hours a day, at the end of one week, all we had to show for our work was merely fleeting snippets of broken signals scattered across forty-five different frequencies.

You have to understand that military usage of the airwaves is entirely different from civilian use. Civilians do not change frequencies. The military, on the other hand, shift frequencies at least three times a day: once in the morning, once in the afternoon, and then once more at night; three days equals one cycle. This means that the lowest-density military broadcast station has nine sets of different frequencies (three frequencies times three days). Generally, these radio stations have anywhere from fifteen to twenty-one sets of frequencies, but certain special stations' cycles could be as long as a month, or even a year. Some do not even have cycles, meaning that they never use the same frequency twice.

To our certain knowledge the opposition had at least a hundred broadcast stations in active use. In other words, we needed to identify a hundred different stations before we could even begin to grasp the situation in the enemy's camp, and before we could accurately deploy strategic countermeasures. If one station on average had eighteen sets of frequencies, then $100 \times 18 = 1,800$ sets of radio frequencies. After one week, we had identified only forty-five frequencies, about 2.5 per cent of the total. At that rate, we would need an additional thirty-five weeks before we could identify all of the enemy frequencies: about nine months before we could implement a new systematic surveillance plan. The problem was that headquarters had given us only three months to complete the mission.

It was quite obvious that we were in dire straits.

Strangely, even though we worked in the same building – he was the officer in charge and I his immediate subordinate – we never really worked closely together, despite the fact that we should have. It was really odd. His name was Tie, Chief Director Tie. Of course we had met briefly once or twice; we had exchanged nods, looks of recognition. But the impression I took away from these encounters was that his position was much above mine. His physique was imposing. He was quite handsome, but emotionally detached. He had the face of a leader: stern; like a guerrilla fighter materializing out of the jungle. Almost everyone in Unit 701 feared him, wary that at any moment he would break the silence with an explosion. It was for this reason that he earned the nickname 'Landmine', meaning that he was someone you wanted to leave well alone. On that day, while I was on the telephone, he suddenly burst into my office. Without saying a word he was standing there in front of me. He grabbed the receiver from my hand and slammed it down. Then he cursed. 'I've been trying to call you for over half an hour, but the line has been busy. Tell me, what have you been nattering about? If it wasn't about work, I am going to fire you on the spot.'

Luckily Chief Wu was there to bear witness. I was indeed on the phone for work reasons, talking to other agents working on intercepts: nothing he could criticize me for. If I hadn't been, I would have been on my way out. It was quite clear that he had earned his nickname of 'Landmine'.

Once things had settled down, Director Tie criticized our efforts to recruit new talent. He felt that we were beating about the same old bushes. He believed that at best all we had accomplished was to enlist a number of high-quality intercept agents, and that was it. But Unit 701's surveillance division needed something more than this. At this juncture, we needed people of unusual abilities – prodigies, maybe even geniuses. The only advice he proffered was for us to break through the circle we had been trapped in and to strike out on a new path. He suggested we make our way into society, into the masses, to find that person of sublime listening talent.

The only problem was, where on earth were we to begin looking for such a person?

Whatever way you looked at it, searching for such a person was perhaps more difficult than identifying the enemy's radio stations.

The Director's unreasonable demand made many think that he had lost some of his marbles. But such was not the case. In fact, he already located such a person: a man by the name of Luo. This man had once been the specialist tuner for the instruments in the KMT's national orchestra and had even played piano for Madame Soong Mei-ling. She had so admired his ability that she gave him the name Luo 'Three Ears'. Before Liberation, the name Luo 'Three Ears' was inseparable from that of Madame Soong's in Nanjing. This even led some to gossip about a possible romance. After Liberation, he changed his name to Luo Shan and moved to Shanghai, taking up a position at the Shanghai Conservatoire. Before we headed out to meet this Luo Shan, Director Tie told us how to make contact with him. He also presented us with a personal summons for Luo, handwritten by a well-known Party cadre. Our orders were to contact him with all due haste and 'request' that he accompany us back to Unit 701.

As I had worked in Shanghai several years before, I was quite familiar with the city. Perhaps that is why Director Tie thrust this responsibility onto my shoulders.

Thanks to the special permit I had received from the Director, not only was I received with courtesy and politeness on my secret mission, but I enjoyed unprecedented support and everybody looked at me with new eyes. Only one thing escaped me, and that was ordinary, everyday luck. I may have had a special permit, but that didn't make me lucky. Barely a couple of weeks before I arrived in Shanghai, the man I was in search of, Luo Shan, or Luo 'Three Ears', had been thrown in jail. The bastard had gone and got the daughter of a prominent member of the Shanghai arts community pregnant.

I thought that if this was how it was, then perhaps my special pass could help in securing his release. Little did I know, however, that the web of misfortune poor old Luo 'Three Ears' had got caught up in would not so easily let him go. The problems of the past were now added to the problems of the present. His only solution, it seemed, was suicide. So the moment he got the opportunity he threw himself from the third storey of the prison.

Perhaps because he simply wasn't destined to die on this occasion he survived. However, he might as well have been dead. When I went to see him in hospital, except for his mouth which stuck out from between layers of bandage, he was a broken shell of a man. His legs were crushed, and from the fact that he was completely incontinent, I reckon that his spinal cord had been broken.

I sat by his bed for about half an hour and told him two things: the first thing was I could have changed his fate, but that now it was impossible because his shattered body was of little use to us – we simply didn't have the time to wait for him to recuperate. Then I asked him if he knew of anyone, anyone at all, with ears as good as his own.

He listened in silence to what I had to say. He did not move, he uttered no sound. He seemed much like a corpse. Then, just as I was about to take my leave, he suddenly called out to me: 'Director!', and proceeded to tell me the following:

'Crossing the Huangpu River, you'll see an oil refinery. Next to it there is a small tributary of the Huangpu. If you walk along this tributary for about five *li*, there is a small hamlet called Lujiayan. There you will find the person you are looking for.'

I asked what this person's name was, and if the person was male or female.

He told me the person in question was a boy, but he did not know his name. He explained, 'It doesn't matter, because once you get there, all you need do is ask any villager about this boy; everyone knows him.'

Bound by the undulating stream, compared to the city of Shanghai, Lujiayan seemed to be much older and yet fairly well-off. The buildings were two-storey, constructed with brick and mortar, and the roads were paved with greenish slate cobblestones. After arriving at the dock at a little past two in the afternoon, I made my way into the village. Before long I came upon a central well that looked very much like a dance stage. A crowd of women encircled it, washing clothes. I began to explain in a somewhat confused way what kind of person I was looking for, but before I had finished speaking two women seemed to know already who it was I wanted. One of them, a woman who seemed to be a little past middle age, spoke to me.

'The person you are looking for is called Abing. His ears can hear anything carried on the wind, they're exceptional . . . he can probably hear what we are saying now. At this time of day he will be in the ancestral hall. If you go there you will find him.'

As she spoke she gestured in the direction I should go. At first I thought she was pointing towards a nearby greyish structure, but I was wrong. She stretched her arm out again and spoke. 'Look! It's that one, the one with the two columns and the pedicab parked out front.'

The building she was speaking of was octagonal in shape and located at the end of the alley, about a hundred metres away. At that distance, how could anyone have heard what we were saying? Perhaps only the newest CR-60 radio from the US could have detected our conversation, and maybe not even that.

I couldn't help but feel this was all very strange.

The ancestral hall stood as the ancient symbol of the town. Its eaves were bedecked with carved dragons, phoenixes, lions and tigers. The town's forefathers had had the menagerie carved in an effort to beautify the hall; now they stood witness to the passage of time. The colours had become mottled and it was not hard to guess that they had lacked care for quite a while. But something of the building's former bearing and presence remained; time had not totally destroyed that. There were many idle people milling about – it was all a bit chaotic. The idlers were a collection of old men, a few women with children, and a number of cripples. It was plain to see that the ancestral hall had become the public square at which the townsfolk gathered and passed the time.

I hesitated in front of the entrance to the hall for a moment, and then went inside. There were two tables of people playing 'carriage-horse-cannon', a type of card game common in the south. There was also a table of people playing chess. Even though I was plainly dressed, and could speak pretty good Shanghainese, everyone stopped what they were doing to stare at me. I wandered about a bit and poked around, hoping that I would be able to guess which one of them was Abing. But none of them seemed right. A small child, perhaps eleven or twelve, his hand all bandaged up, discovered that I was wearing a wristwatch and proceeded to tail after me, trying to satisfy his curiosity and gain a closer look. In the end, I removed my watch, handed it to him and asked whether or not Abing was here. He replied that he was indeed here, that he had just stepped outside to the other hall, and that he would lead me there. 'What do you want Abing for?' he asked curiously.

'I've heard that his hearing is quite exceptional. Is this true?'

'You don't even know that? You can't be from around here, right?' Seeing me nod my head in answer to his question, he immediately warned me in a mysterious manner: 'Don't tell him that you are not from our village. Let's see if he can tell for himself by listening to you.' Laughing, he added, 'I reckon he can!'

Entering the other hall, the child scanned to the left, then to the right, and finally led me to stand in front of a young blind man. In a loud voice he shouted, 'Abing! Here, I want to test you: what family is this fellow from?'

The sightless lad had already noticed my arrival in front of him. Seated on an iron bench, grasping an old, rough bamboo cane, a foolish smile came upon his face; he looked to be not only blind but an imbecile as well. I never would have thought that Luo Shan would recommend such a person to me: a blind idiot. At that moment, however, upon hearing the child's challenge, as though he had been waiting ever so long for just such a challenge, he immediately hid away his foolish smile and his face took on a serious look. He seemed to be waiting for me to open my mouth. I really didn't know what to do: the whole situation took me aback.

'Speak! Come on, say something,' the child persisted.

'What should I say?'

'Whatever you want.'

I hesitated. Excitedly, the child urged me on, 'Speak! Say something!'

I felt uncomfortable. It seemed as though we were tormenting a poor blind child. Without thinking about it at all, in a very polite and vague tone of voice I said: 'Hello . . . Abing . . . I've heard that your listening ability is . . . rather unique, I'm here to . . .'

Before I had really even said anything, Abing began to shake his hands about wildly, claiming, 'Nope. He isn't from our village.' His voice seemed muffled, as though it emanated from a wooden chest.

To tell you the truth, it wasn't because of this incident that I realized that Abing's hearing ability was truly one of a kind. After all, Shanghainese isn't my native tongue, and even if the difference was not all that great, there was still a difference. I thought, if it were me, if I were to close my eyes, if I were to be like Abing, I would probably be able to make out different accents, however slight the variations might be. I am sure I could determine whether a person was from Shanghai or from somewhere else. This is really a simple matter, when you think about it. I began to wonder if this was all he was capable of. Just when my suspicions had reached a crescendo, the situation went from bad to worse. I had already discovered this particular child was rather mischievous, and now he decided to tease Abing, lying to him with a perfectly straight face.

'Ha ha, Abing, you're wrong, this fellow here is from our village!'

'Impossible . . .'

'How is it impossible? He's my uncle who works in Beijing.'

'Impossible!' Abing grew agitated and angry – as his anger grew he began to grind his teeth. In the end, much like a madman, he shouted out: 'Impossible! Absolutely impossible! You . . . you're a liar! A liar! A liar! You . . . you . . . everyone here is a liar! You're all bad! All of you! Liar! Liar! . . .'

As he cursed his face became increasingly ashen, sweat poured down his brow, his body began to convulse almost uncontrollably.

The bystanders to this scene began to gather round. An elderly man who looked as if he came from the big city attempted to console Abing, while a woman brandished her hands in imitation of chopping off the ears of the young rascal who had caused the ruckus in the first place. Her meaning was plain: apologize or else. The boy finally said he was sorry, though it was clear he was putting it on. Calm was restored and after much difficulty, Abing settled down.

To me, the whole situation seemed unreal – indeed, it was totally surreal. If I had first thought that Abing was a fool, it was now I who felt foolish. In the span of a few minutes, I had seen this young man turn from a child to a madman: laughable, pitiful, rude and fragile.

It all seemed very bizarre.

6.

At times the world is so small. The old man who looked as if he came from the city who had consoled Abing used to be part of the same work unit as Luo Shan. Some time ago he had retired and returned to his home village. It goes without saying that Luo Shan came to learn of Abing through him.

It was the old man who told me that Abing was a child of remarkable talents. He was born with learning difficulties, unable to walk until the age of three, and even at the age of five he couldn't utter a passable 'Mummy'. But it was also at the age of five that he developed a terrible fever that put him in a coma for three days and three nights. When the fever broke, he was able to speak, but he had gone blind. No matter what cure was tried, nothing worked. The strange thing was, that even though he couldn't see a thing, he seemed to be much more aware of his surroundings than any of the sighted villagers. When locusts ravaged the farmers' fields, he knew. When a thief stole into the village in the depths of the night, he knew. When someone's wife had an affair, he knew. And if someone's household had a secret underground cache, he knew. All this knowledge came to him by way of his ears. He seemed to now possess an extraordinary pair of lugs: they were able to pick up on anything. If something happened in the village, before anyone had actually seen it, he would know of it because of his ears. Some people said that his ears were carried on the wind, that all they needed was the wind, that even the smallest sound need only be there upon the wind for him to hear it. There were even some who said that every pore on his body was like an ear, that even if Abing's ears were to be thoroughly plugged, he would still be able to hear more than any ordinary person could. Abing's ears were extraordinary, and even though he had lost his sight and had only his ears to rely on, he could still discern everything that was going on.

The old man thought that with his ears being the way they were, Abing should become a professional tuner of musical instruments. For a time he had hoped that Luo Shan would take Abing on as his apprentice, to give him the means to make a living. But after coming to the village and seeing Abing (blind and dim-witted), he wouldn't agree to it, no matter how much Abing's mother begged, nor how many people from the village she enlisted to plead his cause. The old man couldn't help but feel that Luo Shan was a selfish, conceited fool, unable to see Abing's talent. When he learnt of Luo Shan's current predicament (I told him about it), he showed no pleasure in the man's misfortune, though he didn't express any sorrow or regret either.

As we were chatting, another man approached with a baby boy in his arms, wanting to 'test' Abing. The child was little more than a year old and couldn't yet speak; all he was able to do was parrot the sounds of those around him. From the look of them it was easy to see that they weren't from the village; they spoke in Mandarin Chinese, not the local dialect. The person who had brought the child placed him in front of Abing and urged him to call 'Uncle Abing'. Directing his attention to Abing, he asked if he could discern whose family the child belonged to. The child parroted the words 'Uncle Abing', grabbed his cane, and gurgled incomprehensibly as he played with it. At this moment, without the slightest hesitation, Abing spoke.

'This child is Lu Shuigen's third son Guanlin's baby; it's a boy. I remember, Guanlin left home nine years, two months and twelve days ago. He enlisted in the military in Fuzhou. He has returned to visit four times. The last was during the Dragon Boat festival, and he brought his wife along with him. I spoke with her a little, I remember; she's a northerner. This child's voice is like his mother's – very clear, and a little hard.'

Although there seemed to be a buzzing hum to his voice, the previous nervousness and stutter were absent. It felt like he was reciting something from memory, speaking mechanically. It was as though he knew all of these details by heart; they were simply waiting for him to open his mouth so that they could come out.

The old man explained that Lujiayan encompassed an area of several dozen kilometres, that it had over three hundred families, with a total of almost two thousand people. No one in the village could remember every detail about every person, except for Abing. It didn't matter if it was an adult or a child, if the person lived in the village or had moved away, all that mattered was that you were from this town, that your father lived, or had lived, here, and that you had spoken at least a few words to Abing for him to recognize which family you belonged to, to know who your parents were, how many brothers and sisters you had, who was the oldest and who the youngest, to know essentially your entire family history, the good and the bad; Abing was able to recite everything, no exceptions, and usually without error. The child had been born at a military base, and this had been the baby's first visit to Lujiayan, yet Abing could hear and recognize his whole family history.

I was completely stunned!

I thought that this blind and imbecile Abing was truly a freak of nature. He possessed amazing perspicacity and mnemonic abilities, and of course, that was exactly the kind of person I was looking for. Now I simply had to report back to base. But the village had no telephone. Left with little choice, that evening I quickly made my way back to the city in order to call the Bureau Chief and report on my mission concerning Luo Shan, and now Abing as well. The person that I had gone to collect was now out of the picture and the person I wanted to bring back instead was blind and stupid. The Bureau Chief hesitated a moment before passing the receiver onto the Director himself. After listening to my report, he said, 'As the proverb says, in every ten geniuses there are nine fools, and in every ten fools there is one genius. From what you say, perhaps this one is that genius. Bring him with you.'

7

Early the next morning I set off once again for Lujiayan. Thinking of the difficult passage I had made yesterday, and considering that today I would have a blind Abing in tow, I decided to rent a barge to make the round trip.

The barge was waiting for me at the dock.

This was the second time I entered the narrow, meandering streets of Lujiayan.

Not far from the ancestral hall there was a set of stairs winding up a gentle slope and opening out onto a covered courtyard with corridors leading off in different directions. There must have been about seven or eight different households living in the one building. The residents of the village told me that about thirty years ago a platoon of soldiers had arrived one evening and made camp within the courtyard. They arrived late and their departure was before dawn; no one knew from where these soldiers came. But everyone knew that one of them must have taken advantage of the local tailor's daughter. Nine months later, this poor woman gave birth to a child. Thirty years later, with the hum of a sewing machine echoing out from her door, Abing's mother greeted me. She was known to be the best seamstress in the village, and the most unlucky woman. Her entire life was spent taking care of a blind, dim-witted boy, sewing to make a living, never once enjoying a happy laugh. Her face showed the strains of her sorrow and helplessness. I saw a woman whose fate had tormented her night and day. She wasn't yet fifty years old, but she had the look of an old woman well past seventy. Relying on a trade passed on to her by her ancestors, mother and son did not want for food, but they had little else.

At first, Abing's mother thought that I was a customer in search of a seamstress, but once I said I had come for Abing, she immediately understood that I was not from the village. As every-one else in the town knew, since it was still morning, Abing would not be at home; the reason being his sensitive ears. Every night as the townsfolk drifted off into a quiet slumber, the sound of silence would torment Abing immensely, preventing him from sleeping. In order to find the rest he needed, each night he would make his way to the mulberry orchard at the edge of town; only there could he find the quiet he needed. He would normally return home in the early afternoon. The caretaker in charge of the mulberry orchard was Abing's mother's cousin. Each day he would give Abing wood from a mulberry tree to take home with him. The wood was important as it served as the fuel for Abing and his mother to cook their daily meals; it was the only thing that he did for her. But that day, in his haste to hurry back home and greet me, Abing had forgotten to bring along the wood. It wasn't until an hour later, with the two of us already having boarded the barge and set off for the city, that he remembered it. Turning back towards the docks he shouted as loud as he could: 'Mum, today, I forgot . . . I forgot to bring along the firewood. What . . . what can be done?'

Since the barge was still quite close to the dock, I had time to place 20 yuan in a cigarette pack and throw it towards the shore.

When I told him what I had done, Abing burst into tears and said, 'You're a good man.'

I realized then that Abing wasn't an idiot; he was just different from the rest of us.

To tell you the truth, as we set out on our journey that day, quite a few of the villagers saw us off – men and women, old and young. As the barge sailed further and further away, they were finally con-vinced that I hadn't misled them; that I had truly come to take Abing away with me (to educate him to be a musical instrument tuner, they believed). I think that they must have believed that either I was as daft as Abing was, or else I was an incredibly devi-ous and evil-minded person. In the countryside, many old people said that if you were to take the bones of an ill person and roast them and grind them into a powder, the medicine you could make from such a powder would cure that very illness. In other words, if you were to make medicine from Abing's bones, then whole groups of idiots like Abing could be transformed into intelligent men. Perhaps they thought that I was a man with that kind of wicked plan. If not, then I must be completely stupid.

Whatever the case, I felt that there was another possible outcome that the villagers could never have expected. Namely, that Abing would become one of the great heroes of our time.

8.

Even though Director Tie, as well as our Bureau Chief Wu, had already prepared themselves to some extent with respect to his physical and mental shortcomings, upon actually seeing Abing in front of them, they couldn't help but feel disappointed.

Our journey back to Unit 701 was rather arduous. As far as I could tell, Abing never once even closed his eyes; how could he possibly sleep in all that racket? The entire trip was a mess; and what's more, because he was somewhat on edge, Abing's facial muscles seemed to be suffering from some kind of paralysis. His appearance, coupled with the unappealing film that covered his eyes, was almost too unsightly to bear. He looked completely dishevelled and lost, a kind of freakish shadow.

Certainly not something easy on the eyes!

As far as I was concerned, the most worrying thing was that he might have lost his amazing ability to hear, especially now that he was far away from home. With these fears plaguing me on the journey back to Unit 701, I had repeatedly explained to Abing that as soon as we arrived – when we would meet the Chief Director – he had to be sure to show off his abilities. Afterwards, my instructions came back to bite me. Since Abing was certain that I was a good person, he followed my advice to the letter, making sure to 'show off his abilities'. The result was that it didn't matter who the person was, nor even whether or not they were actually speaking to him: he considered everything at this first meeting as a 'test'. It was impossible to have any kind of normal conversation, since he would immediately jump in.

'You're an old-timer, about sixty years old; it's possible that you've just drunk some alcohol . . .'

'You're a heavy smoker; your voice has been blackened by the smoke . . .'

'You're that old-timer that . . .'

'Oh, you're rather young, just thirty I imagine, but your tongue is rather short . . .'

'Oh, you've had voice training, your voice can fly like a kite . . .'

'Aha, you're that heavy smoker again . . .'

As he was speaking, suddenly the sound of two dogs barking echoed in the courtyard and Abing fell completely silent. He seemed to be concentrating all his efforts on listening to the sound. At the same time, his ears seemed to twitch. A moment later, he let out a foolish laugh and said, 'I dare say those two dogs outside are females. One of them is quite old, about seven or eight; the other is its offspring, perhaps not yet two.'

The two dogs were being looked after by the attendant at the guest house. This man happened to be standing next to the Director when Abing made his pronouncement. Naturally, the Director asked, 'Is he right?'

'Well, he's right and he's wrong,' the attendant answered. 'The older one is indeed the mother, but the younger one is a male.'

Abing's face flared red as he shouted with uncontrollable rage: 'Impossible! Absolutely impossible! You – you're a liar! You're – a wicked man, you're – mocking me, a blind man, you . . . What kind of person are you? You – you, you're evil, wicked . . .'

The same terrible scene that I had seen in Lujiayan once again played itself out.

I quickly tried to console him, and in an effort to calm him down, I pretended to reprimand the attendant. To resolve the situation, I suggested that we should all step outside and check for certain. As we walked outside, the attendant whispered to us: 'Ever since it was born, that dog has never been far from my sight. I think I'd know if it was male or female.' But as we entered the courtyard and looked at the two dogs, the attendant was dumbfounded. The younger dog that he had thought was there was nowhere to be seen. His older dog was there, all present and correct, but the other one was the dog belonging to the cafeteria staff. In any case, both of the young dogs were from the same litter – and this one was female.

In the Dark

Upon hearing the attendant's explanation, everyone was amazed.

Afterwards, the Director patted me on the shoulder and said, 'It seems that you have brought back a real treasure.' Turning round to look at Bureau Chief Wu, he issued his orders: 'Prepare food and lodgings for him as you would for any Party cadre, and get him a pair of sunglasses to wear. I'll be back in the evening.'

9.

That evening, Bureau Chief Wu personally escorted the Director and a load of other people to see Abing. The members of the delegation carried with them twenty record–replay devices as well as twenty different telegrams written in Morse code. They set up their equipment in the meeting room in preparation for the special testing of Abing's listening abilities. First, the test involved providing him with a particular signal and giving him a set amount of time to determine the signal's unique characteristics. Then they would randomly give him twenty different signals and see if he could correctly identify the signal he had first been given. This test might be the same as having twenty people sit in front of him, each of the same age and with the same accent – say about twenty years old, and all from the same area. First, it would be arranged for a John Doe to say a few words to Abing and then all twenty would speak, including the aforementioned John Doe. Abing's job would be to pick out of the line-up, as it were, the John Doe who had spoken to him.

Of course, if all of these people were Chinese and if they all spoke Mandarin then I would have absolute faith in Abing's ability to choose the right person. But the reality was far from this because the test involved using Morse code, something completely alien to Abing; he had perhaps never even heard of it. It would be the same as having twenty people speaking some unknown foreign language to him. Needless to say, this was an exceptionally hard test. You could even say, in fact, that the real test was more complicated than even my description, more abstruse, since a test involving a foreign language still meant people speaking to him, still meant listening to the way words came out of a person's mouth. Abing could manage such a test. It would have been the same with a dog. In the evenings in Lujiayan, Abing would sound the alarm whenever a thief attempted to steal into the village, because he could interpret the changes that occurred in the barking of the dogs. He was quite familiar with the sounds made by dogs. But radio signals were something beyond his understanding, something completely alien to him, something he perhaps had never even thought of before, certainly something he had never encountered. As a result, I was deeply pessimistic about Abing's prospects in this test. I thought it was pointless.

But Abing was something special!

Perhaps, if you were to speak of exceptional people, you would imagine that their daily lives are filled with extraordinary events, not the mundane humdrum things that most of us endure. However, we ordinary people still find it very difficult to comprehend how they can cope with these extraordinary things, just like poor people cannot comprehend the way that the rich can simply march in and buy expensive stuff. You get worried on their behalf, but all that this proves is that you and I are not, and never will be, men of exceptional talent or indeed of great wealth.

At any rate, even though the manner by which the exam was carried out was somewhat complicated, its result was clear: Abing was victorious. He didn't get only one right, and he didn't get three out of five right: he won every round. A perfect score in each of the ten tests that he was set. During the test, save for smoking one cigarette after another, it seemed that Abing relied on no special or mysterious tactic – he just plain won.

In truth, the test was quite demanding, but not impossible. You perhaps already know that Morse code is an international method used to transmit text by a series of dots and dashes. It doesn't matter whether it is an open transmission or a clandestine one, all the text is encrypted into code and each unit of code consists of four sets of Arabic numerals. Given that Abing was unfamiliar with such a coding system, for the first test they permitted him to listen to a string of ten characters, perhaps about thirty seconds' worth. This was in order for him to familiarize himself with the model. If during those thirty seconds he was unable to grasp the concept and distinguish its special characteristics, then it would have been impossible for him to take the actual test and listen to a whole string of codes. After he listened to the sample, our people set out to confuse him by playing eight different recordings one after the other, each with a different coded message; and again they only played a string of ten characters. When Abing had heard them, he shook his head first at one and then at the next. The ninth recording was the same as the sample he was given in the first place, just ten characters, but after the fourth, Abing stubbed out his cigarette and said: 'That's the one.'

He was quite right. That was the one.

Abing had won the first round.

The next rounds were done the same way as the first one – the tests were conducted according to the same principles, but the samples got shorter and shorter. So in the second round of tests, the sample was only nine characters, and one bit of code was taken off each time, so by the time he got to the tenth round, the sample consisted of only one character. Without any doubt the difficulty of telling the various messages apart increased massively as the sample got progressively shorter and the listening time decreased. But it didn't seem difficult to Abing; all the tests were equally easy. From the first test to the last, none of them caused him any trouble, nor did he make a single mistake. Not only did he make no mistake; right from the very first exam he did not need to listen right to the end to make his decision. The fastest was the fifth round of tests: he just listened to the first character and then he clapped his hands and shouted, 'Great! That's the one!'

Everyone who was there that night was amazed and delighted!

10

Everyone in Unit 701 was eager for victory.

Once Abing had demonstrated his unique auditory abilities, Bureau Chief Wu took the initiative and contacted the Director to propose that Abing be sent immediately to the radio-listening division to begin work. His proposal had everyone's full support. Towards the end of it, Bureau Chief Wu gave three particular reasons for putting Abing to work straight away:

1. Although Abing didn't truly understand Morse code, as the test demonstrated, in his case it didn't really matter: he could still identify the characters; he was remarkable. If we were to wait for him to actually understand Morse code, that really wouldn't be putting his exceptional talent to work.

2. In terms of the communication systems for our target country and military: no matter how they might change from time to time, they all had a certain number of shared characteristics as well as certain distinct features. At the moment, we had already identified more than fifty of the enemy's frequencies (over the previous few days, a pitiful couple of extra frequencies had been added), which essentially meant that we already had our sample for Abing to listen to. Although the sound of the frequencies that the enemy had switched to that we had not yet identified would not be exactly the same as the samples – indeed, for a normal person they would sound totally different – we ought to have faith in the ability of someone like Abing, who was able to distinguish accurately the parentage and sex of anonymous dogs by

     their barking, to listen through the dense web of airwaves and pick out those frequencies we needed to find.

3. As for Abing's lack of training with respect to using the equipment, that really wasn't an issue because we could easily assign him the most proficient technician we had to serve as his assistant, to operate the equipment whilst he listened. After all, it was Abing's ears that were remarkable, and it was his ears that we needed to use.

I was the only person who didn't support Bureau Chief Wu's proposal. What he and the others had said seemed very clear and logical, and nearly persuaded me to swallow my objections. However, because of my reservations, I still felt the need to explain the reasons for my opposition to the proposal. This is what I said:

'Perhaps I am somewhat more familiar with Abing, so I must ask, what kind of man is he? In all honesty, he is a quite exceptional person, as well as a freak. It is easy to see that he has certain talents, but he is also quite naïve, quite unaware of the larger world around him. I would say that his lack of common sense – his inability to function normally, you might say – shows itself most explicitly in terms of this naïveté. His understanding of the daily routines of life is rather simplistic, and yet those things he determines to be true and accurate must be so – they cannot change; he cannot be doubted. This shows that he has great confidence in his own point of view, in his ability to hear the world around him, but it also demonstrates his weakness – his inability to accept that at times he might be wrong. If such a situation were to occur, not only would we have to endure violent explosions, but there would also be no leeway to put forth opposing ideas. Concerning this point, Bureau Chief: you yourself experienced it first-hand earlier this afternoon, and I have had several days with him, so please understand my feelings on this subject. Abing's weakness and his talent are inseparable: he is much like a sparkling crystal bowl that must be handled with extreme caution, since a single careless strike would shatter it. This is my first reservation.

'Secondly, given Abing's performance in the test, we have ample reason to believe in his abilities; but immediately assigning him to work without proper preparation does not necessarily mean that his talents will simply take over and be on full display – it doesn't necessarily follow that such a gambit will bring us victory. There is a chance, perhaps a fairly good chance, that Abing will succeed; but I don't feel that putting all our eggs in one basket is a chance worth taking. If he suffers one defeat, given his character, quite possibly our defeat would be total. As everyone has already agreed, we cannot view Abing as a normal person. If he were normal and yet still had this exceptional ability, then for sure we could think of victory; we could easily overlook his lack of training and send him off to find the enemy's broadcast stations. If that worked, it would be great. If it didn't, then we could take some time and train him properly, and then put him back to work. The problem is, Abing isn't a normal person: we can't just put him to work; we can't just use him like this. Who's to say that if we did that he wouldn't develop some sort of psychological complex regarding this kind of spy work? Who's to say that later on, if he were to hear a radio broadcast, he wouldn't go into a rage like a madman? A talent such as this could in fact bring Unit 701 crashing down. Is there anyone who would dare to guarantee that if we put him to work immediately he will definitely succeed; that in a very short period of time he will identify all of the enemy's radio stations? Does anyone know how long his patience will last? One day? Two? Or perhaps only half a day? Or maybe even only an hour or two? So I want to say let's not be so hasty: let's give him time to be trained, let him understand the importance of the situation first, before we send him out onto the front lines . . .'

The lingering sounds of my voice hung in the air, waiting for a response from the Director. He stared at the people around him, stood up and made his way over towards me. He spoke in a measured voice. 'I've heard you, and so I give him to you. From this moment on, all of the personnel and facilities of Unit 701 are at your disposal; only make sure that his training works.'

'How much time will you give me?'

'How much do you need?'

I thought for a moment. 'Two weeks.'

The Director ground his teeth. 'I don't have that much time to give you. You have one week! After one week, I want to see him in front of the radio equipment, and I want you to ensure that he will succeed – no excuses!'

11

One week meant seven days.

Seven days meant 168 hours.

Subtracting the hours spent sleeping, how much time was left?

I knew that audio surveillance operatives received eight months of training. That meant over two thousand hours of specific instruction. That was what they needed in order to become operatives in the field.

A northerner by the name of Lin, a woman who had started as a switchboard operator in the central exchange, had, after a month on the job, committed to memory the voices of all the personnel working in Unit 701. In demonstrating this kind of skill, it soon became obvious that she would be ideal for the audio surveillance unit. That's what happened. She joined my class three months before we graduated. At the time, our instructors didn't believe that she could complete all of the training and finish with us at the same time, but upon graduation her scores stood out above the rest of us, especially her ability to transcribe Morse code (our most important skill). She could transcribe 224 characters per minute, double what the rest of us could do. A year later, during a national post and telecommunications competition, she transcribed over 261 characters of Morse code in a minute and earned the nickname 'Heavenly Warrior'.

The reason I mention this is that it should go without saying that one week is in no way sufficient time to properly train an audio surveillance agent, even considering the fact that Abing's preternatural abilities were perhaps ten times greater than that of Agent Lin. Nevertheless, one week was all I had and I couldn't ask for more; no one could. The only option available was for me to slap something together, to jury-rig a training programme that satisfied the essentials. There was certainly no way for me to transform him into a proper agent, but perhaps I could teach him the basics . . . Morse code; he had to be able to understand that at the very least. Secondly, he'd have to listen repeatedly to the enemy stations already identified, to familiarize himself with their unique characteristics and differences; the former he'd know by common sense, the latter by intuition. Nothing more could really be expected, and even this – well, seven days was pushing it.

One day passed.

Two days.

Three days.

On the evening of the fourth day, I went to the Bureau Chief's office to report on Abing's progress. I told him that Abing's level of proficiency, in all respects, could no longer be considered below that of Agent Lin. The Bureau Chief asked me to repeat what I had just told him. 'Seeing is believing,' I said. 'Why don't you bring Director Tie along to see for yourselves?'

Without wasting a minute, the Bureau Chief was on the telephone to report to Director Tie. He too could not believe what he had heard and asked for the Bureau Chief to repeat himself. The Bureau Chief's response was the same as mine: 'Seeing is believing. You'd better come and check this out for yourself.'

12

We were in the same conference room as before.

If anyone ever asks where Abing officially became a surveillance agent, the answer is in this ugly little room.

In order to avoid the possibility of Director Tie and Bureau Chief Wu being suspicious, I turned off all of the record–replay equipment and invited Bureau Chief Wu to draft at least eight strings of Morse code. Afterwards, I requested the equipment operator to use Bureau Chief Wu's text and broadcast at the rate of one hundred characters per minute.

'Dot-dot-dot, dot-dot-dot-dash-dash, dash-dot-dot, dot-dash . . .'

Once the broadcast was finished, we all turned our attention towards Abing: it looked as though he were asleep. His face was blank.

Bureau Chief Wu looked at me with a puzzled expression, and then looked back at Abing. The Director's lips opened and closed as though he wanted to say something, but I quickly gestured for him not to make a sound. At that instant, as if Abing were startled by the silence created by my hand gestures, he seemed to awaken from his dream, exhaled long and hard, and in a clear strong voice recited the set of codes he had just heard:

'X x x x, x x x x, x x x x . . .'

Eight strings of code.

Thirty-two characters in each.

Not a single string missing.

Not a single character wrong.

Exactly the same as the original!

In most cases, it's impossible to keep up writing by hand what one hears. As you transcribe, you have to make use of your memory to keep track of everything; this skill is called 'forced enumeration'. If two transcribers are competing with each other, the difference between the winner and loser depends upon who is more adept at this 'forced enumeration'. I remember that during the competition I spoke of before, Agent Lin managed to transcribe up to the sixth string of code. Right now, Abing was at the eighth. Given that the speed varied, it was impossible for the recording and the transcriber to be totally in unison, but what was easy to see was that Abing had mastered Morse code. As for the sample recordings of the fifty-plus enemy radio frequencies, he didn't need to listen to them over and over again; perhaps just once or twice, and he ought to be able to discern the hidden similarities and differences between all of them – it would be as plain as day for him. In short, even though just half of the time I had been given to train him had passed, Abing had already completed the entire audio surveillance training I had devised . . . and in style. Perfection, to the point where it all seemed unreal.

An hour later, I accompanied Abing into the institution's compound and proceeded towards the political offices. It was there that we arranged the ceremony for Abing to voluntarily swear the oath of allegiance and become an agent of Unit 701. The ceremony was formal and strict, but for Abing it was incomprehensible. Faced with a series of life-or-death requirements and compulsory duties, Abing thought he had rushed into a battlefield heavy with suffocating smoke. It was both exciting and frightening. At last, the official in charge of administering the oaths of allegiance asked Abing if he had any requests to be made of the organization. Solemnly, Abing made the following requests:

1. If he, from this moment on, were unable to return to his home town of Lujiayan, he hoped that the intelligence service would properly resolve his mother's problem concerning the procurement of her daily firewood.
2. If he were to die (in battle), absolutely no one should be permitted to remove his ears for research purposes.

No one knew whether to laugh or cry.

But since he was a voluntary agent of Unit 701, according to the regulations, the organization had to solemnly promise to honour his requests, and make an official record of them.

With the oath-swearing ceremony completed, the three official recordings of the proceedings were signed and marked by those in attendance. Given that Abing did not know how to write, he was instructed to leave his thumbprint, and I signed his name. I realized then that I hadn't yet asked him what his surname was. When I asked, he told me that he didn't have a family name.

'I'm called Abing,' Abing said. 'I haven't any other name.'

However, I knew that Abing couldn't be his real name. He was called it after a once-famous blind man whose tale was told in an *erhu* song entitled 'The Weeping Ballad', part of that famous piece *The Moon Mirrored in the Huiquan Pool*. Our 'Abing' was carrying on the name, as it were, but it couldn't really be a person's actual name.

It perhaps goes without saying that this is another time when we didn't know whether to laugh or cry. Finally, since his mother's surname was Lu, and he came from Lujiayan, we decided to give him the name 'Lu Jiabing'. It was this name that was recorded on the triplicate documents and filed away in the archives of Unit 701.

13.

The sun had just come out when I accompanied Abing in beyond the high walls that sheltered our divisional quarters. To the right and left were hung imposing signs, one large, the other a fraction smaller. Emblazoned upon them were the following:

Army Weapons Research Area No. X
Restricted Access: Authorized Personnel Only

Of course, these signs were only there to fool people.

To be honest, what really went on in this area was beyond what people could fathom. It couldn't consciously register with them, including those who came regularly to Unit 701, such as the guards, doctors, drivers and cooks. They couldn't grasp what we did in here, even if they tried. Every day was the same. It seemed that even time ceased to exist for this place; it was as though we were outside both time and space. Whosoever entered our division would forever find themselves enshrouded within a web of secrecy. They would become part of the nation, part of the People, but they would cease to exist as individuals.

What follows is somewhat vague, but please do not criticize me for this. Everything behind these walls – the buildings, plants, equipment, facilities; the birds in the sky and the insects crawling across the ground – I cannot tell you anything about them. That's because whatever words I use to describe this place will fall under the spotlight of the authorities; the words will be carefully studied, pored over, judged. That's to say, my words could betray me, they could conceivably bring punishment upon me. Although there is perhaps a certain appeal to revealing what I know, don't think that such an appeal will cause me to open my mouth. I've sworn an oath. And that's the only thing I believe in.

There were no sounds of gunfire.

No weapons' discharge hanging in the air.

Abing asked what kind of place this was.

I told him it was a smokeless battlefield . . .

Actually, the battlefield was a first-class structure, built with polished wooden floors and French windows. When you entered you had to remove your shoes since the listening equipment was incredibly expensive and extremely delicate. It was most important for us to be clean and spotless; otherwise we might track in unwanted dust. Once inside, I guided Abing to the sofa and had him sit. Seated to his right was our surveillance division's most accomplished equipment operator, a man by the name of Chen, who held the post of Section Chief. To Abing's left was a small table. On top stood a single cup of tea, one pack of cigarettes, a box of matches and an ashtray. I introduced Abing to Section Chief Chen and said, 'Abing, from now on, consider Section Chief Chen to be your hands. I hope that the two of you will work well together.'

As seemed appropriate in the circumstances, the Section Chief opened the pack of cigarettes, pulled one out, and handed it to Abing. Lighting it, he said how excited and pleased he was to be able to assist Abing in whatever he needed. Abing judged him there and then: Section Chief Chen was like me, a good man. You must understand, in terms of the development of Abing's talent, this was most important. If he didn't like the man now in front of him, Abing would be uncomfortable and out of sorts; he would be easily agitated, and if that happened, his immense abilities would desert him. I very much wanted to avoid such a situation, and I was especially frightened of the possibility that should his ability leave him he might never be able to get it back, just like the filament of a light bulb that once scorched can never light up again. Considering the unique nature of Abing's personality and character, I had to be prepared in advance for any unexpected eventuality. To tell you the truth, a remarkable talent such as Abing possessed is not easily put to use, and to see him now sitting happily in front of the radio equipment was the culmination of our hard work, as well as the result of a large measure of good fortune.

After the two of them had discussed things for a bit, Section Chief Chen began to dextrously twirl the knob of the listening device in his fingers, swivelling it around, whereupon from the depths of the airwaves dormant radio signals – public broadcasts, clamorous yelling, music – and static spewed forth. Abing sat upright on the sofa, the cigarette dangling from his mouth. He began to listen intently; his right forefinger and middle finger began to tap out the signals on the armrest of the sofa.

'Could you speed it up a bit? You're switching channels too slow.

'Still too slow: a little faster.

'A little faster.

'Faster . . .'

We simply couldn't obey his orders fast enough for him, and Abing seemed to be growing anxious. He stood up and asked if he could handle the radio himself. He turned the dials several times, finally settling on a precise number of revolutions per minute. He instructed Section Chief Chen to switch stations at this rate. Chen and I were both stupefied. The rate at which Abing wanted the channels to be switched was five times the normal speed. At this speed, neither I nor Chen could discern anything; the radio seemed to be uttering one long continuous 'dash' or 'dot'. At that speed, all the different sounds seemed to merge into an indeterminate whine. To use an inadequate analogy, imagine that you were attempting to identify a particular signal amongst the airwaves, similar to trying to find a single soundtrack on a recording. Because what you are looking for is mixed up amongst so many other things that everything seems to be more or less the same, naturally you would want to use a normal rate of speed to scan through the airwaves, and even then it might not be all that easy to find what you are looking for. But suppose that as you are scanning through the broadcast waves, someone asks you to increase the speed at which you are working. Of course, such an increase in speed would save time, but everything would blow by you in an instant; it'd all be a blur. How could you identify what you are looking for?

It would be impossible!

Section Chief Chen looked at me and seemed to be at a loss as to what to do.

I considered for a moment and then thought that since Abing had already grown somewhat agitated before, it was better to do as he said. After all, though it was impossible for us, maybe Abing could do it. So Section Chief Chen followed Abing's instructions. To my ears, it all sounded like indistinguishable static and I started to become nervous; it was impossible for me to sit still. But Abing sat quietly upon the sofa, still smoking his cigarette, listening in the same intense manner as before, his fingers tapping away on the armrest.

Ten minutes.

Twenty minutes.

Half an hour passed.

Abruptly, Abing shouted, 'Stop!' He then instructed Section Chief Chen to turn the dial back to the previous frequency; he wanted to listen to it one more time. 'Slower . . . yes, that's it, this one. Save this frequency, tune it a bit more . . .'

Section Chief Chen attempted to fine-tune the signal.

Abing listened for a moment and then began to nod his head. 'Unmistakable: it's this one.' He laughed and then said to me, 'This is more difficult than identifying broadcasts on my radio.'

Listening to the broadcast, it was hard for us to judge whether or not this was indeed one of the enemy frequencies we were looking for. For now, the best option was to transcribe what was being broadcast and have it decrypted. Afterwards we could decide if Abing had indeed identified an enemy frequency. Section Chief Chen took down a page and then handed it to me before continuing with his transcription. I hurried off to the cryptography division and had them set to work immediately decrypting the page. We had to be sure whether or not Abing had discovered one of the missing enemy frequencies. By the time I returned to Abing and Section Chief Chen, the cryptography division was calling us. I listened to their report, put down the receiver and rushed over to hug Abing. 'Abing, you're amazing!' I yelled.

Afterwards, I realized that tears were streaming down my face.

14

Every person of a certain age in my home town remembers that because the Japanese military encountered unexpected resistance in Nanjing that resulted in the deaths of quite a few of their soldiers, they unleashed a series of brutal revenge attacks and murders; what eventually became known as the Nanjing Massacre. Once they reached my home town, they were still in a rage and still hell-bent on revenge. They were determined to destroy the whole goddamn place, and so they slaughtered, looted and raped their way across the countryside, committing all manner of unspeakable evil. That said, my family was relatively fortunate, due in large part to my father's foresight: more than a year before the Nanjing Massacre, he had sent me, my mother and two sisters to Wuxi County in Jiangsu. The small village we lived in was on the banks of Lake Tai. Most of the villagers made a living by fishing in the lake, and my uncle was actually a fisherman of some renown. In the winter when the fish swam deeper and deeper into the depths of the lake, the fishermen usually returned to the village empty-handed, all except my uncle. Not once did he return with nothing. His bamboo basket would always be filled to overflowing with fish and other lake delicacies. His unique method for seemingly accomplishing the impossible was this: on the surface of the water he was able to discern in the mass of bubbles and foam which bubbles were produced by hibernating fish and which weren't. He would then launch his net, a net from which nothing could escape.

The way in which Abing was able to identify the enemy radio stations reminded me of my uncle: it gave me the same feeling. Like him, Abing was able to distinguish which bubbles were made by fish and which weren't, and what's more, he could see all of the different species of fish swimming about. He could tell whether they were carp, crucian carp, or what have you.

No doubt, compared to my uncle, Abing's skills were even greater.

As I've said, everyone in Unit 701 was eager for victory. But before Abing arrived, no one knew how victory could be achieved, and now they began to understand. On the first day, Abing sat in front of the radio equipment for eighteen hours. He smoked four packs of cigarettes, and identified three enemy radio stations and fifty-one frequencies. It worked out to about three frequencies per hour, more than the total Unit 701's other operatives were able to identify in ten days.

Abing's success caused incredible surprise, as well as disbelief.

As one can imagine, in the days that followed Abing continued in his own unique way to identify enemy broadcast stations. His most successful day was the eighteenth after he had begun his mission. On that day, he identified five stations and eighty-two frequencies. The strange thing was, after this most successful day, the number of frequencies Abing found grew less and less as the days passed until finally, on the twenty-fifth day, he identified none. The day that followed had the same outcome; his hard work seemed to be for nothing. In the afternoon of that day, Abing refused to enter the radio equipment room, believing that he had already completed his task.

Could this be true?

According to the progress chart that had been hung on the wall in our offices, it was clear to see that we had identified and catalogued eighty-six stations, using a total of 1,516 radio frequencies. Abing was responsible for identifying seventy-three of these stations, together with 1,309 frequencies, or about 87 per cent of the total. Whilst this seemed to be quite an accomplishment, according to our previous intelligence information, there were still twelve stations unaccounted for, and what's more, these were the enemy's stations dedicated to high-level military use.

These intelligence reports were unquestionable, and they demonstrated clearly that our job was not yet complete. But still we had total confidence and faith in Abing's abilities; we believed that he could finish his task. How could this seemingly contradictory situation be resolved? Faced with such a predicament, the Director convened a special meeting of Unit 701's operatives to go over the data. The conclusion reached was this: the enemy must possess a hitherto unidentified type of radio station that did not conform to any of the models we had already identified. This was the only explanation that fitted; the only reason that explained why Abing could not identify it.

The question that remained was: what kind of radio equipment was it?

Everyone was at a loss.

All we could do was adjourn the meeting.

15

On the following day, I didn't accompany Abing to the radio control room. Instead, I borrowed a car in order to take him for a ride, to clear his mind. I had intended to take him to a mulberry plantation, but I couldn't find one and so settled on a small fruit orchard. I cannot tell you what kind of orchard it was, since if I did, you might be able to work out the general location of Unit 701 – whether it was in the south or the north, the southeast or the northwest. At any rate, the orchard provided a pleasant respite from the confines of Unit 701. We enjoyed breathing in the fresh air, and having a relaxing chat. Abing was very much like a child, excited to be out and about. I, on the other hand, felt like a worried parent. Before we left the orchard, I told Abing the story of my uncle, the master fisherman. I embellished the ending somewhat, making it more like a fairy tale. Abing soaked it all up, believing every word to be true.

This is what I told him: 'One winter, my uncle went out to the lake as usual, but for days and days he couldn't spy any "fish bubbles" floating up to the surface. It was then that my uncle began to think that perhaps he had caught all of the big fish in Lake Tai. As a result, he began to stay at home, relying on the fish he had already caught to feed his family. But one day, whilst his grandson was out playing near the edge of the lake, the young boy witnessed whole schools of fish skimming back and forth in the shallows of the lake. This showed beyond a doubt that there were still lots of fish in the lake; it also showed that they were very crafty and cunning. They seemed to have realized that if they remained in the deep parts of the lake, my uncle would eventually net them all. So they left the deeps and swam towards the shallows near the shore. Although the shallows were terribly cold, there was still enough oxygen in the water for them to breathe, provided they didn't over-exert themselves. The benefit from this was plain: not exerting themselves meant they didn't produce bubbles. No bubbles meant my uncle couldn't find them.'

This was how I explained to Abing our predicament: I told him that there were at least twelve enemy stations that we had not yet identified. How could this be? The answer seemed clear. 'Like the schools of crafty fish, they are hiding.' Hiding somewhere we hadn't yet thought of. Where were they? Well, the only option was to proceed with our scouring of the airwaves, a difficult task to say the least. I asked Abing if he wanted to try.

He replied, 'Let's head back.'

That's to say, he wanted to try.

On the road home, I made sure to pass by a post office so that I could send a money-order for 100 yuan to Abing's mother. I told Abing that this wasn't my personal cash, but rather money belonging to Unit 701. Like me, they hoped that Abing would be able to quickly identify the remaining enemy frequencies. My telling him this had a particular purpose. I knew that Abing was a loving son and I knew he valued comradeship, so I knew it would make him give his all.

Once back in our mountain compound, I went to the archives and brought out eight large boxes of audio tapes – recordings made of the twelve missing radio stations before they went silent. I played them for Abing and told him, 'Right now, your task is to listen to these audio tapes, over and over if necessary, but always carefully. What are you listening for? Well, don't listen to how they broadcast – that is, don't try to identify the special qualities of the radio frequency. Instead, listen to *how the broadcasters "speak"*; listen to their "voices". I believe you should be able to make out how many people are actually "speaking", and therefore you should be able to discern their individual characteristics.'

I thought that since we had determined that the only possible reason why we hadn't been able to identify these twelve stations (at least twelve, perhaps more) was that they were using an entirely unknown radio model, then the only option left for us was to abandon our usual approach and attempt the unusual. If Abing was able to distinguish between the individual operators broadcasting on these stations, if he was able to identify their specific characteristics, then perhaps this could be a shortcut to finding them.

But that was easier said than done.

Of course, theoretically speaking, operators used their hands to control the equipment, not their voices. They each had their own unique accent, however, their own unique differences, even if in reality these differences were incredibly subtle and exceptionally difficult to discern. It is possible to say that there is no simpler language than Morse code as it is based entirely on 'dots' and 'dashes'. Because of this excessive simplicity, it is an exceedingly specialized language, meaning that all of its practitioners need to receive particular training in order to use it. Consequently, everyone who uses it follows a standard method, and since they all follow a standard method, naturally differences will be few and far between – indeed, most people would be unable to make out any differences at all. But they are there. Over the last five years, I've been able to make out one particular operator who has a distinctive habit in their otherwise smooth transmissions: whenever that person transmits five 'dots', there nearly always seems to be one additional 'dot'. But Morse code does not have a string of six 'dots'. You would think that perhaps this would hinder communication, but I guess that when people hear this specific transmission, they simply assume it to be five 'dots' and overlook the sixth. I didn't, and this is how I was able to identify and, let's say, come to know this particular operator. Whenever I hear the extra 'dot' added to the string of five, I know whom I am listening to.

However, such examples of operators not conforming precisely to the code are rare, and for high-level military communications such a person would have already been dismissed. So even though I mentioned this to Abing, in my heart I knew that asking someone to listen for and identify such minute and subtle characteristics of radio operators was not an easy job: indeed, you might as well ask someone to cut you down a moonbeam.

Nevertheless, Abing seemed to have decided to see things

through to the end. On the morning of the following day, I was woken by a telephone call from the guest-house attendant. He told me that Section Chief Chen requested my immediate presence. When I arrived in his office, Chen passed me several sheets of paper and said, 'Abing has already finished listening to the eight boxes of audio tapes (of course, it must have been in a cursory manner, but perhaps that was all he needed?). The results are there on those pages: see for yourself.'

As I scanned through the papers, Chen continued, 'It's almost unbelievable. In fact it's downright unbelievable. Abing! I dare say we shouldn't need more than a few days for him to finish identifying all of the remaining enemy stations!'

I could see the elation in Section Chief Chen's face and I shared it. Not only had Abing listened to all eight boxes of audio tapes and identified seventy-nine specific operators, but for each one he had recorded their specific 'calling card', as it were. For instance:

Operator one: When 3 and 7 crop up together, likes to join them up.

Operator two: When 5 and 4 come together, often makes a mistake, and this should be corrected.

Operator three: The first 'dot' is always quick and fast.

Operator four: A highly accomplished technique, very fluent.

Operator five: When signing off, this operator has a very distinct and eccentric habit; likes to transmit 'GB' as 'GP'.

And so on, and so forth.

In sum, Abing had identified for each of the seventy-nine different operators a distinguishing characteristic – a shortcoming, if you will – that we could exploit. While there was no way for the rest of us to actually verify if Abing's findings were true and correct, one thing we could be sure of was this: the number of operators identified, these seventy-nine different people, seemed about right. That's because in general, with each station broadcasting day and night, a total of six operators would be needed: three for the day shift, three for the night; $6 \times 12 = 72$. Taking into account that at certain times operators would go on leave and need to be replaced, a total number of seventy-nine operators seemed quite logical. Of course, Abing was unaware of this fact, so we could be sure that he wasn't just making a wild guess.

I turned to Abing and said, 'Let's go and get some breakfast – and after we've eaten, Abing, let's go and find those seventy-nine operators!'

I was deliberate in telling him that we were going to hunt down these 'operators' in order to stress to him that the work yet to be done was somewhat different from what he had already completed. Now he would be looking for the 'fingerprints' of the operators and not the 'tone' of the broadcast. Of course, distinguishing between the audio qualities of the broadcasts and differentiating the 'fingerprints' left by the operators were just different ways to achieve the same objective: identifying the enemy radio stations.

16.

Abing's initial success had already surprised and shocked everyone. His second was even more amazing. Identifying 'tonal variations' is one thing; listening for an operator's 'fingerprints' is something else entirely. Increasing the speed at which an operator controls the equipment doesn't really alter the tonal qualities: it still sounds the same. But 'fingerprints' – well, how could you even talk of 'fingerprints'? As a result, this time we would have to proceed slowly: carefully turning the dials, and listening intently. Abing, however, had other ideas: he requested that we bring in another set of radio equipment so that he might listen to two broadcasts simultaneously.

Two broadcasts at the same time just wouldn't work.

Three would be even worse!

And yet we brought in more equipment and more operators. Finally, when we reached six radios, Abing said, 'That's more like it.' He was now surrounded by radio equipment and technicians: the broadcasts and static flowed into one another and a cacophonous buzz encircled him. But he barely moved a muscle. He sat on the sofa quietly smoking away on his cigarettes, his ears listening in all directions, a calm, composed look upon his face. One minute after nine he suddenly stood up, turned round and spoke to the operator sitting behind him.

'You've found it! Did you hear? This person transmits "o" especially strong and hard. It's the thirty-third operator. Unmistakable. That's the one.'

The operator made a note of it.

He began to copy down the transmission. Although it was only the later bit, it would be enough for the cryptographers to pass judgement on it: without a doubt, this was a high-level enemy frequency.

Without verification from the cryptographers, however, no one would have been willing to believe that this could be one of the enemy stations we were searching for – it sounded much too antiquated. Anyone who listened to it would say that the equipment used for this broadcast was ancient, perhaps even from the previous century. That kind of machine had been phased out long ago; no country, not even the poorest, would still be using such outdated communications equipment. Who or what organization would possibly use it? Perhaps a ham radio enthusiast, perhaps some private organization from a desperately poor country – a deep sea salvage operator communicating with its home base onshore, for instance; or perhaps a fisheries processing plant, a forest protection group, a zoo out in the wilds, a travel agency – something of that nature. Most audio surveillance agents would therefore pay little attention to this type of broadcast before switching the dial. Now, though, it was exactly this type of station that was being used for high-level military communications: a truly crafty move whose purpose was clear – to paralyse their adversaries. It's like the thief who, intent on stealing your belongings, sidles up close to you while you look off into the distance for possible threats – you never see what's right next to you. It's a daring strategy, cunning and brave; devilish, you might say.

Still, such a devil was no match for Abing!

With their strategy broken, it was only a matter of time before we succeeded in identifying the remaining radio stations.

Three days later, all fifteen high-level covert enemy stations (we added three to the list) had been identified.

Ten days later, our enemy's entire covert communications system was known to us, in total one hundred and seventy stations, using 1,861 frequencies. All thanks to the tenacious efforts of Unit 701.

17

With unbelievable ease, Abing had resolved Unit 701's predicament and even relieved the immediate danger then facing the nation. In the span of a few months he had done more, and done better, than all of 701's operatives' achievements combined. Thus he ought to have received the reverence, love and respect due to him from Unit 701, as well as honour and decoration for his triumph. If it weren't for the fact that, by its very nature, the work carried out in Unit 701 was secretive, Abing would have become a household name, a national hero even – his abilities and achievements would have received praise and acclamation from all. But the work he did was and is secret. The only other people beside those of us working for Unit 701 who even knew of his existence were the residents of Lujiayan. But what does this matter, really? For Abing, there were only two concerns, and these outweighed everything else: the first was the daily procurement of firewood for his mother. This was something he never forgot. The second involved the power and prestige of his listening abilities; no one should, in any situation, ever doubt his abilities.

It should go without saying that these two problems weren't really problems any more.

After such a triumph, Abing's life was one of considerable comfort. Occasionally he would be asked by his fellow work unit members to assist in 'remedying a problem', but other than that, he passed his time as he wished. The organization provided him with his own personal attendant, a man who used to be the orderly for the Bureau Chief, who was responsible for ensuring that Abing was looked after. Every day after breakfast the orderly would bring him along to the towering walls surrounding the audio surveillance division, where the guard on duty would escort him into the compound. Once inside, his duties were light. Essentially, he would deal with severe problems only if they arose, which was not really that often. Most of his time was spent studying Braille and listening to the radio. But, to be honest, he didn't sit around too much in the office. In the afternoons he liked to go out into the communal grounds and pass the time. He especially liked spending time near the guards' quarters, where he would sit by the playing field and listen to the young soldiers training, singing, competing in martial arts and generally just making a ruckus. Sometimes he would engage in 'listening games' with them. Once I discovered that Abing was frequenting this area, I made sure to give the young soldiers some very important advice: never be disrespectful to Abing and never make fun of him.

In truth, my advice was unnecessary. In our particular quarter, as well as throughout Unit 701, no one showed Abing any less respect than they would show for the Director, and absolutely no one dared to tease him. It was easy for me to see that wherever Abing went everyone would stop what they were doing and show him respect. If necessary they would step out of his way, and always with a smile on their face – even though he couldn't see it. In the history of Unit 701, no one had been accorded the amount of reverence and respect given to Abing, and I dare say no one ever will.

18.

The days passed by.

Winter came and Abing found himself in hospital because of a sudden bout of appendicitis. The hospital was located in the first valley, in the residential quarter; quite a journey from our division on foot, but not so long by car. While he was in hospital, I often went to see him. On one occasion, as I walked into his room, I saw a nurse by the name of Lin Xiaofang changing his IV drip. To my surprise, I actually recognized her. She came from the nearby village. Her elder brother had served as a platoon leader for the security forces, but he had died during a live ammunition training exercise. Because the intelligence service considered her to be the younger sister of a revolutionary martyr, they broke with protocol and brought her into our care. Later she was trained as a nurse and when she became a Party cadre, she was given employment at the hospital.

Since her brother was considered a martyr, Xiaofang was quite hard on herself: she had to live up to his reputation. Her feelings towards Unit 701, however, were the plain and simple emotions of a country girl. When I saw how attentive she was to Abing, something suddenly dawned on me and I quickly relayed my idea to the Bureau Chief. He thought there was merit in my plan, but said that the hospital and its personnel were beyond his jurisdiction and so I should contact the hospital director in person and gauge his response to my idea. With this in mind, I made my way to Director Tie's office to see what he thought.

Director Tie listened and then responded matter-of-factly, 'Hmm, it's not a bad idea – certainly better than just assigning him an attendant. I like it; it all depends on whether or not you can facilitate it.'

'If that's so,' I asked, 'might I be able to use the influence of our Unit to assist in the matter?'

Director Tie never answered my question directly, but suggested that it would not be a problem. 'If I had a daughter and Abing seemed to fancy her, I would use a father's influence to see that she married him.'

I thought the same. Whatever way you looked at it, Abing had saved Unit 701, and so there was really no way we could refuse him anything. I had made my mind up to ensure that such a wedding would take place, and should Xiaofang have any misgivings about marrying someone like Abing, I would use all the power of Unit 701 to assuage her concerns. Talking of this now is quite laughable, and perhaps a little embarrassing. But at that time, at least for Unit 701, it was entirely within our purview to arrange such matters. Actually, my own wedding to my late first wife was arranged by the intelligence service, and while feelings of affection were perhaps absent at the beginning, we did grow to love each other. Unfortunately she passed away prematurely because of an illness, but not before introducing me to her cousin who eventually became my current wife. What am I trying to explain by telling you this? Well, at that time, in Unit 701, we considered marriage and other things of that nature to be all part of the revolution: there was no separation between our private and collective lives. What's more, this type of belief – faith, really – filled our lives with an incomparable sense of warmth and belonging.

Because she was not actually an agent working for Unit 701, Lin Xiaofang had no clue as to the true nature of Abing's work: she assumed that the honour and respect given him was because he had invented some secret weapon or other to safeguard the nation. No matter, her ignorance of the truth had no effect on my aim to arrange a perfect marriage. In fact, once I told her of my plan, she responded in the affirmative without hesitation. She even said that if her brother were still alive he would have wholeheartedly supported her decision to marrying Abing – to marry a man, a hero, responsible for developing an advanced and secret weapon to protect the nation. As for Abing's disability, she believed that to be an important reason for her to marry him: a national hero needed someone to care and look after him.

Lin Xiaofang's display of resoluteness and her noble character were incredibly heartening and morale-boosting. Without wasting time, I hurried to Abing's side to tell him of my plan and Xiaofang's determination. I dare say that this was the first time that Abing ever doubted his own ears, so much so that I had to repeat myself. Somewhat flabbergasted, Abing mumbled to himself, 'Who'd be willing to marry a blind man? In Lujiayan, the only person who'd marry a blind man is a blind woman, but two sightless people living together – well, wouldn't they be even more blind?'

Once I assured him that Xiaofang was absolutely in agreement, Abing seemed barely able to control his emotions and excitement. Half-stuttering he asked, 'Is this really true?'

'Yes.'

'Really?'

'Yes, really.'

This exchange went on for some time.

During the Spring Festival, Abing and Lin Xiaofang tied the knot in a grand ceremony held in the great hall within Unit 701's compound. Everyone from Unit 701 attended, from Director Tie down to the lowliest cook. Everyone expressed their heartfelt congratulations towards the newlyweds. Before long, all manner of wedding presents were piled high upon the stage. Finally, a decorated truck carried the newlyweds, and their mountain of gifts, off to their new residence, which was soon brimming full. Their home was a two-storey structure that had previously housed Bureau Chief Wu's family and my own. In order to provide Abing with the best and most comfortable accommodation, Bureau Chief Wu gave up his residence so that Abing and his new wife could move in and be close to the person whom Abing trusted most – namely, myself. You could say that all the personnel of Unit 701 felt an indescribable joy and satisfaction in providing Abing with the best possible place to live in; he had done so much for Unit 701 that it seemed only fitting for us to arrange such a perfect wedding for him.

19

Just as I had transformed Abing's life after discovering him in Lujiayan, I had once more succeeded in changing his destiny. In all honesty, Lin Xiaofang wasn't at all pretty, nor was she always refined in terms of how she treated other people. But she was amazingly compassionate and understanding. She never once complained nor regretted her marriage to Abing, and it soon became noticeable that he was benefiting greatly from her care: his appearance was much neater, cleaner, and more cheerful. He was enjoying the most pleasant and happy period of his life. Two years later, Xiaofang made him even happier by making him a father.

Considering Abing's special circumstances, and according to Xiaofang's wishes, the intelligence service granted her two years' maternity leave so that she could return to Abing's home town to rear their child. Not only would her salary not be reduced, but the service actually increased it by 10 yuan per month for child support.

Not long after Xiaofang departed for Lujiayan, the postal services of Unit 701 received the following telegram: 'Your son is happy; your mother is doing well. Xiaofang.'

Since we were neighbours, I called in on Abing practically every day. That was how I learnt of a peculiar habit he had developed since receiving the telegram from Xiaofang. As the attendant responsible for taking care of Abing in the absence of his wife told me, and as I soon saw with my own eyes, Abing took every empty pack of cigarettes and folded them into doves: one pack, one dove, on the table, on the bed, in each and every space he could fit one. The paper doves had become so plentiful that there was no longer any space free to put them. That was when the attendant assisted Abing in using red thread to string the paper doves together and then hang them about his house. They were hung on armrests, on the walls, from the ceiling – everywhere. By the time Xiaofang returned to the compound with their son, their house was filled with multicoloured paper doves. According to people's calculations, there were five hundred and forty-three paper doves in total, a number which corresponded exactly to the number of days father and son were separated from each other. When Xiaofang returned, Abing's dreams were satisfied. His son was adorable, and especially striking were his two bright and inquisitive eyes, which couldn't help but delight everyone.

I remember it quite clearly. On the day that Xiaofang returned I was busy preparing a welcoming dinner for mother and son. Perhaps it was because I was so excited to see Abing's son, I don't know – but at any rate, when I went round to invite them over for dinner, I learnt that Abing had a terrible headache and had already taken some medicine and gone off to bed. Without Abing, the welcoming dinner was naturally not quite as joyous, but his boy did surprise and delight everyone present.

The next morning, after I had taken my daily stroll, I returned to sounds of activity coming from Abing's residence. Naturally I knocked on the door and asked how Abing was doing. Xiaofang told me that his headache was gone and that he had already left for the office. In fact, he had left in the middle of the night saying he had something important to take care of. He told her that it was the office that had summoned him. I thought nothing of it at the time – after all, he had been summoned in such a fashion before and so nothing seemed unusual. Just as I turned to leave, Xiaofang called after me and asked me to wait a moment. She had a package that Abing had asked her to give to me. I asked what it was, but she did not know. Abing had told her it contained top-secret files and had forbidden her to look into it.

I opened the package once I returned home. First there was a layer of flannel wrapping, then a hemp one, and then finally a leather case file. Inside were a letter and a tape player. At that time, this type of mini-tape player was rather rare – perhaps Abing was the only person in all of Unit 701 who possessed one (a senior official had given it to him some time ago). I tore open the envelope and discovered several hundred yuan inside. I immediately had a bad feeling about this package; there was something ominous about it. I looked at the mini-tape player and saw that a cassette had already been placed inside. I pressed play and in a moment heard a whimpering cry. Then, in a tearful voice, Abing spoke: '[Sob, sob] . . . although I cannot see, I can hear . . . [sob, sob] . . . the boy isn't my son, his father is the hospital pharmacist, that man from Shandong . . . [sob, sob] . . . my wife has given birth to a bastard child, all I can do is die . . . [sob, sob] . . . every man in Lujiayan follows this rule, if their wife has a bastard child, all that is left for them is death! Death! . . . [sob, sob] . . . Xiaofang is a whore . . . [sob, sob] . . . You're a good man, please give the money to my mum . . . [sob, sob] . . .'

Christ!

How could I listen to any more! I urgently called for a car, hopped in and drove directly to the audio surveillance building. A few minutes later I tore open the door to Abing's office and saw him curled up on the floor. In his hand he was grasping a live electrical flex; his entire body was smouldering: it was an awful sight.

Abing!

Abing!

Abing! !

Abing's ears no longer heard anything.

20

Abing was dead.

The cassette he left me recorded his reason: his wife had betrayed him; the boy was a bastard; all he could do was commit suicide.

Abing's death shocked and pained everyone in Unit 701, but there was no anger towards his wife – I lied to them about that.

It's true. I lied to everyone, even to the intelligence service. What did I do? I never gave them that cassette. No cassette, no confession. How could anyone know that he killed himself? The memorial to Abing simply said that he died of a work-related accidental electrocution. For a blind man, such an accident wasn't beyond the realms of possibility and so no one felt that there was anything odd or wrong about it. Abing's legacy was secure.

Please believe me, I didn't withhold the cassette for any selfish reasons. I did it to protect Abing and Unit 701. To tell you the truth, soon after he arrived, we were no longer referred to as Unit 701, but rather as 'Abing's work unit'. In other words, everyone across the intelligence service knew of Abing and his triumphs. News of such a man's death – due to suicide, no less – would spread like wildfire and do irreparable damage to Abing's good name, as well as to the reputation of Unit 701. In order to guard the reputation and honour of the service, and of Abing, I had to bury the cassette. I had to make Abing's 'last testament' disappear.

Afterwards, however, I kept mulling the situation over in my mind and felt that I should let the organization know. How else could we avenge his death? Informing them of what actually happened was easy enough; all I needed to do was let Bureau Chief An hear Abing's last words. According to the chain of command, however, I had to give the cassette to Bureau Chief Wu first. Of course, I had to tell another lie to cover up my first mistake. I told them that I had only just discovered this cassette. Bureau Chief

Wu became the second person to learn the real reason for Abing's death.

Wu handed the cassette on up to Director Tie, and so the latter became the third person to learn the truth.

Even after all these years, I can still hear Director Tie's words as if he were standing next to me. Once he heard the cassette he let out a tremendous roar of invective: 'Tell them to get the fuck out of here! Both of them! That bitch of a wife and that bastard pharmacist! Now! Inform them immediately! If I see them, they're dead!'

I dare say that had this situation happened during wartime – if they'd been carrying guns – the two of them would have been gunned down in sheer rage. Now, however, that was not possible, nor permitted. Why? Well, partly because memorial services had already been held. Abing's glorious history had been set in stone, and even though it's obvious that a mistake is still a mistake, we couldn't just throw everything out of the window: all we could do was muddle through. Then another problem presented itself: since Abing's official cause of death was accidental electrocution, how could we tell his widow that she had to leave? It was impossible. When I had first withheld the cassette I'd never thought that my actions would result in the real persons responsible for his death going unpunished. I guess you could say that this was my punishment for having selfish motives.

Nonetheless, at least my mistake wouldn't protect that bastard of a pharmacist. The next day, like a lunatic, I grabbed hold of him and dragged him to the train station. Of course, in order to maintain the secrecy surrounding Abing's suicide, we never stated clearly what his crime was, nor could we. Because of this, once at the station, he took on the airs of someone wrongly accused and asked why he was being forced to leave. How was I supposed to answer this fucker without giving away the real cause? Well, at first, I said nothing. Instead, I removed the pistol from the guard's waist, cocked it and pointed the barrel in his face.

'I'll tell you this only once: if you dare utter another word, I'll gun you down where you stand!'

Scared shitless, he remained silent for a moment, then turned and fled like the coward he was.

21

What happened next you'll never guess.

A few days after that Shandong bastard left, I had returned home after a day's work when Lin Xiaofang came round looking for me. When she saw me, she immediately fell to her knees and in a voice choked with tears told me something I couldn't – no, dared not believe. This is what she told me: Abing had no awareness of sex. He believed – like a child believes – that all a man and a woman needed to do was to sleep in the same bed, embrace, kiss, and, *voilà*, he'd be a father. That was how his mother had explained it to him . . .

'You know, he was incredibly filial. He wanted a child so badly – not so much for us, but so that his mother could be a grandmother. A year on and I was still not pregnant . . . he began to feel that it was my fault, that something was wrong with me. He'd get angry, fly into a rage. He wouldn't sleep in the same bed as me; he kept saying we should divorce, that he should find a new wife. I was afraid he was going to get rid of me, and if he did, how could I stay here, at Unit 701? I kept thinking about how I could do right by Unit 701 and my dead brother, I kept thinking, I . . . I . . .'

Finally, she swore that once she knew she was pregnant, she hadn't let that Shandong pharmacist touch her again.

I didn't know why, but for some reason I believed her tears, I believed that what she said could be true; but I still felt no sympathy for her, there was no room in my heart for her sorrow. From beyond the wall I heard the frightened cry of a baby. Wearily and somewhat exasperatedly I stood up and in a cold and detached manner ordered her to leave my house.

As she left she spoke these final words to me: 'I understand that I need to atone for my crime against Abing. Believe me, I will.'

On the following day, a few people saw Xiaofang leave Unit

701 with her toddler bundled in her arms. But no one saw her return, and no one knew where she'd gone. Years later, one winter I was in Shanghai on official business and I thought that I would pay a visit to Abing's mother. Upon reaching Lujiayan, to my surprise, I learnt that after Xiaofang had left Unit 701, she had moved in with Abing's mother. The strange thing was, I didn't see the boy. I asked Xiaofang but she prevaricated, telling me that the child was simply not here. From the way she spoke and from the way she carried herself about the house, you could see that she considered this place her home. And what's more, all the villagers were in agreement: she was the best daughter-in-law in all of Lujiayan. Everyone praised her for bringing good fortune to Abing's house.

In 1983, Abing's mother died of organ failure as a result of diabetes. The villagers told me that once the memorial services for Abing's dead mother were complete, Lin Xiaofang left Lujiayan with the intention of returning to where Abing had worked. But we at Unit 701 knew that she had never returned. In the end, no one knew where she went. To tell you the truth, to this day we still don't know. At first, some people speculated that she returned to her own home town, others said she went to Shandong. But these were all just rumours. Thereupon new stories were told. Some said that she had thrown herself into the Huangpu River; others said that they had seen her on the streets of Shanghai; there were even some who swore that they had seen her at Abing's grave ... Whatever the case might be, I feel that we will never really know what happened to her: her fate, just like the origins of Abing's incredible hearing, will for ever remain a mystery.

Wind Readers

I remember that Anderov once told me that von Neumann was then the best cryptographer in the whole world, and it was as if he had two completely different ways of thinking, one Eastern and one Western . . . At that time he was the only person in the world who had cracked both European and Asian ciphers. He had accepted a number of Asian students, so that they would give him insight into the way that their minds worked . . . Some people said that he was even cleverer than Einstein, that he was the last of the great mathematicians.

An Angel with Problems

She was an angel, but she wasn't perfect.

Yeah, she was an angel with problems.

She was Unit 701's fifth Bureau Chief of the European cryptography division: Huang Yiyi.

There were just as many stories told about Huang Yiyi at Unit 701 as there were about the blind man, Abing, though these stories were much coloured by the opinions and personalities of the speakers. It was fascinating, though, and really made me want to write about Huang Yiyi, the only woman cryptographer ever to have become a Bureau Chief in the history of Unit 701. But I didn't dare, because I hadn't been able to meet the person most closely involved, a man as important to her story as Director Qian was in what happened to Abing. That man was the fourth head of Unit 701, Director An.

Director An was a very, very senior figure indeed: he was one of the nine original members of Unit 701, known as the 'Nine Gentlemen'. Now well past eighty, he was the only surviving Gentleman. His health was still good though: when we shook hands his grip was strong, and he spoke perfectly clearly, though I sometimes had trouble understanding his thick Western Zhejiang accent. He had been living since his retirement in an out-of-the-way little town in the north, a place that was neither his home town nor anything to do with his work, but which had in fact been picked for him by his one-year-old grandson. The venerable Mr An was quite an unusual man: when he retired he didn't want to go to any of the big cities like Beijing or Shanghai; he asked the Party to arrange for him to live in a city he had never been to before. He didn't care which one, just somewhere new! That really did put the Party to a lot of trouble. China is so big, with so many places that he had never been to: so how to choose? In the end he took over the decision-making process himself and got his baby grandson to throw a coin on to a map of China: wherever the coin landed, that was where he would live. It was a fatalistic way of resolving the problem. Ever since then, he had had no contact with Unit 701, and so it was not easy to find him after all that time.

In the end, of course, I did track him down, but getting to meet him and then persuading him to talk was very difficult. There were no doubts in my mind that the reason he had chosen to break off all contact when he left was so that he wouldn't have to talk to anyone about this. I understand that. I don't accept it. In the end, with massive patience and determination, I wore him down, though it was not a complete victory for me – more like a draw. He agreed to talk to me about Huang Yiyi, but he insisted (and drew up a contract to this effect) that this book could say nothing about what he did after resigning as director. He meant something very specific by this. It was something that I had heard about back at Unit 701, and I am sure that if I could write that story, it would be much more worth reading than the tale of Abing or Huang Yiyi. Now, having signed the contract, it is a story that I am never going to be able to tell, nor even to hint at. He also demanded that I allow him to tell Huang Yiyi's story 'in his own way'. That was written into the contract too. So now I have to let him speak in his own words.

To tell the truth, he really couldn't tell a story, and he was terribly discursive – perhaps because he was so old. Hammering this material into the shape you see below was really hard work, ten times worse than writing about Abing, and I am still not exactly happy with it. But what can you do? I wasn't allowed to include any extra information or change anything, just to do some editing and some basic revisions. So here it is . . .

My story starts in Moscow. I was a revolutionary orphan, and I grew up in Moscow. I went to Moscow in 1931, at the age of four, and when I came back home I was already twenty; that was in 1947. While in Moscow I studied wireless technology, and when I returned to the motherland the Party sent me to Unit 701. To begin with I was just doing the most basic kind of radio interceptions, but then because my Russian was so good I was transferred to intelligence gathering and data compilation. In 1957, the Party sent my wife, Xiaoyu, and me back to Moscow: she was seconded by the Ministry of Foreign Affairs to the embassy, while I studied cryptography at the Centre for Code Research at the Department of Mathematics at Lomonosov Moscow State University. That changed my life: afterwards every success and every failure, every reward and every punishment, all my good luck and bad was determined by cryptography. Even now, the fact that I live retired and out of sight is a consequence of that. My supervisor Anderov used to say that cryptography isn't a job, it's a conspiracy – with a plot concealed inside that conspiracy. It is damaging to both mind and body to do this kind of dark, secret and difficult work for any length of time. As time goes on you change imperceptibly, until in the end you find that you can no longer live an ordinary life.

I was supposed to graduate in July 1960, but at the beginning of March of that year I was suddenly informed by the Party that I would have to return home as soon as possible. It was a comrade with the code-name Aeroplane who told me; a woman from Changchun, very tall, with the bright red skin of a professional swimmer: a very healthy colour. She was my handler the whole time that I was in Moscow. Officially I was an overseas student, but I was also an undercover agent – to put it in plain words, a spy: my job was to gather intelligence about American military ciphers cracked by the Soviets. My supervisor at the university was Lev Anderov, who was both a world-famous mathematician and a cryptographer who gave the Americans a lot of headaches. The Party sent me to him in order to use his position to get access to Western military intelligence. During the three years that we worked together we became very friendly; he wasn't just my teacher and my supervisor, he was the person who introduced me to a whole new world. Later on I changed my name to An Zaitian as a sign of my respect. When I knew that I had to leave, I really did not want to go, particularly as I had not yet finished my studies. Having to leave all of a sudden without even being able to graduate is something that I regret very much.

What happened next was even worse. When I had completed the paperwork for leaving university and was just about to buy the train ticket to go home, I suddenly – and it was that sudden – got the news that my wife had died in a car crash. The car in which she was a passenger had crashed into a truck on a mountain road and gone over the edge of the cliff; the car was completely wrecked and everyone inside was dead. The fact that she was dead was one thing, but I wasn't even able to see her body. They told me that when the car went over the edge it caught fire and everyone inside was burnt to a crisp. When they found them it was impossible to tell who was who, and in the end they were only identified by the autopsy. When I next saw Xiaoyu she had turned into a little black box.

A box of ashes.

I took Xiaoyu's ashes with me away from Moscow. I remember that the day I left it was snowing heavily in Moscow, and the train station was covered in a thick blanket of white snow, and I felt as cold as the icy sky and snowy ground. There was a goods train carrying Chinese apples and live pigs standing at the platform, and officials from China and Russia were unloading the goods and checking them. China was repaying its loans in kind. It was exactly as people said: the Russians had really strict vetting procedures – a whole load of conveyer belts had been rigged up around the platform, and the apples were tipped out onto them for testing according to strict criteria. Those apples that were too big were rejected, as were those that were too small. Russian officials were also checking out the pigs, and any that had scars or bruises were sent back.

At that time Sino-Soviet relations were already pretty sensitive, and when I got to the train station my luggage was thoroughly searched. When my supervisor Anderov saw that, he yet again urged me not to go home. For days he had been trying to persuade me to stay, and just the night before we had had a long conversation. He analysed the future of Sino-Soviet relations and my probable future career, and told me that in his opinion going back to China was the worst possible option for me. He seemed to have already had some kind of premonition of the coming Sino-Soviet split, and suspected that when I got home I would quite possibly be set to cracking Russian ciphers, which would sully our deep friendship. He was hoping that I would stay and finish my master's thesis and then go on to study for a PhD, concentrating on mathematical problems. He didn't want me to get caught up in the world of cryptography. 'This whole thing is an ideological issue,' he said. 'It is absolutely nothing to do with scholarship. My experience should be a lesson to you. I can't go back, but there is absolutely no need for you to follow in my footsteps; you can just be an ordinary student.'

But I knew that this was impossible; you could say that from the time I was born I was already an ideological person. I have already mentioned that I am a revolutionary orphan; the Party brought me up, and if the Party needed me now, I had no right to refuse.

When they had finished searching my luggage, my supervisor asked me if I knew what kind of people had been looking through my stuff. I said that I didn't know, and he told me that they were KGB. I guessed that he had already worked out who I really was, but I still pretended to be surprised and said, 'How could that be?'

He laughed. 'My friend, I think you should tell me the truth. Other than being a junior scholar at the Cryptography Research Centre at the Chinese Academy of Sciences, who are you?'

'Why are you suddenly asking me that, Mr Anderov?'

'Because recently you have become very mysterious to me.'

'I have no secrets from you.'

'My friend, you are lying.' He pointed to the box containing Xiaoyu's ashes which I was holding in my arms, and asked me how my wife had died. He said that he didn't believe that it was a simple car crash. I swore that that was all it was. In fact I didn't know myself how she had died. But I had to say that; I had to make him believe me.

In the end, he very formally asked me to remember one thing: that when I got back home, if the Party ever asked me to break a Russian cipher, I should refuse. 'The reason I say this is because it would make me very unhappy, and because you simply don't know enough to make a success of it.'

'Absolutely,' I said. 'That's why I want to come back and continue my studies.'

He shook his head and said, 'You won't be able to. The relationship between our two countries has already gone past the point of no return, and you will never be able to be my student again. We'd better just try and stay friends.'

He looked kind of upset at that, and then he hugged me and said, 'Get on the train. I hope you have a good journey.'

That was how we said goodbye.

Shortly after I got to my compartment, someone knocked on the door. It was Comrade Aeroplane who came in, carrying a black leather suitcase. I had an identical leather suitcase which I had put down underneath the tea table. She put her suitcase down next to mine, and told me the combination of the lock. When she left, it was my suitcase that she took with her – they were absolutely identical in appearance. I have no idea what was in her suitcase, just that it was more important than my life. If something happened during the journey, I was under orders to save the contents of that suitcase, not myself.

Perhaps thanks to Anderov's good wishes, the journey was completely uneventful.

2.

The first day in Beijing someone came to the guest house where I was staying to collect the suitcase that Comrade Aeroplane had given me.

The second day I had an appointment at headquarters with the Deputy Director of Intelligence Operations. His surname was Tie, and he was something over fifty years old, but his hair was already going white, which gave him the appearance of being older than he actually was. When he spoke his voice was very loud and decisive, like a general's might be. He had been the first Director of Unit 701, and because he had such a terrible temper, his subordinates called him 'The Landmine' behind his back. He had left Unit 701 two years earlier, when he had been promoted to Deputy Director at headquarters, in charge of the day-to-day running of the place; now he was responsible for all intelligence operations. His secretary was called Li, a young man with good Russian; we had been colleagues for a few months before I left to go to Moscow. Having only worked together for such a short time, we weren't particularly close, but now meeting again after a couple of years we quickly became friendly. He divulged that Director Tie had really had to fight some of the other senior people in the department to get me recalled.

'You may not be aware of it,' he said, 'but the information that you sent back over the years has been very useful in cracking a number of high-level military ciphers used by enemy powers including the Americans, the British and the Taiwanese. As a result, people at headquarters have come to rely on your intelligence, and several senior officers were most unhappy about the decision to recall you, seeing how well you were doing over there.'

'It would be difficult to carry on, given current conditions,' I said. 'Recently they put me under a lot of restrictions – much worse than before.'

'Yes, things really aren't going too well.' Then he asked me what I thought the prospects were like for Sino-Soviet relations.

I said, not good.

'You're right. Of course, something that is bad for us is good for other people. I don't know whether you have seen it, but the Hong Kong newspapers say that Chiang Kai-shek is getting ready to celebrate his eightieth birthday in Nanjing.'

'He can say whatever he likes; he's just running off at the mouth.'

'Two years ago he was just running off at the mouth, but this time he is definitely up to something. You've been away, so you don't really understand that we're in terrible trouble right now. We've had natural disasters for the last couple of years, and now in addition to the prospect of a Sino-Soviet split there is also tension on the border between China and India. It's just been one damn thing after another. We're in trouble, and he's going to take advantage of that. That's Chiang Kai-shek's plan, the bastard.'

'Ten years ago, when the Korean War had just broken out, didn't he try to take advantage? He sent bombers over every day and wave after wave of special agents, thinking that he could launch a double-pronged attack on the Mainland. And what happened? It didn't work and he practically bankrupted himself.'

'History is repeating itself; the only thing that's changed is the slogan. At that time they talked about "Invading the Mainland"; now it's "Recover the Mainland". Anyway, they have stopped using PORPHORY and switched to a new cipher called RECOVERY.'

I knew that PORPHORY was the high-level cipher that the Taiwanese used to communicate with their agents on the Mainland, which an American expert had created for them. It was reckoned to be secure for twenty years, and so far it had been in use for a decade. We had started to make some headway in cracking it in the last two years, but we were still a long way from the stage where they would have to change it. To suddenly switch to this new cipher suggested that they might well be getting ready to go to war.

'So who gets the job of cracking it?' I asked.

'Your old home: Unit 701.'

This meant that Unit 701 would be faced with a very testing task. Ten years earlier they had been left unable to hear enemy broadcasts; now they couldn't understand them. I asked who was in charge at Unit 701 nowadays, and Li said it was Comrade Luo. I remembered her: a very competent woman. When I worked on radio intercepts, she was my Bureau Chief, but as far as I knew she knew nothing about cryptography. I pointed this out, and he smiled at me and said, 'You're quite right; she has always worked on radio intercepts and knows nothing about cryptography. But providing you know what you're doing, it doesn't matter if she doesn't. From now on you are Deputy Director of Unit 701 and the head of the team deciphering RECOVERY.'

That really did give me a turn. 'I've barely learnt the basics,' I said. 'How could I possibly take charge of such an important mission?'

'It's already been decided,' he replied, 'and the paperwork was completed yesterday. I may as well tell you that you will be meeting Director Tie this afternoon. He's in a meeting right now, but he'll be free to see you later.' He offered formal congratulations on being promoted three grades at once, and explained that I would be the youngest Deputy Director in the whole organization. I was still stunned, and just stood there with my mouth open until he got up to go. Then I stammered out my appeal: I wanted the Party to reconsider their appointment – I couldn't possibly do it. 'This isn't the kind of thing that can be done by hard work,' I said, 'by doing your best. You're putting me in an impossible position.'

He said candidly, 'You're going to have to talk to Director Tie this afternoon; there's no point telling me this. But I really don't think he's going to change his mind.'

Just as he said, that afternoon Director Tie came right to the point and told me there was no way out. 'Stop complaining!' he said in a loud, hectoring tone. 'And stop fussing! Just go to work and you'll soon get used to it. The decision to recall you was a very difficult one to make, but having made it there is no going back.

That's point number one. Secondly, this is a really important job. The Party decided to recall you from your mission working with Anderov because right now cracking RECOVERY takes priority over the work on any other cipher – it is the most important thing that we have to do. Why is it so urgent? Well, it's obvious. Chiang Kai-shek is still dreaming of recapturing the Mainland, and he has adopted a whole series of practical measures to this end. You should know that last year the Taiwanese made a one-off purchase of 1.7 billion US dollars' worth of American military hardware; they've held a whole series of "Recover the Mainland" exercises; they've sent wave after wave of special agents over here; and now they've changed their cipher. All these things coming on top of each other mean that this time they're not just talking about a counter-attack: they're getting ready for something big. Are we going to just sit here ignoring what they're up to while all their special agents run around under our very eyes, committing sabotage here and spreading seditious rumours there? No we are not! This cipher – RECOVERY – must be broken: that is top-priority! Thirdly, if there's something you need, or you encounter a particular problem, then say so, and the Party – and indeed I myself – will do our very best to help you. Bureau Chief Liu tells me that this is the highest-level code the KMT has ever used, and that it's reckoned to be secure for thirty years. Giving special agents such a high-level cipher to use, rather than the military or their own upper echelons, indicates that these people have a very special role to play in the upcoming operation to "Recover the Mainland". You've just come back; you don't know anything about this cipher; and so you have no idea what kind of problems you're likely to encounter – so even if you wanted to request assistance, you don't know what to ask for. That's fine: Bureau Chief Liu understands the situation, so when we've finished our conversation I'll hand over what we have to you and you can think about it, and then write a report for me explaining your plan of action, including any problems that you can foresee and special requests, and I'll do my best to see that you get an answer as soon as possible. How would that be?'

What could I say? I could only agree.

I had been surprised at the news about my new job, but what he told me next about my wife, Xiaoyu, was a shock – a dreadful shock! Director Tie informed me that a memorial ceremony would be held the following day at the Ministry of Foreign Affairs for Xiaoyu, and that he would be attending as one of her former instructors.

'What are you talking about?' I said.

'Don't you think that Xiaoyu was a wonderful assistant? If you hadn't had Xiaoyu's help, would you have found it quite so easy to pass the intelligence that you gathered from Anderov to Comrade Aeroplane?'

Of course not – a student can't be forever rushing off to meet a much older woman without giving rise to comment. It was perfectly true that the vast majority of the information was passed to Comrade Aeroplane by Xiaoyu. She was doing secretarial work at the embassy and Comrade Aeroplane was married to her boss; the two of them got on well and met up regularly, so it was easy for her to transmit information. The thing is that I could have sworn that Xiaoyu didn't know my real job, or that Comrade Aeroplane and I were in contact. But in fact . . . there was another, even bigger secret. Director Tie told me that Xiaoyu knew all about it, that she too had been a special agent, but that she kept quiet about it so as not to add to the pressure I was under, and because her own work demanded absolute secrecy. I understood this to mean that Xiaoyu had even higher security clearance than I did! He was going to attend Xiaoyu's memorial ceremony in a private capacity, though in fact he would be representing headquarters, because she had been one of our people. Her job at the Ministry of Foreign Affairs was just a cover story; it was all a lie.

This was the most terrible shock, and I immediately realized that there was much that I didn't know about the circumstances of Xiaoyu's death.

'There is a lot you don't know,' Director Tie said, 'not just about the way in which she died.'

It was true: there were so many suspicious things that I hardly knew where to start. In fact, a lot of this must have been planned right from the moment that I first set eyes on Xiaoyu. This really was a secret world, where a marriage was an adjunct to your work, a smoke-screen, a security measure. And so the following day, as part of this smoke-screen, the Ministry of Foreign Affairs held a memorial ceremony for Xiaoyu, with a further article in their own internal newsletter, so that everyone would know that while working overseas Xiaoyu had been tragically killed in a car crash, 'dying in the line of duty'. As if that weren't enough, Director Tie ordered Secretary Li to take away the casket containing Xiaoyu's ashes so that when I got to Unit 701 I discovered that her ashes were already in residence: there was a spirit altar in my room, wreathed in incense, and the commemorative photograph of Xiaoyu looked at me through the mist of smoke, as if we were separated by a thousand miles of mountains and rivers.

I understood that this was all being done so that as many people as possible would know that Xiaoyu was dead. How did she die? In a car crash. News would soon spread of the altar in my room, and pretty quickly everyone in Unit 701 would know about it. People in this organization are very thorough.

3

Getting back to the story: that day when I met Director Tie, the Bureau Chief was also present, Comrade Liu.

If Secretary Li represented Director Tie's body – running around doing errands for him, making him tea, fetching and carrying, making sure that everything ran smoothly from day to day – then Bureau Chief Liu represented his brain, his intelligence – helping him to see which way the wind was blowing, coming up with new plans, keeping control of his little empire. Bureau Chief Liu was one of the first generation of PRC cryptographers: his people could be found in every cryptanalysis unit in the country. Not long after I got back from Xiaoyu's memorial ceremony at the Ministry of Foreign Affairs, Bureau Chief Liu came to the guest house to see me. He was very polite and kept referring to me as 'Deputy Director An', which made me extremely uncomfortable. To begin with we were just chatting, talking about some mutual friends and colleagues, then somehow or other the conversation got round to ciphers, since I would soon be taking over this part of his work. While we were discussing RECOVERY, he suddenly asked me, 'Deputy Director An, you were in the Soviet Union for such a long time, I was wondering if perhaps you had heard of a particular mathematician . . . ?'

'Who?'

'Liljeva Sivincy.'

'Of course I've heard of her.' She was well known in the Soviet Union: a very strange woman – a brilliant mathematician but also exceptionally arrogant. I had heard that one time Stalin invited her to lunch but she refused because she wanted to go and watch a football match. Naturally Stalin made her pay for that, and in the end she was forced to seek asylum in the US.

'Do you know what she has been doing since her arrival in the States?' Liu asked me.

'I do. She has been writing ciphers for the Americans.'

'I see that you do actually know something about her. Anyway, at university she was one of your supervisor Anderov's fellow students, and they were pretty close.'

'I know. Anderov often mentioned her. I suppose you know that after she got to the States she wrote a cipher for the US military called DIFFICULT CENTURY which is said to be one of the most complex ever devised. In the end, though, the Americans didn't dare use it. After all, she is Russian.'

Liu said that he knew all about that, and then he asked, 'Do you know what happened to her cipher?'

'No.'

'Well, I do.' He handed me a heap of documents and told me to read them. 'The cipher that we need to crack, RECOVERY, is none other than Liljeva Sivincy's DIFFICULT CENTURY.'

I simply couldn't believe it.

It was true, though. According to Bureau Chief Liu, the Americans did not dare use this cipher themselves but they thought it would be a shame just to waste it, so they gave it to Taiwan. The KMT were absolutely thrilled about it. The documents slipped from my grasp . . . I was in the grip of a strong psychological reaction; everything went dark, my legs buckled under me, it felt as though the blood was draining from my body . . . That night I wrote a report for Director Tie pointing out that this was no ordinary code, but an algorithmic cipher of the utmost complexity. In my opinion, having read the résumés of our current staff, there was no way that we could crack it. If we wanted to break it, we would have to bring someone in from outside, and it would have to be a mathematician of the very first order. I also put it on record again that I was simply not qualified for the job, and recommended that the Party find someone else to lead the team to crack RECOVERY.

The following afternoon, Secretary Li popped up. Trotting along behind him was Director Tie. He came into my room and said with a smile, 'You know more than the rest of us do about Liljeva Sivincy.'

'She was at university with my supervisor, Anderov,' I said.

'So now you should understand why we insisted on appointing you.'

'But there is no way I'm qualified to do this – I'm not a mathematician . . .'

Director Tie cut me short. 'You are absolutely qualified. The fact that you have already come up with a feasible plan of action proves it. Let me be frank: various experts have already informed me that we don't have anyone who can crack this cipher and that we are going to have to bring someone in from outside. The question is: who do you want? This is the homeland of Zu Chongzhi: we have never lacked for excellent mathematicians. We just need to find them and invite them to join us. If you can't get them to join us, I will have a go, and if I can't persuade them then I will find someone who can. Anyway, the point is that we can get them on board, the difficulty is finding them.'

Quite honestly, where was I supposed to look? I was just an ordinary guy who had become involved with this whole thing by chance. I had absolutely no idea what I was doing because I had only just learnt the basics of cryptography from my supervisor. I knew nothing about the situation of mathematics in China, and if you had lined up every mathematician in the country in front of me, I wouldn't have known who to ask for.

Director Tie heard me out, and then he criticized me. 'You are perfectly right to mention the difficulties of the problem we have set you, but you must not be frightened of them. I know the Americans have made all sorts of extravagant claims for this cipher, but we have good reason to be confident about our chances of cracking it. Sivincy is Russian, and any cipher written by her will be framed within Soviet paradigms. In recent years there has been a lot of contact between Russian and Chinese mathematicians – and indeed cryptographers – and this contact has led to understanding. This puts us in a very strong position. And another thing: you've spent a lot of time with Sivincy's fellow student Anderov, and I'm sure you've got a lot out of it. I really feel there's nothing to be so depressed about, and if you continue to find difficulties, you will just have to deal with them, because there is no going back! That's the first thing I wanted to say to you.'

The second thing he said was that I had to start work right away, without delay. Find the right person, and then head straight back to Unit 701 to get busy. We could not wait any longer.

The third thing was that Director Tie had picked a name for our operation. 'They have called this code RECOVERY, and so our operation to crack it is code-named PRIMUS. If you don't want to head the team, that's fine: I'll do it myself and you can be the deputy head. That's the only concession I'm prepared to make. If you complain any more or try to resign again, I really am going to get cross!'

It was an ultimatum.

I had no choice, but I still had no idea where I should even begin. Thank God for Bureau Chief Liu, who was not only a graduate of the Department of Mathematics at Qinghua University, but had also been involved in cryptography programmes for a very long time. He quickly came up with a suggestion for me. This was a man called Hu Haibo, who had studied in America and been winkled out a few years back by Naval Intelligence to crack ciphers for them. His achievements were amazing; in that short time he had decrypted quite a few high-level foreign ciphers, making himself famous in the field.

Bureau Chief Liu said, 'He would definitely be our first choice, but I think it's going to be very difficult to get Naval Intelligence to let him go unless Director Tie makes the request personally.'

After I reported this to Director Tie, he didn't hesitate for a moment. He went straight to his opposite number in the Navy and asked for a meeting to be set up. Since everyone else concerned was already in Beijing, we just had to wait for Mr Hu to get there the following day. He turned out to be somewhat past forty, dressed in a blue naval uniform, with the pips of a captain. He wore glasses and his hair was crew-cut, and when he spoke he weighed up his words carefully. He seemed to me both highly cultivated and extremely intelligent. When I arrived Director Tie and Bureau Chief Liu had already been talking to him for a while, and whatever they had offered him, Captain Hu had refused. Director Tie introduced us, and then with the air of someone who can't stand beating about the bush, he said frankly, 'Well, how about we don't apply for a formal transfer in the first instance, given that this is likely to be extremely difficult even if you want to go forward with it. Let's compromise by just borrowing you for a few months. I'll talk to your boss – is that OK with you?'

The captain thought about this for a moment, then he said helplessly, 'It's not that I don't want to help you, sir, the problem is . . . how can I put it? I can't crack Sivincy's code. She has written a Soviet cipher, and I have never had any contact with the Russians, let alone experience of cracking their ciphers. The whole thing would be pointless.'

'Well, when it comes to experience with Soviet ciphers,' Director Tie said, 'no one has any. Relations between our countries have been so good up until now, why would we need to? The thing is that no one was expecting that Sivincy's cipher would end up in Taiwan.'

'Quite. Up until now they've always used American ciphers.'

'So this is the first time for everyone; we're all starting from scratch. That's why this operation has the code-name PRIMUS. However, I'm sure all ciphers have their points of similarity, and you've cracked so many. There's no one in the country with your experience and skill, and that's why I really hope you can come and help us.'

The captain shook his head with a smile. 'You're wrong, sir. Ciphers simply do not have points of similarity. Russian and American ciphers are constructed on completely different principles. The former are designed to be difficult: they are complex and abstruse, and require an unusually high level of technical knowledge. The latter are designed to be tricky, and they pay a lot of attention to making them mysterious and ingenious. You could say that they are as far apart as heaven and earth. One flies into the sky, the other burrows through the earth – the difference is that great. The specialists who have created these ciphers on both sides have developed this difference intentionally, and the more pronounced the distinction is, the more successful the cipher. There's an unwritten rule in cryptography that people who crack American ciphers don't even try to break Russian ones, because they simply will not succeed. There are some occasions when an inch is long and a foot is short; and people are just the same: you are good at one thing and bad at another, someone else is the opposite. My situation is this: you think I'm going to be able to help you, but you're wrong – as far as RECOVERY goes, it's playing to all my weak points. Pretty much any mathematician you care to name is more likely to crack it than I am.'

Director Tie pointed to me and said, 'He's going to find us a good mathematician, but the idea of putting someone completely untried in charge of this is really nerve-racking: that's why we came to talk to you. I thought you'd be the perfect choice; I really had no idea the whole thing would turn out to be so difficult.'

'If you find the right person,' the captain said, 'the fact that they are untried shouldn't be a problem. Cryptography is like falling in love: just because you've fallen in love loads of times before doesn't mean the relationship is going to work out. Emotional involvement is crucial, as are fate and intelligence.' He suggested that we visit the Institute of Mathematics at the Chinese Academy of Sciences, particularly given that a lot of the mathematicians who had come back from abroad in recent years had ended up there. 'While of course not every mathematician can do this kind of work,' he said, 'the person you need has to be a mathematician. You'll have a lot more choice if you go there. I can give you some material which might help you locate the kind of person that you need.'

The material was all back at his work unit, so Director Tie told me to go with him to collect it. We all left the office together and just as we were standing by the entrance waiting for the car, he seemed to suddenly call someone to mind, and turned back to Director Tie to say, 'If you could find her, I know someone who would be perfect for what you have in mind.' He went on to explain that she had worked for the RAND Corporation in the United

States, and that according to his information she had already broken a couple of Russian ciphers. Director Tie opened his eyes wide and asked how we could locate her. The captain explained that he had run across her at the Harbin Military Engineering University a couple of years earlier, and that she was very young and very pretty. Later on he heard that she had left, but he had no idea where she had gone.

'What is she called?'

'Huang Qian.'

'With a name and address, I am sure we can find her.' Director Tie then told us we would be splitting up. Bureau Chief Liu would be heading for the Harbin Military Engineering University to find Huang Qian, while I would be going to the Institute of Mathematics at the Chinese Academy of Sciences.

4.

The Institute of Mathematics at the Chinese Academy of Sciences was housed on the southern edge of the Haidian district of Beijing in a solitary, almost abandoned-looking building. That afternoon, having collected the documents from Captain Hu's work unit, my route home took me past it, and so I wandered in as any member of the public could do. When I got through the gate, I noticed the statue of Zu Chongzhi shining in the sun. A bit further on there was a young man staring fixedly at the sun: as far as I could tell he was trying to work out the angle of declination. On my way out I spotted an old man, with the thick glasses of someone terribly short-sighted, bending down to pick up some potatoes that had fallen onto the ground from his basket. One of the potatoes had fallen into the gutter but he didn't care, he put it back into his basket as if it were a treasure. Clearly the country was in a worse state than I had realized.

That evening, under the name Yang Xiaogang, I moved into the Institute's guest house. The guest house at that time seemed very fancy to me, but then it was used to house foreign experts. There was a guard on the door, sitting behind a little desk, and he seemed to be keeping a careful eye on everyone who came and went. While I was arranging a room with the front desk, I noticed that there were two foreigners, a man and a woman, sitting in easy chairs in the entrance hall, chatting. I couldn't understand what they were saying so I was sure that they weren't Russian.

Approximately three hours earlier, Wang, the Secretary of the Party Committee at the Institute of Mathematics, had received an important phone call from the principal of the Chinese Academy of Sciences, announcing my arrival. The principal also instructed him, 'Inform me the minute that he arrives.' Before hanging up, he also told him, 'This man is on a special mission: you must guarantee his personal security.'

The minute Wang put the phone down he rushed round to the guest house, waiting apprehensively for my arrival in the newly decorated main hall. Every so often he would go outside into the rain to peer into the distance, to see if I was on my way. Perhaps it was because he had really taken to heart his orders to treat me respectfully that he started looking out for me long before I could possibly have arrived. But when I did finally get there, he barely glanced at me and certainly didn't say hello. There was certainly no sign of the warm welcome that I had been promised.

I guess there were two reasons why Party Secretary Wang cold-shouldered me the way that he did: one is that it was raining outside and the sky was pitch-black, so I had to make a run for the door of the guest house like an escaped convict. Even so my clothes ended up wet through and bedraggled, so I really didn't look like a VIP; the second is that I used an assumed name when registering. I noticed that right from the moment I arrived he was paying attention to me, so that when I walked into the main hall, he was trying to work out who I could be as unobtrusively as possible; taking a good look at me. When I was registering at the front desk he was hanging around beside me, pretending that he wanted to talk to the staff member behind the counter. He would have made a useless detective! When I fished out my letter of introduction, written on perfectly ordinary paper and proclaiming that I was an instructor from some university or other in the south named Yang Xiaogang, he completely lost interest in me, and slipped away. I could feel in my spine that he was walking away from me. When all formalities had been completed and I was on my way upstairs, I saw him pacing up and down by the main entrance, occasionally casting a worried glance out into the rain-soaked night, as if I were still en route and would soon be walking out of the darkness towards him.

To tell the truth, I had no idea that an old habit of mine would result in this poor old comrade enduring more that an hour of completely unnecessary worry. I always used a false name when registering in a hotel; it was part of my job. I had all sorts of different blank letters of introduction on me which I could fill in with whatever name and job description took my fancy when I needed to stay at a guest house, so it all depended which one I pulled out when I put my hand into my bag – the letters were all of about the same dimensions and written on more or less the same weight of paper. That evening the first one I had pulled out was a letter of introduction from the government of a certain northern province for a Section Chief named Xin Xiaofeng, but I didn't think it went with my drowned-rat appearance so I picked another one, the one for Yang Xiaogang. Obviously I was neither Yang Xiaogang nor a Section Chief in a provincial government: in real life my name is An Zaitian, and I was the Deputy Director of Special Unit 701, code-named 705, meaning that I was fifth in the chain of command at Unit 701. If you want to know how many false names I have used in my time, it certainly wouldn't be less than a professional confidence-trickster. In fact from the list of all possible Chinese surnames, I must have used at least half. To give you just one example, on my eight-day journey back to China I used six names: Li Xianjin, Chen Dongming, Dai Congming, Liu Yutang and so on. That tells you that I have been through a lot in pursuit of my profession, and that it has made me cautious. I was cautious but not cowardly. The distinction between the two is like that between being cold in manner and being depressed; from the outside they might look the same, but there is a world of difference inside.

Party Secretary Wang had already reserved a good room for me: number 301. It was a suite, and the first room contained a traditional carved dark-red wooden bed. The bed was piled with silk quilts, and there was a nylon mosquito net, as transparent as a cicada's wing. This room also had an en-suite bathroom. The second room was large and well appointed, with a comfy sofa, modern phone, venetian blinds, cupboard, standard lamp, tea table, tea-set, ashtray and so on. It was on the top floor, at the end of the corridor, so it would not only be quiet but also secure. I needed that kind of room because I worked for Special Unit 701. But that kind of room was reserved for An Zaitian and not Yang Xiaogang. Yang Xiaogang would have to stay in an ordinary room. They had lots of ordinary rooms and I was given the pick, so after discussion they allocated me room 201. This was right underneath room 301, again at the end of the corridor, and also a suite, so even though it wasn't as well appointed as the other, it fulfilled my requirements. Having gone to have a look at the room, I decided to stay there. I was rather tired after my long run through the rain, so having had a quick wash I got into bed and was soon fast asleep. However, I was soon woken by the most almighty clap of thunder, and once awake, I noticed that something or other seemed to be tapping at the window. I had no idea what it could be, so I went over to have a look, and discovered that on the right-hand side outside my window there was a jujube tree nearly as tall as the building. It was the height of summer and so the tree was covered in leaves, and there were a couple of branches that stretched out towards my window, so as the wind blew they had decided to tap against the window frame. When I looked again, I noticed that one branch was growing right up against the wall, and that if someone hadn't lopped off the end, no doubt it would have broken through and be growing into my room. Perhaps it was because it had been cut short that this branch had become extra thick, like a bridge slung underneath my window. Anyone with a bit of agility and no fear of heights could get into my room by shinning up it – all they would have to do was break the glass and they'd be in.

Was this acceptable?

No it was not!

I went downstairs and demanded to change rooms.

The person behind the counter didn't want me to change, and though I made up various excuses, he thought I was just being gratuitously annoying and refused categorically to help me. I wasn't going to be put off and my voice got louder as I got more and more cross. The man wasn't in the least bit bothered; he kept glancing at Party Secretary Wang behind me while treating me with taciturn contempt. In the end there was nothing else I could do, so I decided (in a most unprofessional way) to scare him.

'I am here as a guest of Party Secretary Wang,' I said. 'Can you please help me out?'

You know, although I didn't know it, Comrade Wang was in fact standing right behind me, infuriated by his long wait. When he heard what I said, it seemed as though he still felt a bit slighted, because he was not at all polite when he asked me: 'I am Party Secretary Wang. Who are you?'

'I come from Unit 701,' I said.

'Comrade An?'

'Yes. My name is An Zaitian.'

He um'd and ah'd a bit at that, then he stepped forward and shook my hand. The force of his handshake and his breathing alerted me to the fact that he seemed to have something important to say. I had no idea what he wanted to tell me, but I knew that we couldn't talk here, because it might be awkward. In a very professional (and resourceful) manner I turned his handshake into a hug, and then made use of this to turn my head to say softly in his ear, 'We can't talk here – let's go to my room.'

5.

Of course I got room 301.

When we entered the room I went straight to the window to look at the jujube tree, which was being tossed about in the wind. A sound like the waves of the sea came rushing towards me, and the branches seemed to be doing their very best to strike me, but try as they might they began their recoil when they were still a metre or two away. I thought that it might just about be possible for a cat to jump across to my room, but for a human, only a character from *Outlaws of the Marsh* would have a hope. I admit that I am a cautious person, but then caution was inculcated in every member of Unit 701. As the people at headquarters said, every single member of 701 was worth an army in the field.

It was perfectly true: at the time when a certain country broadcast to us every day on their JOC radios hoping that we'd defect, they put a price on each of us, offering the most senior people several hundred thousand US dollars – even the cheapest was still a good few thousand. For someone like me, you'd be talking not hundreds of thousands but millions. Yeah, if you could have sold me to them, you could have made millions. And some people will do anything for money. To tell you the truth, I wasn't very happy about having to leave the unit right then, so I was feeling particularly jumpy. Perhaps it was because I had been through so much, perhaps it was due to the problems attendant in the circumstances in which I found myself ... and talking about circumstances, as everyone knows the situation then was bad, it was going to continue being bad, and no one knew how much worse it was going to get. When you think about it, particularly back then, no one would have imagined that our big brother, the Soviet Union, would now turn into our enemy. In the blink of an eye we were on opposite sides, and at daggers drawn. With open conflict and with undercover fighting. In addition to that, the situation with Taiwan was getting tenser every day, what with Chiang Kai-shek's wild plan to 'Recover the Mainland'. In that kind of situation I could feel myself becoming more and more nervous, more and more suspicious, more and more cautious. I was very cautious. Caution is not the same as cowardice, but my caution was concealing a certain amount of cowardice. This room was a lot better than the last one, not least because the room next door had two bodyguards in it. I liked that feeling. The feeling of being safe.

The Party secretary didn't seem at all like the person that had been described to me: 'a scholar in an ivory tower'.

Tall, with a large head and an imposing appearance, dressed in a well-tailored Mao suit, speaking with a clear voice, with an unusually refined bearing: that was Secretary Wang. That was the reason that when I saw him in the main hall it never occurred to me that he could be Party Secretary Wang. I thought he was probably a senior figure, maybe even one of the principals. He wasn't even wearing glasses, so he looked totally different from my image of a director of a research facility. But as I was soon to discover, he had the attention to detail and stubbornness that is often found among researchers. For example, at both the start and finish of our discussions he looked at his watch, making it clear that he had a strong sense of time-keeping; and when I made a request, he didn't express an opinion right away but would only reply after he had thought it through carefully. Before our discussion he demanded to see proof of identity, something that could demonstrate that I was indeed An Zaitian from Special Unit 701. He wasn't satisfied with what I gave him, and tried to cross-examine me.

'I hope you don't mind me mentioning it, but when they told me you were coming, they said you'd be arriving in a jeep.'

'And I am sure they told you that the number plate would be . . .'

'So why didn't you come by car?'

'It broke down.'

In the interests of security, I had told the driver to drop me by the gate rather than taking me to the door. I was not expecting the heavens to open during that couple of hundred metres' walk, leaving me looking stupid. He clearly didn't believe my story of the breakdown, but he also had no idea how to call me on it, so he just sat there in silence. In order to gain his trust, I decided to phone up the comrade who had let him know that I would be coming. In fact, when the phone call was made, I was standing beside him. When the call went through, I handed the receiver to him, and told him to take it. He listened to what the principal had to say, and then all of a sudden he was all smiles. After hanging up he grabbed hold of my hand and pumped it enthusiastically, apologizing all the while for having been rude. He dragged me over to sit on the sofa and then hurried about lighting my cigarette and making tea. Having seated myself, I got straight down to business.

'I'm here to find someone.'

He asked me what kind of person.

I thought about it and then said, opening my attaché case: 'See for yourself.'

The first thing I took out of my attaché case was a brown paper envelope, then I fished out a little bottle, like a bottle of ink, and a little brush, and laid them out one by one on the tea table. I then removed a document from the envelope and fanned its pages until I found a loose bit of paper. Caught between a couple of pages, it looked like a bit of scrap paper. I spun the whole thing out for as long as possible, then I laid the paper down on the tea table and showed it to him.

I wanted to have a bit of fun, so I said: 'As you can see, this describes the person I am looking for.'

He peered at it, looked at it from a distance, picked it up, checked both sides, and put it down again. He couldn't see anything.

'It's a blank bit of paper. What are you talking about?' He looked at me suspiciously.

It was a blank bit of paper, and the only thing that might be said to set it apart from any other blank piece of paper was that it was a shade thicker than normal, and that it had not been sized, so the surface was rough.

'No hurry,' I said. 'Everything that you need to know is written here.' I opened the bottle and dipped the brush in its contents, and then started to go to work on the paper. I wasn't writing, but laying down a thin wash, very carefully, as for a painting. Having laid down the wash the paper didn't change colour in the least, but a fine white mist rose up and at the same time there was a very soft crackling sound – as if the paper was burning, and having been dropped into water, the flames were being extinguished.

He was amazed and asked me, 'What are you doing?'

'Watch carefully.'

As I spoke, the words slowly began to appear on the page, one stroke at a time, as if they were being written by an unseen hand; the order in which the strokes appeared was not that in which they were written, but when the first word appeared in its entirety, it read: 'This'. Then the next appeared, and the next, one word after the other, as if by magic . . .

This document was written in a kind of invisible ink.

Why was it written in invisible ink? Of course, it was for security reasons. That way, if anything happened to me en route – say for example I was careless and lost something – even if someone else saw this paper, it wouldn't immediately reveal my identity as a secret agent or the important mission with which I had been entrusted. My mission was to come here – to the home of Chinese mathematics – and find a genius who could crack RECOVERY for us.

Cracking another country's cipher is basically a plot, a dark conspiracy – it is an undercover fight to the death between two countries, or between two political systems. At that time the situation with Taiwan was already so tense that war could break out at any moment, and so cracking RECOVERY was being pushed to the top of the agenda. It was top secret and there was no margin for error: even the slightest rumour leaking out would put us in an extremely disadvantageous situation and might even bring about the failure of our 'counter-RECOVERY' operation; and that would threaten the security of New China. Basically nothing about this operation could leak out. If there was a leak it couldn't come from me, or my life would be ruined. It was that way of thinking, that kind of concern that meant that before I left I had made special arrangements to maintain the secrecy of my mission, spreading a layer of concealing powder on my letter.

The concealing powder had to be laid down in conditions where oxygen and moisture had been eliminated, because when it came into contact with them it vanished into smoke, just like snow melting in the sun. As all concealment was stripped away, my secret mission became black ink on white paper, and I looked straight at the Party secretary. I noticed that he suddenly became very solemn. Then he asked me how many people I wanted. I held up one finger.

'One.'

'One? But ... what are your specifications?' he asked me suspiciously.

'First,' I said, 'it must be a mathematician with a record of independent research.'

He fished out a pen and made a note, murmuring under his breath: 'It must be a mathematician; that's number one.'

'Secondly,' I said, 'it must be someone who understands Russian, preferably someone who has studied there.'

'Understands Russian, preferably having studied in the Soviet Union ...'

'Thirdly, the person must have absolutely no political problems.'

'That's the third point; what is the fourth?'

'We don't want someone too old – preferably middle-aged or younger, and single is best.'

'That's the fourth point; what is the fifth?'

'There isn't one,' I said.

'Is that it?'

'That's it.'

'One person, who answers your four specifications.'

'Yes. The first three specifications are the important ones. We don't want many people – in fact, the fewer the better, and ideally only one. This isn't an ordinary battle where the side with the biggest battalions wins. This is one mathematician deconstructing another mathematician's meticulously created maze; both the mathematician who creates the maze and the one who deconstructs it must be very special; able to leap mountains in a single bound. That's the kind of person we are looking for, and I hope you can suggest some suitable candidates.'

'How many do you want?'

'How many have you got?'

'Maybe a dozen or so.'

'Let me see them,' I said.

'When?'

'As soon as possible.'

'That will be tomorrow.'

'Then set it up for as soon as possible.'

Perhaps it was because I had been so unpleasant to him, or perhaps it was because he was so nervous, that our conversation was very formal and we didn't say anything that wasn't relevant to the matter in hand; there were no jokes, no chatting, and no polite remarks – in fact when he left we did not even say goodbye.

6.

The following morning after breakfast, as I left the restaurant, I saw two people come out of my bodyguards' room next door. One of them was Party Secretary Wang and the other was someone I had never seen before. Party Secretary Wang introduced us, and informed me that the man was here to meet me, that he had a PhD in mathematics and had arrived back from the Soviet Union the year before. He was the first candidate that I saw. After that a stream of visitors came through my room, and by that evening I had interviewed twelve people, of whom two were women comrades. Of these people, only half stayed in my room for more than five minutes. That means that I threw most of them out pretty quickly, including the man with the PhD who had studied in Russia. Afterwards Party Secretary Wang said that he thought he was by far the best candidate, and that was why he had arranged for me to meet him first, and brought him round personally. The fact is that after he entered the room, I didn't even say a word to him; I just watched him for a bit and then told him to leave.

Why?

Party Secretary Wang asked me that question incessantly.

As I explained, when we entered my room, I had deliberately adopted an arrogant manner and did not say a word to him. It was a psychological test. He didn't realize that, and seeing me not say a word and looking like I hadn't even noticed his existence, from start to finish he kept a solicitous, empty smile on his face as he tried to ingratiate himself with me. If I indicated that I wanted to smoke, he came rushing forward to light my cigarette; and he took it upon himself to make tea. The way I thought about it, someone like that would be perfect for a job working with other people, but not for the soul-destroying work of cryptography. Anderov used to say that cracking ciphers is like communicating with the dead.

You don't have to worry about other people's feelings, you don't need to be thoughtful and considerate – you just have to work out a way to listen to the heartbeats of the dead.

Yes, cryptography is like listening to the heartbeats of the dead.

How can a dead person have a heartbeat? It is counter-intuitive, and fundamentally cryptography is massively counter-intuitive. Why do I say that cryptography is the most heartbreaking and difficult work in the world? Well, under normal circumstances a cipher cannot be cracked in anything under its set secure time, and so it is normal not to be able to break a cipher. It is decryption that is unusual. The secret workings of Heaven cannot be revealed, but if it is your job to discover them, your destiny from that moment on is heartbreaking and difficult. That means that our cryptographers had to possess absolute calm – an ability to keep their self-possession in the face of heartbreak and difficulty – as part of their psychological make-up. If, faced with someone pretending to be arrogant you become all confused and forget your own position, doing all sorts of menial tasks to try and please him, then your character is more than a little weak. How could someone like that convince me that the future would be bright? You must understand, at that time the first glimmers of the bright dawn we were looking for seemed as fine as gossamer, and at that time we were still in the midst of the storm. It seemed that perhaps only if we stayed as still as a corpse, not becoming alarmed whatever happened, not changing no matter how alarming the situation, day after day, night after night, that we might get a lucky break.

Of course cryptography is a branch of mathematics, and a profound and incisive mathematical capability was just as important and necessary as the right kind of psychological make-up. The two worked together like a pair of wings, and one without the other would be no good. I wasn't sure whether my method for testing their mathematical capabilities was entirely scientific and logical, for it might well turn out to be arbitrary and favour certain candidates unfairly. But I was absolutely sure that my assessment of their psychology was accurate. It was my principle that I would rather have a lack than a surplus, I didn't want too many people; in this context lots not necessarily being a good thing, while a few was not necessarily a bad thing either. Therefore I insisted on selecting the candidates in my own way, and of the twelve people I saw in the first round, I chose six who would sit the written paper.

The questions in this test were from the material that I had been given by Captain Hu, whereby two middle-level ciphers that had already been broken had been rearranged as two mathematical problems. Of course they weren't complete, but to a certain extent they would reveal the mathematical abilities of the individual, and their familiarity with ciphers. In the current situation, that was the only effective way to test our candidates. I decided to give them the paper with the first question, and two and a half hours to work on it. It was an open-book examination, so they could bring along whatever materials they liked, but they had to work independently. To show my sincere appreciation for their efforts, I invited all the candidates and the people overseeing the examinations to lunch, which would cost 2 yuan per person. I also gave the candidates and the invigilators 3 yuan to cover any additional expenses. I handed Party Secretary Wang 100 yuan, and ration coupons enabling him to buy ten *jin* of rice and ten *jin* of pork at any of the local shops. Party Secretary Wang was just amazed at the sight of the thick bundle of notes and the two really hard-to-come-by ration coupons, and stood there transfixed. Everyone had problems getting enough to eat in those days.

Discipline during the examination was excellent, and the result was OK: there were three successful candidates. Unfortunately the two people particularly recommended by Party Secretary Wang both handed in blank papers. That afternoon I reported the names of the three successful candidates to Party Secretary Wang, and said that I wanted to meet them. He arranged for me to see them one at a time in his office, and I then gave them the second question and told them to work out an answer independently. I had a good reason for not giving them the second question in an exam, because I wanted to test their moral character – to see if they would stick to the rules even if they weren't being supervised.

I don't need to say that the person that I wanted would come from these three. I could tell that the Party secretary was more than a little unhappy about my selection, perhaps because I had not picked any of the people that he had thoroughly recommended. I didn't have any choice: some people like greens and some people like radishes, and I wasn't going to set the menu according to his preferences. In very much the same way, at the banquet that he gave in my honour that evening, even though he wanted us to drink a toast together more than once, I simply refused.

Away from home I never drink; that had been my custom for many years.

At this so-called banquet, which turned out just to be me having the company of a few people while I was eating, the other guests were all important figures or principals from the Institute. With so many people present there was a lot of chat, and the meal seemed to drag on for ever. After eating we left the dining room, and as we walked through to the main room, I suddenly noticed there were a couple of people sitting on one of the sofas. One of them was a woman who stared at me with bold, hot eyes, with something of the air of a femme fatale. She must have been about thirty, maybe a little bit older, and her lips were painted deep red. She wore a narrow-striped black-and-white Lenin suit, and her hair was tied back with a white scarf, somewhat in a Western style. She looked just like a spy in a film. Perhaps it was because of that, I felt her smile was ambiguous. I couldn't believe that this was happening, and hoped that it was just a dream. But either way I felt the same kind of pain as if I had picked up something burning hot, and I was so scared that I did not dare look at her again.

Things then went from bad to worse. Shortly afterwards, I went back to my room after seeing off Party Secretary Wang and the others. She was standing outside the door to my room, and when she saw me she smiled very sweetly. I had the helpless feeling of someone whose world has just been turned upside down, and to disguise it I said accusingly, 'What do you want?'

'I've been looking for you.' Her voice was as sweet as her smile.

'Why have you been looking for me?'

'You're here looking for someone special, and I wanted to know more about it. Why, am I not welcome?' She spoke with perfect self-assurance.

'What do you do?' I asked coldly.

She shook her head like a little girl. 'Guess.'

'I don't want to guess,' I said roughly.

She seemed a bit taken aback, but pretty quickly she smiled again and said, 'Look at you! Carrying on as if I were a KMT sleeper.' She giggled. 'I'm not a KMT special agent, if that's what you're thinking. I'm a patriotic intellectual; a professor who came back from the USA to serve the motherland, invited by Prime Minister Zhou Enlai!'

I heard what she said but was more confused than ever, and for a moment I just stood there. She knocked on the door, and asked me very politely, 'How about opening the door and inviting me in?'

I had put my hand in my pocket to get the key, but I let go of it again. I asked myself whether it would be suitable to just let her into my room, given that I didn't know the first thing about her. The answer was negative. I asked her to go downstairs to the main lobby instead. She didn't seem to be too happy about that idea, and on the way downstairs she suggested that we go to the professors' accommodation block, where there was a coffee shop catering specially to foreign visitors.

'I'm not a foreign visitor,' I said.

'We can pretend that you are.' She then said something in a foreign language, very fluently, but I don't know what language she was speaking.

I was still hesitating when she took out a 10-yuan note and said, 'My treat. Surely you aren't going to say no!'

She didn't seem like a real person to me, more like someone out of a book. Both the way she spoke and the way she behaved made me feel really uncomfortable. In the end, though, I did go with her, and the whole way along the road I kept saying to myself, 'If she tries anything, you're getting the hell out of here.'

She seemed to understand what I was thinking, and said as if trying to cheer me up, 'Don't keep looking at me all bug-eyed, as if I were a wild animal or something. I'm not wild at all, just independent. Round here, everyone else is alike, cut from the same cloth, but I am unique. That's why it's worth your while making my acquaintance.'

In the darkness, I felt that her way of speaking seemed very artificial, and she threw in a lot of foreign words. It gave me goose-bumps to listen to her. I asked myself, who the hell was this woman?

7

Her name was Huang Yiyi, and just as she said, she was a patriotic intellectual. Before coming back to China she had worked for the world-famous mathematician John von Neumann, and she was a fairly well-known mathematician in her own right. I remember that Anderov once told me that von Neumann was then the best cryptographer in the whole world, and it was as if he had two completely different ways of thinking, one Eastern and one Western . . . At that time he was the only person in the world who had cracked both European and Asian ciphers. He had accepted a number of Asian students, so that they would give him insight into the way that their minds worked . . . Some people said that he was even cleverer than Einstein, that he was the last of the great mathematicians.

Lots of people know the story of how Huang Yiyi came to work for von Neumann; it was thanks to her amazing skills on the abacus. Her brilliance with an abacus was hereditary. In the Huang family shrine in Dayuan village, Yingde County, Guangdong Province, there hangs right up to the present day a calligraphic inscription by the Empress Dowager Cixi reading: 'The Best Abacist in the South'. That was her grandfather. As an old man he followed Sun Yat-sen, and for a while he was a manager in the Department of Revenue in the provisional Nationalist government. Later on people deduced from that that he had been Sun Yat-sen's personal accountant. Her grandfather started teaching Huang Yiyi to use an abacus when she was three years old, and by the time she was thirteen and moved to Guangzhou to start middle school, she wasn't appreciably slower than he was. When he was on his deathbed, he gave her his greatest treasure: a very valuable abacus with ivory beads. This made all the other members of the Huang family green with envy.

The abacus that she inherited from her grandfather was about the size of half a cigarette packet. Like a jade pendant, you could fit it in the palm of your hand, and the unusual materials and magnificent workmanship amazed everyone who saw it. The frame was carved from a solid block of wild elephant ivory, absolutely beautifully done, and each one of the hundred and one beads was gilded with pure gold, so that they glittered and shone when you looked at them. It was a remarkable experience to hold that abacus in your hand, because it was so lovely and so special.

Such a tiny and precious abacus isn't really an abacus – it is a piece of jewellery. You can look at it but you can't use it. The beads were so tiny, the size of mung beans, so that an ordinary person couldn't use it, and if they tried, they would have to move the beads really carefully with the tip of a fingernail. But Huang Yiyi could use that abacus at a speed comparable to any expert abacist; for the first few years to move the beads she used her own fingernails, all ten of which had been trimmed to a point. Later on she switched to using false nails like pipa players do, moving her hands with complete confidence. The tiny beads would then be set in motion with the speed of the wind or the rain, with a sound like flying sand or walking on pebbles, and it gave you the same feeling as watching an acrobat walking quickly along a high wire. This was her greatest skill and she was very proud of it. Wherever she went, she always carried her beautiful abacus with her, and whether happy or sad, whether she needed it or not, she would take it out and play with it. Sometimes she would show off with it – to strut her stuff, and let people know what she could do. Mostly though she used it because she was accustomed to having it with her; it was unintentional – she wasn't really aware of what she was doing. But with a skill like that, wherever she went people noticed her, and they remembered her.

In 1942, thanks to her exceptionally high grades, Huang Yiyi was sent on a Republic of China Ministry of Education scholarship to study for a PhD at the Mathematics department of MIT. One day John von Neumann came to give a lecture. Maybe she was deliberately planning to attract the attention of such a famous mathematician; anyway, in the break she got out her abacus and put on her long red false nails, and started click, click, clack, clack moving the beads. In an instant the great mathematician's attention was captured and he watched in fascination. A year later, at the viva for her thesis, she saw him again, and he came up to her beforehand and said, 'One of my assistants has just left. If your thesis defence is as impressive as your abacus use, you are welcome to come and work for me.' She did go to work for von Neumann, which instantly made her famous in the world of mathematics. With the founding of the People's Republic of China, six ministries and institutions (the Home Office, Foreign Affairs, Education, the Chinese Academy of Sciences and so on) came up with a list of patriots who should be invited back to help build a new China. Zhou Enlai himself signed the letters, which were sent to twenty-one individuals, one of whom was Huang Yiyi. She came back to China to become the youngest female professor anywhere in the country – at that time she was twenty-six years old. Later on she went to study for eight months in Moscow and came back with a nickname: Volga Fish. Very few people knew the story behind it.

Of course this was something I found out much later on. That evening, shortly after getting to the coffee shop, we went our separate ways without having said much. Or rather, I walked out. The coffee shop wasn't big, having been converted from a classroom. The owner was a middle-aged woman who looked to be from Xinjiang, though she actually turned out to be Russian, of Kazakh origin. Apparently her husband had been one of the first foreign experts to come from the Soviet Union, and she had opened the coffee shop so that the Russians would have somewhere to go. Now more than half the Russians had left, including her husband, but she had decided to stay. Huang Yiyi told me that she had got together with a Chinese man and could not bear to leave him; she wasn't staying for the coffee shop. With so many of the foreign experts gone, business was pretty bad – in fact when we got there I saw only one other customer. I don't know where he came from, but he was definitely a foreigner. He had a big beard just like Marx and he was listening intently to the song 'Auld Lang Syne' on the gramophone. When the record finished, he asked the owner in halting Chinese for permission to play it again. Since there were no other customers the whole room felt empty, and perhaps it was because of this that Huang Yiyi, while we were waiting for the music to start again, asked me to dance.

'I don't know how to dance,' I said.

'If you don't know, I will teach you,' she replied. She was determined to make me dance.

I was determined to refuse. I felt the whole thing was very peculiar: the idea of dancing with a strange woman in a coffee shop. I didn't dare think about it, let alone actually do it! But Huang Yiyi seemed fixated on the idea, and when she saw that I was absolutely resolute, she went over to the foreigner and asked him to dance with her. I don't know if she was thinking of getting back at me in some way. The foreigner stood up smartly and said thank you to me, as if I had given him something. Before they started dancing, Huang Yiyi went over to the owner of the coffee shop and said something to her in Russian; the owner laughed and came out from behind the counter to sit with me. Her Chinese was pretty good: other than an ugly accent, she could actually speak quite fluently. She asked me if I was Carmen's boyfriend. I asked who Carmen was, and she pointed at Huang Yiyi. I said I thought she was called Huang Yiyi. She laughed and said that clearly I wasn't Carmen's boyfriend. Then she explained to me that Huang Yiyi was her name, but that Carmen was her nickname, and that everyone here called her that. I asked why they called her Carmen, and she said, 'Don't you think she is adorable? Just like Carmen.'

To tell the truth, at that time I didn't know that Carmen was a character in a novel, but I could certainly judge whether she was adorable, and as to that the answer was: No! Not at all! How could you say she was adorable? Mad, more like! A lunatic!

Seeing the two of them circle me like a pair of disgusting flies, I felt really uncomfortable; and so pretty quickly I got up and left. I didn't say goodbye.

The following morning I went to find Party Secretary Wang

because I needed to look at the files on my three candidates. I happened to mention Huang Yiyi, and the Party secretary explained her situation. As he spoke, I could tell that he was very impressed by both her erudition and her capacity for original research. She was directing research on differential mathematics and mass differentials, one of two ongoing projects at the institute that had received much praise from the international mathematical community. On the other hand, he didn't seem to be too pleased with her free-and-easy, independent character.

'I think she's a classic idiot savant. She's obviously brilliant, but in some ways can hardly look after herself, because it seems she can't control her own thoughts and actions. She's always far too self-willed in what she says and does; far too unrestrained and independent. As a result she's always getting into fights, and some people have criticized her for being too bourgeois.' He looked at me and added, 'But then, who on this earth is perfect? Everybody has some shortcomings. She did live for years in the States, so of course her way of thinking has been affected by that. We need to reform her, but we also need to understand her. I do understand her, and I keep trying to persuade her that when in Rome she has to do as the Romans do. Her real problem is that she can't, or perhaps it would be fairer to say that she's not very good at it. But I think that in the end she will learn to fit in.'

I was wondering why, if her work really was that good, he hadn't recommended her. I asked him, and he laughed. 'You've met her, and you think she'd do? As you said, the woman's crazy!'

I thought, yes, how could we choose someone like her? Fundamentally she was just a clever bourgeois element.

As I left the Party secretary's office I put Huang Yiyi to the back of my mind, but it wasn't that easy. Her appearance, her voice, her words, her movements as she danced, came flying in front of my eyes like a persistent bluebottle. The thing is that the Party secretary's praise had aroused my curiosity, particularly as I realized that someone like that in your work unit must cause a lot of headaches. I hadn't expected him to say such nice things, which meant that her work must be absolutely brilliant. A crazy woman but an exceptional scholar: I thought she was awful but some people clearly liked her, like the woman running the coffee shop . . . She obviously wasn't just wild with nothing else to recommend her, and should not be lightly dismissed. I thought that it would be interesting to see her again, but then I remembered that I had put her in an awkward position the night before (walking out without saying goodbye), and if I now went to find her, for all I knew she'd just make fun of me. And of course she wouldn't be suitable for us – after all we were a special unit with particularly strict regulations, so only people whose behaviour and moral qualities were above question could work for us. Thinking like that, I finally let go of her.

I went back to the guest house with the candidates' files, and when I entered my room, I saw two envelopes on the floor. I knew that these would be the answer papers. The previous day I had given the three of them a mathematical maze, and now according to how they had solved the problem – whether they were right or wrong, how quickly they had done it, and how complex their proof was – I would make the final decision about which of them would be employed. Two people had already turned in their finished papers, and I sat down to read their answers, and discovered that both of them were correct, which made me very happy. I had been thinking that if none of the three were able to turn in an answer in the set time, or if they were all wrong, I really wouldn't know what to do for the best. As I saw from their workings, even though each of them had their own strong points, there wasn't much in it from the point of view of complexity and sensitivity, and it would be very difficult to choose between them. That meant that given that I had to pick just one of them, it would all come down to the material in their dossiers. So I was getting ready to go through them with a fine-tooth comb, and then make my choice, when I heard someone knocking on my door. When I went to open it, I discovered that it was Huang Yiyi. She stood in the doorway looking at me with the same dreamy smile as yesterday.

'Do you want something?' I asked.

'Yes,' she said. 'I'm not here to ask you to dance; don't worry.'

'What do you want?'

'Can I come in before I tell you?' Without waiting for my reply, she marched in and said, 'I'm here for the test. You are going to let me take it, aren't you?'

'What test?' I pretended not to know anything about it.

'Aren't you here to find someone special?' She opened her eyes really wide.

'Yes.' I didn't want to talk to her any more; I just wanted to get rid of her. 'But we've found the person we want, so it's over.'

'You mean I'm too late?'

'Yes.'

'You still haven't told me your name, so that I can get to know you.'

'My name is An Zaitian.'

'And what work unit do you belong to, Comrade An?'

'The same as you: a research institute.'

'And what kind of work are you expecting the person you are looking for to do?'

I didn't want to go into details, so I just said: 'The work of a mathematician and good citizen.'

'Mr An, can you please try to be a bit less sour?'

'Don't call me Mister. We're comrades.'

'I can tell you for free, you're still being sour.' Then she burst out laughing. A breath of wind through the window blew away the top page of the test paper lying on the tea table, exposing the question. Huang Yiyi was clearly transfixed by the equations set out there, and glancing at me she asked, 'Is this what you're working on?'

'No, it's for the person I'm here to find to work out.'

'So that's the test?'

'Yes.'

'Can I look?'

Before I had even agreed, she had picked it up and started reading.

I smiled coldly. 'Laughing and joking won't help you with this one . . .'

She didn't pay any attention to me; it was as if she were

quite alone. She was muttering to herself: 'It's a mathematical puzzle . . . someone's gone to a lot of trouble to make this look complicated . . . whoever came up with this is not entirely psychologically normal . . .' She seemed almost to be sleepwalking, and then she suddenly sat down, her lips moving silently. She seemed half awake and half dreaming. I had been startled by the sudden change: one moment she was laughing, the next she was in a world of her own, but without any obvious transition. It was as if there was a switch somewhere, which allowed her to change personality at will.

After a short time spent in a daze, she suddenly came to herself again, and raising her head she said, 'I can solve this equation, but it's going to take a bit of time. Can I take it away with me, or do you want me to work here?' I told her she could take it away, and found another copy of the question paper to give her. She picked it up and walked out, still somewhat disorientated. She seemed to be a completely different person from the one who had first entered my room.

I showed her out and, struck by her dazed look, I felt like a sleepwalker myself.

8

I was sleepwalking.

About half an hour later I heard the sound of her footsteps in the corridor, coming towards my room. The footsteps stopped when they got to my door, but there was no sound of knocking. Instead I saw that something was being pushed under the door. When I picked it up, I saw it was an answer paper, and a note. At the top of the note she had drawn a really cute cartoon of me instead of addressing me directly, and below she had written:

> I got out of the first maze in twenty-seven minutes, and I am sure I got full marks. I have had a quick look at your second maze and I am sure that given time, I can find my way out of that one as well. However right now I don't have time, I have to go and teach a class. From my knowledge of my colleagues, Xie Xingguo, Zhang Xin and Wu Guping have solved your first equation, but only Xie and Wu will have solved the second one; Zhang Xin will have handed in a blank paper. Oh, yeah, and I am pleased to make your acquaintance . . .

I am quite sure that at that moment my eyes were wide open with surprise, because she was absolutely correct: the only people who had solved both equations were Xie Xingguo and Wu Guping! I couldn't help thinking about what she had said, and I seemed to hear Anderov's voice in my ear: 'Most ciphers are decrypted accidentally, and most great cryptographers are also discovered accidentally . . .'

Really, I could hardly believe it, but she had solved the first equation in the time it took me to smoke two cigarettes. Amazing! I was so excited I couldn't sit still, and I kept going to the window, hoping that she would soon be on her way back from class. The umpteenth time that I looked out of the window I caught sight of her walking along carrying a bundle of mimeographed teaching materials, looking for all the world like a princess, her shoulders squared and her back straight. I was so excited to see her. All of a sudden she raised her head and looked straight at me, as if she had sensed something. When our gazes crossed, she seemed both surprised and pleased, and she casually blew me a kiss.

I really don't know how to describe her. What can I say? I made up my mind that whatever personal problems she had, provided there were no political problems, I could make allowances. The minute she solved the first problem so easily, I had no hesitation in putting her name on the list of candidates. I really hoped that she would solve the second equation as soon as possible. It was almost midday, so I decided to get a room at the hostel for her, and demanded that she give me an answer by two o'clock.

'No,' she said.

'What do you mean, no? If you want to take the test you're going to have to complete it according to my conditions.'

'Right. Then you're going to have to tell me what you want the person you are looking for to do.'

'Don't ask. If you're selected, of course you'll be told. Otherwise I will never tell you.'

'That's not fair. If you're asking me to leave here without telling me what I'm going to be doing, how do I know if I want to go or not?'

'You don't have a choice. That's part of the test. You have to be able to put the needs of the country first, and have a revolutionary consciousness that means you're willing to go wherever and do whatever the Party demands.'

'Well, I'm afraid that right now I don't have such an impressive level of revolutionary consciousness.'

'Then give up,' I said. I picked up the answer papers of the other two candidates and waved them in front of her. 'You were absolutely right; only two comrades solved both equations. However, right now you have only solved one, so if I pick you, if I make you the winner of this competition, that won't be fair.'

'I can tell you for free that I know both of them well, and if you're expecting them to be able to work independently, to do something earth-shattering, you're out of luck. Particularly with Xie Xingguo.'

'Why?'

'I know him only too well. He's a very proficient scholar, meticulous in his research, and a classic example of a super-patient person, but he lacks creative ability. If you want to set him to do some kind of theoretical research, he'd be perfect: you just have to tell him your idea, and he'll work out a beautiful proof for you. You won't be able to pick a single hole in it, and it may well be even better than anything you could ever think of yourself. But if you're hoping he'll come up with something independently, you'll find him completely lacking in inspiration. He has neither the ability nor the gumption to create something from nothing.'

'Have you done anything together?' I asked.

She replied in a tone as flippant as that she had used before, trying to keep me in suspense: 'Have we done anything together? Do you mean work or something else? Well, let's just say we've done all sorts of things together. We share an office at work, and as for the rest, that's my private business, though I dare say you can guess.' She smiled wickedly.

I really did not like the way that she was carrying on, so I said coldly, 'I'm really not interested in the rest of what the pair of you have been up to, but I'm somewhat surprised to hear you bad-mouth him in this way.'

'But I was praising him!' she said. 'I'm telling the truth!'

'You know perfectly well that saying those kinds of things about him might well mean that I decide not to hire him. But then that's what you want. You need him for your theoretical research, and you're afraid I might take him away.'

She laughed heartily. 'I'm not as small-minded as all that. Really, what do you think of me! Though I wouldn't mind if he did leave. That way ... well, to tell you the truth, we were having an affair but it didn't work out. These things happen. I guess you know that when people have been having an affair and then stop, quite often they end up as enemies, leaving a kind of festering sore. Who wants to spend all day, every day together under those kinds of circumstances – seeing each other every time you raise your head? If you want him, take him with you. If you want him to be your assistant, or indeed someone else's, that would be wonderful, and I'm sure you've made an excellent choice. He's very conscientious and hardworking. But if you want him to do original work, you're going to cause him a lot of unnecessary pain and suffering, because he simply can't do it.'

I could hear footsteps approaching in the corridor outside. Huang Yiyi heard them too. 'That'll be our Party secretary wanting to invite you to lunch. I'll say goodbye, then. After all, you won't be wanting me to join you.'

'Are you going to take the test?' I asked her.

She smiled and said, 'Nope.' Then she left.

The footsteps weren't actually those of the Party secretary, but one of the canteen staff, who had come up to tell me that lunch was ready. After lunch, I had a meeting with Xie Xingguo and Wu Guping. I had already read their files, and wanted to have a chat with them. It was strange, though: pretty much the only topic that we talked about was Huang Yiyi. She seemed to dominate my thoughts, like having a fish-bone stuck in your throat: you can't be happy until you've got rid of it. Clearly Huang Yiyi's independence had strongly aroused my interest and curiosity. When I discussed her with the others, what I really wanted was to find out the truth. The appraisal of the other two men made me realize that the Huang Yiyi that I had seen was the real one, but only part of her and not the whole. Much more than I had understood, they thought of her as a genius, an eccentric, a shameless woman, an original, a riddle . . . To quote her former lover, in Xie Xingguo's own words: 'She has a good side and a bad side – half angel and half devil.'

I should say that I had had that kind of impression too, so they were just confirming what I thought. It was not a feeling that I had had very often, and so it piqued my interest. I could clearly feel that the non-committal way in which the other two were talking about her, and the evidence that they adduced, was not only not reducing my curiosity about her but even adding oil to the flames; they were just adding to the impression that Huang Yiyi had already made in my mind. When I compared them to her, I could feel that she had a kind of wickedness and brutality about her – that they were domesticated, but that Huang Yiyi came from the wild. Yes, that's exactly what I felt, and it was a very strong impression, so strong that I could not get rid of it.

In spite of everything I was absolutely clear that I didn't want either of them, but I did want Huang Yiyi! Because this was the world of cryptography, and as everyone knows, ciphers are counter-intuitive and inhuman. A counter-intuitive subject is just the same as any other science, and so research and cryptography both require intelligence, knowledge, skill, experience, genius. But at the same time they also need a kind of evil – regardless of whether you are talking about research or cryptography – because both are inhuman. When you get right down to it, ciphers are deceitful, they are concealed, they attack you from the dark. Soldiers do not despise tricks, and ciphers are a kind of weapon, they are just hidden. They are the biggest trick in the world. In a world full of deceit, danger, wickedness and cruelty, perhaps an arrogant, overbearing, difficult and wild person would find it easier to survive . . . Once I got to that point, I picked up the phone and told Party Secretary Wang that I wanted to see him that afternoon.

Some time later, I set off to find him.

The Party secretary's office was on the third floor, and on my way up I passed a woman comrade on the stairs. Why do I remember her? When we passed each other, I noticed that she was crying bitterly – she had one hand over her mouth, and the other was clutching at her chest. Her head was hanging down, and she really did look terribly unhappy, as if she had lost all hope. I realized afterwards that the crying woman must just have left the Party secretary's office, and that was why he was in such a bad mood. When he saw me he was not as polite as he had been at our previous meetings. He asked me what was up, and I said straight out: 'I want to see the file on Huang Yiyi.'

'Huang Yiyi? You can't possibly want her! Are you . . .' The Party secretary fell silent, his expression eloquent with suspicion and scorn. This was something quite different from his earlier attitude of caution and unease. 'I hope you haven't been misled by the fact I said something good about her?'

I shook my head.

'Quite honestly, I said what I did because I was quite sure you wouldn't want her. But if you are thinking of employing her, I can tell you that in my opinion she is unsuitable, completely unsuitable.' Seeing I wasn't going to interrupt, he added, 'Of course, she has her good points. She's very clever, very erudite, hardworking, successful, and she has done some interesting independent research. But . . . I really don't know how to put this . . . You must believe me, the woman has problems – she really isn't suitable.'

I asked what problems, and the Party secretary said that it was private and he could not say. I said that as far as Unit 701 was concerned there is no such thing as a private problem. In fact, it wasn't very clever of him to start talking about something or other being private: it was very disrespectful to us, given that we are ourselves top secret. Besides, who can keep secrets from us? An individual? A country? We investigate other people's private affairs for a living, and they in return try to discover ours. We don't like that feeling, we try to keep it to a minimum, and one of the best ways is to remove the word private from our vocabularies. Excise it. Just like you might excise a disgusting tumour.

The Party secretary noticed that I had gone all stiff, and he smiled and said, 'I can tell you, but you must promise that it won't go any further.' Then he laughed. 'In much the same way as I will not tell anyone about you.'

I didn't reply but waited for him to continue.

He said, 'If you'd arrived a couple of minutes earlier, you would have seen the problem. Comrade Huang Yiyi's problem. About a minute before you came through the door, the woman comrade concerned left here crying.'

'I met her on the stairs,' I said. 'A middle-aged woman, wearing a white dress?'

'That's the one.'

'I noticed she was crying. Why?'

'Go and ask Comrade Huang. After all, she seduced her husband.'

Huang Yiyi's provocative gaze and smile, and the sound of her laughter, immediately sprang to mind. I asked stupidly, 'Are you sure? How do you know who seduced whom?'

The Party secretary said, 'I don't need to investigate. I am quite sure that she seduced this other woman's husband.'

'If you don't investigate, how can you be sure?'

'You don't understand the situation. I do – only too well.' As he spoke he pulled a stack of letters out of a drawer and handed them to me to read. I looked through them and they were all complaints, some anonymous, some signed, but the contents were the same: 'Huang Yiyi's thinking is tainted by bourgeois corruption and she engages in illicit relationships with members of the opposite sex.' Some of the letters named names, saying who it was, when and where. As I read through them, I asked the Party secretary what kind of people were involved. He said all kinds, some from the institute, and some from outside.

'So many? How is that possible?'

'With her, anything is possible. I've asked her about most of the named men, hoping she'd deny it, or at least try to make excuses for herself, but she didn't. She didn't.' He sighed. 'Quite honestly, this has caused an awful lot of trouble. Every time there's a meeting of the directors of the institute someone asks us to punish her or get rid of her. She's very lucky to have a weapon: after all, Zhou Enlai himself invited her to come back. If it weren't for that she would have been thrown out of here long ago. Huang Yiyi, Huang Yiyi . . . You know the saying, "When in Rome, do as the Romans do"? Since coming back to China she still behaves in this completely Westernized way. How can we accept that? How can she behave like that?'

'Does she have a family?' I asked.

'What kind of man would want her?'

'Perhaps she would sort herself out if she was married.'

'Do you think she hasn't been married? She's been married twice, divorced both times.'

'In the US or in China?'

'Once in the US and once here. When she got married in the US, her husband was a chemistry professor, an overseas Chinese from Fujian. The two of them got divorced just before she came back. Not long after she arrived in China, she got together with a cameraman working in the film studios in Changchun, but they divorced not long after the wedding because she was having an affair.'

'So after that divorce she didn't remarry?'

'Remarry? Who would be willing to marry someone like her? She told me herself that she is not expecting to get married again, because no one would really want to marry her. Those men are all just for fun. She's basically given up on herself, and that's why she behaves in this uncontrolled way. Well, this is a research institute, and we give our people considerable leeway. Lots of our people have had experience of living abroad, and we let her get away with it. In any other work unit, she wouldn't have lasted five minutes. She would have been classified as a poisonous weed and been got rid of long ago. Is this really the kind of person you want? Please don't give her the job. The crucial thing is that you don't need her. Let me tell you, Comrades Xie Xingguo and Wu Guping are fine mathematicians; anything she can do, they can do. They don't have any thought or lifestyle problems, so if you take them, they will work well for you. If she goes, maybe even before she has had time to do anything useful, she will have got herself into trouble. When she gets into trouble, will your work unit have any choice other than to get rid of her? And when things get to that pass, even if she wants to work for you, she won't be able to. So why put everyone through the misery?'

The Party secretary had no idea that the blacker he painted Huang Yiyi, the more determined I was to give her the job. I understood that in the trap-filled, dangerous, evil and cruel world of cryptography, only someone arrogant, wild and ambitious would survive. I also thought to myself that while Unit 701 was a much more conservative place than the institute, if she cracked RECOVERY, we could make allowances for pretty much anything. So in spite of all Party Secretary Wang's admonitions, I still wouldn't give up, and demanded to see their file on her.

The Party secretary was in despair. 'Do you really want her?'

I tried to cheer him up. 'I can only decide after I have seen her dossier.'

In fact I had already made up my mind. If there weren't any other problems, I wanted her!

9.

Shortly after I got back to the guest house after my conversation with Party Secretary Wang, I heard someone knock on the door. When I opened it, I found Huang Yiyi. She had taken off her coat, and was wearing a tight dark-blue jumper that moulded every line of her body. Her breasts stuck out like two little cushions. I wasn't intending to look at them, and I turned my eyes away immediately as if I had received an electric shock.

'I've been looking for you,' I said.

'Well, this is the second time I have come here to find you,' she said.

'Why did you want to see me?'

She handed me a piece of paper. 'My answer.'

Although she had said that she didn't want to do it, in fact she had gone home and got on with it. I looked through the workings and found the solution, and she was absolutely correct. I was very pleased, but when I spoke it came out sounding strange. 'Dr Huang.'

'Please don't call me that. Right now I am your student and you are examining me.'

'So how do you think you have done?'

'I have made no mistakes.'

'Well, you are the one with a PhD . . .'

She stopped me again. 'I have already told you not to call me Doctor. Do you know what I think about my PhD?'

'What?'

'During the day I have a PhD; at night I don't.'

'What do you mean?'

'What do you think? PhDs are only human. At night, they're out for fun the same as anyone else.'

As she spoke she started laughing really hard, and ended up

bent over. As she bent, I unintentionally caught sight of her breasts again, bursting seductively out of her clothes. I thought to myself that Party Secretary Wang was absolutely correct: would it be suitable for me to take her away with me? The minute this idea flashed across my mind, I dismissed it. I decided that this was not a question of personal suitability, because only she could do the job.

When she had finished laughing, she asked me politely, 'You said that you had been looking for me. What's up?'

I answered just as politely, 'I need to ask you a couple of questions, and I hope you will answer them truthfully.'

She looked at me coaxingly, and said, 'Don't make them too difficult.'

'They aren't difficult at all, but you must tell the truth.'

'No problem. Ask away.'

'Question number one. Have you ever done any cryptography before?'

'Yes.'

'Would you be willing to do that kind of work again?'

'No.'

'Why not?'

'Because it really is the devil's work!'

'Do you know who I am?'

'I guess you are with the security services, am I right?'

'You are absolutely correct. Are you willing to join us?'

'No. And to join a top-secret unit, definitely not.'

'What is the problem with a top-secret unit?'

'Is that the place for someone like me?'

'What do you mean, someone like you?'

'Independent, romantic, someone who hates having to go by the rules, someone who is happiest when free from ties.'

'Then why on earth did you insist on taking the test?' I was getting angry.

She laughed heartily. 'Do you think that just because I took the test it means that I want to join your unit? I don't even know what kind of unit it is, so why would I want to do a stupid thing like that?' Having finished laughing, she said seriously, 'To tell you the truth, I came to take the test because I wanted to meet you. For the last couple of days my colleagues have done nothing but gossip about you, and I was curious, that's all.'

I was furious, but I was also secretly pleased. The fury was because I felt she was being silly and disrespectful, but I was pleased because I was sure that I was getting the truth, and because no one could have helped her get the answer. She hadn't intended to take the test, I hadn't meant to give it to her: put the two together and what you end up with is the truth, something that will stand up to scrutiny.

Earlier that afternoon I had spoken to Captain Hu on the phone, because I hoped that he would have a look at Xie Xingguo and Xu Guping's answer papers and help me to decide which of them I should employ (at that time I didn't think Huang Yiyi was going to finish). He arrived just at that moment. When he came through the door, he looked at Huang Yiyi a couple of times, and then rushed forward and grabbed her hand. He seemed very pleased, and said: 'Huang Qian! Don't you remember me? I'm Hu Haibo!' Then he turned round and said happily to me, 'This is the woman I told you to find: Huang Qian!'

Later on I found out that she had become suicidal after the painful split from the cameraman. Because of this the Party arranged for her to go as a visiting scholar to the Soviet Union for a year, in the hope that she would cheer up away from home. Perhaps it was in the hope of making a fresh start that she changed her name during her stay in Russia. And again perhaps it was to draw a line under the past that when she finished her time abroad she didn't go back to Harbin Military Engineering University but came here, to Beijing.

In short, she was Huang Qian.

What else was there to say? I wanted her!

So I told Huang Yiyi: 'I can announce officially that you are now working for us, and we will begin the formalities for your transfer immediately.'

'Is this some kind of joke?' she asked with a laugh.

'No joke,' I said. 'We need someone like you.'

'No,' she said, raising her voice. 'You need me but I don't need you!'

Captain Hu told her to keep the conversation civil, and not to get excited. She seemed to be trying to force herself to calm down as she walked over to the window. With her back to me, she said quietly, 'I'm not going with you. You don't understand, I am a . . . bad person . . .'

'I do understand, and I am sure you will be very successful with us.'

She started getting excited again, and shouted, 'But I don't want to do it! I am not going with you!'

'You have no choice.'

She came right up to me and said threateningly, 'It is not up to you.' Then she turned to go.

I grabbed hold of her and asked where she was going, and she said, 'I am going to talk to the principal. I am not leaving here!'

'The principal has his orders,' Captain Hu said.

She stared at me for a while, and then said through gritted teeth: 'Who the hell are you? I hate you!'

Captain Hu got her to sit down, and then I said, 'You clearly don't understand the situation at all, but don't you want to know what is going on? Since I have already decided that we want you, I can now tell you the truth. I am the Deputy Director of the research institute at the intelligence unit 701, and I have absolute power here. If I want you to join us, you have no right to refuse. You will have to come with me.'

'If I don't go?'

'That is not possible.'

'I beg you . . .'

'No.'

After a short silence, I started to persuade her. 'Comrade Huang, you've said yourself, and I know, that you're a patriotic intellectual. The country now needs your help on an issue of national security and I believe that you will not refuse. The work we're asking you to do touches on the sacrosanct issue of the survival of our country. I hope you will not continue showing this antagonistic attitude, but come with me of your own free will.'

She was dead set against it though, and stubbornly refused; there was no way that she would come with me. In the end it was Captain Hu who came up with a trick to make her move. 'He's just a middle manager, there's no point yelling at him. Go with him and tell the senior people what you think. That's more to the point.'

It worked, and she agreed to go with me.

The captain took me aside and told me what I should tell Director Tie to say to her. 'When Director Tie sees her, he shouldn't try and change her mind or appeal to her moral principles: that won't work for someone like her.'

'So what should he say?'

'You must make it clear that she is under your control, that she has to come and there is nothing to discuss. Having made that clear, on that basis you can discuss her conditions. That way it's clear that you respect her, but also that you are very powerful.'

'What do we do if she wants to be unreasonable, and sets us some impossible conditions?'

'Is it possible that she can ask for something that you can't do? Besides, it's just a tactic to bring her under psychological control, to make her understand your determination and your power.'

I realized that he was right, and took her to meet Director Tie. While the two of them were talking, I was waiting uneasily in the corridor outside. I knew Director Tie very well: he was always exceptionally vigorous and decisive, and spoke in such a loud and awe-inspiring voice – but this time I wasn't sure that he could pull it off. Director Tie's manner worked for people like us, but would it work with Huang Yiyi? She was like a wild horse, used to roaming free across the plains and going wherever she liked: she had never been broken to the bridle! I didn't know if Director Tie could do what Captain Hu had suggested and bring her under psychological control. I was so tense that my heart was thumping.

About half an hour later, Director Tie came out looking pleased and patted me on the back. 'Right, she's yours,' he said. 'You can take her away tomorrow.'

I just stood there. I had no idea what Director Tie could have said to make her change her mind, to make her become one of my people. I was amazed, but I also felt a kind of unimaginable happiness spread through my entire body, as though it were being pumped through my veins by the beats of my heart.

When Director Tie noticed me looking so happy, he leaned towards me and whispered in my ear, 'She made conditions.'

'What conditions?'

'When she's cracked the cipher she can leave, and she can take one person with her.'

'Who?'

Director Tie looked at me strangely. 'That's her secret. How should I know?'

I smiled. 'If she can really help us crack the cipher, she can take away a whole mountain for all I care!'

The following morning we set off. I was carrying a suitcase I had been given by Director Tie: a very big and very heavy suitcase, with a red thread hanging from it. Director Tie didn't tell me what was inside it, but when I saw the fuse for the incendiary device (otherwise known as the red thread) I knew that it was top-secret material, probably connected with the cipher that we had to break. I knew that there could be no mistakes. If something happened en route, it was my duty to light the fuse and turn all the secrets inside into ash . . .

10.

Young man, do you think this will do? I can't carry on, I am too tired. Let's continue tomorrow . . .

11

There's no need to be in such a hurry. I want you to look at these photographs.

These are pictures of me as a young man. Look at that one – that's nice and clear. I was pretty good-looking when I was young. Some people admired my nose, and said such a straight bridge and such neat nostrils were a sign I was a reliable man. Some people admired my mouth, with its generous, well-defined lips, and said it was a sign of honesty. Some people admired my forehead, square and with a strong eyebrow ridge, and said it was a sign I would be successful. Look at this picture – you can see how tall and fit I was. Some people said my proportions were pretty much perfect. People said all girls loved men like me – serious, stable, upstanding, good-looking, with a great future in front of me; attractive. But to tell the truth, when I was young none of the girls fancied me. I found it very difficult to get married, and though I had three serious girlfriends none of these relationships worked out, so that in the end the Party had to find me a wife. The reason I'm telling you this is because I want you to understand that other people thought of me as a really outstanding guy. By the time I met Huang Yiyi I was past forty; I had been married and had children; women were no longer a mystery to me. That meant that when Huang Yiyi unfurled like a flower beside me and started murmuring seductive words, it never excited or flustered me: I treated the whole thing as a joke.

I should explain that the journey to Unit 701 was very smooth, though we did have problems getting the train.

At that time there weren't as many trains as there are now, and besides Unit 701 was based in an out-of-the-way little rural county, a backwater – until our work unit moved out there, they didn't even have a train station. Every day the trains just went through with a whistle; they were not willing to stop. Unlike buses, trains are proud creatures: they don't halt when they see people. Of course, it depends on what kind of person you are; for a member of Unit 701, trains go when you want them to and stop when you say so. If there isn't a track, then one has to be laid; if there isn't a platform, then one has to be built. That's why after our arrival at that rural backwater trains had to stop there. There was only one direct service a day from Beijing Main Train Station though, and it didn't stop for long, just three minutes. That train left at eleven o'clock in the morning. Because Huang Yiyi didn't want to go with me, it took ages to get her ready and she kept being tiresome: one minute she wanted to do one thing, the next she wanted to see so-and-so – anyway, what with one thing and another we were delayed. The train left at eleven, and on the stroke of eleven we were running for the platform. Like I say, trains aren't like buses: you can't yell at them to stop. The train was deaf – even as I yelled, it started gathering speed as it pulled out of the station. I could see carriage after carriage speeding past me as it left the platform, each of the windows packed with black heads, and I was so furious that if I could have ripped up the tracks, I would have done!

Well, we'd missed it – we would have to wait until the following day. So another day would be wasted. This wasn't just a question of time, but a security problem: my own personal safety and the security of the secret I was carrying. My personal safety was the responsibility of a whole chain of people; I didn't know what they were up to, but I knew that they had everything under control. Sometimes they were beside me, sometimes they were far away, sometimes they were both. In every sense of the words, they knew me better than I knew myself; before I had arrived, they knew exactly what time I would come; before I had left, they knew when I would set out. I have reason to believe that on that day at eleven o'clock, as they saw the train I was supposed to be travelling on pull out from the platform, they all went home feeling that the job had been well done, and didn't give me another thought. Thinking like that, I gave myself goose-bumps. When people become nervous, it is hard to avoid acting hastily. I found the station guards and showed my pass, asking that they allow me to make a phone call. I wasn't entirely clear who I was talking to, but I had been told that if I encountered some problem that needed sorting out in a hurry, I should phone that number. I started to explain the situation over the phone, but before I had got very far, the person at the other end gave me two orders:

One: not to move from my present location.
Two: someone would arrange for us to be on our way immediately.

Ten minutes later the station master was standing in front of me.

Half an hour after that the station master personally escorted us onto a special train consisting of a single sleeper carriage. The station master informed me that this train would stop specially for a couple of minutes in the middle of nowhere to allow the two of us to get off. I thought with amazement of the mysterious phone call that I had just placed. I didn't know who I had phoned – I still don't know today. But I could sense, and have good reason to believe, that I was talking to someone very powerful, perhaps in Zhongnanhai, perhaps in some other, even more secret place.

Of course, this phone call did not just spare me a potentially very worrying wait; it also allowed me to enjoy a comfortable and safe journey. I had travelled by soft-sleeper before, but always with lots of other people around. This was the very first time I got a whole compartment without any strangers. Given that there were just myself and Huang Yiyi there, it felt like part of Unit 701, so we could discuss things openly, without having to worry and hide. But it was those special circumstances that allowed Huang Yiyi to start to unburden herself to me without restraint.

She said, 'You dragging me to your work unit kicking and screaming – is this because you fancy me and are looking for a relationship?'

In the previous few days I had become very used to her way of speaking, and had come to know a lot about the sort of thing that she was likely to do, so now I wasn't in the least bit surprised. I said calmly, 'What kind of person do you take me for? I have children, a boy and a girl.'

'You may be married with a family, but that doesn't mean you can't have other relationships.'

'That's bourgeois corruption.'

'It's not bourgeois corruption, it's romantic. Don't tell me you've never had a romantic relationship?'

'During all these years of warfare, we relied on the romantic fervour of our revolutionary spirit to bring us victory over every danger.'

'And in the end brought about the liberation of the whole of China,' she continued where I had left off, 'allowing patriotic intellectuals such as myself who had been forced into exile overseas to have their own country and their own home.'

'Yeah,' I said.

'But I still don't have a home.'

'You will.'

'Are you trying to cheer me up?'

'No.'

'But I feel really depressed.'

'Why?'

'Because the person I love doesn't love me.'

'Who?'

'You!'

It was then that she told me that the reason she had come to see me in the guest house was that the afternoon of my arrival, as she walked across the playing field, she had glanced up and caught sight of me standing at the window, staring out. Although I was a long way away, she had been deeply attracted by my handsome and thoughtful appearance.

'I was sure you were looking at me,' she said.

'I was not,' I said quickly. 'The first time I saw you was the day that you came looking for me.'

'Oh. Well, what did you feel when you saw me? Your first impression.'

'Unusual.'

'You didn't fancy me?'

'No.'

'You don't love me?'

'Right.'

'You don't dare to love me.'

'Perhaps.'

'You're a coward, for all that you look like a real man.'

'Perhaps.'

'But I still love you. Please can you take my hand?'

Of course, I refused.

That wasn't the problem – the problem was that something an ordinary person would have the greatest difficulty in putting into words, she would say in such a relaxed, generous, unhurried, thoughtless, open, direct way, as if it were a quite ordinary question, a perfectly normal request. She would just open her mouth and out it came – that really did startle me, time and time again. I had heard of this kind of thing, but never experienced it myself before. So I felt a bit light-headed and tense, as if I were looking down into an abyss. At that moment I really thought she was a devil in an angel's body. Whatever you might think of her, she really did have an angelic side: she was very pretty. Whether you consider her intelligence, her abilities, her position, or her good looks they were all amazing: she was absolutely dazzling. That kind of woman is very special – you might happen across one but you are not going to find one by looking for her. But at the same time I could sense a kind of evil spirit in her, passionate, coquettish, obsessive, daring, bitter, dissolute, selfish, fearless, contemptuous of all authority – shameless, like a witch.

Unique – witch – pretty – passionate – intelligent – dissolute – clickety-clack – clickety-clack . . . The closer we got to Unit 701, the more nervous I became: I wasn't bringing back a cryptographer but a Western capitalist poisonous weed!

12

In a sense you could say that the people I brought back to the unit became part of me. If they did well, that reflected on me; if they did badly, that was also my problem. Thanks to my usual caution, and due to a well-founded concern about Huang Yiyi's unconventional actions and way of speaking, after I got back to our work unit, I didn't tell our superiors too much about her special abilities, nor did I explain that she was particularly suited to the work of cracking RECOVERY thanks to the fact that she had been von Neumann's assistant and had spent time in Moscow. I just vaguely explained that she was a mathematician, somewhat independent and free and easy in character, but that she ought to be suited to cryptography work. It was my intention not to encourage people to expect too much of her – a bit conservative, a bit low-key – so that when she did come up with a result people would be even more amazed, which would give us the upper hand.

It seemed as though the people at Unit 701 couldn't wait, because the afternoon of the day after we arrived, Unit Director Luo summoned all the relevant personnel for a get-together in her office. Among those present were Chen Erhu, one of the Deputy Directors of the unit, and a cryptography Bureau Chief; Comrade Jiang, the manager of the calculations division; and Comrade Jin, the manager of the analysis division, all of them mainstays of Unit 701. This was described as a get-together, but in fact it was intended to be a mobilizing meeting, since we not only had to swear oaths and sign our names right on the spot, but we also opened the steel suitcase that I had been carrying to discover its secrets (which turned out to be a commercial encryption machine invented by Sivincy, three books of mathematical theory that she had written, and a black folder containing a list of the names of all KMT army officers above the rank of major, senior government ministers, and police officers above the rank of chief superintendent), and created a little special working party of which I was the head, having selected ten top-class people from the calculations division and five from the analysis division to assist us in our work. Comrade Jiang and Comrade Jin both volunteered to join the special working party, and I naturally expressed my warmest welcome. I invited Chen Erhu to join as well, but he didn't want to, so I couldn't force him. He mentioned a couple of good cryptographers to me and suggested that I go and meet them and get to know them a bit. Anyone that I wanted, he would transfer to me. I said that would be fine. Huang Yiyi then took it upon herself to start bickering with him. 'And if we want you?'

Comrade Chen said coldly, 'I accept whatever the Party demands.'

As the meeting went on, I could clearly feel that Comrade Chen was unhappy about Huang Yiyi. I felt that this was her fault – after all she had only just arrived and shouldn't speak so rudely to anyone; and when the person concerned was Comrade Chen, she really should be modest and polite, given that he was not only one of the most important people in the unit, but also one of our best cryptographers. At least, before Huang Yiyi arrived in our unit and after she left, he was the very best cryptographer. But in Huang Yiyi's dictionary there was no such word as modest. That was her problem.

When the meeting was over, it was my intention to take Huang Yiyi to the calculations division, the analysis division and the cryptography division to have a look, so that she could familiarize herself with conditions here. But she was in a listless mood and didn't want to go; she wanted me to take her for a walk around the unit. So I took her all round, which I guess counts as letting her get to know the place. I discovered that with practically every step we took, there was a pair of curious eyes weighing us up, as if they had just seen something unusual or discovered a secret. She became really cheerful, looking at this and asking questions about that – if she saw a pretty flower then she wanted to pick it, if she saw a pretty bird she wanted to run after it. In that manner we wandered out of the strictly guarded work area into the living area outside it, and finally we ended up in the guards' little compound. There was a vast magnolia tree in the middle of the compound, which was completely covered in white flowers. The moment Huang Yiyi caught sight of the tree with all its flowers and buds, she emitted an excited squeak. There was a concrete ping-pong table under the tree, and a load of soldiers were standing around watching a game of elephant chess. When they noticed us, they all looked up and gawped at Huang Yiyi. Bureau Chief Yuan of the guards unit saw that Huang Yiyi really liked the magnolia and told one of the guards to climb the tree to pick some flowers for her. The soldier was just about to get up into the tree when Huang Yiyi stopped him. She was looking at the interrupted game laid out on the ping-pong table, and asked which one of them was the best player. They all said it was Comrade Zhang, the clerk in their office. Huang Yiyi said to Bureau Chief Yuan, 'I don't want a reward I haven't earned. I'll play a game of elephant chess with the best player you have, and if he loses then you have to send someone up into the tree to pick flowers for me, OK? If I lose, I'll climb the tree myself.'

Of course, the Bureau Chief agreed.

Huang Yiyi walked up to the ping-pong table and slapped down her chariots, horses and cannons, and then told Comrade Zhang that he could go first. The soldiers all looked at her in stupefaction. But what surprised them even more was that she put down her pieces really quickly, moving her delicate hands all over the board at a speed that made us dizzy, almost as if she wasn't thinking about it at all. Nevertheless she beat Comrade Zhang in no time at all. Then someone went up into the tree and picked an armful of magnolia flowers for her.

Huang Yiyi gathered up her flowers, and followed me happily out of the guards' barracks. Everyone we passed seemed to look at her, staring at the flowers in her hand, or at her appearance. On the way, Huang Yiyi noticed some people walking along the road carrying bowls and chopsticks, and so she asked me if it was lunchtime, and could we go and get something to eat. I thought that she shouldn't go to the canteen looking like that, so I told her to take the flowers home first and get changed. But when Huang Yiyi reappeared at the canteen having left her flowers at home and got changed, everyone's eyes stood out on stalks! Why? Well, she had changed into a very low-cut jumper, which she was wearing without a jacket, and the top two buttons of her white shirt had been left undone – revealing an expanse of pale flesh to the point where you could almost see her cleavage – and she had put on bright red lipstick. When I told her to go home and get changed I was thinking that she'd put on something plainer; I had no idea that she . . . Well, she'd got herself dressed up like a Mata Hari, and when she came to a halt in front of us, we were all stunned. They stared at her and then they stared at me, which clearly meant: What the hell kind of person is this that you've brought back?

You could say that while lots of people used their eyes to ask me that question, only old Comrade Chen came right out and said it.

I met Chen in his office. He had an office, and a cryptography room next to it. When Huang Yiyi and I went to his office, we found nobody there, so we went to the cryptography room. When he heard the sound of knocking, Chen came out, but when he caught sight of Huang Yiyi he immediately shut the door to his cryptography room, as if he had seen a ghost, and insisted that we go to his office. I had heard that Chen was terribly superstitious, and would not let a woman into his cryptography room under any circumstances whatsoever. Cryptographers all have their own idiosyncrasies and taboos, because in addition to knowledge, experience, intelligence and application, the job also requires the kind of luck that comes from far beyond the stars. Luck is a mysterious, elusive thing, and if you want to catch it, you have to become mysterious yourself.

When we got to his office, Chen came straight to the point. 'You're here to pick someone?'

Huang Yiyi got in ahead of me. 'I guess so.'

Chen clearly didn't like the way that she was taking charge, and with some resentment he got out a list of names and gave it to her.

'Everyone's here. Have a look. You can choose one or two comrades off this list to be your assistants.'

Huang Yiyi leafed idly through it and then gave it back to him. 'This doesn't tell me anything: it's just a list of names.'

'What do you want? Do you expect me to call them all in and let you pick them by interview?'

'Not at all.' She walked over to Chen's desk and started inspecting one of the photographs placed under the glass top, asking, 'Are these all your colleagues?'

'Pretty much.'

Huang Yiyi continued her inspection for a moment, then she pointed to an old comrade wearing glasses. 'Who's he? A cryptographer?'

'You can't have him,' Chen said.

'Why not?'

Chen gestured to me to answer, and I explained that the old comrade was not at all well, and that he could not possibly do this kind of work. In actual fact, he was schizophrenic and completely insane.

What I wasn't expecting was that with her next question Huang Yiyi would get right to the point. 'Is he mad?'

'How did you know?' I asked.

'I guessed as much. I looked at his eyes – terribly neurotic, just one step away from madness.'

'He used to be the very best cryptographer we had,' I said.

'People like that are often only one step away from genius.'

'He was driven mad by cryptography. He was under too much stress and his mind just snapped like an over-tight violin string.'

'Like Nash,' she said.

'Who?'

'John Nash, one of the mathematicians behind game theory. He was driven mad by cryptography too.'

Chen suddenly interrupted. 'You're also mad.' He paused. 'We're all mad.'

His words left Huang Yiyi flabbergasted.

I understood what Comrade Chen was trying to say. From start to finish he had his own perspective on the problem of having to decrypt RECOVERY. He thought that our decision to crack it was arbitrary and had not been properly thought through; that it was absolutely absurd; that we were crying for the moon; that this was mad. The previous night he had come to my room to explain his reasoning. Now he repeated it for Huang Yiyi.

'First,' he said, 'as we all know, RECOVERY is one of the world's most difficult ciphers, and it must be reckoned to be secure for at least a decade. That means that under normal circumstances no one can crack it in anything less than ten years. Why have we decided to break it? Because we've decided to take the initiative in the current cross-Straits tension with Taiwan. How long is this tension going to last? A year? Two years? Or will it be ten? Or twenty? I'm thinking a year or two at the most. That means that in order to be of any use, we have to crack this cipher within the shortest possible time – within the next year or two. But the thing is that we might well not even begin to make headway for years. There you are, looking all solemn. You're mad, I tell you, completely insane; and if you don't believe me, just wait and see . . .'

Comrade Chen was that kind of person – mostly he wouldn't say much, but if he did speak it was impossible to argue with him. He didn't beat about the bush, he didn't try and avoid the issue, and he didn't try to be accommodating – he would just tell it to you straight and leave everyone feeling awkward. In fact we understood his point of view perfectly, but this was a decision by our superiors and what could we do other than obey? I said that, but Comrade Chen immediately set on me again.

'I understand that this decision came from our superiors, but we all know it's completely stupid. There's no need to take it so seriously, getting everybody involved and now also bringing in a mathematician specially from outside. Of course, now she's here she's very welcome, but if you ask my opinion, good steel should be left for use in knives, and so we ought to set her to cracking other ciphers, and just put a couple of people to work on RECOVERY, so that it looks OK to our superiors.'

Was this a suitable thing for a Bureau Chief to say? If any of our superiors had heard him, he would have been fired! I knew though that he didn't like being in administration. The cryptography division was a vocational work unit, but even so the better you were at your job the more likely you were to be promoted into administration. He was an uncrowned king.

I had heard Chen speak like this many times, and I couldn't be bothered to argue with him. I wasn't expecting though that Huang Yiyi would take it seriously. She said, 'If I understand you correctly, there is no way that we can crack RECOVERY.'

'Not in the short term.'

'Not necessarily.' Huang Yiyi stepped right into the firing line as she said firmly, 'What is a cipher other than an unusually abstruse mathematical problem? There's nothing to be afraid of there.'

Her words transfixed both Comrade Chen and me. After a long pause, Chen replied respectfully, 'OK. Let's see what you can do.'

'No, you have a part to play too.' She turned her head to speak to me. 'Deputy Director An, I hope that Bureau Chief Chen will join our little cryptographic working party!' Then she walked out and did not stop no matter how much I yelled after her.

Comrade Chen was one of the founders of the cryptography division, and he had now been a Bureau Chief for more than ten years, in addition to which he was one of the deputy directors of Unit 701, though that was in fact largely honorific given that he was also the cryptography Bureau Chief. How could she expect Comrade Chen to go and work as her assistant! But when I went to discuss the matter with her she refused to back down, and insisted that she wanted Chen to take part. 'I don't need an assistant; I need someone to quarrel with!' She was resolute, and spoke persuasively about the reasons why she wanted Comrade Chen to join us. 'Neither you nor I know the first thing about how cryptography is done here, in addition to which they have never cracked a real high-level cipher, so fundamentally they don't have a hope in hell of breaking RECOVERY. That means that if we see the way that they go about trying to crack it, we will know what to avoid.' This put me in mind of something that Anderov used to say: that cracking codes isn't like a duel – you need scapegoats!

You let other people fall into the traps, so that you can walk round them.

I looked at her in alarm, horrified by this nasty idea. But I had no right to refuse her, given that her request was actually perfectly logical. At that moment cracking RECOVERY was our most urgent and high-priority assignment, and this was not the time to worry about what methods we used, whether against the enemy or against ourselves. That's what cracking a cipher is like; it's an unpleasant profession, full of darkness and danger.

Although I wasn't entirely happy with what Huang Yiyi wanted to do, I still went to report it to Unit Director Luo. Unit Director Luo was happy to agree, and she immediately rang Comrade Chen and told him to come round. Right in front of me she ordered him to report to my office. I was expecting him to refuse, but after he had heard her out, he was silent for a bit and then made his position clear: 'Since both you and Unit Director Luo want me to join, I must agree. Even if I didn't want to, I would have to. But I want you to know that I don't believe that we can crack RECOVERY. I can't do it, and I don't think that this expert you have brought in can do it either. She doesn't have any respect for the way that things are done, and in my experience, people like that aren't good cryptographers.'

I said that when she was in the United States she had cracked Soviet ciphers.

Comrade Chen said, 'That's just rumour. I never believe that sort of thing. Do you know why? First and foremost because people who really do decrypt ciphers are very secretive about what they do, and also because anyone who actually has cracked a cipher would never speak as light-heartedly as she does, as if a cipher is just a difficult maths problem. What is cryptography? Didn't your supervisor Anderov say that it was like listening to the heartbeats of the dead and that therefore we have to be as emotionless and untroubled as corpses ourselves? But look at her . . . even though I've only just met her and don't really know her at all, I can see from her eyes that she is full of hope, that she is an impulsive person. I don't know whether all the time you spent with Anderov means you really have learnt the business, but in my opinion whether or not we crack RECOVERY is going to be down to you. That's why I'm happy to work as your assistant and help you out.'

I could only tell him the truth. 'I wasn't actually studying cryptography with him – I was there for other reasons. I was just discussing the matter with Unit Director Luo and we decided to put you in charge of the cryptanalysis work.'

Comrade Chen was obviously suffering when he said, 'Deputy Director An, this is torture! I am past fifty, don't do this to me!'

I smiled. 'Comrade Chen, what do you mean by torture? If we crack RECOVERY, this will be the greatest possible glory. Think of it as adding further lustre to your crown . . .'

Comrade Chen laughed hollowly. It was a very bitter laugh.

13.

That evening while I was tidying up, Huang Yiyi knocked on the door and came in. In amongst the heaps of stuff that I had brought back from the Soviet Union, she quickly rooted out a picture of Anderov and myself. She recognized him immediately, and so the conversation naturally turned to Anderov and Sivincy. She said, 'Anderov is an expert at cracking American ciphers, but RECOVERY was written by Sivincy so it's going to be in the Russian style, which means that your skills are pretty useless.'

I nodded. 'You know that Sivincy wrote a cipher called DIFFI-CULT CENTURY?'

'Yes. She wrote it specially for the American military.'

'The Americans gave Sivincy a job devising ciphers because they wanted to make it difficult for Anderov.'

'Well, Anderov has cracked a lot of American ciphers, and they are really afraid of him. But Sivincy went to university with Anderov, and they were good friends who knew each other very well. Any cipher written by Sivincy will be designed to confuse Anderov.'

'Right, so we can say that when the Americans first decided to employ Sivincy to write DIFFICULT CENTURY, their intention was to deliberately confuse Anderov. And only Sivincy could do that, because she is about the only person who knows his shortcomings.'

'So we can assume that Sivincy will have hidden a lot of traps within DIFFICULT CENTURY that were specifically designed to get Anderov. So if you asked Anderov to break DIFFICULT CENTURY, he would be at a serious disadvantage, being funda-mentally unable to crack the cipher.' She glanced at me and smiled. 'And if we asked Anderov's student to work on it, he would fail.'

I knew that she meant me, but I was thinking about something completely different. I was silent for a moment, then I said, 'RECOVERY is DIFFICULT CENTURY.'

She opened her eyes wide. 'What did you just say?'

I repeated it, and then she said seriously, 'How is that possible?'

'It's a fact. The American top brass were worried about the fact that Sivincy is Russian, and in the end they decided they did not dare use DIFFICULT CENTURY, so they sold it to Taiwan. The Taiwanese renamed it RECOVERY.'

She stood up. 'Is this some kind of joke?'

I shook my head. 'This is important. Is it likely that I would make a joke of it?'

She suddenly started shouting at me. 'If you knew that, why on earth did you take the job? You really do have a fantastic opinion of yourself, to carry on when clearly you don't have a hope in hell. Who do you think you are? Do you really imagine that you can just waltz in and everything will sort itself out?'

I explained to her patiently: one, I didn't know anything about it until I got back to China. Two, the people who did know about it didn't know the first thing about cryptography. She paced up and down the room, muttering, 'Stupid, stupid, calling you in to help us break DIFFICULT CENTURY. They obviously don't have a clue what they're doing.'

I said calmly, 'They didn't call me in, they called you.'

'But I'm going to need assistance, and you can't possibly help me! This cipher is a grave dug specially for your supervisor, and if you try and help me, it's going to be a disaster! If you'd told me this before, there's no way I would have come with you!'

I smiled. 'That's why I waited until we got here before I told you. The fact is that I wasn't really learning cryptography from Anderov. I didn't even study maths to high-school level, so how could I even begin to?'

'What were you doing there?'

'Making use of my position to get information needed by cryptographers here.'

She opened her eyes wide. 'That's spying.'

I didn't say anything.

She shrieked, 'You're a devil!'

'And you're an angel.'

'You're going to drive me to an early death.'

'No way. I may be a devil, but I'm a devil who really appreciates you. When I'd just got back and they landed me with this, I thought the Party had made a mistake. But when I found you, I came to believe that you were the right person for the job. If they'd sent someone else, and he'd met you, he wouldn't necessarily have given you the job, because no one else appreciates you the way I do. Perhaps that's all thanks to Anderov. To appreciate you one needs intelligence and courage, and one needs . . . the experience of having lived abroad, and I have all of those . . .'

That evening, I couldn't stop myself from talking a great deal to Huang Yiyi, as one intelligent person to another, as one fellow sufferer to another. I told her many of my secrets, but I think that she also understood that she was confronted with a difficult task. I hoped that the heavy burden that had been placed upon her would make her more serious, would worry her, would make her concentrate her energies on her cryptography work. But the following morning at the first meeting of the cryptanalysis group, she wasn't there. We waited a while, and then since she didn't turn up, in the end we just had to have the meeting without her.

The most important aim of this meeting was to sort out lines of communication between our personnel and apportion responsibility: Chen Erhu became the deputy head of our working group and head of the cryptanalysis section, with Comrade Yang to assist him; Huang Yiyi was also allocated an assistant, a young woman called Comrade Zha. Apart from that we all got to share a secretary, Comrade Fei, who would also play the role of office manager, making sure that the bosses' decisions were reported to the workforce and the workforce's results got passed up: he would have responsibility for the day-to-day running of our working group. These were all people I had hand-picked from different government organizations, and they shared a high level of revolutionary consciousness, a strong professional attitude to their work, and an uncomplicated family background. This was particularly true of Comrade Zha, who was, like me, a revolutionary orphan, who had grown up in Unit 701. She was a very simple and naïve young woman but also very committed. She seemed to me to be the very best person to act as Huang Yiyi's assistant.

After the meeting was over, since Huang Yiyi still hadn't come to work, I sent Comrade Zha to look for her and find out what she was up to. Well, Comrade Zha found that she had become enamoured of a squirrel and had run off into the forest to play with it! When Comrade Zha dragged her back, I caught sight of her through the window carrying a large red Russian-style backpack, looking from left to right as she walked along the road, for all the world as if she were a tourist admiring the scenery. I couldn't stop myself from getting angry. When she came in I started to criticize her. 'You're coming to work just as everyone else is getting ready to leave. This really is too late!'

She said that she was busy and that she had asked me for the day off, having slipped the note under my door.

I said, 'In future if you want the day off, let Comrade Zha know: she is your assistant.'

When she heard that little Comrade Zha was a revolutionary orphan, she said crossly, 'Why is it that everyone I meet nowadays is a revolutionary orphan – is it because you think I am not revolutionary enough? So you send these people to instruct and reform me. But I am not going to change – do you understand that?'

'No one is going to reform anyone else,' I said, 'but you shouldn't go out of your way to make other people unhappy. Today was the first meeting of our working group and you didn't turn up. Don't do that again.'

'The same applies to you. When you get home, have a look on the doorstep – you never know, there might be a letter from me requesting the day off . . .'

I glared at her. 'Clearly, I'm going to have to take you through the whole thing step by step again, so that you understand exactly who I am and what you are here to do.'

She laughed. 'Don't be cross. I'm sorry. I know. I really wasn't able to attend this morning because I didn't get to sleep until after four in the morning, because I was working on this.' She took out a couple of pages and gave them to me.

I took them and asked, 'What is this?'

'It's a letter I've written to Anderov in your name. Of course there are many things that I haven't got right – you need to rewrite it so that it sounds like you – but the important things are there. I'm hoping you can get some personal information about Sivincy from Anderov – for example, the mathematician that she most admires, her habits, her family background, her marriage, and so on. None of that information is going to hurt our efforts to crack RECOVERY.'

'Isn't sending a letter a bit rash?'

'Well, can you think of a better way? If you can, we'll go for that.'

I put the letter in a drawer, and said coldly, 'I'll think about it. Right now, you're coming with me.' I got up to go, and deliberately did not tell her where we were going.

She ran after me and asked, 'Where are you taking me?'

'You'll find out when we get there.'

I took her to Comrade Jin's domain, the analysis room. The job of an analyst is to look for the cribs in every secret message, to see whether they can pick out any words or phrases. Some people called their work 'autopsying a corpse', because a radio intercept that has not yet been analysed is no different from a corpse, and what they were trying to do was in fact just the same as an autopsy – carrying out dissection and analysis of the body. To use Anderov's words: the connection between analysis and cryptography is the same as that between the words and the text. If you want to write a text the first thing is that you need to know enough words. The analysts teach you the words, the cryptographers instruct you in the meaning. So you can understand how important analysis is to the work of cryptography.

When we walked into the analysis room, Comrade Jin and a couple of his people were autopsying a radio intercept and they had already picked out a couple of words from the message in front of them: PLA, recover, exercise … They had already autopsied twenty-seven messages, but there were nearly a thousand waiting for them. When I was chatting with Comrade Jin, I happened to mention that Huang Yiyi was already a professor, and that she had transferred in at senior level, so she was actually earning more than I was. When Comrade Jin heard that he was amazed, and staring at Huang Yiyi he asked, 'How old are you?'

'Pretty ancient,' she said.

'You look very young to me.'

She laughed. 'Really? Do you know why I look so young?' Comrade Jin was just about to say something, but she didn't wait for him to speak. 'That's my secret, and I'm not telling you!' Then she walked away shaking her head, leaving Comrade Jin standing there, not knowing what to do.

When I came out she said mysteriously to me, 'Do you want to know why I look so young? I can tell you.'

I glanced at her sideways. 'Or you could not tell me.'

'Oh, I want to tell you. It's because I have love. You know, women need to experience love, because if they don't have it they get old.'

'Right now,' I said, 'you need to love your cipher – because if you can't crack it, your hair is going to turn white!'

'What's the hurry? You've only got twenty-seven corpses for me to look at, and if you want me to love my cipher right at this minute, it would be rather like asking me to make love to an under-age boy, which is a crime.'

She was like that – always putting things in such a peculiar way – though actually she did have a point. I remembered that Anderov had said very much the same thing to me: if you're dealing with a high-level cipher, it's better to think about it rather than try to lift the cover too early.

'Can you please be a little more careful about your choice of words!' I said. 'You shouldn't always be joking around and speaking in such a peculiar way, particularly not with your subordinates. You need to think of the effect that your words are going to have, and not crack all these jokes.'

'But I want to make them laugh, so that they feel I'm easy to get on with.'

'You're devious; not at all easy to get on with.'

'And you're a moron.'

'Listen to me! If you keep talking to them in this free and easy way, they're going to think you're stupid and frivolous.'

'You're the one that's stupid. What do you mean by giving me a woman assistant? As the proverb says, when men and women work together neither side gets tired. There are loads of men here, and you have to find me a little girl. I know what you're up to: you're trying to make me feel old and ashamed of myself so that I spend less time on having fun.'

'From this point on you're going to have to stop that. There aren't any men here, or any women.'

'Well, in that case, if you're not a man and I'm not a woman, then we don't have to make a fuss about preserving the proper segregation between the sexes.' As she spoke she reached out to take my hand in a very intimate way, scaring me so much that I snatched my hand away and leapt back. She saw how alarmed I looked, and burst out laughing. Her carefree, open laughter floated through the quiet mountain valley. I just wished the ground would open up and swallow me.

14.

I had been told that Chen never ate lunch – not because he had a poor appetite, but because he wanted to keep his head clear. If you are hungry, the deductive capabilities of your mind are comparatively dynamic, whereas if you have eaten your fill it is easy to become dozy. When people said in the past that eating modestly makes your mind better, that must be what they meant. Comrade Chen, Chen Erhu, was a workaholic, and when he was trying to crack a cipher, he often really made himself suffer. I wished that Huang Yiyi was like that. Or to put it another way, I was worried that she wasn't like that. She hadn't burnt her bridges. As Anderov would say, 'God is just when he creates each individual: clever people lack application, intellectuals like their ivory towers, people capable of doing amazing things turn out not to have the patience.' Someone like Einstein is the exception that proves the rule: God let him have everything, with none of the usual checks and balances. I felt that Huang Yiyi was naturally very gifted, with an unusual mathematical ability. Someone like that is born to crack ciphers, but she was too fond of having fun, and that's a real problem if you want to do great things.

I could understand and make allowances for her, but Comrade Chen couldn't bear it, and wasn't about to put up with it. So the working relationship between the two of them started to go wrong, becoming increasingly awkward and acrimonious. I found out later from Comrade Zha that one day when Huang Yiyi came in to work she gave her a bunch of autopsied radio intercepts and said that they had just come from the analysis room, and that she should look at them immediately and then hand them on to Comrade Chen. Huang Yiyi just flicked through them and handed them back to Comrade Zha, telling her to give them to Comrade Chen.

Little Comrade Zha looked at her in alarm. 'Aren't you going to read them?'

'There's no point,' she said. 'I'm waiting until we have enough material, then I'll look at them.' As she spoke she picked up the newspaper beside her and started leafing through it. She wasn't expecting that the minute the intercepts had been handed over, Comrade Chen would arrive in person. When Huang Yiyi opened the door and saw him, she refused to allow him in, saying, 'Hey, stop right there: whatever it is, I will come to you.' When she came out she told Chen with a laugh, 'Only men are allowed into your cryptography room, and only women are allowed into mine. If you want to talk to me we will do so in Comrade Zha's office.'

He was stunned and a very ugly expression came over his face, but he followed her into Comrade Zha's office, where he waved the intercepts and said, 'Have you looked at all of these?'

'I leafed through them.'

'This is primary data; you need to read through them carefully.'

'I have looked at them.'

'But just now didn't you say that you had leafed through them?'

She was still smiling. 'Bureau Chief Chen, I know you're doing this for my own good, but you're also showing off your power as one of the senior people here.'

'This isn't about power – this is about a sense of responsibility. Look, I'll give them back to you and you can look at them properly.'

She didn't take the documents. 'No. Comrade Chen, if you want to read them, then read them yourself. Right now I'm looking at the papers and I really don't have time for this.'

Chen raised his voice. 'I insist that you read them, OK! Comrade Huang, the two of us are now in the same boat, and we sink or swim together. I hope that in future we will be able to join forces rather than fighting each other.'

She smiled. 'Comrade Chen, maybe you don't want to hear this, but cryptography is like writing a diary – whether you write a lot or a little, whether you write well or badly, it's all up to you. You don't need to worry about me. Quite honestly, even though we're on the same side, we're not going to be joining forces; in fact we can't join forces.'

Comrade Chen just stood there, as if something was choking him; and for a very long time he didn't say anything. Of course later on, when he insisted on coming to find me to complain about her, what could I say? All my bets were on Huang Yiyi, and I really didn't like listening to Comrade Chen criticize her, but I couldn't show it. I calmed him down: she came here because Director Tie gave her a military order to do so, and the fact that she dared to come at all meant that she must have good reason to believe that she could pull it off. We needed to give her time. Time would tell us what kind of person she was, what she could do, what she wanted to do, and so on . . . In fact, it was all waffle.

Fortunately I didn't have to wait too long before Huang Yiyi started to make her presence felt.

That morning, the report on the analysis of the commercial encryption machine that we had brought back from headquarters came out, and I immediately told Comrade Fei to take it over to Comrade Jiang, and tell him to find out how it worked and then write a report. That afternoon I went to the calculations room several times, but they hadn't yet completed their work. I was in a hurry, so I asked Comrade Jiang if it would be possible to get a result before we all went home. Comrade Jiang said that there was no way – there was far too much to do, and even if they all worked overtime it would still take until tomorrow morning. I just had to be patient and let them do their work, and the following morning I would see the results.

The next morning when I got to work, Comrade Jiang – who had been up all night – brought me three copies of the results, a really thick heap. I had a quick look and then handed over the two spare copies to Comrade Fei and told him to give one each to Chen and Huang Yiyi. He was to tell them to look at this immediately and that when they had finished we would be having a meeting to discuss the situation.

The report was very long, and the data therein both complex

and abstruse, and so it was very slow reading for me. But Huang Yiyi finished it quickly and came rushing in to find me. When she saw I was still reading through the report she said angrily, 'Don't look! Don't look! There is nothing to read. Sivincy is a cow!'

I told her to sit down and explain what she meant, and at the same time I got Comrade Fei to call Chen in to hear what she had to say. She was almost bouncing up and down in her chair, desperate to speak. I told her to wait until Chen arrived. She didn't pay any attention, but started in: 'It's a scandal, that's what it is. I am quite sure now that the reason the Americans didn't use DIFFI-CULT CENTURY themselves but gave it to the Taiwanese was because they found out what a nasty trick Sivincy had pulled, and started to have their doubts about her character. If people start worrying about the character of the person writing ciphers for them, is it likely they're going to use them? Particularly not when she has Soviet bones under her nice new American skin!'

What she said confused both me and Comrade Chen, who had arrived in the middle of it all, and we just looked at her blankly.

'What I want to say is very simple,' she explained. 'Both of you have worked in cryptography for so long that I'm sure you're well aware that during the Second World War the Germans used a famous cipher called ULTRA.'

'The Enigma machine,' I said.

'Yes, Enigma.'

'Enigma I know about,' Chen said. 'It was the world's first electro-mechanical encryption device.'

'Yes. In the world of cryptography people talk about ULTRA, because that was the name given to the cipher they used. But the machine those messages were created on was called Enigma, so it's all the same thing.'

I smiled and said to Chen, 'Just like you: your name is Chen Erhu but at work everyone calls you Bureau Chief Chen; it's the same thing.'

'Exactly,' said Huang Yiyi. 'The ciphers they used weren't particularly difficult, but they were developed for a machine, the world's first proper encryption machine. Earlier so-called

encryption machines were basically more like calculators; fundamentally they brought nothing to the original cipher. You could
say that no one up until that time had worked out a way to make
an encrypting machine. Enigma was the first, and it's a landmark
in the history of cryptography. If I told you that Sivincy wrote her
cipher for a commercially available rotor machine which is basically a carbon copy of Enigma, would you believe me? Of course
you wouldn't, because Enigma is so famous, and so many people
have researched it; if you are a thief you don't go and steal something in plain sight, right? But I am absolutely sure that the
machine used is Enigma, and that any differences are superficial –
it has wheels where the original had cogs; thirty-four matrices
rather than twenty-six, with actuating motors rather than gears,
but the underlying principles are fundamentally the same. If you
want a comparison, it's as if someone published a translation
claiming it was an original work . . .'

This discovery really amazed us all. Just as Huang Yiyi said, Sivincy had pulled a very nasty trick on us, the cow. It was very
difficult for us to find our footing when dealing with someone so
unprincipled.

After supper we went for a walk, and Huang Yiyi and I analysed
the motives behind Sivincy's plagiarism of ULTRA. We decided
that the reason Sivincy wrote her cipher for an Enigma machine,
rather than anything else, was because it was part of an elaborately
crafted scheme. It wasn't because she was stupid, or because she
had no choice, but because she was actually extremely crafty. Rip-
ping off ULTRA is like stealing an advertising hoarding on a busy
street, or the portrait of Chairman Mao off the wall outside Tiananmen. If you walk straight up in broad daylight and steal them,
even if the police spot you they aren't going to realize what you are
up to. Sivincy was a famous mathematician; most people wouldn't
believe it possible that someone of her calibre would produce a
rip-off. Just think about it – if someone you would never imagine
stealing anything actually does so, how great are their chances of
success? It was clever, but it was a wicked sort of cleverness. If we
hadn't seen this data that day (given that our job was to decrypt

her cipher), we might well have been completely misled, digging ourselves further into a rut, not realizing that the answer to the riddle was right beside us in our textbooks.

'She deserves all the ridicule she gets,' Huang Yiyi said.

'But she's achieved her objective,' I said. 'A cipher is a tool, and if you can't break it, then it has been successful. No matter how you look at it, you have no right to sneer at her.'

'Clearly we are going to have to be just as devious as she is,' she replied.

I asked her what kind of thing she had in mind, and she wanted me to write to Anderov and find out more about Sivincy. I knew that Anderov was very sensitive and careful, so it would not be at all easy to get anything out of him. That was why I still had not sent the letter. But in the current impasse we had no other way to learn about Sivincy, so it seemed that I would have to give this a go.

That evening, as instructed by Huang Yiyi, I wrote a letter to Anderov.

The contents of the letter seemed entirely innocuous, but I thought very carefully about my choice of words. I can't remember exactly what I wrote, just that since coming back I had been very busy organizing Xiaoyu's funeral, and that was why I had not had time to write to him, and that I hoped he would forgive me. I also told him that I had recently started work in a new work unit, a code school, and that now I would be teaching other people everything I had learnt from him. Apart from teaching the students encoding, I was also teaching them a bit of history, mainly the history of Russian codes. As part of that I was teaching them about some famous Soviet experts. I wrote down his name, and followed it with a list of the names of other Russians, one of whom, of course, was Sivincy. I said I didn't have enough material for my classes, and hoped that he would do his best to send me some personal information about each of them. All this was just to hide the fact that we were trying to get at Sivincy through him.

I sent the letter, but hardly dared hope that he would actually write back.

15.

Originally I had imagined that once Huang Yiyi had grasped what Sivincy was up to, plagiarizing ULTRA, she would be buoyed up by this success to carry on devoting her time and attention to RECOVERY. I was not expecting her to go back to her old ways, running crazy. One day she was in the woods feeding biscuits to the squirrels, the next she had run round to the guards' compound to play chess – and she even found something to amuse her at the carpenters' workshop, because she seemed to be there every five minutes. When she was in her office she kept the door shut and wouldn't talk to anyone. She also wouldn't read reports. She clearly didn't care if she put everyone's backs up. Chen complained all the time to me about her insouciance: 'Look! Look at her! Is that acceptable?'

It really was not acceptable.

That evening I went to her house for a serious talk. The moment I got through the door I just stopped dead. Do you know what she was doing? She was telling her own fortune with a pack of cards, and as far as I could make out she wanted to know if she would be lucky in love, because she was roaring with laughter when it came out. I asked her what on earth she was doing and she asked me seriously, 'Hey, I've heard that your wife is dead. Is that right?'

'It has nothing to do with you,' I said crossly.

'Of course it does,' she said confidently. 'Can't you see what I'm doing? I'm telling fortunes. I want to know if you and I are destined to be together.'

'The only thing I want you to do is concentrate on the cipher!' I shouted.

She smiled at me. 'All love is a kind of cipher which two people have to decrypt together. I've already decrypted your cipher, and the answer is me.'

That evening when I got home I took the little altar that I had set up to Xiaoyu in the library, with the casket containing her ashes, an incense burner and some candles, and moved it into the living room. I wanted Xiaoyu to tell Huang Yiyi that any relationship between us was impossible. Although Xiaoyu was dead there was no room in my heart for any other woman.

It didn't work like that, because Huang Yiyi used it as a weapon against me. One evening when she came to find me, the first thing she spotted was Xiaoyu's altar, and after a moment's surprise she lit an incense stick and with tears pouring down her face she started to tell her deepest feelings to Xiaoyu's picture. She addressed Xiaoyu as if she were a member of the family, and said that she hoped that in paradise she would look with sympathy on the fact that she loved me and help her, make me accept her love.

'I really love him,' she said. 'Heaven, and your soul in paradise, can testify to that. I gave up the job that I loved for him, and came to this rural backwater from Beijing. I love every hair on his head, every hair in his beard, even the most delicate of hairs on his body . . .'

I simply couldn't listen to it any more and dragged her away, shouting, 'That's enough!'

She collapsed against my chest, biting my lower lip, searching for my mouth. I had to leave her, like a murderer who has committed a crime in someone else's house and then runs away. Like a stray dog, I hung around outside not daring to go home, waiting unhappily for her to leave. In the darkness I once again had the horrible suspicion that what I had brought back with me was not an angel, but a devil.

After that I ignored her for a couple of days, until Comrade Chen came to see me, to report crossly that Huang Yiyi was banging about in her office so that he couldn't possibly concentrate on his work. 'If you want to play around then go ahead – go to the forest and feed the squirrels, go to the barracks and play chess with the soldiers – just don't make a racket in your cryptography room. Bang, bang, bang – some people want to work!' Comrade Chen's face showed that he had absolutely had enough.

To begin with I didn't believe Huang Yiyi had taken her tiresomeness to that point. But when I went with Comrade Chen to his cryptography room, I could hear the occasional sound of banging from Huang Yiyi's room next door, as though there was a carpenter at work. I was angry with her, and went over to hammer on her door, but no matter how hard I knocked she didn't open it. I banged again and shouted, 'Huang Yiyi, open the door: I want to talk to you!'

I heard her quick steps coming over, and then she opened the door abruptly and stuck her head out. She looked extremely cross, and yelled at me: 'What the hell do you think you're doing? I thought you were ignoring me, so what's all this shouting?' Then she shut the door with a bang without even giving me the opportunity to get a word in edgeways, as if it wasn't her that was bothering other people, but me who had come to disturb her. I was so cross that I was about to kick the door open, but thinking better of it I controlled myself.

'You see – how can anyone work with someone like that?' Comrade Chen complained. 'You bring this Bodhisattva here, and not only does she not do anything to help, she makes everyone else's life more difficult. How are we supposed to crack this cipher? To tell you the truth, after all this time I don't have the slightest idea of how to go about it. I simply don't have any feel for this at all.'

I tried to cheer him up. 'It doesn't matter; that's normal. Modern ciphers are always very difficult to get started on, but once you've found a way in you'll be fine.'

Anderov used to say that modern ciphers aren't mazes, they are black holes. You can get into a maze but you can't get out, so even though you can't crack the whole cipher you can crack individual intercepts, because it doesn't matter where you enter, there is only one way to go. A black hole you can't get into, and if you do there are hundreds of different paths through it, so the problem is finding the right one – which is much harder than finding your way out of the most complex of mazes.

When Comrade Chen said that he didn't have a feel for this at all, I wasn't surprised. I knew that the reason that Huang Yiyi wanted him to take part in the cryptanalysis work was because she needed a scapegoat, just like shock troops and mine-clearers on the battlefield. You send them out to die, using their flesh and blood to clear the obstacles and find the traps so that their comrades can pass without danger. Otherwise how can you expect your troops to go and assault mountain fortresses and win?

That wasn't the problem. The problem was that Comrade Chen was a much respected cryptographer in Unit 701, and from start to finish he didn't know what his real role was in this working group. Even after Huang Yiyi cracked RECOVERY, he still didn't know. For decades after, I felt bad for old Chen for that reason.

Of course, that all happened much later . . . we're talking about Huang Yiyi.

One afternoon Unit Director Luo came in person to deliver a letter from Director Tie that had just arrived by plane. On the envelope it was clearly written that it was to be handed to me in person. Unit Director Luo thought that it was something to do with RECOVERY, but it wasn't. What was it? I will tell you later. It seemed as if Unit Director Luo must have heard some gossip about Huang Yiyi, because that day when she saw everyone hard at work and realized that only Huang Yiyi was missing, she said to me, 'I've heard some bad things about her; people say she doesn't have a good attitude.'

'That's not entirely fair,' I said. 'Everyone has a different way of working. She may seem to be a bit . . . Well, she may seem not to be working very hard, but when you actually talk to her you realize that she takes her work very seriously.'

Unit Director Luo pointed to her empty office. 'Does it look like she takes her work seriously? This is office hours, but heaven only knows where she has gone.'

'Maybe . . . she is working at home.'

Unit Director Luo looked at me, and then she said with a smile, 'You always speak up for her. Are you getting emotionally involved?'

I denied it flatly. 'Not at all. Absolutely no way.'

'There's nothing wrong with that – you have every right to fall in love again. Look, I really think you should hold a funeral for Xiaoyu; you can't keep on putting it off. She's dead, and it's time to let her rest in peace.'

'Not yet,' I said. 'I'm waiting until we have cracked RECOVERY.'

Unit Director Luo thought about that. 'OK. But I really think you need to talk to Huang Yiyi and get her to understand the importance of the task she has been set. She needs to concentrate and not . . . I've heard that she treats Comrade Chen very disrespectfully. That's not right. You need to find some way to get the two of them to set their differences aside – we don't want co-workers going around despising each other, and we particularly don't want them breaking out into open conflict.'

Unit Director Luo's words reminded me that I really did need to speak seriously to Huang Yiyi. I needed her to understand my feelings, so that she would not get bogged down in her emotions, which after all might well affect her ability to crack RECOVERY. She seemed to know intuitively what I was thinking, because that evening when I got home after dark, I found a bag hanging from the door handle. Inside there was a wine bottle, a letter, a book, a pack of playing cards and a note. The note was only a couple of lines long: 'Here are four ciphers. Please crack them in order. You have half an hour. As I am sure you will have guessed, this puzzle comes to you from Huang Yiyi!' Though I was rather surprised at the whole thing, I took the bag into the house and laid the items out on the table, and then got to work on her ciphers.

I looked first at the wine bottle, and realized that it didn't have wine inside it, but a long strip of paper about an inch wide. I took it out, and saw that it had been written on all over: there was Chinese, there was English, there was some Russian, and also some apparently random scribbles. It was completely mysterious. I thought about the paper for a bit, and then decided that it was probably a 'Roman cipher' and the wine bottle was actually the scytale. I wound the paper strip around the bottle, and when I got it right the random rubbish turned into a perfectly clear message:

Good wine and I are equally intoxicating, you are just as important to me as RECOVERY is!

I shook my head and laughed over the idea that any woman in this day and age could compare herself to a fine wine, and say that she was equally intoxicating!

Then I took out the envelope. This was empty, but there was a line of nonsensical Russian written on it that I cracked really quickly, to produce one line of plain text:

Russian is a really complicated and profound language, so will a Russian code be very abstruse?

After that I looked at the book, which was Nikolai Ostrovsky's *How the Steel Was Tempered*. Inside there was a sheet of paper covered with numbers. Just as with the previous one, I immediately realized what I was dealing with, and flipping back and forth between the pages of the code book, I finally picked out all the words, arriving at the message:

Tonia does actually love Pavel as much as Pavel loves the revolution.

The cipher concealed in the pack of cards was also quick to crack. When I put the cards back in the right order by suit, the message written on their sides was easy to read:

It's ages since you wrote to Anderov, why hasn't he written back?

That really did make me think. Yes, I had written to Anderov more than a month ago, but he still hadn't replied. Why not? And another thing: why had Huang Yiyi gone to all the trouble of setting me these four ciphers – surely it couldn't be just for fun? What was she up to? And another thing: recently she had been holed up in her office all day banging away at something, so what was she doing? If Chen was right and she was just messing about, why would she be so mysterious? But if she wasn't messing about, then what was she doing? Cracking ciphers is hard work – you don't want your office turned into a workshop with lots of noise and banging about.

While I was still all confused, Huang Yiyi knocked on the door and came in. The second she came through the door she asked me if I had cracked the ciphers. I pointed to the four plain-text messages and said something about her being full of energy. She retorted rudely, 'You're so unimaginative. Even though this may seem just a bit of fun, why would you criticize a cryptographer for creating this sort of puzzle? At the very least it means that she lives in a world of ciphers.'

I asked her to come to the point and tell me the real reason why she had set me the four problems. She explained that they represented four different types of ciphers: the bottle was a transposition cipher, the letter a substitution cipher, the book a book cipher, and the playing cards an algorithmic cipher. Nowadays these are all basic cipher forms.

'But,' she explained, 'it doesn't matter whether it's a mid-level cipher or one of these new high-level ones – they are all just more or less complex variants of these old types. For example ULTRA (that is, the Enigma machine) is an algorithmic cipher encrypted with a substitution cipher. The complexity comes from the encryption – modern ciphers are all based on algorithms.'

I understood what she meant. 'And when you use that method to make them more difficult to work out, they become mathematical puzzles.'

'Exactly. So when you encrypt them in the most difficult way to work out, how many kinds of cipher are there?'

'There are only a handful of viable possibilities: first, a super-large-value algorithmic cipher encrypted with a medium-large-value algorithmic cipher. The second is a super-large-value algorithmic cipher encrypted with a transposition cipher. Third, a super-large-value algorithmic cipher encrypted with a substitution cipher. Finally, a super-large-value algorithmic cipher encrypted with a transposition and substitution cipher. Those are the most important kinds; any other kind of cipher is impossible in conjunction with an algorithm.'

'Exactly,' she said. 'We can be sure that RECOVERY is an algorithmic cipher, so now what I want to ask you is: given your knowledge of Sivincy, when she was designing RECOVERY twenty years later, what kind of encryption method would she use? I don't want you to think about it, just tell me straight out.'

'Number one: a super-large-value algorithmic cipher encrypted with a medium-large-value algorithmic cipher. If you give me a second choice, I would say . . .'

She cut me short. 'You don't get a second choice.'

'So which would you pick?'

She sighed deeply. 'To be quite frank, I have no feel for this, and it's giving me a headache. Up until now I've always had a kind of sixth sense for this sort of thing, but this time it's simply not working.'

'Maybe Sivincy's tiresome traps are affecting your feel for it.'

'Do you think she has more nasty surprises in store for us?'

'Well, as I just said, if I were given a second guess . . .'

She said shortly, 'You don't have a second choice; your second guess is pointless.' After a short pause she added, 'I really wish that I was talking to Anderov himself rather than one of his students. If Anderov made the same choice I could eliminate it straight away. Why do you think Anderov hasn't replied to your letter?'

'No idea,' I said.

After that she demanded that we go for a walk. On the way home she insisted on inviting me in. I said no, it was already late and I wanted to go to bed. She said that it was still early, just past nine o'clock, so let's go. That whole evening we had done nothing but talk about ciphers, so I didn't want to annoy her. I actually thought that she wanted to carry on talking about ciphers, so even though I was uncomfortable about the whole thing, in the end I went with her.

It was the first time I had ever been to her room, and she had arranged it very nicely, and very distinctively. On the wall above her bed she had stuck a poster of the American film star Marilyn Monroe which really caught my attention: she was bending down so that her hands were on her knees, but her head was raised to look out at you, her generous lips slightly parted, her whole body expressing longing!

I couldn't help wondering what kind of person admired that sort of film star.

Huang Yiyi was busy rushing around the room, making tea and hunting out some biscuits. She had even managed to find some really expensive cigarettes, which at that time were very difficult to get, and said she had bought them specially for me. She pulled one out of the packet and gave it to me, saying that she liked the smell. I lit the cigarette and then said through a cloud of smoke, 'Do you think I should try writing again to Anderov?'

She said at once, 'Oh my God, you really are annoying sometimes. We've done nothing but talk about work all evening. Can we please talk about something else!'

I asked her what she wanted to talk about, and she looked at me curiously and suggested that I tell her about being a spy and about my wife, Xiaoyu. I told her a bit about what I had done in the Soviet Union, and a few things about Xiaoyu. Naturally I said nothing at all about what she had really been doing there. Those were the rules, and I obeyed them.

Suddenly Huang Yiyi asked me, 'In films spies are all really romantic figures. Female spies always seem to use sex to carry out their covert operations, so were you ever seduced by one?'

'I had Xiaoyu with me, so of course not!'

'So people knew that you were married?'

'Even if people hadn't known, I wouldn't have done it!'

'Not even if it was necessary for your work?'

'That is never necessary for work. That kind of behaviour is corrupt and degenerate.'

'It's not degenerate, it's romantic. Don't tell me you've never been romantically involved with anyone?'

'I've told you before: during all those years of warfare and unsurpassed hardship, we relied on the optimistic spirit of revolutionary romanticism to conquer every difficulty and danger, gaining victory after victory.'

She caught hold of my hands and said, 'Why are you so selfless? Don't you realize that the more you're like that, the more I love you? Do you understand how much I love you?'

I gently freed my hands and got up to go.

She didn't try and stop me, and without moving from her seat she said quietly, 'Just now you mentioned several times wanting me to give you a second choice, but in fact I already know what your second choice is; it's the fourth possibility. That would break all the usual rules, using all the possible ancient encryption methods to create a single cipher.'

I could only admire her insight. 'Yes,' I said. 'Because, as you said, Sivincy is a cow and completely unprincipled, so she's very likely to overstep all boundaries and pull some weird trick on us.'

'That's exactly what I thought, and it's been affecting my usual sixth sense, so I really can't get a handle on this. But it doesn't matter whether she's actually gone down that route or not, because I've been inspired by her to create one like that.'

I couldn't stop myself from asking her, 'What do you mean?'

'I designed an algorithmic cipher, and the four previous ciphers represent four different encryption methods. What you need to do now is to go home and look at the four messages together, because I used four different encryption methods in conjunction with my algorithmic cipher. What I want to tell you is hidden in the final cipher – so you go away and read it. I can give you a clue though: the key to cracking the cipher is "four", the number four.'

I went back and put the four messages together in order and then using the key she had given me, I circled the fourth word of each message. Immediately the words that I least wanted to see were in front of my eyes.

The message was: 'I really love you.'

16

The moment I got to work the next day, Huang Yiyi came to my office and asked me if I had worked out what it was that she really wanted to say to me. I looked as serious as I could, and glared at her. 'I really don't think you should say that sort of thing to me! If that's all you have to say, go back to your office, because I have nothing to say to you.'

'Clearly you don't understand in the least what I mean,' she retorted.

It was only much later on that I realized that she was using this method to test her theories about RECOVERY. 'I really love you' – these four words have an unusual characteristic: you can arrange them in any order. 'I love you really', 'Really I love you', 'You I love really', and so on, and the meaning never changes. That's a special kind of language, and she had been wondering if RECOVERY might not be that kind of cipher, which worked whether you ran it backwards or forwards – just like a ring of dominoes, where there is no start and no finish. Or rather the start and finish are man-made, and could in fact come anywhere. The clack, clack, clack sounds emanating from her office came from falling dominoes.

I found this out by chance when the support for my washbasin broke and the whole thing would no longer stand up properly. I went to the carpentry shed to ask for a nail, and came across the master carpenter, Comrade Zhang, who was cutting holes in a piece of wood. Beside him there was a hand-drawn plan for something that looked a bit like an adding machine, with measurements. I thought that it looked like Huang Yiyi's handwriting, and felt curious, so I asked the carpenter and he said that Comrade Huang had asked him to make it, but he had no idea what it was for. On my way out, I noticed a pile of things in the corner, some round, some conical, some cylindrical and some spherical, and asked the carpenter what they were for. He said he had made them for Comrade Huang some time ago, but now she didn't need them any more and had brought them back to be broken up. My interest was even more piqued – what on earth could Huang Yiyi want such bizarre objects for? All the racket from her room, was it because she was playing with them? I couldn't see that these toys could bear any relation to the decryption of RECOVERY. Later on when Huang Yiyi explained her idea, I was very impressed. You just had to be impressed: an ordinary person is an ordinary person and a genius is a genius – if you meet one you know about it.

That day when I left the woodworkers' shed, I found Huang Yiyi in the nearby forest. I was expecting her to be there feeding the squirrels, but instead she was standing underneath one of the trees discussing something with the madman who spent his time running around the forest. The madman raised his head to look at the treetops, or perhaps it was the sky; maybe he was talking to her, but then on the other hand maybe he wasn't – he could easily have been talking to himself, lost in a world of his own. He was the man Huang Yiyi had asked about the first time she went to Chen's office, the lunatic. His name was Jiang Nan, a cryptographer who had joined us at the same time as Chen, and who was eventually driven mad by decrypting PORPHORY. He knew too many secrets to be allowed to leave Unit 701 even though he was mad. We couldn't even let him see his family, so we let him roam through the mountains, spending his days running through the forest. He had the silent trees, he had the flowers and squirrels, he had this whole beautiful, illogical world for company. If he saw a stranger he would stop them and say, 'I cracked PORPHORY, the most difficult of all the KMT ciphers. No one else could crack it, only me . . .'

The people he stopped were always very polite to him, and would say kindly, 'Yes, of course you cracked it: you really are amazing.'

Then he would be really happy, and spreading his arms wide like the wings of a bird, he would run along the road shouting, 'I cracked PORPHORY, I really am amazing, I really am amazing . . .' Everyone who saw him felt deeply sorry for him.

That day, I didn't say much to Jiang Nan, but I lit his cigarette for him and sent him on his way as politely as I could. Then I asked Huang Yiyi what she had been talking to him about, and she said she had asked him how he'd found the key to PORPHORY.

I said jokingly that she should have asked me – well, it wasn't entirely a joke; I could have told her.

She answered the question I hadn't asked. 'I saw you leave the carpenters' shed – you've been checking up on me.'

I tried to sound convincing when I denied it, and told her that it was purely by chance that I had discovered she was making some mystery machine, and I hoped she would tell me what it was for. She then explained her domino theory. It seemed very strange to me, and I wanted to ask her more about it. She said, 'That's enough – I've already given up on it, but I do have a new idea. Last night I had a dream. In the dream I was holding a fistful of hornets, and the hornets stung my hand and then flew away, leaving all these holes. My hand looked like a sieve full of holes, and Arabic numerals came tumbling through them . . .'

There are many people in this world who don't believe in dreams, but for a cryptographer, dreams are a secret passage that those who fight using only their intellects use to reach the opposite bank victoriously. In the history of cryptography, there is no lack of examples of people who succeeded thanks to some sudden illumination in their dreams. Huang Yiyi told me excitedly that her dream had reminded her that the key to unlocking RECOVERY, that is the key to the cipher, might well be an original and modern cryptographic bombe! To use her imagery, it would be a sieve that created a domino effect. The sieve was separated into nine layers, and each layer would have 365 holes, so that in total the sieve would have $9 \times 9 \times 365 = 29,565$ holes, and each day's radio messages would correspond to one hole. That would mean the messages could only be decrypted through one hole, but if you found that hole, the entire day's output could be read. If we compared the numbers in the radio intercepts to grains of rice, and used a sieve to sieve and re-sieve them, in principle once one grain of rice had come through the system and fallen through the final hole at the other end, then we had cracked it, and all the other grains of rice (the remaining radio intercepts picked up on the same day) would all roll through as well. That is the domino effect – the difference being that traditionally with dominoes the first action that sets everything in motion is human, whereas what she had in mind was a sieve-initiated effect. To put it another way, the dominoes weren't set up to form a line but a circle, a single plane, but once you cut it and lined up the first set of numbers against the first set of holes, once one had found the right path, then the rest would follow suit in order. In very much the same way that if you have a bucket of water and pierce a hole in the bottom, the water will form a stream.

I was very excited and urged her to continue. Huang Yiyi said crossly, 'I hadn't realized you were so impatient. If you were equally excitable in emotional matters that would be wonderful.' Since that was her attitude, it was obvious that she hadn't given up hope in spite of all my efforts. She then made a request, saying that she would only continue talking if I sat down next to her. Really! But as it happened we had already walked into the wood and there was nobody else around, and I was tired, so there was no reason why I shouldn't sit with her. I guessed that if I sat down that would be followed by a whole series of other requests, so I made my own demand: that after I sat down she would have to do what I said. She agreed to that, and then we both sat down and she carried on her explanation. She said that the current trend in cryptography was to make the key to the cipher highly complex, but that this process was limited by the constraints of wireless technology, particularly in cases where the communication had to be sent vast distances or to numerous places, so mostly the key was hidden in the message.

'For example ULTRA, which was a high-level cipher – do you know what its key was?'

'The first three sets of numbers on even-number days, the last three sets on odd-number days.'

'Right. And it was concealed in the message text. Why did they want to make it part of the message?'

'Because they were using a lot of different wirelesses and it was during wartime, so the sets were moving around a lot and there was a high turnover in personnel. If they hadn't done it that way – if, for example, they had used a key from a one-time pad, if the person with the pad got killed, communications would be crippled.'

'That's the point. RECOVERY is the cipher that Sivincy designed for the American military, and since the end of the Second World War the US army has been involved in many theatres, with bases all over the world. With their bases so spread out, and their communications networks so numerous, we can be sure that it is impossible for RECOVERY to have its own one-time pad.'

'Mmm. A one-time pad also wouldn't suit the uses that the KMT are putting it to now, letting their special agents use it.'

'Right. The KMT are using RECOVERY as the cipher through which Taiwan communicates with their special agents on the Mainland, and so we can be sure that the key is part of the message. The special agents have to split up – they need to be able to work in the widest field possible – so if the key isn't part of the message, the whole system could easily break down.'

'Mmm.'

'So I believe that the key to RECOVERY must be hidden in the message. But where is it hidden? If it were just like ULTRA, and on even-number days it was this set of numbers and on odd-number days it was that set, neither Sivincy herself nor the American army that was employing her would have been happy with it. Within the limitations imposed by her cipher, she would certainly want to work out an unusual and clever new key. After I considered that for a bit, I remembered that Sivincy at an earlier stage in her career discovered a mathematical principle which is called the Shadow Principle or the Light Principle, popularly known as Honeycomb Theory. The substance of this theory is that if you take any given honeycomb structure, with the help of a moving light source, you can distinguish black and white, shadow and light. Right now I don't have the equipment, so I can't demonstrate it for you.'

'I can imagine it. For example, if the roof was in fact made of some honeycombed substance, we'd see pinpricks of light.'

'Exactly. And what's the point of all this? It means that if you make sure you are forever moving at the same speed as the light, you can always keep yourself hidden in the shadows. This has significant implications for astrophysics.'

I felt she was wandering away from the point. 'Let's get back to our key.'

'Right now I'm making my cryptographic bombe. When it's finished we'll give it a run-through, and then you'll understand.'

I opened my eyes wide. 'So all that banging about in your room, and those things like bottles and bowling balls was all preparation for a cryptographic bombe?'

'Yes. What did you think I was doing?'

I was embarrassed. 'Chen thought you were playing some stupid game.'

She sniffed. 'You people really do look at everyone else in such a negative way!'

I quickly apologized for misunderstanding her, but I wasn't expecting her to giggle and say charmingly that as long as I understood that she loved me, she didn't care about anything else. As she spoke, she reached for my hand. Fortunately I had already made my request that she should obey me, otherwise she would have caused even more trouble on this occasion.

That day, after Huang Yiyi had left, I stayed in the forest alone and walked round and round one of the trees like the madman, Jiang Nan. I looked up at the treetops, and at the sky above the treetops, and thought about the holes that the carpenter was cutting in that piece of wood, and I seemed to see light streaming from each hexagonal hole, followed by every secret encrypted in RECOVERY. At that moment I understood why Jiang Nan spent every day walking round the trees talking to himself, and yet was clearly so happy; it was because he had experienced the strange pleasure of having cracked PORPHORY. That day, I really identified with the strange pleasures of a madman.

17

About a week later, Huang Yiyi's cryptographic bombe was delivered from the carpenters' workshop, and I called all the members of our special working group into the conference room in order to listen to her explanation.

The cryptographic bombe wasn't actually particularly complicated. Both in shape and in the way it worked it was somewhat like those machines you see on street corners for measuring your height, where the scale rod moves independently. The difference was that the scale rod on the bombe was a wooden honeycombed board, about thirty centimetres high and as thick as a piece of card. At the bottom there was a square tray, and on all four sides there were troughs, in which you could place the radio intercepts.

Huang Yiyi demonstrated how it worked as she talked. 'This is the cryptographic bombe I've designed. As you can see, we have an upper plate in which there are many round holes in a honeycomb pattern, and on this gauge there are thirty-one notches to represent the thirty-one days of the month. The upper plate is mounted on rollers, so that it can move up and down of its own accord; again, it can be raised or lowered by thirty-one notches. At the top of the gauge there is a light source, and right here, in the hollow underneath, is where we put the radio intercepts. We can clip them in like this. This tray can also be moved sideways along its thirty-one notches, and again one notch represents one day. Now we must imagine that in addition to the upper plate moving up and down and the tray moving from side to side, our light source is also in constant motion. If the group of numbers illuminated by our light is the cipher key that allows us to read that day's messages, then we can calculate how big the key must be: there are three hundred and sixty-five possibilities, which means that it is one whole year before the cipher key has to be repeated.

Now if we want to make it more difficult for our light source to reveal the key, for example by adding another plate, then that gives us twice as many possible combinations; and extrapolating from that, the more plates you add, the more years it is before you have to repeat your cipher key. Now my first demonstration model has nine levels of plates . . .'

Chen got up and cut her short. 'Comrade Huang, let me say this: if this bombe helps us crack the cipher then that is wonderful, but to my knowledge no cryptographic unit anywhere in the world uses a machine to generate cipher keys. Have any of you ever heard of such a thing?'

'Have you ever heard of anyone daring to steal the portrait of Chairman Mao off the gate at Tiananmen?' asked Huang Yiyi.

I laughed. 'Only Sivincy.'

'Exactly. Just as I told Deputy Director An, I am now more and more convinced that Sivincy's plagiarism of the Enigma machine isn't a straightforward rip-off; it is because she is so intelligent and so cunning that she is always up to nasty tricks – she enjoys break-ing the rules.'

Comrade Chen said, 'But have you considered, Comrade Huang, that the key to the cipher isn't actually part of the cipher itself, it is an adjunct. Not having it will stop the novice but not the expert, so why would Sivincy go to so much trouble to hide it?'

'Why? First, it actually isn't a lot of trouble; this is such a simple machine that our carpentry workshop could make a rough approximation of it. Secondly, it is a very valuable tool, given that it would be a good few years before you would need to repeat the cipher key. That makes it very difficult indeed. If they had created a one-time pad specially for this occasion it would have to be so big that it would cover the wall over there. We can now be abso-lutely sure that they are not using a one-time pad because it is too impractical and would cause so many residual problems – it really could not be used successfully for real-life communications. If they are not using a one-time pad but have incorporated the cipher key into the message, there would be massive limitations. It doesn't matter how you do it – the first two groups of numbers, the first

In the Dark

three groups, the last two groups, the last three groups, a middle group, a middle three groups – you can't possibly create such a big cipher key. Thirdly, Sivincy would be interested in creating a machine that generates cipher keys. You may have realized already that the reason I thought she might have done this is that Sivincy started working on this branch of mathematics at a very early stage in her career. Fourthly, I realized from her books, and indeed from her actions, that Sivincy isn't a very profound person. She is not a black hole: in her eccentricities, cunning, changeability and slipperiness she is more like a chameleon, and that makes her very good at misleading people. Since she herself lacks depth, the ciphers that she creates can't be that difficult or complex. Given the limitations on the level of difficulty intrinsic in her cipher, she would want to make up for that by adding to the complexity of the adjuncts, like the key to the cipher.'

'What do you think, Deputy Director An?' asked Comrade Chen. 'Do you really think it is possible that they are using a machine to generate their cipher keys?'

I didn't answer him straight away, but turned to Huang Yiyi. 'I am currently working on the supposition that your theory is correct and that the enemy really is using a machine to create their cipher keys, so the next step is that we need to create a copy. Making a copy relies on deductions; it is easy for them to make the original, but it is going to be difficult for us because we can't afford to make any mistakes – a centimetre's error could create massive problems for us. Of course I understand that what we actually need to copy is the mathematical formula, so do you have the data to work it out?'

She handed me a folder. 'The formulae and figures for the exercise are all here.'

I took the folder and saw that it contained a thick stack of papers, each page covered in formulae and the data for the calculations. The formulae were all very complex and there was a mass of figures to work through – so densely packed that as I read through them my eyes widened. I said, 'Oh hell, this is going to be a huge exercise.'

'Of course it is big,' she said. 'Each stage in the separation process is a living thing: when the top plate moves, the others all change; when the left figure moves, so does the one on the right. If you have to work through a whole stack of calculations even to get to the starting point, there is a limit to how small the exercise can possibly be.'

I handed the folder over to the manager of the Calculations Office, Comrade Jiang. 'You have a look and estimate roughly how long this is going to take you to do.'

Comrade Jiang looked at it and said, 'If we split our people into three teams and work round the clock, it will take us about a month.'

Huang Yiyi gave a sharp exclamation. 'That long!'

'We don't have the facilities or the people to do it in less.'

'If only we had computers.'

'What happens if you're wrong?' asked Comrade Chen. 'That is one hell of a waste of time!'

Comrade Chen's word of warning startled everyone, and we all looked at each other, including Huang Yiyi; and then in the end all eyes turned to me, waiting for me to make the final decision. You know, right at that moment I found it very difficult to know what to do. It was a massive exercise which would involve an awful lot of time and effort, and what happened if the premise it was based on was wrong? That would be a disaster! But then I thought about it from another point of view: breaking a cipher is like looking for a needle in a haystack, so what is the chance of getting it right first time? But if you don't go into the tiger's den you can't capture its cubs; if you don't carry out the exercise how do you know whether the premise is wrong or not? So I was silent for a bit and then resolutely made my decision: 'If you are right, we have made a massive step forward in cracking RECOVERY. For that, a month is worth it!'

You can guess how we spent the next month. Everyone in our special working group was entirely caught up in the work of the calculations division, and although they came into work they couldn't concentrate on anything. It was as if they were in a trance:

the only thing they could think about was the exercise going on in the Calculations Office; their ears were filled with the sound of moving abacus beads, like the swish of nuts being swirled across a roasting pan. During this time, even I who am normally so serious and calm found myself becoming increasingly restless; in the course of a single day I would go many times to stare out of the window in the direction of the quiet single-storey building housing the team working on the calculations – just like a shipwrecked sailor on a desert island, scanning the horizon for the ship that would rescue him.

Of course, Huang Yiyi suffered the worst. She couldn't eat, she couldn't sleep, she kept running round to the Calculations Office to look at their results. She was so nervous that she almost stopped laughing, and when I cracked a joke with her, she hardly reacted. She just lifted the corners of her mouth, like a sleepwalker whose soul is far away. I saw that she was getting thinner day by day, and I found myself feeling a kind of wordless sympathy for her. One day, as I was going upstairs with her, I don't know exactly what happened but her foot seemed to give way under her and she fell down the stairs. I helped her up and took her to my office, telling her that she ought to relax; this exercise wasn't that important. She saw that I had tears in my eyes, but nevertheless she shouted at me as though she was trying to pick a quarrel. 'How can I not take it seriously? This is the first time I have suggested a premise for cracking RECOVERY since my arrival at Unit 701. If Comrade Chen is right, everyone is going to laugh at me!'

That was the very first time I felt like taking her in my arms and hugging her tight. Of course I immediately realized that was a really bad idea; and my emotions were under iron control, thanks to my love for Xiaoyu and my long experience as a secret agent. At all times and in all places my self-control protected me. I knew that nothing in this world is perfect, and we had to accept pain and suffering.

On day twenty-nine, the exercise reached its final conclusion. Everyone in the special working group rushed to the Calculations Office, to wait for the final result. On the dais in the office, the data was piled up in heaps two or three feet high, but there were still a couple of people there reciting numbers without stopping, like the traders at a stock market: '1234567890. 0187654329. 2345678901.'

When all the data had come in, Comrade Jiang, the cynosure of everybody's eyes, sat down in front of a large abacus and prepared to make the final calculations. Huang Yiyi and I were both unbearably nervous. Everyone had their eyes fixed on Comrade Jiang's fingers, and watched unblinkingly as his hands flew across the abacus. There was not a single sound to be heard in the whole of the vast Calculations Office, just the click of the beads on his abacus. The sound was tiny, but it thudded in our minds like the blows of an axe.

In the end, his fingers seemed to receive an electric shock. They convulsed and then hung in the air unmoving – but beneath his rigid fingers there were still several beads up by the central bar! That meant that the result of this calculation was an infinite number: we could never work it out. Or to put it another way, it meant that Huang Yiyi was wrong!

Comrade Jiang was appalled and just stood there, not daring to report.

A dead silence reigned in the Calculations Office, but there was a tension in the air that could explode at any moment.

Huang Yiyi lost control of herself and shrieked, 'It's not possible! You must have made a mistake!'

I pulled myself together and went over to comfort her. She suddenly seemed to go mad and got up, grabbed hold of an abacus, and then threw it violently to the floor, before bursting into tears and running out of the Calculations Office.

The beads of the abacus scattered across the ground, bouncing and rolling around our feet.

That was how an amazing theory and an enormous effort ended in failure.

That evening I went to Huang Yiyi's room for a second time. I was intending to try and cheer her up, but she seemed to have done that herself, and so she was comparatively calm. I found her lying on the sofa reading a foreign fashion magazine. When she saw me come in, she sat up and said shamefacedly, 'I'm sorry. I . . . behaved really badly.'

'It doesn't matter: everyone understands how you feel. If you hadn't smashed the abacus, quite possibly I would have done.'

When I said that, she became very cheerful and said, 'Really? I was afraid you'd be angry because I made you look bad.'

'The person who made us look bad is Sivincy.'

She ground her teeth and swore. 'That witch! I thought this time I'd got her, but we've come away empty-handed.'

'I wasn't expecting it, either. I really thought you'd pull it off.'

'And that's why you made such a big decision, roping everyone else in to help me out. And now I'm a laughing stock.'

'No one is laughing at you. This is cracking ciphers, not spreading nets to catch fish. This was an unusually large exercise and our comrades all worked extra hard on it, and so you might expect that they are extremely disappointed it didn't work out. But they all understand what you are going through, because they get to see Jiang Nan wandering around outside their windows every day. They see him every day, they think about it every day – that even though cracking ciphers is an intangible achievement, it can make you pay a truly terrible price.'

She was deeply moved. 'I don't know what to say . . . that's terribly kind of you. Thank you.'

I smiled. 'Thank you for your praise: it is a great compliment.'

She said seriously, 'It's true: I have a lot of respect for you. You don't seem to mind when things go wrong. I simply am not like that – I can't do it.'

I tried to cheer her up. 'You mustn't let this get you down. This isn't a failure, this is just one of those setbacks that any cryptographer has to face. Cracking a cipher isn't like doing a crossword, where a moment of inspiration gets you the answer.'

Her eyes sparkled and she put her hand down lightly on my shoulder. 'I understand. Don't worry, this won't get me down. Before leaving Beijing I went off to bow to the statue of the god of mathematics, Zu Chongzhi, and made a wish. I believe that the gods will protect us.'

I took her hand with the intention of getting it off my shoulder, but she grabbed hold of me and said seriously, 'Zaitian, I know that you don't dare to love me, and so I have been doing my best to forget you, to move on, but it's not working. What am I supposed to do?'

I quickly whipped my hand out of her grasp and got up to go. She didn't try and stop me, just asked me to sit with her for a little longer. I was worried that she was up to her old tricks, and insisted on leaving. She was clearly upset but still walked me to the door, turning expectant eyes upon me. She clearly wanted to talk to me and was holding herself back painfully, which made me feel profoundly uncomfortable. I sensed that if I stayed there any longer I might no longer be able to resist her, so I was even more determined to leave. On the road home, I couldn't stop myself from thinking of something that Anderov once said to me: 'Until you have cracked a cipher, only an idiot would be sure that he can do it. This isn't a plot of land and a cipher isn't a potato, from which if you plant it and look after it carefully you can be guaranteed a harvest.' Involuntarily I found myself becoming more and more depressed by the horrible nature of cryptographic work, and I didn't sleep the whole night.

18.

Late one evening a few days later, just as I was getting ready to have a wash, I suddenly heard a knock on the door. I went to open it somewhat suspiciously, and it was Huang Yiyi who was standing there. I was more than a little surprised. 'It's really late, why aren't you at home? Is something up?'

She stared at me but didn't speak. I saw that her hair was in a mess, and she didn't look at all well – in the yellowish lamplight she looked as white as a sheet, as if there really was something wrong with her. I was worried that she might be getting ill, so I quickly told her to come in, and asked, 'Are you OK? You really don't look well – are you coming down with something?'

She suddenly seemed to become completely boneless as she pitched forward against my chest silently, her eyes closed, as if she had fainted. I got her down into a chair, called to her, felt her forehead, and rushed around in a panic not knowing what to do for the best. I had just decided to put her down and phone for help when she suddenly opened her eyes, shook her head, and said, 'I'm fine, don't bother phoning anyone.' Then she looked at me silently, lovingly.

'You just fainted,' I said. 'What's wrong with you?'

She nodded as if she were at the very end of her resources. 'I'm tired . . . I am so very, very tired . . . Between you, you . . . and RECOVERY . . . have worn me out . . .' As she spoke, she took hold of my hand.

I tried to remove my hand from her grasp. 'What's wrong with you?'

She held tight to my hand, staring fixedly at me, and then after a long pause she said, 'Zaitian, you must believe me, we need God's help. Do you remember that before leaving Beijing, I went to pray in front of the statue of Zu Chongzhi?'

'Of course I remember.'

She said in a sad and despairing voice, 'But how can someone like me, unwanted by men, possibly be loved by God? Zaitian, do you really think that I can crack RECOVERY like this?'

I had a feeling that we might be working round to that old tune, so while I was trying to get her to let go of my hand, I said with a laugh, 'What are you talking about? I, more than anyone, am sure that you can crack RECOVERY.'

She simply wouldn't let go of my hand. 'Love me, Zaitian. I need your help, and God knows I love you . . . If God sees you don't love me, then how can He love me? Really, Zaitian, this time . . . this failure . . . Zaitian, help me – for you to love me would be the biggest help . . .'

'Yiyi, how can you . . . what are you saying . . . ?'

'Otherwise we can't crack RECOVERY . . .'

I cut her short. 'You're wrong!' I wrested my hand free and stood well back, looking for all the world like a recaptured prisoner, begging to be forgiven. 'Yiyi, please don't do this to me.'

She ran after me and grabbed hold of me. 'Why don't you love me? Zaitian, I love you, I really love you . . . and I know you love me . . .'

I was absolutely furious, and looked across at the casket of Xiaoyu's ashes standing on the altar. Then I dragged her to the door and pointed at it: 'Out! Just get out!'

She was completely at a loss. 'Zaitian, I don't know what to say . . .'

'Don't say anything. Out!'

'I'm not leaving.' She threw herself against me. 'Zaitian, love me, hold me . . .'

I flung her aside and took a step back. 'Don't come any closer . . . just go away . . .'

She stood there, and there was both bitterness and anger in her wet eyes. 'Zaitian, I really don't know what to say . . . I know I shouldn't be here now demanding your love . . . I should wait until we've cracked RECOVERY . . . but, Zaitian, this failure was a terrible setback for me. God isn't helping me, God isn't on my side . . . I ask myself all the time, why? Why isn't God helping me? And it's because I haven't made you love me . . . Someone who isn't loved by a man can't hope to be loved by God . . . Zaitian, believe me, I love you, I need your love . . .'

I walked round to stand in front of Xiaoyu's altar and pointed at the casket containing her ashes. 'Huang Yiyi, please show a bit of respect for me, and don't ever again mention love in front of my wife. You have no right to love me: I'm married!'

'But Xiaoyu's gone, and I'm sure . . . she'd understand.'

'To you, maybe Xiaoyu is dead, but to me she's going to live for ever. Go away, and in future show me a bit more respect.'

'But you don't respect me . . . Zaitian, hold me, I need you, I love you, please . . .'

I couldn't stand it any more and shouted, 'Stop that! I don't love you and I never will! You have no right to love me, so will you please leave! Get out of here!'

She sat down on the sofa. 'No.'

'If you won't leave then I'll go!' I started marching towards the door, and when I got there, I couldn't stop myself from turning back to say, 'Don't you think you're behaving really disgustingly? How can you say you love me?'

She looked at me, and then collapsed back against the sofa.

That evening Huang Yiyi sat in my room for over an hour, and then slowly and hesitantly she walked away. She didn't look to left or right, but just walked straight ahead like a sleepwalker. Once I had seen her disappear into her own building, I went quietly home.

There was a note on the tea table, just a single line: 'An Zaitian, I hate you!'

I quickly struck a match, and having turned my back to Xiaoyu's altar, I burned the note.

The following morning I went to the canteen for breakfast, but though I waited a long time, I didn't see Huang Yiyi. I started to get worried. I kept looking around in all directions, and just then Comrade Wang, the head of the training centre, came over to me and asked, 'Hey, what was wrong with your new mathematician last night?'

I was surprised to suddenly be asked such a question by someone from the training centre, which stands a long way away from our cryptography division, so I replied somewhat coldly, 'What do you mean?'

Wang said that the night before, just as he was on his way home from the guest house through the lashing rain at about two o'clock in the morning, he had seen Huang Yiyi wandering around looking like a lost soul, soaked to the skin, and she had refused to go home whatever he said.

I knew exactly what was the matter, so I got my food and started gulping it down. My idea was to eat up and then go and find Comrade Zha to see if Huang Yiyi was OK. I wasn't expecting that Comrade Wang would get his breakfast and then come and sit down next to me, looking inquisitive. I had no idea that later on this same man would cause such terrible trouble in our efforts to break RECOVERY, nearly destroying both Huang Yiyi and myself! If I had had the slightest premonition, I would have ordered him to leave the table. But I had no inkling of the future, and there was no way for me to know what was in store. However, I had always hated outsiders trying to find out what was going on in my division, particularly anything to do with Huang Yiyi, and the moment anyone started in on it, I got cross. So when Wang was getting ready to ask his questions, I looked as unhelpful as possible, shovelled in a few more mouthfuls and left.

I went to her office, but I didn't find Huang Yiyi. I asked little Comrade Zha, who was cleaning up the place, and she said Huang Yiyi hadn't come to work. An hour later I went back and asked again, and Comrade Zha said she still hadn't come in.

I got angry and criticized her. 'You're supposed to be her assistant, don't you care that she hasn't come to work? Go to her home and get her.'

Comrade Zha said in a put-upon tone: 'I've already been and there's nobody there. I have no idea where she's gone.'

I stood there for a moment, and then a horrible thought suddenly crossed my mind. I was scared practically witless, and ran to find her with Comrade Zha at my heels. We went to her room first, banging hard on the door, shouting and calling to her, but there was no response from inside. But I could sense that she was in there. I went round to the neighbours' to rustle up some strong young men, and they broke the door down. We found Huang Yiyi lying unconscious on her bed, running a high temperature. We immediately phoned the hospital, telling them to send an ambulance, and they took her off to hospital.

They gave her a check-up and discovered that there was nothing much wrong with her other than a really bad cold. I could relax.

19.

Young man, it's getting late, let's carry on tomorrow.

You know, time lets you forget many things, but there are some that you remember all your life. What I need to tell you now is something I have tried hard to forget, but have never been able to . . .

20

I think I have already mentioned that as a young man I had three serious girlfriends, but that none of these relationships worked out, so that in the end the Party had to help me find a wife. To tell you the truth, I didn't have much experience with women, and particularly not a relentless nagger like Huang Yiyi. I really didn't know what to do. I did have one weapon though, and that was stubbornness. During the course of my life there have been a number of successes that I owe to stubbornness and determination, and I believed that I could use these qualities to sort out the problems I had with Huang Yiyi. I thought I could resolve the situation so that no one got hurt and the country benefited.

Looking back now, you could say that was a terrible mistake. Or maybe it wasn't a mistake, but at the very least it didn't work out the way I wanted. But at that time and in that situation, did I have any choice but to make that mistake? I had no choice! This seems like a paradox. But then decrypting ciphers is a paradox, and there were many people in Unit 701 who had to live with that. I don't know if that is impressive, or tragic.

Let's not talk about that any more: it's time to get back to the main story.

The following afternoon, I went to the hospital to see Huang Yiyi. She had already discharged herself. It was just a bad cold – these things come on quickly and leave just as fast; all she needed was to take some medicine and it sorted itself out. On the way back from the hospital I debated with myself whether I should go and see her at home. In the end I thought it was my duty as her boss, so I decided to get together some fruit and then go and see her. I didn't know if she really hated me or was just pretending to be cold and distant, but when she saw me she was positively icy and her words were cutting. I asked her if she was feeling any better, and she glared at me and said, 'That's nothing to do with you. I guess you'll be happy when I'm dead!' I just stood there not knowing what to say. Seeing me all silent she got really angry, and shouted at me: 'Say something!'

'I don't know what to say. You should rest. I will leave.'

She immediately became furious and cursed me, saying that she should have guessed I wasn't really concerned about her.

The only thing I could do was to stay and say, 'Yiyi, I really wanted to see you.'

She smiled coldly. 'I guess you came here to make fun of me.'

I raised my voice. 'Can't you say anything nice!'

Seeing I was getting angry, she got me to sit down and play a game of *go* with her. I didn't want to play because there was no way I was good enough. She paid no attention to me but started scrutinizing the board, black pieces in one hand and white pieces in the other, helping me to play against her. She looked like a complete lunatic talking to herself: 'Ah, I knew you would take that spot . . . if you put your piece there then mine goes here . . . the next piece someone at your level would put here. Actually that's a really stupid move, but what can you do, that's the level you play at . . .' In the end I was forced to take over my *go* pieces and start playing against her properly.

We played, and then the board ended up soaked in her tears: we were back to square one! She was asking me again why I didn't love her.

'Can we please talk about something else?'

'But I want to talk about it. I want you to tell me why you don't love me.'

I thought about it for a moment. 'Because I love someone else.'

She looked at me. 'Who? You mean . . . your late wife?'

I nodded.

'Don't you think that's a bit weird?'

'I think . . . until the dead person has been buried, to find someone new would be wrong.'

She smiled coldly. 'Your wife is dead. Don't you think it is disrespectful to leave her unburied, sitting on your little home-made altar?'

'I'm waiting for the right day.'

'When will that be, the anniversary of her death? Christmas? The anniversary of the founding of the PLA? Or are you planning to wait until National Day?'

'No, none of those.'

'You're not telling me you're going to wait until we've cracked RECOVERY?'

'Yes.'

There was a strange light in her eyes, and she looked at me fixedly for a long time, then she said, 'You mean ... if I crack RECOVERY you will love me?'

I laughed bitterly. 'You carry on about love day in and day out; is love really that important?'

'Is there anything more important than love?'

'Right now cracking RECOVERY is the most important thing for me, more important than everything else put together. If you're talking about love, that's the very greatest kind of love. It is the living embodiment of our love for the country, our love for the Party, our love for the people, and for Communism.'

'But our Party, our country, our people and Communism don't say that you can only love them; that you can't love anyone else.'

'All other kinds of love are subordinate to those. The only thing I care about right now is cracking RECOVERY: nothing else.'

'I want to crack RECOVERY too, and I am sure that if you promise me one thing, I can do it.'

'Provided it is nothing to do with loving you, any other request I will grant.'

'There is nothing I want right now. If I can't crack RECOVERY, I don't want anything. But if I do crack it, I want you to promise me something.'

'What?'

'Marry me. I want you to marry me!'

What could I say to that? It was a perfectly reasonable request. When Abing helped us out, the Party wanted to find a wife for him, and if Huang Yiyi really did crack RECOVERY, her achievements would far outstrip anything that Abing had done. In that case we would do whatever was necessary to make her happy, providing it wasn't actually against the law. I, especially, would do anything for her. If she cracked RECOVERY, I would be one of the beneficiaries, so I had no reason to refuse her request, either as a private individual or as her boss. If there was not a very special reason, I would say yes without hesitation; even if I didn't love her I would still be willing to marry her. Besides which – how could I not love her? She was so pretty, so talented, so attractive, what kind of man could resist? Any man would fall for her, and if she seemed to have a problematic lifestyle, no doubt it largely came about because there were so many men who fancied her. She was so seductive, and on top of that she had lived for a long time abroad, which perhaps gave her a more free and easy manner with men than most women then had. As a wife, that would of course be a shortcoming, but I think that as far as most men were concerned her attractions would always outweigh her shortcomings. I would even say that if she cracked RECOVERY, even if she had nothing going for her at all, and had this problematic lifestyle, I would still have been willing to marry her. Just like Lin Xiaofang, I would have been proud to devote the rest of my life to such a heroine!

But I . . . couldn't.

Why?

Because Xiaoyu was still alive.

It was all a lie, an elaborate cover story cunningly constructed by headquarters. The aim was to give Xiaoyu a secure identity for her espionage work after I left Russia. After her 'death' she changed her name and moved from Moscow to Leningrad, giving up her job at the embassy to become an illegal arms-dealer. Just like Comrade Aeroplane she had become a full-time spy. At that time, apart from a few senior people at headquarters, no one was in on the secret, not even Unit Director Luo. To begin with I didn't even know myself. How did I find out? Well, it was Director Tie who told me. It seems that while he was in Beijing he heard some gossip about Huang Yiyi pursuing me, and so he sent me a letter in which he honestly informed me about what had actually happened. That was the letter that Unit Director Luo had given me. That day I was of course very shocked, but I also suddenly understood why the Party had demanded that I make such a show of bringing Xiaoyu's ashes home, and why the Ministry of Foreign Affairs had held such a large memorial ceremony, and told me to set up an altar at home . . . It was all done to publicize her 'death' as much as possible. We wanted as many people as possible to know that I had lost my wife; that was crucial for her safety. And the opposite was also true: the more people who knew she was alive, the greater the danger.

That evening I had no choice: Huang Yiyi had pushed me to the point of no return. I had only two options: one was to agree to her demand and marry her after she cracked RECOVERY, the second was to tell her the truth and let her get over it. I chose the second, because I thought the first was impossible; it would hurt her too much. It would have been a double lie, with the damage twice as deep. I simply couldn't bear it. So I made her swear an oath (that she would keep this a secret and never let anyone else know) in front of a statue of Chairman Mao, and then I told her the truth. She seemed to be very shocked at the whole thing, and watched me in silence. Then she suddenly seemed to explode – she burst into tears, wailing and covering her face with both hands. She ran out, and though I called to her, and went after her, she paid no attention to me.

That night I walked up and down outside her building until I saw the light in her room go out. Seeing nothing unusual, I went home. I was sure it had been a terrible shock to her, but at least now she would be under no illusions. The problem was that I had no idea how she would cope with the situation. Would she insist on leaving Unit 701? She was always so decisive; she didn't think about the consequences. I was really worried that she would do something hasty, and both she and the Party would suffer from it. It was for that reason I wrote her a long letter that night and pushed it under her door, in the hope she would face up to the whole thing squarely.

I don't know if it was because of my letter or for some other reason, but she arrived on time at her office the next day – which was pleasing, but scary. I quickly realized that she had changed: she wasn't as cheerful as she had been before, she spoke less and seemed colder, particularly towards me. Her eyes shone with an icy glitter, which left me uneasy and at a loss.

One afternoon we had a meeting which was intended to help Huang Yiyi come up with a new avenue of approach after the recent failure. She didn't say a word from start to finish, and so I was left to mention the two main points: one was to do with the rate at which analysis was proceeding, which reflected the standard of our performance. To begin with we were having problems even reaching the rate of two in a thousand, but now we were achieving five in a thousand, and both the speed and extent of this increase were very pleasing. However, looking at it from a cryptographic point of view, even though the rate of analysis was improving rapidly, the gold content wasn't very high. What did I mean by that? Even though we were picking out some words and phrases, and some numbers, we were getting only a tiny proportion of the key words and phrases. The majority of what we were finding were the code-names for army units, their designations, people's names and dates. I would guess that we were getting roughly 87 per cent of the people's names. That means that we were picking out the ordinary stuff but not what actually mattered, and that was not a good state of affairs. In a good situation maybe the rate of analysis isn't so high, but you get what matters, even if the rest is a tissue of holes. Right now we had far too many holes, and what is worse the holes were all the important ones. The second thing was a request, or perhaps it would be better to say a demand. I wanted the comrades in the analysis department to take back all the intercepts that they had worked through and analyse them again. There was a good reason for doing that, which was as follows: we were getting our newspapers about ten days to two weeks after they had been published, which means that we were losing any connection with events on the ground. If we did the analysis in the light of what was being reported on the day, we might make new discoveries.

As the facts subsequently demonstrated, my idea was right, and there was a great improvement in the quality of analysis of the radio intercepts. Comrade Chen was the immediate beneficiary of this: a couple of days later he burst into my office to tell me the good news. He had decrypted one entire message. The contents of this secret communication were: 'Operation Wolf' was under way, and the agents should wait in the usual place for 'Banana' . . .

That was what old Comrade Chen was good at. Thanks to his understanding of the way enemy intelligence operations worked, and the vast and swelling sea of information he had accumulated over the years, he could build something out of nothing. It was as if a writer were such a genius that he could write a whole book without knowing anything about grammar. Twenty years earlier, before cryptography was computerized in other countries, being able to read a message in its entirety was priceless, because it could set in motion a domino effect whereby the whole cipher would be laid bare.

We then held another meeting, to discuss how to proceed in the light of Comrade Chen's reading of this secret message. It seemed that Huang Yiyi didn't think much of Chen's achievements, because at the meeting she said, 'First of all I would like to congratulate Comrade Chen on his little breakthrough; for the first time we can read an entire radio message. That means that we can now be sure that we are on the right track. But Comrade Chen seems to be under the impression that this has been a massive advance for our cryptographic work and determines the next steps in the process, and I am afraid I don't agree with him. In my opinion this is a very simple message and will be of no help at all in our work on cracking RECOVERY. This is just a single hair when we are dealing with nine head of oxen. While from the presence of the ox's hair we can be sure of the existence of the oxen, we mustn't be too optimistic, nor should we make a hasty decision that sends our decryption down the wrong route.'

Comrade Chen retorted, 'What do you mean, a hair? In the past we often found the whole ox by starting from a couple of hairs.'

'That was in the past. At that point ciphers relied on human encryption skills, so that one message could lead you on to the next, and then to the third and fourth. Modern ciphers are mathematical problems, and if you want to solve them you have to work out the equations on which they are based, how they are formulated and how they develop. Otherwise one is one and two is two, and you can't hope to get one and then have the rest fall into your lap. You must not be under any illusions about that.'

Chen glared at her and asked her to come up with something better instead. She waved her hands and said that she had nothing to suggest.

'So,' said Chen rudely, 'I suggest that you stop trying to bite off more than you can chew and settle down to working through the information and intelligence seriously, whereby you deal with actual concrete radio intercepts. Every message decrypted is another step forward, and I am sure that once we have reached a certain point, a chain reaction will be set off.'

Huang Yiyi said, 'Of course if you now go on to decrypt another thousand messages, then you've cracked it. However, by the time you've done that, this cipher may well have long been taken out of use and the messages will have become irrelevant. As I just said, this one message text is not a goose that is going to lay golden eggs; and having decrypted one isn't going to help us with the rest. This message is it: it's a gander, which not only doesn't lay eggs but also can't turn into a phoenix. Just think about it, Chen: if it takes you a week to decrypt one message, how long is it going to take you to do one thousand?'

Chen said angrily, 'Well, it's better than your stupid carryings-on.'

Huang Yiyi raised her voice. 'What do you mean by stupid carryings-on?'

Things were going from bad to worse, so I quickly started

trying to calm them down. Huang Yiyi was clearly not going to let this one go at that, and said nastily, 'You know, Comrade Chen, in the past your work might have been called cryptography, but now you're nothing better than a high-level cryptanalyst.'

Chen was very upset. 'What? I'm just a cryptanalyst? There are many, many cryptanalysts in this building – how come I have never seen one of them decrypt a cipher text? Haven't you noticed them hard at work day after day, analysing messages and picking out cribs – though even then they often get them wrong.'

'They are ordinary cryptanalysts; you are a high-level one.'

Chen was so furious that he bolted out of his chair and glared at her. 'Humph. Many thanks for the information. Now it's my turn to say something to you.'

'Please do. I'm all ears.'

Chen ground his teeth and said, 'If a silly little piece like you can crack RECOVERY . . .'

She looked at him with interest. 'Then what?'

Chen glared at her, stretched out a hand, and said, 'I'll use this hand as a grill to cook a fish for you!'

Huang Yiyi laughed. 'I'll be waiting. I dare say the fish will be delicious, particularly with overtones of human flesh.'

Chen got so angry that he walked out. When the meeting was over he came to my office, and the moment he got through the door he started shouting at me, complaining about Huang Yiyi's behaviour. I spoke up for her, which really didn't please Chen, and he started to blame me for what had happened. 'It is not that I want to criticize you, but sometimes you seem to trust her and give in to her too much. That's a bad thing. I've been really puzzled that you support her over this idea of finding the key in order to decrypt this cipher, which is a topsy-turvy approach.'

'What do you mean, topsy-turvy? It's a new way of dealing with the thing.'

'What do you mean, a new way? It's clearly a dead end. Humph. I've been cracking ciphers for more than twenty years, and I've never heard of trying to find the key first. What is the key anyway? It is like the key to a room, and if I give you that key, you can open the door; but if what you want is actually in the safe which you can't open – what's the point? On the other hand, if I can open the safe I don't need a key: I can climb in through the window . . .'

I shook my head and looked silently at Chen. He really was getting past it: he didn't know about the advances in Western computing, or understand that a revolution had taken place both in the development of ciphers and in their decryption. In modern ciphers the key is given as part of the cipher text: they are indivisible, in the same way as modern metallurgy transforms aluminium and iron into a completely new material. How can you separate the constituent elements?

It was that day, after my conversation with Chen, that I suddenly got the idea of going to the Soviet Union. If Anderov wouldn't write back, that didn't mean that I couldn't go to Russia and find him myself, did it?

21

My idea was supported by my superiors, and Director Tie told me to get things organized and do the round trip as quickly as possible. The day before I set out, I decided to go and talk to Huang Yiyi. I found her in the woods, feeding biscuits to the squirrels. From the moment she learnt the truth about Xiaoyu she had been ignoring me. She caught sight of me but pretended she hadn't seen me, and walked deeper into the woods. I had to shout at her to stop. She stood under a tree and waited for me to catch up with her, and then she said in a depressed way, 'Are you here to try and raise my revolutionary consciousness? Or are you afraid I'm suicidal, or that I'm going to stop working for you?'

She didn't wait for my reply. 'Don't worry. I don't have your complicated history, nor your great commitment to the revolution, though I do have my own little commitment. So there's no need for you to worry. I'm not going to commit suicide, which would be a crime against my parents; I'm also not going to stop work, which would be a crime against the Party and the Chinese people, and unfair to Director Tie, Unit Director Luo and you. From now on I will go to work regularly. Don't worry.'

I said abruptly, 'I'm going to Moscow tomorrow.'

She seemed a bit surprised at that, and asked if I was going to see Anderov. I said yes, and she expressed some misgivings. 'He wouldn't write back to you – do you think he is going to see you?'

I said he would; if I was there in person he would certainly want to see me. She said that if I popped up suddenly like that, even if I did see him he wouldn't say anything useful, people like that being very sensitive. I said that I had a really good excuse for going to see him, given that I wanted to perform a 'summoning the soul' ceremony for Xiaoyu. Xiaoyu's soul was still lost and far from home, which meant that she could not rest in peace. It was imperative that her soul be summoned. I didn't care if he really believed in that kind of thing or not, what mattered was that it made a viable excuse. 'The reason I have come to see you is to ask, what kind of thing is it that you want to know from Anderov?'

That question seemed to go right to the heart of things, and she immediately got excited and said, 'Fantastic! I'll write you a list this evening.'

I said this evening would be too late since I was leaving first thing in the morning, and besides something like that probably shouldn't be put into writing: she should just tell me.

She thought about it, and said: 'If at all possible, I'd like to know what Anderov thinks of Sivincy's cryptographic skills: whether she is likely to pull any particularly nasty or unexpected tricks, and whether she is capable of producing a super-difficult cipher. If she isn't, then we can eliminate one of the four possibilities that I discussed with you: RECOVERY can't possibly be a super-large-value algorithmic cipher encrypted with a medium-large-value algorithmic cipher. Finding that out would be crucial, because if RECOVERY really is that kind of code it would be bad news for our chances of decrypting it. The calculations required would be massive, and we simply don't have the capacity: we can't deal with it. In that case we won't be able to crack it for at least another couple of years.'

Then she asked me how long I was planning to spend in Moscow. I said I was desperate to get there, see Anderov, get the information that I needed and come back, and if possible I would like to do it all the same day.

'You seem to be in a real hurry.'

'Well, I am in a hurry, but if you think I shouldn't be, then I'm not.'

'Thanks for informing me. I won't see you off tomorrow, but I hope you have a good journey.' She then walked further into the wood.

Seeing her solitary, lonely shadow, I felt a sadness, disappointment, desolation and pain that is impossible to describe. It was as if I was never going to see her again.

The next day Bureau Chief Yuan of the guards unit accompanied me to the nearest town, where I got on board a whistling train and began my journey to Moscow. This was my third visit to Moscow, but it seemed that every time I went there dreadful, unexpected things happened. Moscow has been an unlucky place for me. I had made a big decision in going there, but I did not even get to hear Anderov's voice, let alone actually see him. Every day I roamed through the streets of Moscow like a detective, trying to find out what had happened to Anderov, and everyone told me a different story. One person told me that he was being held under house arrest by the KGB, someone else told me that he had claimed asylum in France, a third person said that he was dead . . . and so on and so forth, no two stories the same. It was as if Anderov had been carried away by the icy blast of the Siberian winds, never to return . . .

It was more than a month before I returned, defeated, to Unit 701.

I handed out souvenirs from Russia to all the members of the team, and then – following closely on each other's heels – Huang Yiyi and Comrade Chen both came to my office to ask how it had gone and whether I had got anything out of it. I shook my head and said that I hadn't been able to see Anderov. I explained the problem and as Huang Yiyi listened she became more and more anxious, and asked, 'So you came back empty-handed?'

Not exactly, I said, and took out the documentation I had collected in Moscow about Sivincy's life, and her correspondence with Anderov since her arrival in the United States, which I had inadvertently discovered was in the possession of one of his former students. When I passed through Beijing, Director Tie had given me documentation from the Ministry of Public Security concerning the latest sabotage operations by KMT secret agents on the Mainland, and I handed that over to them and told them to look at it. Finally I told them something that none of us had known before, that when Sivincy was a teenager she had been gang-raped by White Russian soldiers!

Chen was confused. 'Is that going to help us crack her cipher?'

I said, 'Of course it is going to help us; it enables us to understand her character. For a young person to go through such a terrible experience is going to have an enormous impact on her; it will affect everything for the rest of her life. If you take that into account it is not hard to understand why she decided to plagiarize Enigma, or why she refused to attend the banquet that Stalin gave in her honour. A completely sane person wouldn't do that sort of thing, but she has suffered great psychological damage, and so her actions are not entirely normal, and may seem perverse. Her wicked intelligence and her nasty tricks may all be connected to this experience.' As I spoke I took out a photograph of Sivincy and gave it to them to look at. The icy gaze and arrogant mouth of the ageing woman in the picture startled both Chen and Huang Yiyi.

Comrade Chen said, 'Bloody hell, she looks a nasty piece of work!'

Huang Yiyi said, 'I have a feeling.' We asked her what feeling, and she stared at Sivincy's picture and said, 'I don't see a woman but a black hole, a dark pit crawling with poisonous snakes and vampire bats!' She wanted me to give her the picture of Sivincy, and I agreed.

Just then Unit Director Luo rang me up, having heard that I was back, and wanted me to go round and report to her, so we finished our discussion there. That evening Unit Director Luo invited me to our guest house for dinner, to welcome me back. Afterwards I was walking past the office block in the dark, when I noticed that the light in Huang Yiyi's office was still on, so I went in to see her. I found her sitting in front of her desk staring unblinkingly at the photograph of Sivincy in her hand. I asked her what she was doing, and she replied that she was in deep communication with Sivincy. I asked whether she had found anything out, and she said, 'A lot.'

I remembered I had brought a little present back from Moscow specially for her, so I asked her to come to my office. It was a pretty Russian doll, and she loved it the moment she set eyes on it. 'This is a pair to the one I have at home: a prince and a princess.'

'I noticed the prince in your room, so I bought this one for you specially to make a pair.'

She praised the princess's prettiness for a bit, and then she raised her head and said, 'Why are you being so good to me?'

'What do you mean, so good? It was easy, and the princess wasn't expensive.'

She looked at me, and then as if something had disappointed her, she said to herself, 'I don't understand you, you are . . . too mysterious for me.'

I said cheerfully, 'It doesn't matter if you don't understand me: all we want is for you to understand RECOVERY.' I asked her if she thought I was right, that Sivincy's experience of being raped as a girl would have had a great effect in perverting her character. She said of course, it was quite sufficient to explain her abnormal psychology.

'Would it be possible for someone psychologically abnormal to conceal that fact?'

'I don't think so. Even if she wanted to, she wouldn't be able to hide every trace. Say I myself wanted to pretend to be reserved, I might take everyone in for a bit but I wouldn't be able to keep it up for a lifetime. Now pretty much everyone in the unit looks at me askance. Why? Because the fox can't hide its tail for ever. The same goes for you. Mountains may crumble and rivers change their course, but human nature is hard to change.'

'You ought to remember that when you gave me the choice of picking which principles Sivincy would have used to construct RECOVERY, I chose a mathematical cipher created by encrypting an algorithmic cipher with a second algorithmic cipher. Do you know why I picked that? It was because Sivincy, to use your own words, had already pulled a very nasty trick on us, toying with the cryptographers trying to break her cipher. So I guessed that when she was thinking about her cipher she would do her very best to create an exceptionally difficult one, which on the one hand would prove her abilities and on the other would demonstrate that her plagiarism didn't arise from stupidity but was in fact entirely intentional, a joke that she was playing on other cryptographers.'

She looked at me a bit startled, and then asked me to carry on talking.

'Now we can be sure that she is psychologically abnormal, and, as we just discussed, such a person may want to conceal the fact but would not be able to. That means that when she set out to create RECOVERY, an exceptionally difficult cipher but one designed according to standard parameters, she might have had the intention but not the ability, because she found that her personality made it impossible to stick to the rules. She might have wanted to make DIFFICULT CENTURY a conventional if abstruse cipher, but she couldn't.'

She said, feeling her way forward, 'You mean RECOVERY cannot be an algorithmic cipher encrypted with another algorithmic cipher?'

I nodded my head.

She looked up at the ceiling and said, 'If you're right, normally there would be only one way to understand RECOVERY: it is an algorithmic cipher encrypted with a transposition cipher.'

'Why can't it be an algorithmic cipher encrypted with a substitution cipher?' I asked.

'Because that's the route that Chen has been trying out, and he has got nowhere.'

'So what are you going to do now?'

'I don't know.'

'I thought you just said there was only one way?'

'I said normally . . .'

I was listening carefully to what she was saying when suddenly she stopped speaking and indicated that I should pay attention to something outside. I could hear someone pacing up and down the corridor, and you could feel the impatience in the footsteps. I smiled. 'It must be Chen. I dare say he wants to report some new development.'

She said, 'I'll go and call him in.'

'Tell me what you think first.'

She cleared her throat. 'I'm sure you remember the four cipher texts I gave you, which when combined gave you a four-word plain text: "I really love you".

I felt very uncomfortable. 'Why are you bringing that up again?'

'You're scared, aren't you? Well in that case I won't carry on, and anyway there are people waiting to talk to you.' She got up to go, but I stopped her and got her to carry on. She looked at me disdainfully. 'Don't worry, I will never talk to you about love again: that's history and it's all in the past. I want you to think about this sentence and what is special about it. I will read it aloud, and you can work out what is special about it. I really love you – Really I love you – You I really love – four words that you can put in any order without affecting the meaning.'

I looked at her curiously, for it was as if a fluttering and fast-moving beam of light had suddenly appeared in front of me, illuminating a strange and brilliant new world.

'That was my first deduction concerning RECOVERY,' Huang Yiyi went on. 'This isn't an ordinary cipher and it also isn't particularly difficult, but in its cunning, artfulness, innovativeness, fascination and cleverness, it is more like a wonderful magic trick. A magic trick may not be very difficult to perform, yet it can perplex you in the same way that a cipher can. Sivincy may well have constructed a magic cipher, to trick other cryptographers.'

'An eccentric genius like Sivincy might well enjoy pulling that kind of trick,' I said.

'Right. That was the reason I made this deduction.'

I was getting interested, and rubbed my hands together. 'Fascinating! Really fascinating!'

Huang Yiyi showed that she wasn't entirely happy with her theories when she said, 'When my deductions about the cipher key didn't work out, I was very upset, and I started to wonder if all my ideas were wrong. That was when I came up with a new theory: that this is an algorithmic cipher encrypted with an algorithmic cipher. If you asked someone like Sivincy, with such a massive reputation and with such impressive mathematical abilities, to create a conventional cipher, she would certainly choose that route because it would allow her to demonstrate her talents as a mathematician. But I have been moving that way for such a long time and I simply don't feel I have got anything out of it, so perhaps it is time to wrap it up. You think that Sivincy wouldn't have designed RECOVERY that way either?'

I nodded.

She then said: 'I have a very strong feeling that Sivincy is most likely to have incorporated classic encryption techniques into RECOVERY, and even though my theories didn't work out, this feeling has never gone away.' She sighed deeply. 'Maybe I do have to go right back to the beginning.'

That day the longer we talked, the deeper we became caught up in what we were doing, and the more excited we became, until we found that we had been chatting for several hours. We discussed with complete freedom the theories that we had and the ideas that had struck us. It was wonderful! But while Huang Yiyi and I were chatting so happily, I couldn't help hearing Comrade Chen's footsteps pacing up and down the corridor many times, ever more impatient and stubborn. At that time I had no idea what Chen's angry footsteps meant, and when I did understand, it was too late.

22

That evening I stayed in my office for a while after Huang Yiyi had left, putting the documents and letters I had amassed in Russia into some sort of order, then I set out for home alone. I bumped into Chen just as I turned into the housing compound; it looked as if he had been waiting for me. I thought that he wanted to talk to me about some new ideas for how to crack RECOVERY, so I said I was feeling a bit tired and whatever it was would have to wait until tomorrow. Chen stared at me, but he didn't say anything. We walked on together in silence, and in the distance I could see the light shining from Huang Yiyi's windows. I sighed and said, 'She was working in her office until past eight o'clock. It's really late now and look, she still hasn't gone to bed. I guess she is working.'

Chen sniffed and said disdainfully, 'She'll be waiting for everyone else to go to sleep, because then she can go out.'

'Go out? Go where?'

'To the training centre.'

'Why on earth would she go to the training centre?'

'You don't know?'

I asked what was going on, and he said that it was to do with Comrade Wang, the head of the training centre. I asked what the two of them were up to, but he said nothing.

'Tell me what is going on, Chen, please!'

'No one has told you?'

'If someone had told me, I wouldn't be asking you.'

'Find someone else; I really don't like to say.'

I was getting angry. 'I am asking you, and I expect you to tell me!'

He said unwillingly, 'What do you think – they're having an affair.' After a short pause he added, 'Going by what people say, she goes to the training centre every evening and comes back at dawn.'

To get from the cryptography division to the training centre you would have to cross two mountain ridges. If you walked along the main road it would be about eight kilometres, while if you went along the paths you could cut it down to maybe four, but it would still take over an hour. The regulations said that people from the cryptography division could go to the training centre, but not the other way round. So if the two of them were having an affair, it would be Huang Yiyi who had to go to him. But I really found it hard to believe, first because Wang was married and certainly wouldn't dare do something like that, and secondly Huang Yiyi was so young and so pretty, how on earth could she fall for someone like him?

There was no point speculating. If I wanted to know the truth I would have to call Comrade Wang in and ask him.

Wang was only a departmental cadre, but he was nevertheless an important figure. Although in name I was Deputy Director of Unit 701, I was still junior to him in Party ranking, and organizational matters were outside my remit. As a result I had to ask Unit Director Luo to question him. When Unit Director Luo heard my report she was even more shocked than I had been, and immediately phoned Comrade Wang to summon him to her office. I was not expecting that the minute Unit Director Luo started questioning him, the bastard wouldn't even try and deny it, but just caved in and admitted everything.

According to him the two of them had got together while I was in the Soviet Union. That bastard Wang really was bloody audacious: having an affair and not just with any woman – with our treasure, destined to do great things for the Party! Unit Director Luo was absolutely furious and didn't have the least sympathy with any of his pleas for mercy: she immediately summoned all the senior people in the unit for a meeting to discuss how to punish him. At the meeting Unit Director Luo said that she had already reported the matter to our superiors at headquarters, and headquarters had requested that we come up with a means of punishing him which they would then consider. She was clearly in favour of the most severe punishment, severe and quick, and she was not going to listen to any excuses or allow any face-saving measures. 'It is completely unacceptable, a married man, a government official and Party member of almost twenty years' standing, to behave in such a corrupt and decadent manner! I can hardly believe it!' Unit Director Luo said angrily.

Deputy Director Zhong, who was responsible for discipline within the unit, asked the head of the political affairs division what kind of punishments had been handed out in this sort of situation in the past. Unit Director Luo said, 'I don't care about precedents, the nature of this offence is particularly serious because this isn't an ordinary affair: he has been interfering with our treasure, a comrade expert who is going to do great things for the Party. This is very serious because if we don't deal with it root and branch it might have a detrimental effect on our ability to complete this mission on time.'

Deputy Director Zhong said, 'Well then it is a "Triple Loss": he loses his government position, his Party membership and his job, and we send him home.'

Chen said, 'A Triple Loss is pretty severe; it would be better to leave him a shred of dignity.'

Unit Director Luo asked which shred he had in mind, and Chen suggested that he should keep his job. To begin with Unit Director Luo didn't agree, but in the end she caved in and he kept his job, though he would be moved to Lingshan farm on the back mountain to raise pigs. She asked us what we thought of that. I agreed but I recommended that when Comrade Wang was punished, we shouldn't drag Comrade Huang's name into it. Chen immediately agreed. 'You're right. We must preserve Comrade Huang's reputation or it might have a disastrous effect on her work.'

Unit Director Luo agreed to that, and told the head of the political affairs division to write a carefully worded document as soon as possible so that she could send it up to headquarters, get a decision quickly, and then that bloody Wang could piss off to the farm.

Approval was immediately given for our plan, and formal notification was sent to every division. The wording of the document was deliberately vague, saying that Wang was 'morally corrupt and an extremely bad influence on others'. It didn't go into details.

But Huang Yiyi really didn't appreciate our gesture, and so the afternoon the verdict was delivered she came bursting into my office and started calling me to account: why were we punishing Comrade Wang like that? I really had no idea how I had managed to contain my anger at her behaviour for so long, and this was a wonderful opportunity to express my resentment. I just exploded with rage, and shouted at her, 'How dare you come in here like this!'

'What do you mean?'

'You know perfectly well!'

'I don't know!' In a voice loud enough to shout me down, she added, 'The verdict didn't say why you were punishing him, just that he's "morally corrupt and an extremely bad influence on others". What do you mean by that? I don't know. If you mean that we are having an affair, then I can tell you that it is not his fault, I seduced him, and if you want to punish someone it should be me and not him!'

'Do you think we are going to listen to you?'

'This isn't about listening to me, it is about the facts. If you want to punish someone you need to prove that they have done something wrong, and I have just told you the fact of the matter.'

'The fact is that we went to massive trouble to bring you on board, and that was not so that you would cause trouble but in the hope that you would take up a heavy burden and do something useful!'

She curled her lip contemptuously. 'I told you ages ago, I am a bad person . . .'

I cursed her. 'Are you completely stupid? He's a married man – what's the point of getting involved with him?'

She smiled coldly. 'What's the point? There are some things that you need a man for, right?'

'There are lots of men out there. Why couldn't you find one of them?'

'Do you think I haven't looked? I found you, but did you want me?'

I was so furious I could hardly speak, and yelled at her to go to hell.

She hung her head. 'This is my own business, but . . . it is a fact and I . . . I am not going to deny it . . .'

'You can't deny it.'

There was an ugly expression on her face, and she said quietly, 'I think that you . . . shouldn't punish him like that.'

'Why not?'

'It's too severe.'

I laughed coldly. 'What? Are you pleading on his behalf? As far as I can see you've gone completely mad!'

She was silent for a long time, and then she said, 'I know there's no point saying anything to you right now; you won't believe it. But Zaitian, please can we still be friends? I am begging you, don't punish him.'

I smiled coldly. 'So that you can continue your affair?'

'No. Don't you think it would be too farcical if I begged you for that?'

'You don't find yourself farcical anyway?'

'If I beg you for this, then I can be at peace with myself, knowing that I have done the right thing: that's not farcical. I know you wrote those things in the verdict to protect me, but that makes me very uncomfortable. It makes me into someone who doesn't take responsibility for her own actions, someone whose comfort is bought at other people's expense. I can't stand it.'

I cut her short. 'You're going to have to put up with it. He has to be punished.'

'But . . .'

'No buts. There is nothing to discuss. You can leave now.'

She didn't leave but just sat there, then suddenly she shouted, 'An Zaitian, I hate you!'

'I know: you were hoping that I'd save your lover, but I won't. I'd save a dog before I'd save him. He's worse than a dog!'

She watched me for a bit, then all of a sudden she burst out crying and cursed me through her tears. 'You bastard, you don't even dare face up to the fact that you love me . . . This is all your fault . . .

you're the real criminal here, you've turned me into this . . . I hate you, An Zaitian, I hate you!'

I stood up and shouted at her, 'That's enough!'

She was surprised into silence. I told her in a milder tone of voice, 'Go home.'

She took two steps and then stopped. Wiping away her tears, she asked me, 'Do you know where he is now?'

'You still want to see him?'

'If he leaves under such a cloud, he'll hate me.'

'Do you think that he loves you?'

She went as white as a sheet, and with a bitter smile she said, 'Love . . . What love? . . . Love always turns to hate . . . I don't want people to think that I'm completely heartless . . . If he leaves like this he'll think that I . . . betrayed him. Please tell me where he is!'

I said nastily, 'He's where he deserves to be!' Then I turned my back on her and wouldn't say any more. She stood there and glared at me, her eyes filling with tears, then she left.

Just after Huang Yiyi had gone, Comrade Fei brought a letter, and said that when Comrade Wang had been taken under guard to the farm on the back mountain, he had given it to Bureau Chief Yuan at the guards' barracks, and asked him to give it to me. When I heard that the letter came from him, I felt a stabbing pain in my heart. I quickly waved at Comrade Fei to leave, and then I opened the letter. Guess what the letter said? This is what he wrote:

An Zaitian, I know that you hate me, because I slept with your woman. But guess what? I hate you even more, because as far as she was concerned, I was nothing but a substitute for you. I am paying for having loved a woman that I shouldn't have, but I hope and believe that in the end you will pay for not having loved the woman that you should have!

I was so furious that I ground my teeth, and having read the letter I ripped it into pieces and threw them into the rubbish bin.

I thought the thing with Wang was all over. I had said everything that needed to be said, and everything was perfectly clear. Whatever happened Huang Yiyi couldn't come back begging for mercy for him again. I didn't realize that she hadn't given up, and that she was about to play her trump card and blackmail me by threatening to throw up her job!

One evening just after I got home she was there banging on my door, shouting, 'Open up, An Zaitian – I'm not here to try and seduce you! I need to talk to you.'

I opened the door and invited her in. She walked straight up to the sofa and plunked herself down, looking neither left nor right. I could see that she had recently been crying, and that she was struggling to control her emotions. It looked as though she could break down at any moment. To try and calm her down, I said, 'Let me get you a glass of water.'

She said coldly, 'It's not necessary. Sit down. I've got a couple of things to say to you, then I'll leave you in peace.'

I sat down and heard her out. The first thing was that she said she hoped whatever she'd done wrong, that I could forgive her. The second thing was that she would like us to reconsider the verdict on Comrade Wang, and reduce his punishment, not sending him to the farm. She explained, 'I am making this request not because I love him, but because I believe you are punishing him unfairly: he's being treated like this because of me, and I can't stand that. I hate owing other people, and I really don't want people thinking that I am completely heartless.'

'That's impossible,' I said. 'He has to be punished and the verdict has been given.'

'Even people condemned to death can be reprieved on the scaffold.'

'Other than you, no one has the least bit of sympathy for him, including me.'

She looked at me for a bit, then she suddenly said in a low voice, 'If you want me to crack RECOVERY, I hope you will show some respect for my opinions, and give him another chance.'

'You mean if we don't do what you tell us, you won't crack it?'

'I can't crack it.'

I was so angry I got to my feet, pointed at her, and started shouting. 'Huang Yiyi, don't think you can play games with me! Let me

tell you, Comrade Wang is being punished because of his relationship with you. The only reason you haven't been punished as well
is because you're working on RECOVERY. If you now decide that
you don't want to carry on trying to crack it, fine: I'll phone Director Tie tomorrow and get headquarters to write another verdict
just the same, but with the name changed. They'll put "Huang
Yiyi" instead, and then in future you'll be raising pigs with him on
the back mountain.' The more I spoke, the more furious I became.
I really wanted to rub her nose in it. 'Who the hell do you think
you are? You've been here for ages achieving nothing, and you still
think you can waltz in here and throw your weight about! How
dare you! Get out of here! Go to hell!'

She didn't go and she also didn't apologize; she just sat there in
silence. I went for a walk outside, and when I came back she still
hadn't gone, but was sitting there in the same place – in fact it
looked as if she hadn't moved at all. I was still angry with her, and
so I carried on yelling at her. 'I've told you to leave! Is this a sit-in?
Or are you on hunger strike?'

Two lines of tears suddenly coursed down, but there was no
sign of it in her voice, which was completely even. She said, 'It's my
fault, I . . . seduced him. Can you tell the Party not to punish him?
I'm begging you.'

Seeing the tears rolling down her cheeks, I could feel my anger
abating, and I asked her in a low voice, 'Do you really want to rescue him?'

She nodded seriously. 'He is innocent, after all.'

'Things have got to the stage where it is useless to talk about
innocence, but there is still one way that you can save him.'

She asked me enthusiastically, 'How?'

I was toying with her. 'That's up to you.'

She was very clever, and worked out what I meant straight away.
'You mean I have to crack RECOVERY?'

'Yes. If you can crack RECOVERY quickly, then you are a
heroine, and you can do anything. Whatever you want, I will
agree to.'

'How long is quickly?'

'As soon as you can.'

'A year?'

'OK.'

She heard me say the word, and then she said firmly, 'OK. I want you to remember what you have said: you've given me a year!'

Then she rushed out of the door.

23

Anderov used to say that impetuosity is the devil, and so impetuous people often make mistakes. I have an impetuous nature, even though I always try to appear serious. That day, listening to what Huang Yiyi said, looking after her as she rushed out, I could feel myself getting excited. I was thinking that if I put her under pressure, and she really threw herself wholeheartedly into cracking RECOVERY, perhaps she'd get lucky. As I have said, and as everyone who has ever worked in cryptography knows, cracking a cipher requires knowledge, experience and a touch of genius; but more than that you need a luck that comes from far beyond the stars. Luck is a mysterious thing, but it might be attracted by a display of diligence on Huang Yiyi's part, because she was certainly amazingly gifted, and her training and mathematical abilities were unequalled. If she plunged into RECOVERY, she would dive deeper and go further than anyone else could; and luck is to be found in the deepest and most distant places. For someone without those kinds of abilities, luck is something that moves through the darkness: though you may want to grasp it, it's pure chance whether you stumble across it or not. But for someone who can dive deep, luck may be at the edge of the horizon or it may be just in front of you, dancing around you, and even if you don't try and grasp it, it may still come to you. There's a saying: 'Luck is unavoidable', and that's exactly what it means. RECOVERY was a very difficult cipher, but Huang Yiyi was no ordinary mathematician; she had been von Neumann's assistant, she was at the very top of her profession.

Other people might not know this, but I did.

This is why, when everyone else – including Chen – had given up hoping that Huang Yiyi might crack RECOVERY, I continued to invest heavily in her. You might say that this was a secret investment, because I never told anyone else about her unusual background. As I have explained, this was part of my plan. More than anyone else in Unit 701, I hoped she would crack RECOV-ERY. If she did, everything would work out for both of us. Both Bureau Chief Chen and Unit Director Luo were coming up to retirement age, and if Huang Yiyi cracked RECOVERY without too many problems, they would indubitably appoint her as the new head of cryptography, and I might well replace Comrade Luo as Director of Unit 701.

That was my secret, and my fate.

My fate was not in my own hands, but in Huang Yiyi's.

However, I was deeply depressed by what Chen and Comrade Zha told me about Huang Yiyi ... Early one Sunday morning I was eating breakfast in the canteen, when suddenly Comrade Zha came running in and told me that someone had seen Huang Yiyi leave early that morning, dressed in long trousers, a big overcoat and galoshes, a straw hat on her head, and with an army-issue rucksack and Thermos flask strapped to her back. It looked as if she would be going quite a distance. Where could she be going? I didn't have time to think about it, but rushed straight to the main gate, with Comrade Zha at my heels, to ask the sentry. The sentry said he hadn't seen her all day, so we ran to the back gate, and the sentry there told us that Huang Yiyi had left about an hour earlier. Comrade Zha asked where she was going, but the sentry said he didn't know. I asked the sentry which direction she'd gone in, and he pointed to one of the mountain paths, and said, 'She went that way, that path.'

I raised my head to look at the winding mountain path, and sighed deeply. I'm sure that at that moment I had a very grim expression on my face. That path went to Lingshan farm on the back mountain. I knew exactly where Huang Yiyi had gone, and why. I looked at that narrow path snaking into the woods and suddenly felt as if everything had been ruined.

I was in a really bad mood all day, and I couldn't settle to anything, so I just sat around at home. In the end I couldn't stand it one moment longer, and went for a walk round the mountain. On my wanderings, I caught sight of the lunatic Jiang Nan. He was holding an injured pigeon, and looking up into the sky he said, 'Hello. I know you're bringing me another cipher . . . They all say I'm mad, that I can't crack ciphers . . . They wouldn't know, I help them crack ciphers every day, one cipher in the morning, another during the night . . . hee, hee, I'm a cryptographic genius. When other experts hear my name, they're all panic-stricken . . .'

I listened to him in silence, and suddenly the image of Huang Yiyi came to my mind, bringing me to the verge of tears.

She came back at dusk, completely exhausted. I was hiding in the woods watching her, and when I saw her looking so tired and haggard, the last strands of my self-control snapped and I trampled the bushes around me like a lunatic. When I had smashed them to bits I went home in a rage. Having got home, I found I still couldn't settle to anything. I felt as if my chest was packed so full that it was about to explode. I had to go and find Huang Yiyi. When she opened the door and saw it was me she sniffed and asked what was up. I didn't look at all well; was I ill?

I said that I was unhappy.

She said teasingly, 'If you're unhappy, why come and find me? Though of course who does a single man take his troubles to? Well, since you're here, you're here, and I'm a single woman too – so it's six of one and half a dozen of the other.'

I said sneeringly, 'Since when were you a single woman?'

'You're behaving really oddly today.'

'That comes of spending the whole day trying to keep your temper.'

She looked at me curiously. 'What's your problem? What have I done to upset you this time?'

With a grim expression on my face, I asked her where she had been all day. She started, and said, 'It's a Sunday – why should you care? I went for a walk in the mountains, is that OK?'

'Of course it is,' I said. 'The problem is that you weren't just going for a walk, you went to meet someone.'

She sat up straight. 'Who could I be going to meet? Unless it was one of the mountain ghosts!'

I laughed coldly. 'Maybe he is a ghost; he's certainly got some kind of supernatural power, to bewitch you to this extent. I really don't understand it – going that far, getting up at dawn and getting back after dark, walking five or six hours through the mountains, running the risk of being bitten by a poisonous snake – and all for the sake of a depraved and corrupt element, a moral degenerate!'

She was silent for a moment. 'Gossip travels really fast in this place. OK, I'm perfectly happy to admit to what I have done, so I can tell you for free that I did go to see him, OK? Do you have some sort of problem with that? He isn't a criminal, and besides which even convicts are allowed prison visits.'

'If he receives prison visits, they can't be from you!'

'But I wanted to go – and besides which, it's my business. It's nothing to do with you.'

'I have a question for you: who exactly do you think you are? You're a mathematician, you are an intellectual singled out for special attention by the Party and the leaders of our country, and you still seem to find it appropriate to get together with a degenerate. What the hell do you think you're doing? This is wrong!'

'There are lots of things that are wrong in this world, and more of them apply to you than they do to me!' I knew she was alluding to Xiaoyu, and the fact that I had set up a spirit altar to my wife when she was still alive. But that was a revolutionary necessity, and when I explained that, she said, 'Well, as far as I'm concerned, this is a revolutionary necessity too. I need someone to love – that's how I get my inspiration.'

'That's not love – he's going to ruin your life!'

She glared at me. 'If anyone has ruined my life, it's you.'

I was silent for a moment, and then said earnestly: 'Huang Yiyi, let me say this again: I want you to leave him.'

She didn't even think about it, but said stubbornly, 'No!'

My whole body was shaking, and I fumbled for a cigarette. She wouldn't let me smoke in her room, but I ignored that and lit it anyway. She grabbed the cigarette out of my mouth, threw it on the floor and stamped on it. I jumped up, glaring angrily at her, and shouted, 'Huang Yiyi, what the hell are you thinking of?'

She glared right back. 'What do you think?'

'Don't you want to crack RECOVERY?'

'Of course I do. In fact, I want to crack it more now than ever before. Do you know why? I want to be, to use your words, a heroine who can do anything. I want to be able to save other people.'

'But how can you decrypt anything when you're not concentrating? Do you think that RECOVERY is an ordinary mathematical puzzle? Do you think you can solve it while messing about? We went to a lot of trouble to find you, we have treated you as a treasure, you get the highest salary, the very best treatment, you can do pretty much whatever you want and we close our eyes to it, we do our very best to understand you and forgive you, we give you the best working conditions that we possibly can, in the hope that you will concentrate on the job at hand. But what do you do? Time and time again you have caused trouble – one day you're quarrelling with someone, the next you've flown into a temper – either you're kicking up a massive fuss or you're trying to throw up your job: how do you ever think you're going to achieve anything? You're an adult; you ought to understand that if you want to achieve great things you have to work hard and think deeply. Our job requires you to slave away, to rack your brains. Have you slaved? Have you racked your brains? Do you think you are a magician and that by simply saying "Abracadabra!" your dreams will come true?'

She laughed. 'What are you lecturing me for? I'm not a magician but I'm also not a small child. I know what I'm doing – what the hell gives you the right to criticize me like that? What's wrong with going to see him? I went on a Sunday, not in office hours. On Sundays I can do what I like and you have no right to interfere!'

'Anything which is disadvantageous to your work, I have the right to interfere in.'

'In my opinion it will not affect my work at all, other than for the good.'

That stuck in my throat to the point where I couldn't speak for a long time, and just glared at her.

'Don't look at me like that, An Zaitian. You shouldn't use your own standards to measure other people's actions. As the proverb says, in any group of a hundred people you will find all shapes and sizes. I am a very different kind of person from you, who can give up everything to achieve your ambitions, who can control your desires, working day and night behind closed doors. If I tried to behave like you do, I would never achieve anything, because that's your way of working and not mine. There's more than one way to skin a cat, and everyone has their own way of doing things. You do your thing and I'll do mine, and we leave each other alone, OK? You need to stop trying to control me.'

I glared at her for a long time, and then finally I said through gritted teeth, 'Fine, then go. Go every day!'

She was completely relaxed as she said, 'Why on earth would I want to go every day? I'll go on Sundays.'

'Don't you want to be together? Why not go every day?'

'But I have a job to do. I need to crack RECOVERY. Didn't you say that if I decrypt RECOVERY then I am a heroine and can save him? That way we can get married, we can leave this place, we can start over and never have to lead this kind of horrible life again!'

My eyes nearly fell out of my head; I had no idea that she was still so obsessed with him, that she was still thinking like that! I stamped away angrily, thinking that if I had stayed one moment longer, I would have exploded with rage . . .

24.

There was nothing that I could do – I had to tell Unit Director Luo that Huang Yiyi was sneaking out to the farm to meet Comrade Wang. Unit Director Luo was absolutely furious and said, 'How can you allow it? Won't it affect her work?' Then she decided that Deputy Director Zhong should take Comrade Wang away, back to his home town in Jiangsu.

That was another mistake I made with Huang Yiyi. If Comrade Wang hadn't gone, when Huang Yiyi cracked RECOVERY perhaps they might have got back together. As it was he went home to his wife and children, and so there was no chance of a happy ending. This of course belongs to a later part of the story.

Comrade Wang had left, but Huang Yiyi didn't know that. So on Sunday she bought a lot of things, put a straw hat on her head, picked up her army-issue Thermos flask and headed out for the back mountain to see him. I didn't stop her; I didn't tell her what had happened; I let her go. I thought: this time you'll realize that it's all over!

It got to four or five o'clock and she still wasn't back. I noticed that black clouds were massing, and the trees in front of my window were being whipped back and forth by the wind. There was a big storm coming! I was worried that something might have happened to her, so I quickly called for a jeep and went to the back mountain to look for her. Just as we pulled out of the main gate of Unit 701, raindrops the size of copper coins started coming down, hammering on the roof of the car.

The jeep took me to the mouth of the valley at the foot of the back mountain; after that there wasn't a road. The driver and I had to put on our raincoats and get out of the car, braving that appalling weather to stumble along the winding path leading to the farm. When we had fought our way through the rain across two ridges, we caught sight of Huang Yiyi caught up in the storm, weaving from side to side as if she were drunk. She had lost her straw hat, and was soaked to the skin. In that hammering rain she kept on tripping over, forcing herself up, and then falling over again. She looked like someone who had lost their soul, leaving an empty shell to wander around through the punishing storm.

I shouted to her and started running, catching her in my arms. Her eyes fluttered and her lips moved as if she wanted to say something, but before she could get a word out she fainted. She had hit her forehead on something and cut it open, and the blood had mixed with the rain that soaked her face and body. I was now really worried, and held her tight as I shouted, 'Huang Yiyi, wake up! Yiyi, wake up!' I shouted until I was hoarse and on the verge of tears, but she didn't open her eyes.

It was only when we'd got her to hospital, where they stitched up the wound, gave her a shot, and put her on a drip, that she finally came round. I was standing by her bed, and pointing at her bandaged head, I tried to make light of the whole thing by saying, 'They've put two stitches in you; you're very lucky.' She looked at me coldly and then turned her head away. I knew that she hated me, but I tried to make light of the matter. 'Yiyi, guess who the hero was who carried you down from the mountain today?'

She sniffed scornfully, then she turned her back to me and closed her eyes.

I suddenly felt deeply hurt, and sat down on the edge of the bed. Looking out at the drizzle outside, I said, 'Yiyi, when I carried you down from the mountain today, I felt like crying. Do you know why? I felt . . . it wasn't you I was carrying, but that I was giving a piggyback to my daughter. She's nine this year, but I've never even been able to give her a piggyback, and I really wish that I could – I'd like to do something for her as a father. Yiyi, this is an invisible battle line, but it's crucial for preserving the security of the Party and our country, and having chosen it, we have chosen a revolutionary life. That means that personal advantage, hopes, ideas and our futures don't matter any more; they are all subordinate to the necessities of the revolution. A revolution demands sacrifices, it demands discipline, it demands selflessness – that you forget about yourself. Every individual has to throw themselves whole-heartedly into the revolution, to make it even more glorious, even more brilliant.'

She opened her eyes and told me not to preach at her. I said that we were doing an important job here. She got cross and shouted, 'Stop all of this "you" and "us" stuff, like I'm a complete outsider!' I was startled, and she continued, 'I'm a tree, and having been planted here for so long I've become one of Unit 701's trees, so there's no need for you to preach at me like that. I'm going to crack RECOVERY, but not for your sake. You've always carried on as if RECOVERY is yours – your ideas, your future – but the fact is, RECOVERY isn't yours: it's mine. It's my proof that you are an utter bastard. So whatever you do to hurt me, I am not going to give up on it. I know what you're up to: you've done something you're ashamed of and now you're afraid that I might pack in my job, and so you've come to try and talk me round – well there's no need. You can go now. I'm tired and I want to get some rest; the sooner I'm better, the sooner I can get back to work.'

I opened my mouth to say something, but she cut me short. 'Don't say anything. Save your strength and go home. You've done what you had to do; you've also done things that you shouldn't have. All that's left for me now is to do what I have to do – and I will, don't worry about it.'

'I'm not worried –'

She cut in, and said with a cold smile, 'You have nothing to worry about, but you still can't let things rest. You really are a nasty piece of work, you bastard!'

I wanted to explain, but she wouldn't let me. 'Don't say any-thing. You do your thing, I'll do mine – there's no need to explain. I've said everything that I want to: you can go now.'

I had to leave.

That evening after I got home I sat in my room and looked in silence at the memorial photograph of Xiaoyu. I was beginning to feel that I might have been too cruel to Huang Yiyi. In the photograph, Xiaoyu's eyes were bright; only she and I knew the secret behind them.

I held Xiaoyu's photograph, feeling absolutely heartbroken.

The only thing that cheered me up was that Huang Yiyi behaved completely differently after that, concentrating entirely on her work. What surprised me though was that she had cut her hair into what was then the most popular style, a short bob; and when I saw her in running clothes setting out for a jog first thing one morning, I was amazed. I knew she was trying to make a statement: she had made up her mind and was getting ready to start the assault on RECOVERY.

Not long afterwards, at one of our regular weekly meetings, she set out a very daring plan. After spending a certain amount of time feeling her way forward, she had gone back to her original idea, that RECOVERY was a cipher created by combining three of the original encryption methods: a substitution cipher, a transposition cipher and an algorithmic cipher. It was shape-shifting, complex, cunning, but that did not necessarily mean that it was also particularly difficult. Chen didn't agree with her ideas at all; he said, hadn't she got stuck in her old rut? The exercise last time proved that it was a dead end! She said that she had changed some of her original ideas, and that even though the exercise had demonstrated that there were problems with her theory, it hadn't proved that it was a dead end. There were two options which could explain why the exercise hadn't worked.

'What two options?' I asked.

She said one possibility was that her ideas about the key to the cipher were not correct; or that she was right about most of it but wrong in some of the details. At that time she was still convinced that she was right in principle, but there was a problem in one of the links in the chain. The other possibility was that she was completely right about the key and that there was something wrong with RECOVERY, that there was some kind of intrinsic problem with it.

'What do you mean?' asked Chen. 'There's a fundamental problem with RECOVERY?'

She explained, 'There are mistakes in every cipher – just like when we write a document we get things wrong and misspell words. If there aren't too many mistakes and the error rate isn't too high, so that it's within accepted parameters, it's allowed.' She had designed the last exercise on the understanding that RECOVERY was an ordinary cipher, with the normal low error rate. If on the other hand there was a serious problem with RECOVERY, the rate of errors would be much higher than normal, and so our calculations would not support her theory.

'So you now think that the rate of errors in RECOVERY is higher than normal?' I said.

She shook her head. 'I don't think it's very likely, which is why right now my most important task is to prove my method for finding the key, in the hope that I can then quickly discover where the problem lies and come up with a new approach which takes account of it.'

'And if you prove that there is nothing wrong with the method you have developed for finding the key?'

'Then I would suspect that there is a fundamental problem with RECOVERY, and hence there is an unusually high error rate.'

Chen said, 'So either way, you don't believe the results of the exercise; you only believe in yourself.'

'I have faith in my theory,' she replied, 'but I am worried about the deductive process – that's why I want to check it again and come up with a new plan.'

'And when will your new plan be ready?' asked Chen.

She smiled bitterly. 'That's very difficult to say. If it's quick, it might be really quick, but if it's slow, I might never come up with anything.'

Comrade Chen shook his head. 'That's pretty cold comfort!'

'Those are the conditions under which every cipher ever created was decrypted!' she said.

Chen looked at me and shook his head. I said, 'She's right.' I wasn't about to side with him.

From that point on, either Huang Yiyi didn't come to work at all, or she would head straight for her cryptography room and lock herself in. Comrade Zha brought both lunch and dinner to her office. When she was at home, the light in her room was often burning until three or four in the morning, and sometimes it was on all night. I understood that she was using her exceptional courage, resourcefulness and intelligence to pit her wits against the dangerous and tricky Sivincy; that they were locked in hand-to-hand combat. In this duel to the death we would see sabre pitted against sword, and blood would flow like a river. It reminded me of something that Anderov often used to say: 'Decrypting a cipher is like asking a man to give birth to a baby or a woman to grow a beard; under normal circumstances it is impossible.' But we had to make the impossible possible, and there is only one way to do that: you have to shut yourself up and burn the midnight oil, racking your brains, busting your gut. If you don't put yourself through that, if you don't have that kind of mind, then cracking a cipher is just empty words.

During that time, I often went to stand outside Huang Yiyi's building when her light was still on, silently praying for her, hoping that one day she really would give us a wonderful surprise, that all her hard work would eventually result in a brilliant success!

One evening she came to find me, looking completely exhausted. I quickly got her to sit down, and asked her what was up.

'Nothing much. I've already checked more than twenty thousand of the seventy-four thousand, two hundred and eleven possibilities, and I haven't found the slightest problem.'

I thought about that for a bit, and then I asked: 'Why do you think the problem is at this end, rather than intrinsic to Sivincy's cipher?'

'I'm working on the theory that RECOVERY isn't a particularly abstruse cipher, for all that it's so difficult; so the error rate ought not to be particularly high. Besides, Sivincy wrote it. The Americans use computers now for this sort of thing, so it's easy for them to check the capabilities of any given cipher. If they tested it and discovered it was fundamentally flawed, there's no way they would have sold it to Taiwan.'

I was silent for a bit, then I said, 'There's a possibility that I don't know if you have considered . . .'

'What possibility?'

'RECOVERY was tailored by Sivincy to the specifications of the US army, but now this particular dress is being worn by someone quite different. So the dress doesn't fit any more and needs altering, right?'

'It wouldn't be difficult, and surely Sivincy would be happy to do it?'

'Under normal circumstances, yes. A tailor makes a garment for you, you give it to me, it doesn't fit, so I take it back to the tailor and he's happy to make the alterations. But Sivincy is not like the rest of us; her mind is dominated by hatred and revenge, and she cannot tolerate the slightest difference of opinion or criticism. To her, the relationship between America and Taiwan is not one of equals; it's the relationship of a superpower and a Third World country – one is rich and the other poor, one is strong and the other weak. She made this dress for a princess to wear, but now it has fallen into the hands of a maid. If the maid asks her for alterations, is she likely to do them? I don't think so.'

She looked at me in stunned silence and then suddenly got excited. 'I know what you're trying to say! The Taiwanese couldn't get Sivincy to help them, so they tailored the cipher themselves. As a result the error rate increased beyond normal levels!'

I said yes, that seemed quite possible to me.

She was thrilled. 'It's only too likely. How come I didn't think of that myself? And you . . . why didn't you say something earlier? I could have got to work on the cipher itself long ago!' She then rushed out without another word.

You know, I really wasn't expecting that my idea, which anyone could have had, would make Huang Yiyi so happy. That very day she worked out a way to prove her theory, and then quickly found her way through all the residual problems, forcing her way out of the bottleneck that had been holding up our cryptographic work for so long.

That was the last big problem with RECOVERY: solving this structural issue allowed her to correct the cipher's mathematical formulae.

You can probably imagine what happened next. Huang Yiyi basically moved into her office and shut herself in, working flat out without sleep and forgetting to eat. Sometimes when Comrade Zha hammered on the door shouting at her to come out and eat she paid no attention at all, and it was only after Zha knocked for ages that she would finally notice. One day I bumped into her in the corridor as she was leaving the lavatory, and her haggard appearance gave me a turn: she'd got a lot thinner, her eyes were bloodshot, her forehead deeply lined, her hair a bird's nest! I wanted to say something to her, but she quickly shushed me. I knew she was worried I might break her train of thought.

All through those days our little team kept circling Huang Yiyi's office. I went to talk to Unit Director Luo about getting her the very highest grade of food, then I went every day to the canteen to personally arrange the menu they would cook for her. Comrade Zha and Comrade Fei were responsible for data transfer; Comrade Zha would pick up the data from her office and give it to Comrade Fei, who would then take it to the Calculations Office; he would then take the results they had come up with back to Huang Yiyi. In the end even Chen, who had consistently loathed Huang Yiyi, got sucked into the job of data transfer – running backwards and forwards from our office building to the Calculations Office along with Comrades Zha and Fei; running until he was sweating freely and his breathing was stertorous. One time Chen even came to my office to talk about how hard Huang Yiyi was pushing herself. He said – and he really was concerned about her – 'I really hope she cracks this bloody RECOVERY soon, and stops working like a demon, because otherwise she's going to break down!'

By day fourteen, even Unit Director Luo was on tenterhooks, and she came to me to find out what was going on. 'What's happening; is there any news?'

I shook my head. 'She won't see anyone other that Comrade Zha. She's avoiding us.'

'Maybe she's worried about losing concentration?'

I nodded. 'Her train of thought is now like gossamer – a breath of wind could break it, and then we'll be in trouble.'

'So what do you think?'

'I don't know . . . it's difficult to say . . .'

Unit Director Luo sighed. 'She really is a strange creature: one moment we're all worried because she's not working, but now she has gone to work she's going flat out, which is going to ruin her health if she's not careful.'

'There's nothing we can do about it, that's just the way she is. Once she's caught up in something, she doesn't care about anything else.'

Unit Director Luo looked at me and said, 'I really hope she succeeds this time. Then you can lay Xiaoyu to rest, and I can have a bit of peace and quiet myself. You have no idea what it's been like. Headquarters keep writing us warning letters, telling us to stop protecting her.'

I thought about it, and then I said seriously, 'I'm sure she can do it.'

Unit Director Luo laughed and said, 'I believe you.'

25

The day we had been waiting for for so long finally dawned.

At that time my feelings were somewhat as if I had been marching through the desert for so long that the blood in my body, and even the tiny bit of water in the tips of my hair, had all been parched by the hot winds. But just as our strength was exhausted – or perhaps it would be better to say, just as we felt our final hour had come – we suddenly caught sight of a deep blue spring, the bubbling waters spraying our faces, refreshing us, making us shudder with pleasure and surprise.

Our lives were trembling in the balance, our souls were trembling in the balance!

There was no advance warning that our great victory was nearly upon us: it came out of the blue, so suddenly that we really weren't ready for it. That was why we all exploded in such delight and amazement . . . It was a perfectly ordinary weekly meeting, but beforehand Comrade Zha mentioned that Huang Yiyi had said that today she wanted to attend. So we all waited for her in the conference room. But she didn't come. To cheer everyone up, I explained that she had only gone to sleep at six o'clock that morning, so I requested that everyone just wait patiently a little longer. Comrade Chen suggested that we hold our meeting now, and then reconvene when she got out of bed. Little Comrade Zha said that we should wait, because before she went off to sleep Comrade Huang had left a note specially to say that she wanted to attend this meeting, and quite possibly she had something to announce to everyone. Comrade Jin, the head of the Analysis Division, said, 'Do you think she's really done it?'

Comrade Jiang of the Calculations Office said, 'Possibly. Our Comrade Huang is a strange creature, but this time I think she's onto something.'

I laughed. 'Chen, maybe this time your hand is for it.'

Chen said, 'Well, if I lose it I lose it – providing we crack RECOVERY, I don't care if you kill me.'

We all burst out laughing at that.

You know, the way everyone was speaking that day was just an expression of their hopes. We none of us realized that Huang Yiyi, who had caused me so much trouble, who had gradually come to be called a 'strange creature' by everyone else, was just about to make our dreams come true! Just as we were joking, she suddenly came rushing into the conference room, parked a thick stack of papers on the desk, and said, 'I'm sorry, I've kept everyone waiting. But I have some good news for you all – at four o'clock this morning I finally worked out all the mathematical equations that make up this cipher. Of course, I've only worked it out on paper; whether I have got it right in practice is going to have to wait for the calculations to come out. I've already set out the programme for you, but I'm afraid it's going to involve a lot of work. Comrade Jiang, I really hope this time I'm not putting you to a lot of trouble for nothing.'

Comrade Jiang, the head of the Calculations Office, said, 'Well, it wasn't a lot of trouble for nothing the last time either; in the end it proved that your theories were correct.'

Huang Yiyi handed a heap of papers to me. I looked at them and then handed them on to Comrade Jiang: 'Let's do it! Let's find out if it works!'

Day One.

Day Two.

Day Three . . .

The calculations went on day and night, day after day, as the exercise proceeded step by step. On the ninth day, as the calculations entered their final stages, Huang Yiyi couldn't help getting more and more nervous, and she would put her hands together, close her eyes and pray silently. When all the data was in, just as Comrade Jiang was preparing yet again to make the final calculations, Huang Yiyi suddenly addressed him. 'Just a moment, Comrade Jiang. I would like to do it.' Everyone turned their eyes on her, and then she walked out to go to the bathroom where she filled a basin full of water and then in front of everyone she started to wash her hands, washing them again and again, as if she were trying to wring something out of them. Everyone was completely silent, watching her hands. They all looked nervous and solemn.

She washed her hands again and again in the basin, like a doctor going into surgery, and then she held them out in front of her, allowing the water to drip slowly off them. She looked at everyone and then at her own hands. Then she kissed them and said, 'Today you've got to do me credit!' Then one step at a time she slowly climbed the stairs and sat on the dais in the Calculations Room. I raised my head and let out a deep breath, then calmly watched as she soberly put her hands down on the abacus. The moment she touched the smooth and delicate abacus beads, her hands seemed to take on a life of their own, seemingly moving entirely of their own volition. As the sound of 'ping, ping, pang, pang' assaulted my ears, I couldn't stand it one second longer and I went out to stand in the corridor, leaning my head against the wall, praying silently as I waited for the final result of the calculations.

It was only about twenty minutes or so, but during that time I suffered agonies. Cold sweat and hot broke out on my forehead, on the palms of my hands, my feet . . . my hair was standing on end. The terror absolutely exhausted me. But it was all already over, and suddenly the most amazing roar broke out from inside the room:

'Zero!'

'We've done it!'

'We've done it . . .'

I opened my eyes but tears were blurring my vision. I rushed into the room and saw everyone coming to hug me and Huang Yiyi, crying with happiness . . .

26

Huang Yiyi's achievement in cracking RECOVERY was so great it's hard to know where to start when describing it. After we broke RECOVERY, headquarters was able to round up most of the Taiwanese and American special agents working on the Mainland, as one after the other they blew their cover. People said that at that time Chiang Kai-shek was absolutely set on his plan to 'Recover the Mainland', to the point where there was even talk of celebrating his birthday in Nanjing, but that in the end they didn't do anything simply because we broke RECOVERY. We got rid of Chiang Kai-shek's eyes and ears on the Mainland, making him blind and deaf overnight! A blind man can't even walk along the road with any ease, so how would he be rash enough to launch some stupid military operation from the other side of the Straits? The fact that we cracked RECOVERY didn't just prevent a major operation by special agents, it preserved the security of our country and the peace of its people!

Rewards from headquarters were pretty quick in coming: every member of the special working group was awarded honours of the second class, while Huang Yiyi and I both received honours of the first class. Although the fact that RECOVERY had been decrypted was top secret, the unit nevertheless held a high-level celebration ceremony, and Director Tie himself came out from headquarters. We lit firecrackers, and all of us wore red ribbons – it was all most splendid. Huang Yiyi, who had played the most important role in the cracking of RECOVERY, was naturally the cynosure of all eyes, the queen of the day. When she went up to the platform to receive her reward and put on her ribbon, we all called out to her from below and clapped. She smiled as she looked out at us, and her achievements made her seem like the moon, hung high in the firmament. We felt an unparalleled respect and admiration for her.

After the ceremony Director Tie went specially to talk to Huang Yiyi, and said, 'Comrade Huang, you really are a genius. I have an idea that I'd like to discuss with you.'

She understood immediately what he was talking about. 'So you're not going to keep your promise, sir?'

Director Tie nodded and said, 'I would be delighted if you stayed and took over from Chen. He's very hard-working, and has done some good stuff, but asking him to take charge of other people is really not appropriate. I know he wants to give up that part of his job; he would much prefer to be able to concentrate on decrypting his ciphers. Now you've done so well, and he seems to hate being a Bureau Chief as much as he ever did. I know exactly what he's up to, and he doesn't seem to care how much I yell at him. What do you think? Do you want to stay and be our youngest ever Bureau Chief?'

Huang Yiyi didn't hesitate for a moment but shook her head. 'No. I want to leave.'

Director Tie smiled at her. 'And do you still want to take someone with you?'

'I can't,' she muttered.

'Why not?'

'Because he's married.'

'Oh, really? Do you mind telling me who you wanted to take away?'

She hesitated for a moment then whispered the name in his ear. He started and turned to look at me. I was standing not far away, chatting to Unit Director Luo. Director Tie glared at me and then turned back to Huang Yiyi with a laugh. 'Fine, we'll stick with the original agreement. If he wants to go with you, then you can take him away; if he doesn't want to, then it is not our problem.'

He had been a special agent, and under no circumstances would he show the predicament in which he had been placed; he used his hearty laugh to disguise his shock. I don't need to tell you that Director Tie had no idea that the person Huang Yiyi wanted to take away was me, and I . . . he knew that Xiaoyu was still alive and so I wouldn't go. Therefore he cunningly changed tack and left it all up to me. There was no need to do that, because Huang Yiyi already knew my real circumstances. And it was for that reason that Huang Yiyi was very unhappy when she heard what Director Tie had to say, and was angry enough to add a final sentence: 'Don't laugh, sir: if anything you should be crying.' Then she rushed out.

Director Tie watched her leave, and immediately started to worry whether I had told her the truth about Xiaoyu. After I confirmed his suspicions, he was so furious that he let forth a savage stream of invective. Of course it was top secret and I had had no right to tell anyone, at any time, under any circumstances. I had escaped from Huang Yiyi's clutches by telling her a secret, and now I was going to be punished for it. Naturally I had realized long ago that if I hadn't told her the truth, she would never have had an affair with Comrade Wang. Wang was absolutely right when he said in his letter that he was a scapegoat for me: he was Huang Yiyi's Parthian shot, her revenge, her response to my refusal, and in the process both jade and stone were crushed, and two people were irreparably damaged. I had no idea though that my actions would also harm Huang Yiyi again in the future. That is the next step in this story.

Whatever happened, I had to go on playing the part of Xiaoyu's inconsolable widower, and so I had to go back to my home town to hold a funeral for her 'ashes'. The evening before I set out, Huang Yiyi came to see me, and told me that she wouldn't be there when I got back: she was returning to Beijing, and wanted to say goodbye. I told her not to go, to stay and take over from Chen. She didn't say a word, but took out the Russian doll that I had given her, and said, 'This stays here, not me.' Then she walked out without saying goodbye.

I watched her depart in this cold, unfriendly mood, and then collapsed onto my suitcase. I didn't move for a long, long time . . .

27.

Young man, sometimes love makes you suffer much more than hate. I didn't sleep at all last night . . . I couldn't sleep, because all the things I have to tell you from now on are really painful.

They caused me a lot of pain.

I have to accept this, it is my fate . . . The journey to Shanghai and back took a month. The reason it took so long was that I wanted to avoid having to see Huang Yiyi again. I was afraid to see her, afraid to see her great big eyes watching me, whether in love or in hate. It made me very unhappy to see her like that, so I kept delaying my return, thinking that she would have left and gone back to Beijing. We were like two stars whose paths had crossed by chance, brought together from far across the universe only to separate again, and all the heartache and pain would be lost as we continued our trajectories. However, when I got back, I discovered that contrary to every expectation, Huang Yiyi was still there. She had been terribly ill but was better now, and the Party had already appointed her as a section head in the cryptography division, replacing Comrade Chen. Chen had refused the promotion he was offered to become acting Deputy Director: he just wanted to be a cryptographer and not have to bother with what was going on outside his own four walls. It was what he really enjoyed, and he was happy. Eventually Chen became a very successful cryptographer, and I think that this had a lot to do with the way that Huang Yiyi had needled him. Of course that happened much later.

When I heard that Huang Yiyi hadn't left, I was pleased but surprised, and that evening I couldn't stop myself from going to see her. She wasn't particularly friendly. I gave her some specialities that I had brought back from Shanghai. Just a few snacks, but she wouldn't accept them. She said, 'Give them to someone else instead.'

I was amazed and asked her, 'Yiyi, what's the matter?'

'Deputy Director An, please don't call me that. You can call me Huang Yiyi or Bureau Chief Huang, either will do, just don't call me Yiyi again.'

I was stunned.

She said very calmly, 'In future I want us just to keep to normal relations between a boss and an employee, nothing else.'

I was silent for a long time, and then I said, 'You hate me.'

She shook her head. 'No, but I think that this is better.'

I looked her in the eyes and said, 'I heard that you have been really ill.'

She avoided my gaze, and said lightly, 'Yes, I was in hospital for a couple of weeks.'

I asked her what was wrong with her, and she said that she hadn't really been ill, just overtired to the point where she hadn't felt like getting out of bed, and if she did she felt dizzy. I said she had been overworking. She smiled bitterly. 'Yes, I was tired, really, really tired. If there is nothing else . . . ?' She was trying to get rid of me.

I didn't leave. I said, 'Is it normal for an employee to try and throw her boss out?'

She smiled again. It was an unhappy, cold smile. 'Just go away. In future if you need to talk to me, do it at the office.'

I didn't move, and trying to drag out the conversation I asked her, 'Why didn't you go back to Beijing?'

She said coldly, 'Could I go back?'

'Director Tie agreed, so who could stop you?'

'Then let's just say that I didn't want to go.'

'You made the right decision.'

She sighed and said with a bitter smile: 'This isn't about having made the right decision. I have no idea why I am even alive, so wherever I go it would be the same. At least here I have been able to make a contribution, people respect me. Maybe that's why I didn't leave. I am not staying for your sake, or for any other man, but for my own, OK? Do you think you can understand that?'

I looked at her helplessly. Her unfriendly arrogance made me feel cold and strange in a way I had never experienced before. In the past I had often hoped that she would change her ways, but now that she really had, I felt bereft, a pain deep in my heart. However, the real pain, the kind that etches into your bones, was still waiting for me.

The following day, when I went to report to Unit Director Luo, she told me that Huang Yiyi had not wanted to stay, but that Director Tie had ordered that under no circumstances whatsoever was she to be allowed to leave. Director Tie had agreed, so why didn't he let her go? I thought it was very peculiar. Unit Director Luo said, 'I have no idea how Director Tie found out, but apparently Huang Yiyi in the course of her work inadvertently became aware of something that headquarters has declared top secret, so if she leaves she would pose an enormous security threat. I'm afraid that she will just have to put up with having to stay.' I asked what the top-secret information was, but Unit Director Luo said she didn't know. 'If even my security clearance isn't high enough, it must be very important,' she said crisply. 'That's why I always tell my cadres, "Don't ask about the things you shouldn't know about, because if you do know then you have to take responsibility for them." Look at Huang Yiyi! I know she's desperate to leave, but it's her own fault for finding out whatever it is, and now she has to take responsibility for it.'

What could it be that she had found out? I wondered at the time if it was about Xiaoyu, and later on Director Tie confirmed it. According to our rules, Huang Yiyi would have to wait until Xiaoyu's mission was completed before she could leave.

It was all my fault!

Huang Yiyi went on hunger strike and ended up making herself seriously ill. I understood why she had decided to stay, why she had taken over Chen's old job – it was because she had no choice, and was trying to make the best of things. Her life was in ruins, but she couldn't be bothered to talk to me, she couldn't even be bothered to complain, and just warded me off with politely worded generalities. I guessed that she must hate me, hate me to the point where she was left helpless and mute, and so she had written me out of her life, not wanting to have anything to do with me ever again.

Sure enough, from that day onwards unless it was necessary for work, Huang Yiyi never said another word to me. I understood that this was her way of punishing me, and that it was my fate. Since it was my fate, I had to try and make it look as if I accepted it . . . Day after day, Huang Yiyi and I would meet on the road and walk past each other without a word, as if we had not seen each other.

This went on for nearly a year, and then suddenly one afternoon Huang Yiyi came to see me and asked for help from the Party with solving a problem. I asked her what the problem was, and she seemed to be sunk deep in silent thought. After a long pause she raised her head and said it was about Zhang Guoqing from the communications section. I was most puzzled; what on earth could have happened to Zhang Guoqing that he needed her to sort it out? She said: 'Don't you know that his wife and son have been sent back home as punishment?' Of course I knew. I asked her what she wanted done about it. She said, 'You promised me that if I cracked the cipher I could save someone.'

'That's right, you can bring Wang back to work. I've been wondering why you haven't mentioned it recently.'

She sniffed. 'When Director Tie forced me to stay, I didn't want to live, and I really didn't have the energy to think about anyone else. Besides which he's gone back to his old home town to try and make things up with his wife. He'll be watching her every mood day in and day out; he won't love me any more.'

She was absolutely right; I had hurt her time and again. I wanted to apologize, but she cut me short. 'It's fine, I don't want to talk about it. I'm here to tell you that I want to use my power not to help Comrade Wang but Zhang Guoqing. Please do your best to help Zhang Guoqing bring his wife and son back to Unit 701.'

I was confused. What was Zhang Guoqing to her?

Everyone in Unit 701 knew Zhang Guoqing. He used to work in the confidential documents division, and all secret and top-secret documents generated by Unit 701 passed through his hands. His wife was a nurse at our hospital, a woman from Jiaodong, very tall and strong, with a real temper. It was said that Zhang Guoqing was afraid of his wife, because if they started quarrelling she would pick up anything that came to hand and throw it at him. One time what came to hand was a scalpel, which flew like a sliver of silver to bury itself in Zhang Guoqing's shoulder. I guess that was when the story about the domestic violence he suffered first started. But people said that she really loved her husband and that he didn't have to lift a finger at home – she would even wash his feet and clip his nails for him. She was always talking about how wonderful Zhang Guoqing was, how much she loved him and couldn't bear to be apart from him, to the point where she couldn't sleep if he was away from home, and so on and so forth. The thing is that Zhang Guoqing was often away from home, because his work demanded that he travel regularly to headquarters. On one occasion three years earlier he was on his way back from headquarters – he always used to go to the office first on his return, to lock the confidential documents in his filing cabinet before he headed off home. But on this occasion the train had been delayed by many hours, so by the time he got to Unit 701 it was already well past midnight, and if he had gone to his office before going home it would have taken at least an hour. He just couldn't bear the prospect, so he went straight home, not thinking that this would result in terrible consequences.

If the following day he had got up early and gone to work, nothing would have happened. But as he was about to get out of bed, his wife reminded him that today was a Sunday, meaning that he might as well sleep in a bit longer. Sleeping late was a bad idea. That bad idea caused all sorts of trouble! When he finally woke up it was past ten o'clock and the house was empty, both his wife and son having gone out. He knew why his wife wasn't there: this was a Sunday and so all the wives living in the compound would have taken the bus provided by our unit to go to the nearest town to shop. They went once a week because that was their only chance, and if they didn't go food, and indeed other necessities of life, would be a real problem the following week. Mostly the wives wouldn't take their children, and in this case Zhang Guoqing was at home and could look after the boy. But perhaps because his wife wanted him to be able to sleep in peace and quiet, she took the child with her. The boy was only seven and had just started primary school, and in the past every time his father came back he had brought presents. This time his father had come back in the middle of the night, so he didn't know what presents he had brought: therefore he decided to search his father's briefcase. His mother had gone to the canteen to buy buns, his father was still asleep, there was no one else at home, and so he opened his father's briefcase and immediately found his present: a paper bag of sweets and a box of biscuits. He twisted a sweet out of its wrapper and ate it while he carried on looking. He then flipped through a folder of confidential documents. The child was not at all interested in the contents of the documents, but he was attracted by the paper, so white, so shiny, he just had to feel it, and having felt it, so stiff and smooth, he knew it was the perfect stuff to make paper planes out of . . .

It was at that moment that Zhang Guoqing's life started to go seriously wrong. His son noticed that there were loads of papers in the folder, bound into individual documents. Given that there were dozens of documents, would anyone notice if he took one? So he put one in his school bag. After breakfast his mother told him to come with her, and he thought that he could play with paper planes when they went out, so he went to pick up his school bag. His mother said, 'You're not going to school – we're off to town to shop, so why have you got your school bag?'

He said, 'I have some homework to do, so while you are shopping I will sit in the bus and do it.' When his mother heard that she was pleased to see her son being so good.

Two hours later when Zhang Guoqing got up, he immediately noticed that his briefcase was standing open. He was a confidential documents courier, more than a decade of experience made him exceptionally sensitive to the material that he carried, and the moment he looked he realized at once: one document was missing! He was pretty sure that his seven-year-old son was responsible, so he rushed out to find him. He searched the compound and asked all the neighbours, but they had not seen hide nor hair of the child. Then someone suggested that he might have gone with his mother into town. That scared Zhang Guoqing practically witless, because if his son really had got hold of one of these documents, it was going to be crucial whether he had left the compound or not. In the end it was that point that condemned them all.

I will cut a long story short. When Zhang Guoqing met his wife and son coming back from town, the boy was clutching a paper plane made out of half a sheet of paper. Going by what the boy said later, because the sheets were so big (A3 size), he tore them in half so that each page could make two paper planes. When his mother went shopping he did not go with her but stayed at the bus station under the pretext of doing his homework. In fact he was playing with one of the other children from the compound. Since that document consisted of four pages, they had the wherewithal to make eight planes. And that's what they did. As it happened, each of the two children had one paper plane left; as for the rest, some had got stuck on roofs, some had just disappeared into the crowds of people, some had been stolen by boys from the town. When we searched the bus station and surrounding area, we found four of the planes, which really is not at all bad. But we never found the other two, and that kind of loss was as serious as if they had been real aeroplanes. Every member in Unit 701 was deeply scared by this development, and it was discussed in the most alarming terms.

Punishment was unavoidable, and it had to be severe.

In the end Zhang Guoqing's wife lost her job and had to take the boy back to their home town. There were two things that saved Zhang Guoqing. One was that he was a Party member, and there's the saying, 'Losing Party membership takes three years off'. That means that in return for being stripped of Party membership, you could avoid a prison sentence of three years or less. The other reason was that he was a confidential documents courier, with very high security clearance, and there was no way that he could be allowed to return to civilian life. Just because we wanted to fire him doesn't mean that we could. So he kept his job, but had to leave the confidential documents division and go and work for the communications section. His rank within the Party was then reduced from level 21 right down to the very lowest grade: 24. There actually was no such thing as a level 24 cadre in the national Party structure, the lowest was actually 23: level 24 was a grade operated by work units themselves. The first year after applying for Party membership, or the first year after graduating from university, you'd be treated as a so-called level 24 cadre, kind of like getting you ready to be a Party member. If during that year you didn't do anything wrong, you'd be formally enrolled.

Some people said that the punishment meted out to Zhang Guoqing's wife was too heavy – and it was true, she was punished because he couldn't be. She suffered for the sake of her husband and child; it was her duty, and she didn't complain. She didn't complain, and of course there was no way that the Party was going to revise the verdict, and no one was expecting Huang Yiyi to come out and ask for mercy on their behalf. I asked her why she wanted to do this and she said something vague about feeling sorry for them; that it was unfair that the lives of three people should be wrecked because a seven-year-old child did something wrong.

'Comrade Wang doesn't have a fun life either.'

I had been expecting her to 'redeem' Comrade Wang, because after all she was involved in what happened to him, and she had made me promise. Instead she took my pawn with her queen.

'Well, if you would sort things out for both Comrade Wang and Zhang Guoqing, that would be wonderful.'

'I meant to deal with Comrade Wang first.'

'No. If we have to prioritize, then Zhang Guoqing comes first.'

'Why?'

'No reason.'

Everyone would have understood it if she had wanted to save Comrade Wang, but it seemed completely inexplicable that she would go to all this effort for Zhang Guoqing. Since I didn't know what was going on, I set out to make some basic inquiries, and thus discovered a new bombshell – she was having an affair with him! They had got together completely by chance and in a very simple way: one Sunday Zhang Guoqing had borrowed 20 yuan from other people, to which he added his own 5 yuan, and was on his way to the post office in the nearby town to send it to his wife and child who were suffering in the famine. He filled in the documentation and just as he was handing the money over at the counter, someone suddenly rushed forward, grabbed the money out of his hand, and ran off. Zhang Guoqing ran after him but didn't catch him, so he squatted down in the road and burst into tears. He kept saying that it wasn't money that had been stolen – it was the lives of his wife and child! And so on and so forth. Anyway, Huang Yiyi and Comrade Zha happened to be walking past the post office and bumped into him. Huang Yiyi saw him crying in the road like that and felt sorry for him, so she fished out all the money that she had on her and borrowed some from Comrade Zha to make up 25 yuan, which she then gave to Zhang Guoqing. She told him to hurry up and send it to his family. Zhang Guoqing was stunned when he saw the money in Huang Yiyi's hands; this was after all the time of the three years of natural disaster when people were starving all over the country, and 25 yuan was enough to buy three or four hundred *jin* of rice. His wife and child would be able to eat for more than six months on that!

From that point onward, without saying a word, Zhang Guoqing was often to be found helping out Huang Yiyi: he'd be sweeping the floor, or washing it, or putting new paper in the windows, or cleaning her bathroom – in the end he also washed her clothes, including her underwear! Thanks to all this, the two of them gradually got closer and closer. So she was having an affair with him just as she had with Comrade Wang, but the difference was that this time most people didn't know. This was because the pair of them lived in the same compound, so they would meet regularly anyway without attracting any attention. Comrade Wang on the other hand had worked in a different unit, so any relationship was easily detected. There was also another factor. Zhang

Guoqing was generally agreed to be a good husband, not the kind of person you would believe this of, so anyone who discovered the affair would be sure that it was Huang Yiyi who had seduced him. But she was in a very different position now, whereby we could forgive any mistakes that she made, because she had done so well for us. So this particular piece of gossip hadn't gone very far and neither Unit Director Luo nor myself was aware of it.

Having discovered this bombshell, I decided to deal with the situation in a completely different way from that with Comrade Wang. So rather than reporting to my superiors, I made an appointment to see Huang Yiyi. I needed to make her understand one thing: although at present very few people were aware of her relationship with Zhang Guoqing, if the Party acceded to her request to resolve the problem of his wife and son, the whole of Unit 701 would know about them and her reputation would be ruined.

'Really,' I reminded her, 'you can't carry on being single.'

'Why not?' she said in a half-teasing voice.

'If you love Zhang Guoqing, this won't help him.'

'You mean I should make him get a divorce and then marry me?'

'Yes.'

'It wouldn't work, and besides it's impossible. I know him, he'd almost rather die than get a divorce. He couldn't bear it.'

'Leaving that on one side, you still shouldn't do this for him.'

She asked why, and I told her that she was currently in a wonderful position: the Party had already put in motion steps to find her a husband, so if she made a fuss right now, people would gossip about her relationship with Zhang Guoqing, which would be very bad for her efforts to get married. I kept coming back to the same point: in my opinion she shouldn't interfere in Zhang Guoqing's affairs – not that she couldn't, but that it would be a bad idea, because it was a genie she couldn't put back in the bottle, and she would just get hurt. It was a fact, and she did think seriously about it. However, her final decision was very disappointing.

'I've promised Zhang Guoqing,' she said, 'and I'm not going to go back on my word. Besides, anyone who cares about that sort of thing wouldn't be a good choice as a husband; we'd split up right away.'

'Everyone cares about that sort of thing – every man, at any rate.'

'Well in that case I am doomed to stay single.'

'The Party is doing its best, and we need you to cooperate. Please don't make any further representations about Zhang Guoqing.'

'I can keep quiet for a bit, but I'm not going to let it go, OK? Stop dragging it out: I'm going to see that Zhang Guoqing's problems get sorted out, and as for everything else we'll just have to see how it goes. I'm not that farsighted, nor that patient; I really can't be bothered to look eight generations into the future before I decide what to do. The only thing that matters to me right now is to help Zhang Guoqing – first, because I promised him I would, and second, because you know what he's like, he's completely open and honest, and if I don't help him, who will? Being honest won't solve his problems, will it? And if his problems aren't solved, how can he ever be happy? That's why I want to get involved, and if you don't want to help, that's fine, I'll find someone else who will.'

Since I was now painted into a corner, I had to help out. At that point in time she was a goddess – she could summon the wind and raise the rain, she could turn base metal into gold – and what she said went. If I didn't do this for her, someone else would. And if someone else stepped forward to help her, then I would have annoyed her, and that could bring down a lot of trouble on my own head. Whenever senior people came, did any of them not want to meet her? They all wanted to see her! She could easily take the opportunity either to complain about me or to say something nice – something as easy for her as leading a lamb, but it could change my destiny. What is meant by one word changing your life? Right then, every word she said could change your life. I certainly wasn't stupid enough to annoy her and then let someone else take advantage of that fact. So since she was insisting on helping Zhang Guoqing, and also mentioned that she'd really like

Comrade Wang's problems sorted out as well, I had no hesitation in doing my very best for her. I had to make a special trip to head-quarters, and then everything was done.

To tell you the truth, right then the Party would have taken ser-iously any request that she cared to make, and would have done their best to fulfil her every wish. The problems that Zhang Guo-qing and Comrade Wang had were actually internal, and could be solved within the work unit, so the minute she made her request, it was fixed – it was really no trouble.

28.

Unit 701 was usually sealed, and the people inside were allowed no contact with the outside world. Perhaps it was for that reason that gossip flourished so readily. Zhang Guoqing and Comrade Wang's situation was known to everyone in the unit, and when Huang Yiyi saved them, that really was a fresh bit of news – before we knew where we were, everybody had heard about it. They called Huang Yiyi 'Angel' or 'The Angel with Problems'. Thinking about it, they were perfectly correct. What kind of person could have brought them out of hell? No ordinary human being, only an angel! And if you think about it, what kind of person could have cracked RECOVERY like that? Only an angel! Calling Huang Yiyi the Angel was doubly appropriate, and so everyone started calling her that.

About the same time as people started calling her Angel, rumours about her affair with Zhang Guoqing started to spread. I was expecting that; it was nothing to be surprised about. Any gossip worth their salt could have guessed, and having guessed could investigate, could get proof, could talk. But if Zhang Guoqing's wife came back to work at the hospital in Unit 701, given that walls have ears, sooner or later she would find out. So for 'security reasons' we sent her to work as a nurse in the People's Hospital in the nearest town. Comrade Wang asked not to return to the training centre – I guess he felt he had lost too much face – he chose instead to go to one of Unit 701's branch offices at the other end of the country. Clearly he was breaking off all contact with Huang Yiyi.

Zhang Guoqing's wife's situation was different; even though she worked in town, she came back every day, since her home was in Unit 701. What was she called? I've been trying to remember, but I can't. It's on the tip of my tongue, but I just can't quite get it. I need her name because she's a part of the rest of this story, and it's annoying not to be able to remember. But since I can't call it to mind, I will just have to carry on regardless. She – Zhang Guoqing's wife – was someone I had never had anything to do with before, and I had managed to completely ignore her existence. But since Huang Yiyi was having an affair with her husband, I had to pay attention to her after she came back, because I was afraid she would find out what was going on and cause trouble. I had heard people in the hospital say she was a real shrew. There is a saying that in this world there are two sorts of people that you really need to watch out for: shrewish women and toadying men. Both are the kind that causes trouble. In this case, the problem was obvious, and I was worried that if she found out the truth and started creating scenes, Huang Yiyi's reputation would be ruined, with concomitant damage to her work. Outsiders didn't realize, but after cracking RECOVERY, our superiors set us a new assignment: breaking Russian military ciphers. Given that Huang Yiyi was familiar with Soviet methods, she was the first choice to take charge of this project.

It is true for everyone that if a relationship goes wrong or they have a personal problem, it affects their work. For some people it wouldn't matter, or at least I wouldn't worry about it, but anything affecting Huang Yiyi was serious. She was now not only the head of a division but a key figure in our cryptography programme and a model worker in Unit 701. If anything happened to her it would affect all of us, so it was our duty to protect her. Protecting her security, making sure that she was healthy and well-fed – that was easy; the problem was that we had no idea what Zhang Guoqing's wife would do when she found out. I wanted to protect Huang Yiyi but I didn't know how. Not only did I not know how to prevent disaster, I had no idea how I was going to minimize the damage if the worst happened. The whole thing was a real headache, but it seemed as though all I could do was wait.

Zhang Guoqing's wife came back.

One month passed.

A second month passed.

Everything was quiet on the Zhang Guoqing's wife front; there wasn't any sign of trouble. The possibility I was most worried about seemed to have been averted, and the thing I most wanted to have happen did: within the space of six months Huang Yiyi cracked three mid-level Soviet military ciphers one after the other; it was wonderful news! It was an excellent omen. You see, regardless of whether you are thinking about Zhang Guoqing's wife or about the ciphers, the first couple of months were going to be crucial. Having got safely through them, everything else seemed to be easy. The saying about how the beginning is always the most difficult really seemed to apply here!

Having got safe and sound through that first six months, I felt as though I must have a guardian angel somewhere looking out for me. Everything was going well, and I don't need to tell you how pleased I was. The only thing that wasn't going according to plan was the search for a husband for Huang Yiyi. The whole thing went completely wrong: the Party came up with a list of suitable men and asked her opinion, but she very tactfully said no to all of them. She had good reason to do so: everyone in the unit knew that she was having an affair with Zhang Guoqing, gossip had seen to that. The only person who didn't know was Zhang Guoqing's wife. In the circumstances, picking someone from within the unit really wouldn't work – after all everyone needs a bit of self-respect. So in the end the Party moved to Plan B: finding someone from outside. It is easy to say, 'Oh, we'll just find someone suitable for Huang Yiyi', but there weren't that many men of the right age with the requisite education and self-confidence.

Why did we want someone self-confident? Well, the first couple of candidates we found seemed OK on paper but when they actually met her, and saw how pretty Huang Yiyi was, and heard about how much she had done for the country – that was it; they didn't dare have anything to do with her. It was as if they surrendered before they could lose. Later on we found another man, a colonel from the nearby garrison. The two of them seemed to get along all right, and they met three times in the space of a month, but there wasn't a fourth time. It was over. We asked what the problem was, and the colonel said that she was far too free and easy; having met

each other just three times and really not knowing each other at
all well, she was already wanting to hug and kiss him, and in broad
daylight too! What did she think that looked like? Clearly he had
been scared off by Huang Yiyi's manner. There was another one
who Huang Yiyi liked, a professor from the university at the provincial capital. A few years earlier he had been denounced as a
Rightist and his wife had divorced him. He was about the same
age as Huang Yiyi and had studied abroad. They enjoyed each
other's company a lot, to the point where you could almost say
that they fell in love at first sight. The professor also had plenty of
gall: the second time they met they spent the night together. They
carried on like that for a couple of weeks and then Huang Yiyi
came running to see me and said, 'He's the one.' She told us to get
on with the security check.

The security check wrecked any chance they might have had of
getting married.

Why? Well, the professor's father had been a high-ranking official in the KMT, and he had maybe seven or eight siblings, some
of whom had gone to Taiwan, some were in Hong Kong, and some
were in the US. Given the security considerations of Unit 701, it
was strictly forbidden to marry anyone with family connections
overseas. Those were the rules, and no one dared to break them.
They applied to our superiors and they applied to us. So yet again
Huang Yiyi's marriage plans didn't work out.

According to my information, in the six months after Zhang
Guoqing's wife came back, Huang Yiyi had no contact at all with
him. Later on though – I don't know why, perhaps it was to do
with the fact that she couldn't find a husband – the two of them
got back together. One time I saw with my own eyes Zhang Guoqing leaving Huang Yiyi's house early in the morning, and that
really did give me a turn. Given that we all lived in the same compound, sooner or later the woman was bound to find out. So I
went in person to see the mayor and asked him to get the hospital
to give Zhang Guoqing's wife accommodation in town. If they
were all living in town, Zhang Guoqing's wife would have no reason to come up the mountain, and if they went their separate ways

the chances of anyone letting the cat out of the bag were much reduced. Most of the time after work Zhang Guoqing would go down to town to join his family, but every so often he would stay overnight with Huang Yiyi on the mountain. I made time to call several times on Zhang Guoqing's family, to tell his wife that he was so busy at work that he would not always be able to get home, saying something about how I hoped she would support him . . . I went to a lot of trouble to protect them – I used my power, I told a lot of lies; to use Huang Yiyi's own words, I pandered to them. Quite honestly, the whole of Unit 701 pandered to them. Even the dogs living on that mountain knew they were having an affair. Everyone was very careful, and they all played their part in making sure that Zhang Guoqing's wife never found out, no matter what.

Of course I knew perfectly well that this wasn't a long-term solution and that we would have to find Mr Right so that Huang Yiyi could get married and have a proper home. So on the one hand we were trying to keep a lid on things, while on the other we were searching high and low for someone suitable for Huang Yiyi. That was hard, but we had to carry on looking. This wasn't Huang Yiyi's problem any more, it was Unit 701's problem; a government problem. Maybe you don't believe it, but it's true.

One afternoon the following spring, Huang Yiyi suddenly burst into my office. The second she got through the door she said, 'I want to marry Zhang Guoqing!'

I was surprised and didn't know what to say, so it was only after a long pause that I replied, and with a stupid question at that.

'What are you talking about?'

'I mean what I say. I want to marry Zhang Guoqing.'

'Is this some kind of joke?'

'No.'

'What on earth is going on? Why have you all of a sudden decided you want to marry him?'

'I can't stand seeing him go back to his wife every day.'

'Is that the problem? I will tell Zhang Guoqing not to go home so often. You don't have to marry him.'

'No. I want to get married.' She said it very calmly, very firmly, and had clearly thought it through beforehand.

I was cross with her. 'If you wanted to marry him all along, why did we go to all the trouble of bringing his family back –'

She cut me short. 'That was then and this is now. I want to marry him, so you tell him to get a divorce.'

She then walked out and didn't stop, no matter how much I yelled at her.

After she left, I just sat behind my desk in a daze. The whole thing seemed more than a little peculiar: if she wanted to get married to him, why had she come to tell me before even mentioning it to him? She seemed to be carrying on as if getting married was a task that I'd set her. And another thing, she had never wanted to marry him before, so what could have put that idea into her head all of a sudden? It was a bad idea from start to finish, and we had all been put to an awful lot of trouble for nothing! Oh well, come what may I had to sort it out for her. Even though it wasn't really my job, when you get right down to it, it was work. I knew what she was like: if things didn't go to her liking she could do absolutely anything, including going on hunger strike, or taking to her bed for three days, until I was completely desperate. Well, she was the Angel and I was just an ordinary mortal, so what could I do? I had to do what she wanted. So I went to find Zhang Guoqing and explained the situation, and finally I asked his opinion.

His answer was very straightforward: he would listen to the Party.

The Party wanted him to get divorced.

So he got a divorce.

In fact, even if he had not wanted to follow the Party's wishes, he would still have had to divorce his wife, because there was no room for manoeuvre there. This decision came from the Angel. The amazing fact that the Angel was cracking one cipher after the other told us one thing: the more angelic she was, the more we had to dance to her tune; but as long as we did so all would be well.

A divorce here, a wedding there: they were in such a hurry there was no time for discussion – they didn't even really think about the rules, just like a pair of ignorant teenagers. The wedding was very simple, just the people from their divisions, me and a few of our superiors. All in all there were enough guests for two tables at the unit's dining hall. After the meal we went round to the newly married couple's home to eat wedding-sweets. We wished them well and cracked a few jokes, as seemed appropriate to the situation. We got to see her retching again and again, and then we understood everything: she was pregnant!

Now we all knew why Huang Yiyi had been in such a hurry to get married: it couldn't be more clear. What nobody knew was that in addition to the obvious reason, there was another that was much more important and much more mysterious. Huang Yiyi had been married twice already, and had had innumerable boyfriends. But in spite of all those men, and over such a long period of time, she had never once been pregnant. This was the first time! Even Huang Yiyi was amazed that after so many men Zhang Guoqing was the first for her, and even with him nothing had happened to begin with – they had to go through a certain period of getting familiar with each other and waiting. It was as if there was a lock on her womb, which Zhang Guoqing had only gradually worked out how to open.

Having found Mr Right, and now also being pregnant, I should have been happy for her. But every time I thought about her having to stop work, even if only temporarily, I was really unhappy. This simply wasn't the right moment for Huang Yiyi to have a baby. Everything has its time and place, and if the same thing happens in two completely different times and places, the result is totally different. But how could I tell her that? This was so important to her, besides which she was already well into her thirties – so how could I ask her to put it off? There it was: the national interest on one side and her happiness on the other, neither of which could be ignored, and I was caught in the middle. What to do for the best? I was deeply worried.

In the end I came down in favour of the national interest and made a suggestion to Huang Yiyi that really wasn't within the scope of my duties.

I was anticipating that she would refuse, but I was not expecting what actually happened next. One day Zhang Guoqing came to ask me for permission to take a car out, because Huang Yiyi was feeling ill and wanted to go to hospital. The hospital was next to the training centre, a good few kilometres from the housing complex. In the past, when she was having the affair with Comrade Wang, she had regularly walked there and back, but this time she clearly wasn't feeling at all well and needed the car.

The car brought Huang Yiyi back from the hospital less than two hours later. She came straight to my office, and stood in front of me. Then she said something very peculiar: 'Happy now?'

When she got to the hospital they told her that she had a cold, and although they could easily have given her medication for it, the doctor refused on the grounds that it would be bad for the baby. Huang Yiyi counted up on her fingers; during the course of her pregnancy she had in fact taken this medication on at least a couple of occasions. The doctor found a box and took out the instructions leaflet with the words 'contraindicated for pregnant women', and gave it to her to read, combined with a verbal explanation that made her skin crawl. It was too late for regrets now though.

Actually the doctor was being far too alarmist: the baby would have been fine. But weighing up the options as she had been told them, Huang Yiyi made the decision which she thought would make me 'happy now': she would abort the baby and try again later.

I was happy. But that feeling of unexpected happiness is now inextricably linked with the shadow cast by Huang Yiyi's death. A few days later, when I went to see her ice-cold body in the hospital mortuary, my legs suddenly buckled under me and I almost fell to my knees beside her. Right at that moment, I could have killed that alarmist doctor, for it was she who tolled Huang Yiyi's death knell.

29

She didn't die during the operation; she died when it was over.

She didn't die in one of the wards, but in the lavatory.

Later on, I went to look at the lavatory with its two wooden cubicles, both of which had spring-mounted saloon doors, which could swing either way. One of the cubicles was out of order and there was a sign up: 'Pipes Blocked. Don't Use.' That cubicle had a lavatory throne and was reserved for patients; the other was a squat toilet. They said that the old springs on these doors had been out of action for ages, so that you could open them but then they would not close again. No one paid any attention, but then about a month earlier, just before an inspection by hospital managers, the springs were replaced. Now, thanks to the new springs, the doors closed properly. When you pushed the door open, it would close itself, though if you weren't careful it might well hit you on the back on the return swing.

This wasn't Unit 701's own hospital, but the county People's Hospital. Our hospital didn't have an obstetrics and gynaecology unit, so any problem of that nature had to go to the county hospital for treatment. Our office was in contact with their obstetrics and gynaecology unit, so that any women comrades who had to go there would be guaranteed the very best treatment. That day when Huang Yiyi went to the county People's Hospital for an abortion, the office arranged for her to be accompanied by a comrade with particularly good contacts at the hospital, so it goes without saying that she was treated well. Someone met her at the door, the operation was performed in the best theatre by the most experienced doctor, and the whole thing went without the slightest hitch. After the abortion, they put her in a single room to rest, and gave her a cup of sweet tea. Everyone did their very best, and they deserve only praise. Perhaps God wanted her to feel looked after in the moments before she died.

Having rested for about an hour, she started to feel better. It was already eleven o'clock, and seeing that time was getting on, she told Zhang Guoqing to collect her things and get ready to go while she went to the lavatory. She went in and didn't come out, until the people waiting outside decided that something must be wrong and went in to look for her. She was half lying, half seated on the floor, and they could not wake her up. To begin with they thought it was an ordinary faint, but as her pulse got weaker and weaker they realized that it couldn't be. In fact when they found her she was already past human aid.

It was a cerebral haemorrhage.

When she fell, she hit the back of her head on a bend in the pipework in the corner, which caused the haemorrhage.

The doctor said that for that type of injury, only immediate surgery at one of the big hospitals in Beijing or Shanghai could have saved her life. We didn't have that kind of surgeon or that kind of equipment, but we could see her face getting paler and paler, her pulse weaker and weaker, her body colder and more still . . . Everyone was desperate to save her, and right up to the very last moment people were rushing around trying anything they could think of, but there was nothing they could do. This was a problem for a top-class hospital, and the people here couldn't even make an accurate diagnosis, let alone save her life. In fact they only found out that it was a cerebral haemorrhage at the autopsy. It sounds really weird that someone could die like that without breaking their head open, without even a bruise. There was just a small scrape with a thin line of blood, and even that was covered by her hair. If you weren't really careful you could easily miss it. It seemed that Huang Yiyi's skin was as tough as leather, but that had not stopped the skull underneath from fracturing like an eggshell.

That was how our wonderful cipher-cracking Angel left us.

Huang Yiyi's death was the most terrible shock, the worst

tragedy that we ever had to face. I kept thinking that if someone was responsible for her death, no matter what the consequences, I would rip them to pieces with my bare hands and then trample the remains to a bloody pulp. But no one was responsible; everyone with whom she came into contact that morning had treated her with the utmost respect and concern. The abortion was done as carefully as they could, and after she collapsed they did their very best to save her. It was regrettable that they didn't have the equipment to save her, but you couldn't blame them for that. If anyone was to blame, it was the hospital managers who had not had the lavatory throne repaired in time. Why had Huang Yiyi fainted in the lavatory? She had always been someone who fainted easily, and on top of that she was feeling weak after the operation, so squatting down had been too much for her. When she stood up again she felt giddy and fell. That was all there was to it.

Huang Yiyi's death undoubtedly put our cryptography unit under a lot of extra pressure. After her relationship with Zhang Guoqing came out, people called her Angel to her face, but behind her back they still called her 'The Angel with Problems'. Actually, when it comes to cryptography, she didn't have any problems: she really was an angel, a cipher-cracking angel. In my opinion, if you put all the cryptographers who ever worked for Unit 701 together, they couldn't beat one Huang Yiyi. I am talking about ability, basic cryptographic talent and ability; because later on there were people whose achievements surpassed hers. In some ways, though, you could say she was the very best, because she only worked for us for a very short time, just a bit more than two years. However you look at it she really was the best, and because she came to our assistance, because she achieved such a signal success, she left a shining mark, so that ever after cryptographers at Unit 701 didn't dare become arrogant or overweening, they just had to grit their teeth and get on with it. She was like a bright beacon that shone for a short time before disappearing for ever, remembered by those who came after her, talked about, commemorated, whispered about, until she became a legend towering above us, encouraging her successors to venture ever further into the dark.

Decrypting a cipher is like looking for a needle in a haystack; it is like trying to listen to the heartbeats of the dead.

The dead never come back. But once Huang Yiyi had passed away, Zhang Guoqing remarried his ex-wife. Just talking about it, I can feel all my old hatred for them revive. I really don't want to discuss them, particularly not Zhang Guoqing's wife. She deserved everything she got! I wish I could have killed her with my own bare hands!

She murdered Huang Yiyi.

I really don't want to talk about her any more than I have to, but I need to tell you the facts. At the time no one thought about the possibility that someone had killed Huang Yiyi; we all thought it was an accidental concatenation of events, so there was no proper investigation. So she got away with it, and got to live happily ever after. One year followed another, but somehow or other in the autumn of the third year rumours started to circulate that Huang Yiyi had been murdered by Zhang Guoqing's wife; some people saying that she had taken advantage of her position at the hospital to administer a lethal injection, others that she had smothered her with bandages in the lavatory, or that she had beaten her to death with a stick. Anyway, there were lots of stories about the methods she was supposed to have used to kill her, but the whole thing seemed laughable to me. I was quite sure it was fantasy. Of course everyone knew about the situation between Huang Yiyi and Zhang Guoqing's wife, and we quite understood that she hated her, so it seemed that these stories had sprung up from this slender basis.

But then one afternoon I bumped into Zhang Guoqing in the corridor, and he seemed unusually nervous, as if he had seen a ghost. That immediately made me suspicious. Later on, I got his boss to call Zhang Guoqing in, though I really wasn't at all sure what I was going to say to him. But the minute he got to my office he was so scared that he started crying, and through his tears he said, 'Deputy Director An, arrest her, she killed Huang Yiyi . . .'

Later on, when we interrogated that awful woman – Zhang Guoqing's wife – we found out that when Huang Yiyi entered the lavatory, the ex was squatting in the cubicle, and hearing someone come in she made her presence known. Huang Yiyi responded politely. Of course they had seen each other in the past – you could even say that they knew each other – but not well enough to recognize each other's voice. So on this occasion, even though they spoke to each other, neither realized who the other one was. If Huang Yiyi had recognized her voice she would have got the hell out of there and nothing would have happened to her. That is just a supposition though. In fact Huang Yiyi didn't go anywhere, and thus two enemies met in a narrow lane . . . According to what that horrible woman said, when she came out of the lavatory cubicle and found herself face to face with Huang Yiyi, she was absolutely furious and cursed her with the most disgusting swear words she could think of. Huang Yiyi didn't respond, other than to ask her to keep a civil tongue in her head; and she tried to move away, making it clear that she didn't want to quarrel with her. But the ex-wife didn't stop: she stood blocking the doorway as she continued cursing.

A neutral observer might say that Huang Yiyi was the trouble-maker and the other woman a victim, and so for her to get angry and say some nasty things was perfectly understandable. So Huang Yiyi kept herself under control and didn't try to answer back, though a disdainful expression played across her face. Then she shut her eyes, as if she were not listening to a word the other woman said. If the person you are cursing isn't paying any attention then it is pointless, and so the ex decided to give up. But as the harridan explained, having decided to leave she looked at Huang Yiyi standing there with her eyes shut, and thought how pleasing it would be to smack her a couple of times in the face. Though she thought she would enjoy it she didn't dare actually do anything because she was scared of getting into trouble. On her way out she noticed how strong the spring on the door was, and realized that she could use the door to hit Huang Yiyi and get back at her that way. So she deliberately pulled the door back as far as it would go, the spring at full stretch, and then suddenly let go. The door hit Huang Yiyi with full force as it swung back. Standing there with her eyes shut, how could she get out of the way? She lost her

footing and as she fell, she hit the back of her head on the project-
ing bend in the pipework. She cried out and crumpled into a heap
on the floor.

When that awful woman saw Huang Yiyi had fallen, she walked
out happily, feeling that for once she had got the better of her. She
didn't know that Huang Yiyi was dying, that life was slipping away
into the darkness. She also didn't know she had just signed her
own death warrant, though thanks to delays it was not actually
served until three years later. She had to pay a heavy price for that:
Zhang Guoqing went to prison as an accessory after the fact, as a
result of which their little boy was left effectively orphaned and
homeless.

Everyone agreed that if she had confessed straight away she
might well not have been sentenced to death, and Zhang Guoqing
certainly wouldn't have been dragged in. That way their boy would
at the very least have had his father to look after him. But that's all
supposition; the fact is she only told the truth three years later, and
during that time the knowledge of what she had done tormented
Zhang Guoqing into a shadow of his former self. Her evidence
cleared him of any actual involvement in the crime, but the fact
that he had helped cover it up was quite enough to send him to
prison.

I feel sorry for Zhang Guoqing.

You might say that Zhang Guoqing's wife was also a victim, but
I can't find it in my heart to feel sorry for her.

30

Finally, I would like to say something that has nothing to do with Huang Yiyi. Originally I hadn't planned to speak about it here, but since I have already mentioned Xiaoyu, it seems appropriate to explain what happened to her. People in my line of work, regardless of what terrible tragedies overtake them, can only suffer in silence. It is a horrible feeling, having to keep these things bottled up, and I have already been made wretched for decades about what happened to Xiaoyu. Now I want to use this opportunity to bring it all out into the open, for a kind of release.

It must have been fate that not long after Huang Yiyi died, Director Tie suddenly rang me up and told me to come to Beijing immediately to see him. Why? He didn't tell me on the phone, and I didn't ask. It was one of our rules, and I was used to it: if your superiors don't tell you, it's best for you not to ask. When I got to headquarters he put a black wooden box down in front of me. What could it be? How right you are: it was a casket of ashes.

But what you won't have guessed is that it really did contain Xiaoyu's ashes.

This time it was true; it wasn't a cover story. The strange thing was that Xiaoyu really did die in a car crash. No one has ever worked out the reasons for the crash; some people say that the weather had warmed up and so there was black ice on the roads – very slippery – and that Xiaoyu (who was driving) had accidentally crashed the car. But other people said that the KGB had found out who she really was, and that they arranged the car accident. In fact, how she died is of secondary importance, what matters is that at that time Xiaoyu's identity had not been declassified, so that meant that even though she was now dead it could not be announced, since she was supposed to have died much earlier.

The people at headquarters told me to keep the matter strictly secret, and to take her ashes away and give them a quiet burial. To tell the truth, at that moment I felt a helpless abhorrence of my work that I had never experienced before. I hated the brutality and heartlessness of it all! Afterwards I went back to Unit 701, and late one night I made my way out into the forest and buried the casket containing Xiaoyu's ashes next to Huang Yiyi's grave. I don't know why I did that, but I felt that the two of them ought to be together. They were sisters-in-arms fighting on an invisible front line, so it seemed appropriate. Besides, the two of them had been so unhappy. This way, with someone to keep them company in the darkness, perhaps they wouldn't feel so lonely.

They wouldn't feel lonely any more, but what about me? I had to go on living. I remember that that night I cried silently, and sat for a long, long time next to Huang Yiyi and Xiaoyu's graves, right up until it got light. It must have been nearly May – the trees and the grass were all green, the flowers were open, and their scent was spread by the night dew, brimming with life. But I felt death around me, as if the very air I was breathing was rotten. For the rest of my life I have lived only for my work. I don't have any emotions, any enjoyment; those feelings all died on that spring day.

I have lived with that death until the present day; I don't know if that is a sign of my weakness or my strength. However, now I have a sense of peace, for I know that I don't have much longer to live, and then I can go and keep Xiaoyu and Huang Yiyi company. There is a saying, I don't know if you know it, which goes: 'All roads lead to Heaven'. I have been thinking about what that means, and in my opinion my most heartfelt wishes, perfect love, are things that can only come true in Heaven. Maybe other people don't believe in Heaven, but I do. Of course I am an atheist, but I still believe in Heaven. It was Anderov who made me believe. Anderov often said to me, 'How can humanity live without Heaven? Where do people's souls go?' Xiaoyu, Huang Yiyi and I are all just the same; if we can't hope to meet again in Heaven, then what? How can we console others? How can we comfort ourselves?

All roads lead to Heaven, what a wonderful thing that is to know . . .

The Shadow of Chen Erhu

By 1987, Old Chen Erhu was no longer a healthy man; he'd die in the spring of that same year – seventeen years ago now. Most Unit 701 operatives' personal files would have been declassified long ago. But Old Chen was no ordinary agent: he was a witness. A witness to what, you may ask. Well, to everything. Nothing that went on in Unit 701 escaped his watchful eye, no matter how small and insignificant. He was privy to all the inner workings of the cryptography division, privy to a vast storehouse of still top-secret information. Without exaggerating, making his personal file public would mean that half the secrets of the cryptography division would be revealed to the world. Perhaps that was the reason his repeated entreaties for the declassification of his own documents met with no success. It was also the reason, I imagine, why my efforts to get to the bottom of the matter had hit an impasse.

On 25 October 2002 I was witness to the very peculiar way in which information was released on Declassification Day. Beginning at 08.30 and continuing throughout the day, people walked up to the record clerk's office counter, produced a notification form, accepted a file folder from the clerk, and left. It was just like the workings of a post office, except that the exchange between the clerk and the person requesting such-and-such a file revealed much more good will, friendliness even – something you don't often see in a post office. At any rate, during the comings and goings of these people, I did notice one particular man amble in, supporting himself on a cane. He didn't seem all that old, actually, perhaps around fifty or so; the age of an administrator of some sort or other. However, two years before I met the man, he had been unlucky enough to contract a serious eye infection that gradually destroyed his eyesight. No matter what the doctors attempted, nothing seemed to work. The world now appeared to him as completely blank, forcing him to use a cane to get around. Of course, work was out of the question, and his blindness was the main reason he had left active duty at Unit 701. Well, leaving doesn't really describe his retirement. After all, when he 'left' Unit 701, he was, in a sense, abandoning his youth, his skills, his friends, his comrades, his correspondence over the twelve years of his service, his diaries, and all sorts of other papers and notes – everything; his whole life. All of it remained within the compound's walls. Some of these things he would never see again. But some other items, namely his letters and diaries, he could take home with him today. His file had been declassified.

Later, I learnt that he was in fact Chen Erhu's former aide and confidant, a man by the name of Shi Guoguang. What made me even more excited about meeting him was the fact that in the declassified documents which were handed over that day, there were many letters and diaries that dealt directly with Chen Erhu. This discovery raised my hopes that one day soon Old Chen's personal file would be made public. But until that day, all I can use to reconstruct and put together the pieces of the life of Old Chen are these letters and notes made by Shi Guoguang.

I do not need to tell you that the depiction of Chen Erhu that you read here is nothing approaching a complete picture of the individual; it's just a shadow of the man. That's what I meant by the title of this section: 'The Shadow of Chen Erhu'. I couldn't have got this far without the help of his disciple, Shi Guoguang, so I'm very grateful to him and wish him all the best with his recovery.

Even though I have only this 'shadow' of the man, as it were, what's plain to see and understand from reading through Shi's notes is that whilst Old Chen was a very unusual character, he was still a man full of life. The puzzling thing is, the image painted by Shi contrasts greatly with the description given by Director An. Indeed, in Director An's portrayal of Chen Erhu, Old Chen was an obscure and dark figure, someone who operated in the shadows, and was a shadow himself. Perhaps this was because Director An wanted to give all the credit to Huang Yiyi and so felt the need to dull Old Chen's lustre; or perhaps there was another reason – I simply don't know. But one thing is clear: once I had read through Shi Guoguang's letters and diaries, my respect for Chen Erhu grew.

What follows are Shi Guoguang's papers: enjoy . . .

Diary Excerpts: 25 March 1987

Dormitory. Night. Raining.

Today, the son of my former *shifu* telephoned. At first I thought it was a woman speaking because the voice was so faint and distant. I asked who it was and he told me he was Chen Sibing. I mulled it over for a bit but I couldn't place the name. Finally he said that he was Chen Erhu's son.

Chen Erhu was my *shifu*.

I was quite startled by the phone call, mostly because he was rather rude. All he asked was whether or not I had received a letter he had sent. I told him that I hadn't, and he started to hang up. I thought perhaps it was inconvenient for him to call from wherever he was, so before he let the receiver fall I asked for the telephone number there – so I could call him instead. He said there was no need, and that he would contact me again tomorrow, and then he hung up. I couldn't shake the feeling that something had gone very wrong. What was this letter he spoke of? It was all very peculiar and a bit out of the blue. The truth is, even though I was fairly close to his father and his family, I don't know much about this young man. He was reared by his maternal grandmother in the city and didn't often come out to the mountains (the first valley compound). After he began studying at university, I would occasionally see him during the winter and summer holidays, usually on the volleyball court. He was fairly tall and he could jump exceptionally well. His prowess on the court always attracted attention. Because of my relationship with his father, when we met it was generally quite cordial; we'd even exchange small talk from time to time. He had quite a way with words – he was very entertaining, and his words were always accompanied by gestures: his hands would move this way and that, his shoulders would shrug up and down; he reminded me somehow of a foreigner. He'd also always lean to one side, putting most of his weight on one foot – he gave the impression of someone without a care in the world. From his words and how he said them I could discern a key difference between father and son: Sibing had a care-free demeanour, he was talkative and optimistic – a young man full of life; his father, on the other hand, was usually silent and reticent – he had a cold and hard demeanour, and was a solitary figure. At first I was quite surprised by this difference between them, but later, as I considered it some more, it didn't seem all that strange – there are plenty of sons who aren't a bit like their fathers. Nonetheless, I didn't know Sibing all that well. I didn't even know his actual name: everyone just seemed to call him Ah-bing. This was of course a nickname, and it was only today that I discovered that his real name was Chen Sibing.

What is this letter he has sent me? I've told myself not to think of it now, but rather wait until it arrives.

26 March

Office. Night. Still raining.

Could it be that the rain has delayed the letter? It didn't come today, but Ah-bing did telephone. It certainly seemed as though he had something important to ask me, but since I hadn't received the letter, there was no way for him to press the issue further. From the sound of his voice, he seemed to be in a better mood than when we spoke previously; he had a lot more to say this time. He told me of his work unit, how he had finished his studies and was now working for a publisher in the south, presumably as an editor. But an editor of what I don't know – he didn't say. Still, considering what he studied at university, an editor seems most fitting. After all, he studied contemporary European literature – so if he wasn't an editor, what could he be? I certainly can't think of anything else.

I've been to the city he works in once. It was a pretty little place. The streets were lined with flowers, all very romantic. Most of them were cherry trees, which practically every city has now planted along their main arteries. It was easy to imagine the scene in spring, when the trees would be in flower: the streets would be painted in a pinkish brilliance, blossoms would fill the sky like snowflakes, they'd drift along like white downy clouds, the air would be filled with a sweet fragrance. I could swear I caught the scent of the flowers myself.

I also knew something else about this city, something I learnt from history books. According to those books, a century ago it was ravaged by a massive earthquake; countless people had perished, perhaps in the tens of thousands. Fifty years ago, it was the scene of a famous and incredibly bloody military campaign. According to those same books, countless people had died in the fighting. I often thought that the land under the city must be filled with the bones of all of these dead, perhaps several tons of human remains. Cherry blossom and human remains certainly didn't seem to go together, but I couldn't think of one without the other. Ah, what does it matter? Being aware of certain truths, certain connections isn't necessarily wrong. Being aware of too much could be considered an illness, but most definitely not wrong. And since it's not wrong, it shouldn't matter if one speculates on it a bit. In truth, I know, thinking of such things is my way of distancing myself from something else. My mind's in a mess, a complete and total mess.

27 March

Dormitory. Night. Fine.

I finally received Ah-bing's letter today. I spent the last two days wondering what the letter might be about, but never once did I think it would be news of my *shifu*'s death! He had died on the second of March, almost a month ago now. Ah-bing's letter told me that when death was nearly upon him, my *shifu* had wanted to see me. He had actually telephoned my work unit, but I was on leave at the time, and there was no way to get in touch with me. Finally, he decided to leave me some last words, instructing Ah-bing repeatedly to deliver them to me. That's what his letter was about.

Shifu had written the words himself, but his handwriting was worse than a child's. The characters were all over the place: some were huge, others nearly too small to make out; none were straight and none followed the lines on the page. I was familiar with his handwriting, so I could tell from this letter that when he wrote it he must have been terribly weak, his hand barely able to hold the brush; he must have been labouring horribly – these words scrawled across this page painted a picture before my eyes of an old and feeble man; a man whose heart was heavy, whose hand trembled . . . This is the first time I've received a dying man's last words: I never thought they would affect me so much. Looking at the words, I couldn't help but be fearful. His words drew me in: there was something murderous about them, something ferocious; they were like a sword working its way towards my heart. I began to cry, the tears rolling off my face and onto his last words.

This is what he wrote:

Little Shi, it seems as though my time has come. Before death takes me, I need to warn you: that certain matter – you have to believe

me that it is incredibly important, no matter what, you must ensure
that it remains a secret, buried for ever. It must never be divulged
to outsiders. Chen Erhu. 1 March 1987.

What was 'that certain matter' he spoke of?

It's enough to make anyone think, and no doubt Ah-bing has
become obsessed with the whole thing. He telephoned again
today. He knew that I had received the letter, and wanted to know
what the 'certain matter' was. He refused to take no for an answer;
he had to ask me what the letter was about. Since his father had
accorded 'that matter' such importance, and since he was his son,
he thought he had a right to know, and hoped I would tell him. I
understood completely – only he had to understand me: his
father's last words were clear. Under absolutely no circumstances
was I to reveal this secret. I had to keep it buried *for ever*. The letter
made no mention of exceptions. No exceptions meant I was not to
tell anyone, not even his son. This was a dying man's last wish and
I intend to honour it.

In fact, even without this last message, I still wouldn't be able to
tell him – it involved national security. As a specialized work unit,
you could say that everything we did at Unit 701 was top secret
and classified. It was our responsibility, our life, our past, present
and future – everything. What's more, my *shifu* – Chen Sibing's
father, Chen Erhu – well, he was at the heart of Unit 701, the secret
buried within the heart of the enigma. How could I talk about this
man to an outsider? Impossible. I can't tell his son – I couldn't
even tell the Son of Heaven what was going on. To tell you the
truth, I understood quite clearly what 'ensure that it remains a
secret' meant, and it wasn't directed at people like Ah-bing; rather
it was meant for those who worked in the cryptography division.
That's right. It was meant for the insiders, for my old comrades.
No one else knew, only me. 'That matter' is a secret pertaining to
the cryptography division; it's a personal secret concerning Chen
Erhu, a secret he kept hidden from the intelligence service, from
the cryptography division itself, from Unit 701. This is how it was.
In Unit 701, Chen Erhu was not an ordinary man; he was extraor-

dinary, and he had received perhaps more honours than any other agent. These honours were like a suit of shining armour, and even though he is now dead, Unit 701 will not forget him; they will in fact commemorate him, respect and praise his memory. I'm convinced his memorial service will be grander than grand, and that the tears of Unit 701's personnel will fall interminably; but all of this will happen only because people don't know what 'that certain matter' was. I was the only one who knew, and I understand why, on his deathbed, he had so solemnly warned me to keep it secret. Actually, this wasn't the first time he had told me to make sure I held my tongue. That's to say, even without these last words, I knew I had to keep 'that matter' secret from everyone, even from his son. To be frank, Chen Sibing doesn't have the proper qualifications; I will never talk to him.

I realize of course that my refusal to tell Ah-bing what had happened will weigh heavily upon his mind. It will be difficult to bear, like having a precious and rare heirloom broken. Most likely from this day onwards Ah-bing, and perhaps the rest of Chen Erhu's family and relatives, will be tormented by my refusal to divulge this secret. They will perhaps feel much apprehension about it – brood over it, even. In a sense, you could say that Chen Erhu's last words have enveloped them in a dense, impenetrable fog of confusion and unknowing; they are haunted by them as if by some terrible tragedy they can't understand or accept. They refuse to believe that someone they spent their entire lives with would entrust an outsider with such a mysterious and obviously very important secret. No doubt they turned it over and over in their minds: just what was this secret, what other life did Chen Erhu have, could this secret be concealing some unknown danger, might it bring misfortune onto the family? And so on, and so forth: they'll wonder, worry, expect and fear. I'm sure that's what they're thinking. Even though he wrote so few words, they won't be able to stop mulling them over, scouring the recesses of their memories for some clue as to what this secret could be. They'll certainly torture themselves trying to figure it out, wishing they could prise it apart and discover its hidden meaning. But their efforts will be futile; inevitably they'll begin to be apprehensive around me, wary of me; they'll try to figure out what I'm up to, they'll begin to suspect me of something, to consider me an enemy. I soon realized that Chen Erhu couldn't have asked me to bear a greater burden. I thought that if I had been able to see Old Chen on his deathbed, his last words would have been given to me directly – they wouldn't have passed through other people's hands; they'd be mine alone. Even though Ah-bing handed them on to me, I'm sure he did it unwillingly – his desire to know what was being concealed from him proved that. He knew his father had written 'ensure that it remains a secret', and still he had to ask me; his request was as purposeful as it was brazen. What's more, I can't shake the feeling that in the days to come, I'll receive more letters and telephone calls, more requests to know the truth, or perhaps more rudeness. I had no trouble in saying no to Ah-bing, of course, but I can't say the same about future letters and phone calls. These future letters and future calls will eventually come from his older sister.

To be honest, I would much rather be faced with a letter than a phone call.

28 March

Dormitory. Night. Windy.

The letters and phone calls I worried about never came. I knew, however, that I was not yet in the clear. Ah-bing continued to ring me constantly, and judging by his voice on the phone yesterday, he still had high hopes of getting me to give in. If he hasn't given up, he'll be calling in reinforcements in the form of his older sister. Her name is Chen Sisi.

Chen Sisi is tall. A large, dark mole graces her chin, setting off the whiteness of her skin. In my home town we had a saying about people who had this kind of mole: 'A man's mole must draw attention; a woman's must shun it.' This meant that a man with such a mole used it to catch the eye; the more eye-catching it was, the greater his fortune; for a woman, it meant the opposite. That's to say, Chen Sisi's mole was in the wrong place; or rather, it meant that she was an unlucky woman. Good fortune is a mysterious thing; it's difficult to say who has it and who doesn't. As for Chen Sisi, I can't say that I didn't understand her – in truth, she was much like her father: quiet, reticent; she kept things inside; she didn't like to talk much; there was always a modest, shy, bashful smile on her face. To be honest, her silence and bashfulness were quite alluring, so much so that her father, years ago, had been able to see how fond I was of her. As my superior, he was much more gracious, much kinder to me than usual in such a relationship. In a sense, I, too, was his son. He had served for longer than I had been alive, and so tended to treat me with the same affection he showed towards his own children. One day, he asked whether or not I had a girlfriend, to which I answered that I did not. He said he'd like to introduce me to someone. That person was his daughter, Chen Sisi. We ended up dating for about half a year. The relationship really only amounted to a couple of trips to the cinema and one walk through the park. It was during our walk that she said she hoped that our relationship could return to what it was before we had started dating. So that's what we did. I should explain that it wasn't because we didn't love each other that things worked out that way, not at all. We went back to the way things were before, meeting occasionally because of her father. Things remained that way until I left.

I left Unit 701 in the summer of 1983 and came here. Where is here? Well, it's a sub-bureau of the cryptography division. Because this sub-bureau is important – increasingly important as it turns out – some say that we are the second Unit 701, no longer just a sub-bureau. Why did I transfer here? I had two reasons: one was work related, the other personal. My personal reason was that I had just got married and the sub-bureau was much, much closer to the city in which my wife lived than headquarters. As it turned out, I was one of the few people who volunteered to be transferred here; everyone else came pretty unwillingly. I remember that on the night before I left the valley compound, Chen Erhu gave me a commemorative notebook. He had written the following inscription on the flyleaf:

> We both live amongst secrets, some of them we have to use all our efforts to crack, others we have to protect with the same vigour. Our job requires a large amount of luck. My heartfelt good wishes that you will succeed in all your endeavours!

From then on, I felt as though this notebook allowed Chen Erhu to be always by my side. I also felt that there was a particular reason why he had given me the notebook with this specific inscription: he wanted to remind me to keep a 'certain matter' secret. In other words, this notebook served as Chen Erhu's talisman to ensure my silence, no matter how far I might actually be from him. Compared to the frankness of his last words, the inscription on the notebook was much more tactful. At any rate, through frankness or tact, I knew how much 'that matter' meant to him. It was something that had brought Chen Erhu enormous glory as well as lifelong regrets. He was constantly fearful that I would be unable, intentionally or otherwise, to keep it buried, to keep it secret. That was why he took every opportunity to remind me – I understood this. But I couldn't help feeling that his last letter was a miscalculation on his part. First, his previous admonishments were sufficient, he didn't need to emphasize the importance of the situation any further. His method of reinforcing his message, by putting it in his last letter, was wholly inappropriate; he was guilty of protesting too much, of drawing too much attention to it. To be honest, we were the only two who knew about it, no one else did, and no one even asked – that was best. Now, though, how many more Chen Sibings will come asking? Chen Erhu's dying words have peeled away the layers that had surrounded this buried truth, they have shorn it of protection, left it naked and out in the open. I have no idea how many people have seen Old Chen's letter, but I know that each and every one of them, no matter how many, will now try to dig up this secret, something I had kept hidden for so long. They will all try to test my allegiance to Chen Erhu. At present, I am most worried about Chen Sisi: I know that her entreaties will be coming next, and I know she will make unreasonable requests. I'm waiting for her letter or phone call. It's like waiting for my doom.

2 April

Dormitory. Night. Clear.

Chen Sisi's letter arrived even faster than I expected, but now it was here, now I could feel its weight in my hand, I could tell it was no ordinary letter. No doubt its contents included any number of means to dredge up my secret. I kneaded the letter between my fingers for what seemed like forever. I didn't dare open it. Of course, a letter must be read, only . . . I needed to prepare myself for what was inside. To give me strength and to reinforce my defences, I took out Chen Erhu's photo and last words and placed them in front of me. When I finally opened Chen Sisi's letter I had Chen Erhu and his scrawled missive watching over me.

And so I began to read the letter from my former love. Once I had finished reading, however, I discovered that my concerns had all been for naught. From beginning to end, she didn't once mention her father's last words: it was almost as though she knew I was fearful of her raising the issue and so she deliberately did not. I began to suspect that perhaps she was unaware of what was in her father's letter to me, so I telephoned Chen Sibing to ask. He told me that his father had made him promise not to tell a soul what the letter contained, not even his sister. That was how I was finally able to refuse Ah-bing's demands. I told him, 'Your father did this because he knew I wouldn't be able to resist her interrogation, given our previous relationship, and so he deliberately concealed the situation from her.'

Once Ah-bing had listened to my explanation, he seemed to come to some kind of conclusion. He sighed and said, 'So that's how it is.' Then he hung up. I knew he wouldn't ask me about the secret again. That was good. Very good.

The only thing I didn't expect was how long Sisi's letter was. Over eighteen pages, every page filled out completely, not like a letter at all. Looking at it, seeing the slight changes in handwriting, it was easy to see that she had written it over several days, the final day being the twenty-fifth of March, the same day I received the first phone call from her brother. Its contents read more like a novel than a letter. You could say that the pages were soaked with emotion; the narrative was exciting and very moving.

The Letter: Day One

... A red enclosure, its wall are high, wire netting adorns the top, two large, black iron doors forever closed, the opening is a window that looks very much like a small iron door, armed sentinels march back and forth, they ask for identification from whoever they see. When I was small, I and the other children would steal out of the compound and into the mountain. Standing outside the iron gates, we'd watch as the grown-ups would walk up to the doors and disappear inside. We thought we'd take a look inside the grounds, but none of us were permitted inside and no one told us why. Once I'd grown up, I understood. I knew that my father dealt in secrets, and so what was behind those red walls was also a secret: no ID meant no admittance.

Even to this day we're still not sure what the actual nature and content of our father's work was, but considering the amount of respect everyone in the organization accorded him, I believe that the work he did was vital, and no doubt very arduous, very exhausting. When my mother was still alive, she used to nag him to retire early because she could see how the work was draining him of life. As every year passed he looked older and more feeble. I often used to wonder when my father would be able to stop working, when he would be able to leave those red walls behind, to be a normal man and live a normal life. The year after you were transferred, 1984 it would've been, that day finally came. He was already sixty-five years old; he should have retired years earlier.

After his retirement, I thought he would be able to live a quiet, relaxing, normal life, to live in ease and comfort – I thought we would be happier than ever before. Perhaps you don't know, but since my father's life had revolved around work, he didn't much care for family life and he didn't show much concern for us. But our feelings for him were deep and real. We never complained that he spent little of his time with us. In truth, we understood him, supported him, respected him. We believed that his golden years would be filled with happiness because, up until now, he'd known only work. In order to give him something to do after his retirement, we planted a flower garden round the house and began to raise a few birds and fish. Once the holidays came, we took him to see our relatives and also for strolls in the park. At the time, Ah-bing hadn't yet begun his graduate studies and he didn't talk much about girls. I just wanted him to keep Father company and not to burden him with his own personal concerns. That's what he did. The two of them would just chat about trivial things and go for walks together, all very relaxing. Ah-bing was raised by our maternal grandmother. Afterwards he performed his mandatory military service, and then went to university. So you could say that the relationship between father and son was rather cold and distant. Now that they were often together, I worried at first that they would have difficulties talking and getting along with each other, but I soon realized that my worries were groundless. They got along marvellously, much better than I had expected. Afterwards, I thought this might be because they had never had much to do with one another before: they were like two long-lost friends getting re-acquainted with one another. They always seemed to have something to talk about, and they'd talk and talk for hours non-stop. For the first little while after his retirement, everyone was incredibly happy.

But it didn't last. A month later, perhaps less, Father had grown tired and annoyed with this kind of purposeless life. He had no patience to look at flowers; he couldn't be bothered to watch his birds; and it seemed as though he and Ah-bing had exhausted all topics of conversation. His temperament changed: he became gruff and unpleasant to be around. Without provocation, he'd let loose a litany of complaints – hurling insults at this, blaming that – it was as if everything in our house exhausted him, tormented him, made him uncomfortable. Now, whatever we said or whatever we did seemed to displease him. Even when we tried to get close to him, he'd become upset and wave his hands, shouting at us to go away. In such a short period of time, life had become a burden to him, something unbearable. He would spend the whole day shut up in his room, reduced to a shadow of his former self as he paced up and down. Needless to say, it made all of us feel terribly worried. I should say that Father never used to be so temperamental, so unpredictable and difficult to please. He never used to make unreasonable demands on anyone, but now he seemed to be a complete stranger. He was pernickety, harsh, peremptory, violent and unreasonable. One day – I don't know whether someone had said something to him – he suddenly went wild. He went out onto the balcony and tore open the bird cages, releasing them into the air, and then he set about smashing all the flowerpots, one after another. A month before this, he seemed to like his birds and his flowers very much, but now he had turned against them. Father seemed to get bored with his toys like a child, but the problem is that he wasn't a child. Every day he'd get up incredibly early, but he wouldn't go anywhere, he wouldn't do anything, he wouldn't open his mouth. From morning till night, he'd mope about looking discouraged and dejected. He'd sigh, he'd get angry, he'd stare blankly at nothing. He gave the impression of a man at the end of his tether.

One day, I noticed that he'd spent ages just standing on the balcony, a blank expression on his face. Several times I asked if he'd like to go for a walk, and each time he rudely refused. I asked him what he was thinking – if there was something making him unhappy, or if he needed us to do something for him. He uttered not a sound; he just stood there looking sad – pathetic, really – not moving a muscle, like a wooden puppet without a puppet master. The winter sun slowly worked its way over his body, illuminating his head of grey hair, giving it a shining brilliance. I walked up to the balcony window and looked out. You can easily imagine the look on his face in that moment – it was an expression absolutely familiar to me: his face was taut, deep lines were etched across his forehead, his eyes had a vacant quality about them – unmoving, they seemed to be embedded within sagging eye sockets from which they could, at any moment, come loose and fall silently to the ground. But if you looked attentively at that empty mask, if you looked beyond the spectre of death hanging about it, you could see under the surface the confusion he felt, the restlessness, the sense of expectation for something that would never come, the utter despondency.

Father's moods made him seem a stranger, and yet he remained familiar. This often made me very unhappy. In the beginning, we thought that the reason he did not wish to go to the old people's recreation centre was that he didn't like the atmosphere there, so we asked some of his old comrades-in-arms to come and pay him a visit. But even after these friends arrived, Father remained cold and indifferent; no friendship was rekindled. After a few commonplace remarks and some unwelcoming looks, he managed to get rid of them pretty quickly. It soon became obvious to us that Father was friendless, and that this was mostly his own doing. When he was dying I noticed that the only people who came to pay their final respects were a few senior officials from that red-walled compound and our relatives; no one else. The only person he wanted to see was you; you were perhaps his only friend, if you could call your relationship with him friendship. My father must have got along poorly with the people in his work unit. I wondered how this happened. What was it that made him keep people at a distance? Was it honour? Or character? Was it the work? What made him so solitary, so bad at normal relationships? What was it that left him friendless, can you tell me? Ah, forget it. Perhaps it's better if you don't tell me. But let me tell you why he was unable to enjoy his golden years, unable to live out his days happily as other old people do.

One day, even though it was after dark, Father had not come home for dinner. We went out to look for him, scouring the whole area. We finally found him out by those red walls. He was sitting next to the iron gates, alone, the ground around him littered with cigarette butts. According to the guard, he'd spent the afternoon sitting there. He had shown the guard his ID, but knew that he would not be permitted inside, so he had just sat there like that – and yet to look at him, he seemed at ease, peaceful. He just couldn't let go of his former life behind those red walls! He just couldn't let go of the work! I knew then why he had been unable to enjoy retirement. His heart had remained within those walls; it had remained with all those mysteries and secrets. Nothing else could steal it away: he was infatuated with the place, with the work. He'd been intoxicated by what went on behind the walls; his heart had become divorced from the world outside the compound. This special work, this oh-so-secretive career, had required him to sever all connections with the real world. It was as though he had been confined within a web of secrecy. Year after year the outside world and its inhabitants grew ever more remote until finally they ceased to exist for him. To make him leave this world of secrets, to suddenly force him out of that red-walled compound – well, what he saw, what he heard, what he felt could only mean nothing to him. It was all so unrelated and alien to him; snippets of a life he had long since abandoned. As a result, everything bored him. It was all so meaningless. It was an ossified form of life, unendurable. You could say this is the attitude of a 'company man': for such a person normal life is fragmentary, superfluous, pointless. I remember General Patton once said, 'There's only one proper way for a professional soldier to die: the last bullet of the last battle of the war.' I think my father's sorrow stemmed from this. He hadn't been felled by some bullet fired from within those red towering walls. The last bullet never found him.

Oh, Father, why do we call them your golden years! Today, here, describing your last days to your only friend, I can't help but feel how terrible those days were for you. How difficult it is for me to put this down on paper. Right now I have only written the beginning, but I already feel that I can't go on, my heart weeps. I want to forget everything, I don't want to remember it . . . but I am your daughter. And I think your friend deserves to understand, deserves to know you, the real you. It is only by seeing your end that he can understand the rest of your life. Your last years were so painful . . .

Day Two

Once he was fed up with tending to his flowers, for nearly two months he simply did nothing but sit upon the sofa, always with a dejected look on his face, his body slumped over, smoking cigarette after cigarette, punctuated only by fits of coughing. At the same time his health began to deteriorate and his blood pressure soared. It went as high as 200/90 when normally it'd stand at around 160/90; it really worried everyone. Then he developed chronic bronchitis: he'd cough and cough, so loud it seemed that the earth shook and the mountains trembled. For certain this was caused by all the heavy smoking he had been doing recently. Father's love of tobacco had always been quite serious: normally two packs a day wouldn't be enough, but during his retirement, he smoked even more, lighting one cigarette after another. We tried to tell him he should cut down, to which he replied that he bought his cigarettes with his own money, not ours, and so it was none of our business. Later we heard that he had been repeatedly contacting the work-unit supervisor requesting to be reinstated, to be permitted back inside those red walls. His requests were always denied. I couldn't help but think all his requests must be becoming an annoyance to the authorities, and I was right. One day, Director Wang came to speak to me. He implored us to think of some way to deal with the situation, to find some way to placate Father so that he'd no longer bother them. I wanted to ask him what he thought we'd been doing. Nothing? We'd already tried everything we could think of; we'd exhausted ourselves trying to make him happy, all to no avail.

Some time later, one day in winter, Father had finished his dinner and, as usual, planted himself down on the sofa with his cigarettes. Bluish-grey smoke soon began to billow out from his mouth and nose like a spirit exiting its mortal shell. The haze blanketed the room with a heavy, suffocating shroud. Everyone became tense and nervous, fearful even, which only provoked Father's bad temper even more. Ah-bing turned on the TV, hoping to find a programme that would catch his attention. Once the screen flickered on, the image of a *go* board came into view. Black and white pieces appeared. They seemed to be scattered across a white wall in a disordered manner. A man and a woman seemed to be demonstrating various strategies. To the uninitiated it would have seemed deeply mysterious. Ah-bing, however, was addicted to *go* and so was drawn to the image on the television screen. I, too, enjoyed the game (mostly because of Ah-bing's influence), but I thought Father wouldn't be interested and would yell at him to change the channel. Ah-bing turned round to look at Father. His eyes were narrowed, his face blank; he looked to be overcome with boredom. Ah-bing asked whether or not he wanted to watch this, but Father seemed not to hear him, nor did he answer. When Ah-bing changed the channel, he told Ah-bing to go back to the *go* game. It seemed as though he hadn't heard his son's earlier question. As the *go* game flickered back on, Father asked Ah-bing what game it was. It was *go*, he said, and then explained the basic rules. Father listened to the explanation, but made no response. His face remained expressionless. He just sat there, watching the programme until it finished.

On the following day at the same time, Father watched another lecture on *go*, but this time something was different – his face had a different look to it. He watched the programme intently, concentrating on what was being said; his mind seemed to be going over the intricacies of the game. I asked him if he understood what they were talking about, whereupon he challenged me to a game; this surprised me so much that it took some time for me to respond. Even though I'm a pretty average player, I believed I'd be much better than my father. After all, he didn't even really seem to understand the game. As we began, Ah-bing came and stood next to Father, prepared to assist him if necessary. In the beginning, he was happy to let Ah-bing give him instructions, but before long he stopped listening to him; he said he wanted to play the game by himself. He was quite slow in making his moves; each one seemed to require an inordinate amount of time and consideration. When he finally shifted a stone, he did so in quite an unorthodox manner. Given his illogical moves, he seemed to be heading for sure defeat, but by the time the game reached the halfway point, both Ah-bing and I were stunned. A moment ago his manoeuvres seemed to lack precision and skill, but now he went on the offensive. In a series of strange and eccentric moves he began to put pressure on me, harassing my stones, forcing me to slow my pace and think more deeply about each and every piece. I soon discovered that it would be difficult for me to regain the initiative. He was advancing with every move and consolidating his position. There seemed to be fewer and fewer avenues open for me to break through the stranglehold he was building. I had no idea what move to make.

On the one hand, Father pressured my every move – he closed in on me, cut me off and besieged my pieces. Although he was greatly stretching his forces, he continued his relentless attack. He was tenacious, unyielding. Nevertheless, all his moves seemed to be part of a larger plan; a plan I could not discern. I was at a loss. His intentions remained hidden, and yet he carried them out ingeniously; danger seemed to be all around me. The board changed repeatedly: black and white stones crisscrossed each other, forming strange, bizarre patterns; the battle for dominance was increasingly bitter and hard-fought, and I began to doubt and question my every move. Then the endgame arrived. Father played his advantage, but – perhaps because he was too anxious for victory, I don't know – he managed to grab only one of my stones whilst I took several of his. Later, although he had exhausted his strategy, he hit out in all directions, striving to regain the initiative, fighting against his impending doom, but it was all for nothing. This is how our first game ended. Father lost by three pieces.

But he didn't lose the rematch.

We played three more games. Father won them all, each one more easily than the last. Our final game ended before I had even played half of it. Afterwards, Father played Ah-bing. In total seven games. The result was the same: Ah-bing won the first match before losing the next six. I thought: just a few days ago, Father was completely ignorant of the game, he didn't even know the squares from the circles, but in the blink of an eye he seemed to have mastered it – he had destroyed the two of us. We were both left speechless.

On the following day, Ah-bing invited over a fellow *go* enthusiast. They belonged to the same work unit. Ah-bing's friend was a more accomplished *go* player. Generally, Ah-bing was able to take two of his stones, but nothing more. I remember that day clearly. The sky was crystal clear. There was a freshness in the air that had come with the newly fallen snow. It had been the first major snowfall of winter, and the hurried and sudden blast of cold had covered the landscape with a soft blanket of whiteness. I should say, it was an absolutely perfect day to play *go*. In the first match, Father started poorly and by his twentieth move he knew he would lose. I don't know if you are familiar with *go* or not, but you need to understand one thing: to realize that you have already lost shortly after beginning is not something an ordinary player is capable of.

Do you know the ancient parable, 'Defeat or Victory in Nine Moves'? It's the story of an ancient chess master by the name of Zhao Qiao who travelled over land and sea, over the entire realm, all in search of a worthy opponent. Finally, on the banks of the River Wei, at the foot of Phoenix Mountain, he encountered a woman with long, glistening black hair. The woman's husband had enlisted in the army and was far away at the frontier. Her house was barren and empty, without even a bowl of rice, and she made a living by playing *go*. So by the banks of the river and in the shadow of the mountain, the two sat down to play. After Zhao had made nine moves, the woman conceded defeat and began to gather in her pieces. Zhao did not believe her, and so the woman explained: each game of *go* is quite clear and logical, from up in the mountains water begins to flow, unceasingly it makes its way down, but there is only one outcome. Zhao listened to her explanation and humbly conceded defeat: the woman was his master. In other words, since Father was able to determine the outcome of the game after his first nineteen moves, it meant he possessed a far-reaching insight; he was able to see across and into the board. I realized then that the man who had come to play him would ultimately lose, for the most important ability when playing *go*, regardless of the quality of the opposition, is to be able to see your moves in advance, to know what you are going to do before you do it. As expected, Father won the next five matches. Ah-bing's friend couldn't believe it when we told him it was only last night that Father had learnt how to play.

I think I can say that Father's sensitivity for the game was amazing. It was like . . . love at first sight. They seemed to share an implicit mutual understanding. The game of *go* saved my father, and helped us immeasurably. For a long time after this, Father was fascinated with everything related to it. If he wasn't reading some book or other on the game, he would be searching for an opponent. His life was finally satisfying; he was his old, vigorous self again. People's minds are not easy to understand . . . We had expended so much energy and thought on trying to solve Father's problems, without success, but then, in one night, everything seemed to be resolved – all because of a game.

In the beginning, he spent most of his time playing against opponents who lived within the neighbourhood, usually in the work unit's recreation centre. It was there that you could find the *go* enthusiasts. Some were quite accomplished players, others not so much. Father played each of them, one by one. About a month later he had gone through the ranks; there was no one who had not conceded defeat. Of course, there were any number of *go* masters still to be challenged, but those types of players would never come to play in such a place. I mean, really, what would they do there? They'd easily tire of the social niceties and interactions of such a place, much preferring the peace of their own homes – hidden away, as it were. This is what happened to Father; he turned into one of those *go* players. You could say that it was the recreation centre that had forged him, and had broadened his understanding of the game, but the level of play at the centre never changed, and now Father was unable to find a suitable opponent – no one matched his ability, or presented a challenge to him. What's the fun in playing *go* without a worthy opponent? Victory now meant nothing to him, it held no appeal; and thus there was no need to go to the recreation centre. It was then that he began to venture out into the garrison town to find an adversary, someone to measure his abilities against. But even before the warm breezes of summer arrived, there was no one in the town who had not suffered defeat at his hands. It took him only six months to become the best-known and most feared *go* player in the area!

Afterwards, Ah-bing and myself, as well as my husband (you can call him Little Lü), would often go into the city to find an opponent for Father. Once we found someone, we'd invite them over and arrange a game. That's how we satisfied Father's love for *go*; satisfied his addiction. Even though this was a tiresome task, once we saw Father absorbed in the game, fascinated by it, we felt nothing but happiness. At the beginning, the search for adversaries was somewhat annoying, mostly because we had to rely on other people's introductions, and so the range of abilities of these opponents was extremely large, the good mixed in with the bad. Some, for instance, had quite a reputation, but a very limited outlook, and even less ability. They were very difficult to convince to come round, and when they did, they often left angry . . . their abilities were just no match for Father's. Later, Ah-bing was able to arrange, on the recommendation of a friend of a friend's father who happened to be head of the membership committee, for Father to become a member of the local *Go* Association. From then on we were able to invite over a load of opponents, some highly skilled, others not so much.

The *Go* Association had a membership of about thirty or forty people. These were the most highly proficient players in the city. Amongst them, there was a small group that had achieved a 5th *dan* ranking. These were the city's champions. They were all exceptionally seasoned players who played with style and sophistication; they were like silent killing machines waiting in the darkness. To them, Father was, at most, a beginner who demonstrated some talent. As you can imagine, the first match ended in disaster; Father was shattered like an egg smashing against a rock. But that wasn't the end of it – something rather strange happened, practically unbelievable, really! The best player in the group wanted to do battle with Father, so the board was set up. But things didn't turn out as expected. Whilst the match began with him employing his superior skill, Father quite quickly began to catch up, began to take his stones, and eventually surpassed him, by a large margin in fact. Facing such superior opponents, it was perhaps to be expected that Father would lose quite a few games, but it wasn't long before he began transforming every defeat into victory, ultimately becoming an unbeatable opponent. It was as though in the span of a single night Father's *go* skills had grown by leaps and bounds. Yesterday he was easy to beat, but today he was invincible. The truth was, basically, no one could challenge Father, at least not for long. Quite a few well-known *go* players did pay him visits, and for more than a couple of weeks, Father would be continuously locked in battle with these adversaries. In most instances, the expert players would win the first match, they'd be the lords and masters of the game, but the result always turned out the same: without exception, they would all lose to Father in the end. Father truly was a formidable player; eventually every opponent would fall against him. It practically became routine! Later on, Father would often say, every time he began a match with a new opponent, he'd never worry about defeating them, he was only ever concerned about them defeating him. Father understood that it was getting difficult for us to find him a challenger, especially if they had no chance of winning. Not only did this depress us, but it also greatly annoyed him. He always longed for a challenge. He loved coming face to face with an imposing enemy and then destroying them, conquering them – giving his all to achieve victory. He couldn't stand not being able to find a worthy foe; not being able to play a game of *go* that didn't already have a foregone conclusion. And so, as with the tediousness of normal life, he soon began to grow weary of the game.

I remember it was in the afternoon of the day before the Mid-Autumn Festival. I was on the balcony reading, Father was playing *go* with the city's champion player in the living room – they played game after game, from early midday until late in the evening. Throughout the afternoon, over and over again, I heard them begin a game and then finish, and then start a new one. The conversation between them was brief, but I could hear that Father was winning. Occasionally I stepped into the living room to refresh their drinks. Father's expression was always calm and level-headed as he sipped at a bowl of tea or smoked a cigarette – he was happy, joyful even. The champion, on the other hand, smoked not one cigarette, nor did he drink a single bowl of tea. Both his eyes were glued to the *go* board, and there was hatred and vengeance upon his face. He was unyielding, determined to struggle on. He gritted his teeth, occasionally reaching out his hand to grasp a piece, and then suspending that hand in the air, the stone wedged between his fingers. It didn't seem like a *go* stone at all, but rather a bomb. Should he put it down or not? And where? These were the questions he struggled with. He was cautious, careful, hesitant. His consternation was obvious, his face contorted, resolute; his entire body seemed to be dedicated to making the correct move. In contrast, Father was a picture of serenity, peacefulness, calmness; it looked as though his train of thought had already left the game in front of him – already flown off into the ether. Later I heard them conclude the match, and then the champion spoke. 'How about another game?'

I heard my father's reply; it was firm and peremptory. 'It's like this – if we play another game, I'll have to start with a handicap and I don't like playing that kind of game.'

This was how Father rudely ended all possibilities of a rematch, by saying that he had no desire to inflict defeat upon yet another opponent. Needless to say, his form of curt refusal drove people mad. What's more, in this case, the opponent was a revered champion *go* player. As he left he fired off these words at me: 'Your father is a *go* prodigy, there's no one he cannot defeat.'

That's what the champion said. There's no one Father cannot defeat.

As you can imagine, there was no one in this city who could challenge my father.

No one!

Absolutely no one!

Speaking of this, I can't help but feel that Father was a stranger to me, mysterious, imponderable. Perhaps you want to ask, was all of this real? I tell you it was, every word. All true. And, yet . . . I can't help but have my suspicions that perhaps it wasn't . . . it's just so unbelievable, beyond the realms of possibility.

Day Three

. . . It's mid-afternoon, but my three co-workers still have not arrived. Perhaps they won't be coming. It's raining outside – maybe that's why. I guess there's some logic to it . . . However, thinking of my father: what would have served as a legitimate reason for him not to report to work? As far as I can remember, Father never once failed to enter that red-walled compound. Not once. Occasionally we'd ask him to take the day off – Mother needed him, there was some family emergency; he had to stay at home, at least for half a day. On those occasions Father would halt mid-step and stand still for a moment, mulling it over. We'd look at him, trying to use our eyes to implore him to stay. But he wouldn't look at us, he'd deliberately avoid our eyes; he'd look at his watch or stare off into space, hesitating, deciding whether to go or stay . . . it was a difficult choice it seemed. Nearly every time we would mistakenly believe that perhaps on this occasion he would stay, and we would walk up to him and take the permit from his hand, reach for the hat he held in order to hang it up. But just as we reached for it, Father would seem to make up his mind; he'd take back the permit and say firmly, 'No, I have to go.'

It was always like that.

His reasons for refusing were always simple and effective – impervious to argument. Even though we would use any number of excuses to implore him to stay, none of them worked. Even when Mum's illness became really serious, when she had only a few days left with us, Father still wouldn't spend those last remaining days by her side.

My mother died of that illness. Perhaps you didn't know – it happened the year before you arrived, that would've been 1972. Thinking back, her symptoms developed quite early on, during the Spring Festival of that year. Without warning, her stomach would cause her terrible pain. At the time, we didn't think much of it, nor did she – I guess she thought it was just a passing problem. She'd drink a bowl of warm, sweet water and take a couple of aspirin. Once the pain subsided she'd forget about it; it would be business as usual and she'd head off to work. I heard that her career had begun in some provincial office or other. Then, once she married Father, she transferred to this work unit . . . but it wasn't Unit 701 proper, it was somewhere else, several kilometres away. She would ride her bicycle back and forth every day. She also took us to and from school, cooked our meals, washed our clothes – for years it was the same. To be honest, the way I saw it, Mum was the only person that kept the family together. Father did nothing. You know, our house was only about two or three kilometres away from the red-walled compound, about thirty minutes on foot, but Father rarely came home; at most once a month, and even then it would be late at night when he'd arrive and he would leave early the next morning. I remember one evening – we hadn't seen Father for ages, and we were at the table having dinner . . . My mother's ears were like her eyes. Father was still some distance away, and we didn't hear anything, but Mum's ears were sensitive to his approach. She turned to us and said, 'Your Dad's back.' As she spoke she put down her bowl and chopsticks and went into the kitchen to prepare for his arrival. We thought she was imagining things – hallucinating – but as she came out of the kitchen with a bowl of warmed water for him to wash his face, Father's heavy footsteps sounded at the door . . .

When he was at home, Father rarely spoke. His face and eyes were cold, and he didn't seem like someone's husband, let alone a father. He never once sat down and chatted with us, and on those rare occasions when he did speak, it always sounded like a command – he never minced his words. Whenever he was home, the whole house became tense and nervous; we all felt like we were walking on eggshells. We would lower our voices, fearful of upsetting him. If we did upset him – cause him to get angry, to curse at us – Mum would enter the fray and reprimand us, not him. She was always on his side. Don't you think that was strange? I think

I can safely say that, as a husband, Father's life was much happier than most other men's. Mum's life was devoted to his. If it seemed as though his life had been given to the red-walled compound, then surely her life was his – given to this man who had been bewitched by something she could never understand!

I've never been able to comprehend life or the things around me according to logic. To everyone else around us, it seemed natural that my mother belonged to my father; but they didn't marry because of love, they married because of 'revolutionary necessity'. Mum said that for everyone in Father's work unit, the organization decided whom they would marry. Potential partners had their political, social and family backgrounds vetted by the intelligence service; their present and past circumstances were thoroughly investigated. This was how Mum married Father: it was arranged by the Party. She was only twenty-two but Father was already past thirty. Mum also told me that she had met him only once before they actually married. They had spoken very little, perhaps only a sentence or two. I can imagine that Father must have been terribly embarrassed the time they first met; he probably didn't dare look her in the face. I guess you could say that once outside those red walls, he was simply a man who didn't know where to put his hands and feet. He didn't come from the real world; he came from somewhere else – a special laboratory, outer space, some dark, hidden corner. If you forced him out past those red walls and into the real world, into the world under the sun and blue sky, he'd be like a fish out of water; he'd be all out of sorts, a sorry wretch of a man – this was something we could all imagine. But there was something we couldn't understand: a month after they met, Mum married him. She believed in the intelligence service, more than she believed in her own parents. I heard that at the beginning, my grandmother had not been in favour of the marriage, but her husband had. He was an old Red soldier, an orphan at birth, a revolutionary by fourteen; the Party had raised him, educated him, given him a family, a fortunate life. Not only did he feel thankful to the Party with all his heart, but he wanted his children to feel the same, to consider the Party and the intelligence service more important than parents, more important than family. And so my Mum, from very early on, had complete faith in the organization. If they said that Father was a great man, she believed them. If they said he was exceptional, she believed that, too. So they got married. It wasn't for love; it was for the Party, for the revolution. You could say that she married him out of political responsibility . . . If Mum could hear me speak like this she'd be angry, so let's forget about it.

By May of 1972, my mother's stomach pain was much more severe. She'd often be in so much pain that she couldn't get out of bed. She'd just lie there, her whole body covered in sweat. At the time, Ah-bing was away completing his military service and I had been sent down to the countryside. Although it wasn't too far away – just a neighbouring county, about a hundred-kilometre round trip – I couldn't go home often. Just once a month, and only for one night at a time. As a result, I really didn't know she was so ill. My father was worse: he didn't have a clue. I don't want to say that he didn't know Mum was ill, it's just that he probably wouldn't even have realized if he was ill himself, to say nothing of the fact that she deliberately concealed it from him. Just think: she spent her whole life being concerned about us, but when she needed our concern, none of us were there for her. But Mum just continued to look after us, to make sure the three of us were fine, always busy . . . How could she find time to look after herself? There was no room in her heart for herself; we had already occupied it completely. This was a woman who had grown up with an old Red Army soldier for a father, who had been taught to love the Party and the intelligence service more than her own parents. My mother loved us as a parent ought to love her children, real human love, but she was unable to love herself. Mum, how tired and exhausted you must've been in such a dysfunctional family! You were seriously ill, and yet you concealed it from us – you lied to us. You seemed guilt-ridden, as though you had done something wrong. Mum, I realize now that you and Father were cut from the same cloth: you both had no place for yourselves, you were buried within your faith and idealism – but all it did was drain your blood, drop by drop, until nothing was left. And yet, both of you were satisfied with your lot in life, both of you were happy.

But you couldn't know – nobody can – that in our hearts is buried an endless amount of remorse and guilt!

Finally, I discovered that she was ill. I had just returned from the countryside one evening. It was already late, the house was dark and the lights had been turned off. I turned on a lamp and noticed my mother's bedroom door was ajar, but she didn't come out to greet me as usual. I called out but there was no answer. All I heard was the quiet sound of someone moving about. I went into her room, turned on the light and saw Mum squatting down on the floor, her head propped up against the bed frame. Her face was distorted with pain, it was unnatural-looking. Tears streamed down her cheeks, her hair was a tangled mess. I rushed over to her. She grabbed me and immediately began to weep like a child. I asked her what was wrong. She cried out in a choked voice that she was dying. She called out again, asking me to take her to the hospital. Her tears and sweat glittered under the light of the lamp. I'd never seen Mum cry out in pain before. I had never seen her in such a state – her body had gone limp like vegetable leaves wilted by a frost. In the dusky glow emanating from the lamp, she looked like a mass of wrinkled clothes. The following day the doctor told me that my mother was suffering from liver cancer, already in its terminal stages – there was simply nothing that could be done.

To be honest, to write this hurts . . . it hurts so much! I was never willing to talk about it before, but talking about it now . . . I somehow feel a little better. I think, it doesn't matter if Mum was somehow a part of Father; it seems as though we all belonged somehow to that red-walled compound, we are all somehow a part of it. Mum was Father's wife, but she was also his comrade-in-arms; she had given her whole life to him. When I light an incense stick in memory of him, I must remember to light one for her as well, and to cry . . .

Day Four

Darkness has already shrouded the courtyard, but still the smells and sounds of it creep in past the metal window frame. The glow from the lamp is soft and indeterminate, it illuminates my mood. Staring at the draft paper next to the lamp, I notice that at some point it had become a *kifu*, a record of *go* games. An image of Father appears in my mind – his hand seems to move in and out from the shadows in a confused way. He longed to play a game of *go* again.

But who could play with him?

By the autumn of 1985, Father's skill at *go* had surpassed all boundaries, and we could no longer find a willing partner to challenge him to a game. Because his reputation had spread beyond our town, occasionally uninvited guests would come in search of him – but as we expected, not only did their arrival not make Father happy, it actually often made him angry. Unimaginably angry; furious even. He had no desire to engage in a match of *go* with these average players and he abhorred the idea of letting them win. Could anyone still consider Father to be anything other than remarkable? No one. For over a year now, Father had immersed himself in studying the game, in learning its various techniques; he clearly understood its mysteries. He had competed with connoisseurs from all directions, and had learnt by constantly comparing notes with them and engaging them in battle. These contests had forged his talent, and he had reached an incredibly high level, at least for this city.

But our inability to find him an opponent meant he wasn't able to play the game. So his life relapsed into one of dejected boredom. He had become trapped again – the danger of intellectual decrepitude lurked everywhere. Again we had to think of ways to keep him occupied, to give him something to do. We thought of travel, calligraphy, painting, qigong, t'ai chi – anything that might make him take an interest. But nothing worked. He was once more cold and detached – we were terribly discouraged. Once, a qigong teacher arrived in our residential area and many people decided to learn t'ai chi. I doggedly urged him to attend, for days, then a week; finally he agreed to study with a group of elderly people, about thirty men and women. Occasionally I went along with him and practised the moves, but even though Father had been going every day, and studying constantly, he still couldn't perform the most basic moves – his movements were all over the place. He'd remember the first part of a move and then forget the final part; it was completely infuriating. Needless to say, his performance demonstrated his clumsiness. He seemed to be two different people: one a sublimely skilled *go* player possessed of immeasurable intelligence; the other, a clumsy old man unable to master the most basic moves of t'ai chi. It was quite bizarre. On the one hand he was a superman, a man of towering intelligence and skill; on the other, he was incorrigibly obstinate, slow-witted – nothing more than a drone. He was a man easily stuck in a rut, pigeon-holed into one particular thing that he couldn't extricate himself from – so in a sense he was very limited. The only thing I had misgivings about was this: what was it, exactly, that allowed him to display such remarkable skill in the game of *go*? Was he truly a talented player who understood the game inside out, or was there some other reason for his success?

In my experience, *go* is a kind of test: it can uncover a person's hitherto untapped abilities. There is a grim difference if it's compared with other forms of chess. Chinese chess, for instance, is a more involving game that requires a greater number of pieces, but *go* is more complicated, more mysterious – sublime. There is no particular property for each stone in *go*; they can all perform the same function. They can be a general or a soldier – it all depends on where you place them and how you move them. Everything depends upon the player's knowledge and skill, or lack thereof. Chinese chess is different – chariot, cannon, horse, all have their unique qualities: the chariot can move orthogonally, but it can't leap over intervening pieces; the cannon can capture opposing pieces, but only by leaping over them; the horse moves orthogonally and then diagonally, but it cannot jump; the elephant moves two points diagonally to capture its opponent, and it, too, cannot jump; the soldier must advance straight towards the river, but once past it, can move diagonally to capture an opponent – but there is no retreat for the soldier. These differences, which are really limitations, mean that playing Chinese chess is comparatively easy, and not particularly profound. But the situation in *go* is entirely different. You could say that for Chinese chess there is a limit concerning the skill and intelligence involved, and that the opposite is true for *go*: the nature of its challenge is limitless. No stone has a particular property; its power comes from its placement on the board, and, in certain places, that power can be exceptional. Consequently, *go* requires you to have a special ability to combine things – to structure things to your advantage. You must provide the stones with the place at which they can be most effective; you must strive to connect them, to link them all together, and the connections must grow – only by growing can they survive. But this combinatorial style is also without limit: there is no set form, or rather, the form is formless. This limitlessness is sublime, alluring, imaginative – it is almost an intelligence. Victory or defeat does not depend on crafty tricks or random chance: the game is an intense battle of wits and insight, it's a contest, a challenge. The game strengthens one's character. The laurels of victory rest upon wisdom and intelligence, a resoluteness of character. For those who have a talent for the game, their powers of imagination, of perception, patience and technique are similar to those of mathematicians, poets and composers; the only difference is in how they combine these skills to create. The amazing ability that Father demonstrated in playing *go*, the unfathomable manner by which he achieved victory, as well as his obvious disdain for social niceties, his arrogant pride, aloofness, eccentricity and unwillingness to lose were not only puzzling to us, but to all those opponents who came one after another. They also couldn't seem to grasp what he was all about; how he was able to win game after game.

It's obvious that explaining the phenomenon of Father's *go* ability as random chance is dissatisfying, but then, what else can explain his incredible prowess? Naturally, I must consider that mysterious world behind the red walls. To me, that compound was the strangest place in the world. For all those years it monopolized my vision, day and night. It possessed my mind, but never once did it let me look on it. Its walls were built high, its security was terrifying, its secrets concealed: it was a place entirely unknowable. I don't know, nor can I know what kind of secret work Father did behind those red walls, but I couldn't help but feel that somehow his work was intimately related to the game of *go*, that there was some sublime connection between them. That is to say that *go* perhaps played some part in his secret work, and through karma it had found him after he had been expelled from those red walls. And just like the work behind those ramparts, *go* didn't allow you to just dabble with it: once you became involved, you'd be in thrall to it, just as he was to his work. Because this was an addiction, his body was not his own . . .

Day Five

Father was an amazing *go* player. His skill had grown faster than anyone could have hoped for. By the following autumn, there were no opponents left for him, and yet he still seated himself in front of the *go* board, waiting for his dream challenger to arrive. He believed that within the tens of thousands of people who lived in this district there had to be some who possessed consummate skill in the game. Perhaps they were living in seclusion in some unknown corner of the city; perhaps one day they would get wind of the fact that in this corner there lived a *go* player of immeasurable skill, and they would race over to engage in combat. But month after month passed and the only people who came to seek him out could not be considered true equals, true challengers – in fact, they hadn't come to fight him at all but rather to learn from him. Watching Father at these times, you could see he felt no cautious modesty.

Generally those who came were strangers, people he hadn't played against before, so he usually looked quite pleased and happy, at least at first. After a couple of games, however, his face would transform: he'd become silent and that familiar and expert look of dissatisfaction would appear. At times, his opponent's level would simply be too low and so he would berate them, exasperated by their overall inability – it was very embarrassing. They all left feeling really upset, and I realized that the numbers of people showing up to learn from Father would become fewer and fewer; and so Father's chances of finding a truly worthy opponent would likewise grow slimmer and slimmer – perhaps impossible. At that point I talked things over with Ah-bing, and advised him to plan to do his graduate studies in the provincial capital. I even thought if he eventually went off to study there, we could move the whole family to the provincial capital. That would have pleased Little Lü as well, since his parents lived in the capital. To tell you the truth, though, I didn't think of this for Little Lü, I thought of it for Father. I thought perhaps he could find new challengers in the provincial capital – that there were bound to be more worthy opponents there than here. In fact, that's why Ah-bing decided to go to graduate school. But by the time he was preparing for his final undergraduate exams two years later, Father would no longer seem to have a reason to go to the provincial capital . . .

One afternoon, a man came round to play *go*. They played five matches and, quite unexpectedly, Father failed to win a single game. This had never happened before. At first, we mistakenly believed that this man had played extraordinarily well, so we didn't give it much thought. In fact, we thought it was incredibly fortunate; we thought that Father would now be able to satisfy his addiction to the game. But over the next few weeks, Father continued to lose every game he played, no matter who came to see him. He lost again and again, match after match. It seemed the lustre of previous times had gone. Of course, these people then went out and told everyone they could find that they had beaten Father. At first no one believed them, so there was one telephone call after another asking if it were true. We told them that, yes, Father had lost, and they all felt it was most peculiar, especially since those who had now beaten him were terribly undistinguished players. As expected, the numbers of people showing up to play Father grew and grew, and nearly every one of them had once been bested by him. Now, however, Father continued to lose. He even lost to me and Ah-bing. It seemed as though he simply couldn't play the game any more; that all of his inordinate ability had deserted him overnight. He soon took on the look of a inveterate loser.

How could this have happened?

Gradually, we discovered that his game had become 'sick'. It was as though he didn't or couldn't believe his own eyes. Even when an obviously good move was in front of him, he'd make some inexplicable move instead. It almost made you want to cry – so much so that we even tried to let him win a few games. It never worked:

he'd still lose. What was even stranger, however, was that now Father didn't even seem to care whether he won or lost – not like before when he would get angry at losing. Now losing seemed to make him happy, as if he had won. We couldn't help but feel that this wasn't normal, but he seemed so happy, so much more at ease than ever before – he was so much more candid and open with everyone – perhaps selfishly, we didn't want it to go back to the way it was before.

Everything seemed fine until one evening when Ah-bing returned and Father mistook him for you. He called out your name and embraced Ah-bing. He seemed to have lost his mind. We expended much effort explaining to him that Ah-bing wasn't you, but he wouldn't believe us; he really seemed to be going senile. This really alarmed us and so we decided that we had to take him to the hospital. What we were not expecting, however, was that when Ah-bing returned to the living room after having changed his clothes, Father seemed to recover his senses – he no longer thought that Ah-bing was you. This was the first time we had ever seen Father ill. But it was a strange illness, something we could never have imagined.

The doctor at the hospital believed that Father's illness was the natural beginnings of senility, a common ailment of the elderly, and nothing else. He instructed us to ensure that Father got plenty of rest and avoided excitement. Naturally, we ceased looking for *go* opponents and began to administer a mild sedative to him. Without the game I feared that Father would be unable to bear staying at home. I thought of Ah-bing and his impending graduate studies, but I was thankful that for now at least his work unit was being incredibly considerate by allowing him to take extended leave to look after Father. Every day when I returned home from work I'd see the two of them sitting at the table playing *go*. I would ask if Father had won any games and Ah-bing would always shake his head. Father's skill with the game was growing increasingly erratic; even if we tried to lose it wouldn't work.

Father's skill being this bad, I feared that his senility would grow worse. As expected, it did. One morning, very early, when the sky was still hazy and Ah-bing and I still asleep, we were suddenly woken by the fuss Father was making out in the living room. I went to look first and he mistook me for Mum. He asked where he was: he didn't recognize the place. I told him he was at home, but he flatly and doggedly refused to believe me; he wanted to leave. Then Ah-bing came into the room and Father stood for a moment, stunned and frightened. His whole body began to tremble. He kept apologizing to Ah-bing: he seemed to think that we – himself and his 'wife', me – had entered the wrong house and he hoped that this 'stranger', Ah-bing, would forgive him. Of course, we took him back to the hospital and this time asked if he could be admitted for treatment. He was, but later that same day, in the evening, he tried to run away. Nothing seemed to console him, nor could anyone stop him from going. He believed that he wasn't ill. The doctors ran a battery of tests and confirmed that he wasn't suffering from anything that they could detect. His state of mind was sober and clear-headed; he certainly didn't seem to be suffering the onset of dementia.

But we knew that Father had a problem, it was just that it manifested itself in peculiar ways. He would seem to fall ill and then not be ill – it was as if the things surrounding him were playing hide-and-seek, tormenting him ceaselessly. One evening, as I was taking him for a walk, we saw near the main gate a red leather ball that some child or other must have left. When we returned from our walk, the ball was still there. Father stopped and stared at it, then turned about. I asked him where he was going and he said he was going home. I told him that we were already headed in the direction of our house, but he didn't believe me. He turned to face me and pointed at the ball, then explained: 'That ball is not normally in front of our house. Since it isn't normal for it to be there, its appearance is meant to confuse; but for a confused person such things cannot always remain the same . . .' and so on, and so forth.

After he'd spoken I was mystified. I had no idea what he meant. Why was he so concerned about that bloody ball? So, when his attention was diverted for a moment, I kicked the ball off into the shadows. When he noticed it was gone, he began to mumble incomprehensibly and then returned home. During those days, he mumbled constantly to himself. However, neither Ah-bing nor I could make head or tail of what he said. Sometimes it seemed as though he were reciting some poem or other, at others it seemed as if he were teaching someone something. But on that day, during the incident with the ball, I was finally able to make out what he had been mumbling. This is what it was: 'You certainly are not you . . . I certainly am not me . . . The table certainly is not a table . . . The blackboard certainly is not a blackboard . . . Today certainly is not today . . . The sunshine certainly is not the sunshine . . .'

What did this mean? It didn't seem to be a poem, or a song, or some folk tune. Had he remembered this . . . whatever it was for very long? It was really strange. Once we got home I asked Father what the words meant. He gave me a vacant stare, and then asked me what I meant. I repeated to him what he had been mumbling outside. Immediately, to my surprise, his eyes became wide and round. He asked me where I had heard this, as if it were some confidential information that I shouldn't know about. I told him the truth and his face paled with fright: he implored me to forget what I had heard, and then declared in no uncertain terms that he had never spoken these words. He acted as though he had inadvertently let slip some top-secret information. Seeing Father so alarmed and anxious, I immediately realized what this was all about, these words were somehow related to what went on behind those red walls . . .

Day Six

Red walls!
Red walls!
What mysteries do you keep hidden inside you?
How is it that you always make people so nervous, so strange?

I kept thinking that at his age, my father's eccentricities were OK. I was resigned to his illness; though it was certain it had some connection to the secret work that went on behind those red walls. In other words, it was perhaps a sign of an occupational disease – the lingering traces of it. Because his occupation was so ineffable, it seemed to make sense that his illness would likewise be unusual and bizarre – something ordinary people couldn't understand or grasp.

Even a small bell can wake a person. I thought, 'If Father's illness is the result of his work, perhaps someone behind those red walls will have the means to deal with it.' And so one day I went to find old Director Wang. He'd visited our house several times in the past, and given me the impression that he was concerned about Father's well-being. Director Wang listened to my description of Father's illness, and for a long time afterwards he didn't speak. He didn't seem surprised, nor did he show much sympathy; instead, his expression was blank. He asked me where my father was, and I told him he was at home. He made his secretary get him two cigarettes and said that he would return home with me. Once we arrived there, we discovered that the door was open and Father was nowhere to be found. I asked the old man who served as concierge if he had seen him leave the compound, to which he answered that it was absolutely impossible for him to have left as it had only been half an hour since he'd seen Father in the courtyard. Still, we looked and looked and could not find him, nor did we see any trace of him having been there; it seemed as though he had disappeared into thin air.

Where do you think he got to? He was over in the building opposite ours, wandering through the corridors with his house keys in his hand, repeatedly trying to open doors, trying to find out which one worked. Absurd, don't you think? He didn't even recognize his own home! We brought him back, but as soon as we entered, he abruptly turned round and insisted that he wanted to leave because this wasn't our home. I really didn't know what to do. It was then that Director Wang thought of a solution. He told me to take my father outside for a moment and wait for him to call us back. A few moments later, we heard Director Wang's voice. Once we went back in I noticed that slight changes had been made: the sofa cover was gone, the vase of flowers that had been on the dining-room table was on the small tea table, and a few other small decorative items had been shifted around. But Father, having seen these slight changes, now believed that this was indeed his house.

Wouldn't you say this was strange? It was downright bizarre!

That day, as he took his leave, Director Wang told me how to deal with Father if he should become confused again. Afterwards, whenever Father had one of his episodes, we simply shifted around some of the things in front of him and he would relax. To be honest, in the beginning I didn't believe it would work, but after doing it several times I could see how well it worked – for example, when he'd suddenly mistake Ah-bing or myself for someone else, we'd simply change our clothes or rearrange our hair and he'd recognize us again as if he had just woken from a dream. Other episodes were the same: all we had to do was make several small changes as the situation demanded, and Father would seem to come to his senses. Sometime later, and without even trying, we discovered a particularly useful method: whenever Father had one of his moments during which he argued that this wasn't his home, all we needed to do was turn on the television or the radio and he'd be fine. Perhaps this was because the image on the television and the sound emanating from the radio were always changing. But whatever the reason, after making this discovery we had certainly eliminated a major headache. At least now when we brought him home we wouldn't have any more trouble. Unfortunately, new problems began to present themselves one after another. At times, he would mistake such-and-such a person for someone else; or he'd misunderstand what someone said. There was always one damn thing after another; some crazy or bizarre social gaffe or other that he'd commit. Whilst those behind those red walls might possibly understand, what about everyone else? Eventually, the other families in the compound all said that Father had gone mad, and they all avoided him.

As you can imagine, who would dare let this kind of man, who could lapse at any moment, out of the house on his own? I wouldn't – after all, who knew what kind of trouble he might get into? Anything could have happened! Consequently, Father never went outside unless someone was there to accompany him, to make sure he was all right, and that he'd come home without causing some fuss or other. He was like a child. If we turned our backs for a moment, it was quite likely that we'd end up having to look all over the place for him. While Ah-bing was at home this wasn't really a problem, but in another couple of months he would be off to the provincial capital to begin his graduate studies. As I've told you, originally we had thought that we'd move to the capital along with Ah-bing (to find new *go* opponents for Father), but now this was unnecessary – and what's more, it was impossible. Father being the way he was, how could we take him somewhere else? He could only stay in the courtyard in front of our house! Everyone knew us here: if Father had a sudden accident or caused an incident, people would understand and make allowances for him. It was also safe here. In the provincial capital no one knew us; it'd be a miracle if nothing bad were to happen. But Ah-bing was leaving – I'd be the only one left at home, and I had to work. I couldn't stay at home and take care of Father all the time. What was I to do? I thought the best thing to do was to go and see Director Wang, but he couldn't think of any answer either. Mulling it over, it seemed that there was only one solution: Father should be admitted to hospital.

I knew that he'd be unwilling to go, but Director Wang said that this was a directive issued by the organization, and he didn't have a choice. Father wouldn't challenge an organizational directive. As a result of Director Wang's hard work and effort, we didn't have to worry about Father being admitted to the local psychiatric ward. In fact, he was admitted to the Lingshan Convalescent Home. At first, I was very pleased and happy with this solution. When we took him there and I saw the environment, the conditions and the atmosphere, as well as the scenery we travelled through to get there – well, everything seemed better than I could have imagined. I was overjoyed. At the time, I certainly didn't realize that within three days my joy would turn to regret. A deep, profound sense of regret . . .

On that day, the convalescent home rang me. Something had happened to Father. Director Wang and I immediately went to 'resolve the situation', but when we got there and stood just outside the building where my father was living, I could hear him shouting himself hoarse. I raced up the stairs, but when I got to his room I saw an iron chain securing the door. He looked like a confused and distraught old man, like a man who has been wrongly accused of some crime. I asked him what had happened, but he told me he did not know; all he could tell me was that they had locked him in like this for the last several hours; it was nearly four in the afternoon now and they hadn't even given him his lunch. Director Wang took me to see the hospital administrator. Both of us wanted to register a complaint against them, but once we heard the administrator's explanation of the situation, we didn't know what to say.

It seemed it was to do with one of the hospital's nurses, a woman by the name of Shi. She was very young – everyone called her Little Shi. You know that my family also used to call me Little Si; perhaps that was the reason for what happened, that brought on one of Father's episodes. He thought she was me, and in the morning when she came to tidy his room, he became a little over-affectionate with her, which made her quite angry. Finally freeing herself from his hands, she went to leave. Father, however, chased after her, repeatedly calling out to her. The whole situation frightened Little Shi terribly. As a result, the hospital staff believed Father was some sort of potential rapist and locked him in his room. We asked for some explanation of their treatment of him, but they retorted forcefully, with the conviction of someone who has been unfairly accused, that it wasn't they who were at fault but us, since we knew but had not told them that father suffered from such moments. In short, we shouldn't have brought him here in the first place; this was a convalescent home, not a psychiatric hospital. Neither Director Wang nor I could say that they were wrong because, in truth, we were the ones who had made a mistake. What made me angry was that one of the hospital staff suddenly said that we should apologize to Little Shi and compensate her for emotional damage. The gall of some people! My father had already suffered such massive emotional damage. Who should we look to for compensation?

The situation at the convalescent home was patched up. When all was said and done, it was decided that Father would spend the next three days there, a sort of trial period. If it turned out that they simply couldn't take care of him, he would have to be returned home. I was at a loss, however. I really didn't know what to do. I simply couldn't think of a way to allow Father to live out his days peacefully. I no longer dared to think that I could make his 'golden years' happy, I just wanted him to be at peace. That's all; that would be enough. I was advised to put Father in a psychiatric ward, but I just couldn't do it: wouldn't that be tantamount to giving up on him? I thought the best thing I could do would be to quit work. I just couldn't send him to such a place. No matter how I looked at it, this was a problem that couldn't be dealt with rationally – it was a problem of the heart. My heart just wouldn't let me make such a choice.

Sometime later – Father had been back from the convalescent home for about a day or so – I had just come home from work when I saw him smiling quite contentedly. He didn't wait for me to ask him what was going on, he just told me in an excited voice that the organization had given him a new assignment, and he was going back to work!

For that whole day, Father was so happy and delighted.

In the years when he was working, we had continuously looked forward to, had hoped for, the day he would leave those red walls behind. I never thought that the day would come when he would be planning to go back. I was so unhappy about the whole thing. I really didn't want him to go! When Director Wang asked my opinion on the matter, I told him the truth. I told him no; I said I couldn't bear it. I also told him that I was planning to quit my job and stay at home to take care of Father. Father was really furious with me afterwards for what I had said. Then I realized I really didn't have any power to oppose this new assignment, so my opposition was pointless. What if I had resigned my position, intending to look after him every minute of every day, how was that going to be? Father's illness would still be the same as before; the problems would be the same as before: we simply couldn't make him happy. There was nothing we could do to make him happy, but there was something that they could do. I remember his face on that day. You can't imagine it – he was so pleased, he'd spent more than two hours on the phone with Ah-bing. The topic never veered far from what was making him so content: he had a new assignment; he was going back to work.

On the following day, Father really 'went back to work'. I remember it clearly. It was 1986, a cold, windy, wintry day – cold enough to freeze you to the bone. Slushy snow wet the ground. I escorted Father out to the gate of our housing compound to the car that was waiting to carry him back behind the red walls. As the car pulled away, as I watched his back recede into the distance, my mind returned to those red walls, the large iron gate, to the image of him disappearing inside . . . unable, unwilling, perhaps, to turn round and give me one last look.

Father! Dad!

Those red walls!

And that was how, 827 days after he exited Unit 701, he was welcomed back into its bosom.

At first, I was very worried that Father would have another one of his episodes whilst at work, and there would be no one there to look after him. Who's to say that he wouldn't cause a serious disturbance? I was also worried about his physical health – after all, he had been away for quite a long time; would he be able to handle the strain of going back? In a sense, now that he had returned to those red walls, he took my spirit with him. I was flustered and confused, I couldn't sleep well, I couldn't remember things clearly, I spent my days distracted and absent-minded. I couldn't shake an ominous sense of foreboding. But a week passed, then two, and then a month, and nothing happened. Not only did nothing untoward happen, but things actually got better. Whenever Father came home to visit, his face would seem spirited and full of energy; he looked truly invigorated, satisfied – so very contented. I felt pleased and gratified. Ha, I know you don't believe me at all: not only had Father's spirit returned since he went back inside, his health had returned as well. The problems he had experienced when retired never reappeared. He had recovered; it all seemed as though it had never happened. Those red walls seemed like a large magical protective screen: they had spared him from the disasters he had created; they had rescued him from himself. To use Director Wang's words: when Father returned back behind those red walls, it was like a fish returning to water.

It's true: Father was reborn!

Now, when I am in a depressed mood, I often use these thoughts to blame myself. I think: the cosmos will change, but my father won't. His life belonged behind those red walls, his heart and mind had already been bound incontrovertibly to that place, so they could never be separated from it; if they were, they would decay and die. Those mysterious red walls and the compound they held were his native soil; they'd also be where his body would be welcomed back into the earth. In the end, he would die inside . . . speaking of him dying, my hand has begun to tremble, I cannot believe that he's dead. I don't want him to be, I don't want it! I want my dad!

Dad!

Dad!

Dad!

Where are you?

Day Seven

. . . I no longer have the energy to write any more, I'll just use a few words to finish up.

Sunday was Father's day to visit home. After he had returned behind those red walls, Sundays became the day he'd come round to see me, he'd stay the night and leave in the morning. If he couldn't make it, he'd telephone. On one particular Sunday, he didn't call and so I expected him home. At around three in the afternoon I went to the market to buy food for dinner, I bought four fillets of crucian carp. Father said that chicken aided the feet, but fish was good for the brain. He loved to eat fish. This preference had stayed with him all his life, he never once felt tired of it. I got back home at close to four, and until 4:30 I prepared dinner. Suddenly the phone rang. The man on the other end said that Father had had a heart attack and was now in the hospital emergency room; they wanted me to come over as quickly as possible. It was the work unit's hospital, inside the compound, but by the time I made it to the iron gates they told me that he had been transferred to a hospital in the city. This meant that he was in a very serious condition; within moments of hearing this tears began to stream down my face. Tears of fear. I managed to stagger my way to the city hospital. Once there, the doctor told me that his heart had already stopped once but they had been able to revive him. As I stood in front of him, I didn't know whether I should be sad or happy. Father smiled at me, but he didn't speak. Five days later, at 9:03 in the evening, Father smiled at me once more and then departed for ever . . .

Two Old Letters

To Chen Sisi

Just a moment ago I went up to the roof and turned towards the faraway southwest, where I imagined was the direction in which your father – my *shifu* – was buried, and observed a solemn moment of silence for longer than I needed to. I believe if your father is a spirit up in heaven, he must have heard me saying goodbye. I spoke for quite a while – even if I had wanted to, I wouldn't have been able to keep silent. I seemed to be possessed. I called out his name repeatedly, offering my heartfelt condolences, my best wishes, my deep feelings of love, over and over again. Because I had so much to give to him, I ended up feeling somewhat light-headed, like a feather drifting through the sky. I felt as though I were flying. It was almost a feeling of being torn asunder, but it wasn't painful, only unobstructed. I was reconciled to having my mortal shell disassembled.

Now I'm at my writing desk, writing you this letter.

I have a feeling that I'm going to write a lot, but to be honest, I don't know when you will be able to read it. You will certainly have to wait a long time; probably several years, or a decade – perhaps even several. I just don't know. I only know that so long as your father's file remains classified, you won't be able to receive this letter. In a very real way, I'm writing a letter I can't send, and I don't know when I will be able to. Still, even though this is how it is, I still want to write it, and once it's done, I will send it. This doesn't mean I'm being irrational; rather it's because I am rational and clear-headed that I'm writing it. I mean, I have faith that one day your father's secrets will be declassified, I just don't know when. Secrets, after all, are a counterpart to time. Fifty years ago, the Americans decided to hunt down and kill the general responsible for Pearl Harbor, Yamamoto Isoroku. Of course, this was an enormous secret at the time, but now they've made a movie out of it and what was once a secret is known to everyone. Time will eventually open a window to all secrets, for there is no such thing as a secret that can never be revealed. Sooner or later everything can come out into the open. Thinking this way gives me faith that this letter might bring you some happiness. I know – perhaps more than anyone else – that you hope that I can explain to you why your father experienced so many difficulties in his so-called golden years, why he endured so much pain and torment. This letter will tell you everything, but when you see it don't blame me for making you wait so long. This letter needs time, like some old sore that requires patience to heal.

You've told me before that the outside world says Unit 701 is busy developing advanced, top-secret weaponry. But in truth we do no such thing. What do we do then? Well, we are an intelligence-gathering organization, nothing more, nothing less. Our main responsibility is eavesdropping on the radio frequencies of X Country and decrypting their transmissions. Every country has this type of intelligence-gathering service – today and in the past; big countries and small. So you could say that this secret is known to everyone. Every country does it, that's self-evident. I've often said 'to know thy enemy is to know thyself'; then and only then can you always be victorious. 'Know thy enemy' – well, that's intelligence gathering. In war, intelligence gathering works like a crowbar, a lever that prises open the enemy's defences. Just as the physicists say, give us a suitable opening, give us the needed information, and we can prise open the secrets of the universe. With enough accurate information, any army can win any war. But there's only one way to gather this intelligence, and that's stealing; there is no other way. Sending special agents to infiltrate the enemy's military apparatuses, scaling their defences: both approaches are forms of stealing. Quietly sitting in front of radio equipment intercepting transmissions is the same. The only difference is that the latter is much safer, and produces more results. In order to combat this type of theft, secret means of encrypting transmissions have been developed and, in tandem, secret means to decrypt these transmissions have likewise been devised. Your father was engaged in decryption.

You could say that decrypting is at the heart of Unit 701. At the very core of the heart.

Decrypting these transmissions is, in its form, like a game of hide and seek. Those who create the ciphers are engaged in hiding whilst those who decrypt them are the seekers. The art of concealing has its own mysteries, and so too does the art of seeking. After going through the baptism of fire that was the Second World War, both aspects of cryptography have developed into a science. Many of the brightest minds from all over the world have been recruited, especially mathematicians. Some say that decrypting is the work of one genius trying to crack the work of another genius, like hand-to-hand combat between two very skilled warriors. To put it another way, those who engage in decrypting are the greatest mathematical talents of our time. Where does our organization recruit these men? Well, that's easy to answer: in the nation's universities. Every summer some of our people, armed with extraordinary powers, show up on university campuses and take away student files. Later, they pore over these files, thoroughly scanning through all of the information, and then finally they select perhaps one or two of the very best students, and take them away. Forty years ago, a student in the mathematics department at S University was 'recruited' in this fashion: he was your father. Thirty years later, your father's alma mater had another mathematics student 'recruited': that was me. No one knew what work I was going to be doing. I didn't even know myself. It wouldn't be until several months later I would learn that what I had been chosen for was cryptography.

If it were possible for one to choose one's own destiny, then frankly speaking I wouldn't have chosen the path my life has taken. It is a lonely, solitary career, forever in the shadows. It twists and warps your character; it strangles you. I remember clearly the night I was escorted away from S University by the men from headquarters. I remember sitting on a train for hours, then in the middle of the night the train stopped at some unmarked station. There was no nearby village, no shops, nothing – it looked like a desolate and deserted station in the middle of nowhere. At the station we got into an unmarked jeep and began driving into the darkness. Finally, the man who climbed in after me offered me a drink of water; he seemed to be full of concern for my welfare. God knows what he put in it, but whatever it was, it knocked me out completely. When I awoke, I was in a cold and cheerless barrack courtyard: the secret training ground for future cryptographers. There were five of us in total to be trained, four men and one woman. For the first month they taught us how to 'forget'. The aim was to forget who we had been, our pasts. This was followed by a month's training on how to conceal and protect secrets. Finally, we had three months of professional instruction. This was how half a year passed, in an atmosphere of secrecy and tension. Then we were removed from that place, with our eyes blindfolded. I still don't know where it is . . . East? West? South? North? I haven't a clue, I only know that it was somewhere deep in a forest, an almost primeval woodland.

During those three months of professional training, several cryptographers came to lecture us. Their lectures usually focused on the basic principles of the work and their own personal experiences. One day, the comrade in charge of the base told us that the guest instructor today was a high-level cryptographer. Within the intelligence service he was known as the 'double bull'. What exactly did that mean? Well, it meant that he got angry like a bull, and he was bullish in his work, always attacking things head on. Since his temperament was haughty and bullish, as well as his approach to work, he was the 'double bull': overbearing and sure of himself. With this type of disposition, we had to be sure to pay attention during his lecture; we should not anger him in any way. Once he arrived, as expected we all felt he was quite strange. His topic was supposed to be his personal experiences, but once he entered the classroom he didn't even look at us. For a long time all he did was sit in front of the class, smoking cigarette after cigarette without regard for anyone – he spoke not a word. Silently we looked at him as seconds passed by and the smoke from his cigarettes continued to encircle him. Soon minutes drifted by. We began to grow uncomfortable in our chairs and several students couldn't help but cough, clearing their throats, perhaps trying to get his attention. It worked. He raised his head and looked at us, stood up, walked around us once, returned to his seat and picked up a piece of chalk. He asked us what it was. He asked student after student and got the same answer each time: it was a piece of chalk. Then he put the chalk in the palm of his hand, he looked ready to recite something. This is what he said:

'If this is truly a piece of chalk, then it means that you are not cryptographers; conversely, it shouldn't be a piece of chalk. Many years ago, I sat in the very same chairs you are seated in now, listening attentively to a senior cryptographer, just as you are now. This is what he said to me: "*In the world of cryptography, there is nothing that can be seen by the naked eye. Whatever you see with your eyes is not what you think it is*" (he gestured with his hand) "*you certainly are not you, I certainly am not me, the table certainly is not a table, the blackboard certainly is not a black board, today certainly is not today, the sunshine certainly is not the sunshine.*" Everything in the world is like this: it is often the most confusing thing that is the simplest. I think this is all I need tell you today. Class dismissed.'

Upon delivering these cryptic words, he stood and left the classroom. None of us knew what to do. Nevertheless this very strange lecture stayed with us always, and we never forgot what it was he had said. In the days that followed, as I became more familiar with actual ciphers, I discovered – more and more – that what he had said during that class summed up the work perfectly. Some people may say that decrypting ciphers is a lonely job, a shadowy career that takes place in yet deeper shadows. Perhaps that's true. But besides the necessary skill and training required, besides experience and a measure of innate ability, decrypting ciphers needs luck more than anything else – a luck that comes from far beyond the stars. Such good fortune isn't something you can strive for, let alone demand. You simply have to trust in it. You need to learn how to grin and bear the inevitable failures, you need to study how to be patient. Even if you burn with anxiety you need to wait, perhaps even beyond the end of time. And yet this reasoning, this description of my career . . . it still doesn't compare to what he said. That strange speech has been etched into my memory. What he said was so simple and yet so penetrating. He took something that seemed so profound, so abstruse, and summed it up in just a few words. With that speech, he allowed me to see what career it was that I had begun to devote my life to; he expanded my horizon, he allowed me to take hold of it.

He really understood the nature of cryptography.

The man I am talking about was your father.

Half a month later I was assigned to Unit 701's cryptography division and began my long association with your father. I've told you if I had been given a choice, I wouldn't have chosen this career, but since I didn't have a choice, coming to know your father, working with him day and night, was the most enormous piece of good fortune. To be honest, I still have not met anyone in the world of cryptography who has the sensitivity and ability to decrypt ciphers that your father did. He had some spiritual connection to ciphers, like the relationship between a child and its mother. There just seemed to be a natural connection between them and him, a blood tie as it were. He was an extraordinary cryptographer. He also possessed another exceptional quality: determination. No matter what the cost, no matter how hopeless the situation, he would persevere. His knowledge and determination complemented each other. They were compatible, they worked in unison, and they were more than double what normal people had. The way he went about his work, calmly but with the confidence of vast experience, couldn't help but boost your morale and also make you feel feeble and powerless at the same time.

I remember one day, not long after I had been assigned to Unit 701, not long after I had entered beyond those red walls. I was in your father's office for a moment and I saw upon the wall a series of black Xs. They were arranged like a poem. This is what I saw:

```
X X X X X
X X X X X
X X X X X X X
X X X X X X X X
X X X X X
X X X X X X X
```

These black strokes obviously meant something.

I asked your father what it was, and all he said was that they were a cipher, a key to decryption. Then he asked me if I could solve it. He looked at me without making a sound, and it reminded me of something. Then it came to me: I had heard him say this once before. I thought it over for a bit and understood. The markings on the wall matched the number of words he had spoken to us during his one and only lecture. I simply had to put it together, and then I would know which sentence belonged with which set of marks.

This is what was written upon the wall:

> You certainly are not you
> I certainly am not me
> The table certainly is not a table
> The blackboard certainly is not a black board
> Today certainly is not today
> The sunshine certainly is not the sunshine

After he spoke those words during that lecture, a few of us had taken to chanting them out loud, but I never imagined that your father had spent his entire life with them. Later I learnt that every night before bed and every morning when he woke up, he would read these words as if reciting a prayer. At those infrequent times when he had nothing to do, he would retrace the words again and again, so the markings on the wall always looked bright and fresh. Following your father's example, I did the same. I wrote those words on the four walls of my room, and every night before bed and every morning when I woke up I would recite them. Over time, I learnt that for those of us working in decryption, these words are incredibly important.

Someone once asked me, 'What kind of person is most suited for this line of work?' My answer was, 'A lunatic.' As you can imagine, if someone could follow the same line of thought as a madman – that is a completely random sequence – and devise a cipher based upon it, then without a doubt this cipher would be unbreakable. Why are ciphers so often decrypted nowadays? Well, the reason is plain: it's because their creators are not truly madmen; they only pretend to be insane. Consequently, they cannot in fact achieve true irrationality when they construct a cipher. In order to crack a cipher all that is needed is the faintest trace of rationality to it. If such logic exists, then its door can be found and eventually prised opened. Who is most suited to this kind of work? Again, it's a madman, and that's because decrypting is the other side of the coin. In fact, when all is said and done, encrypting or decrypting is the kind of work that is very much akin to insanity. If you can draw close to that insanity, move further away from the way normal people think, then you can create ciphers that are ungraspable and impervious to being cracked. The same is true for decrypting. If you can draw close to the irrationality of madman, then you can be that much closer to the mental state of the cipher, and you can be that much closer to solving ciphers. So the more normal your way of looking at things is, the greater the difficulties you will face in decrypting ciphers, because you will be so easily distracted by the surface appearance. The truth of any cipher is buried deep within it, in the bowels of the cipher itself. If you cannot crack through the surface, you will not be able to prise it open. This is the most crucial aspect of decryption.

To employ an analogy, here are two sentences:

> You certainly are not you
> I certainly am not me

Now, let's create two hypothetical ciphers.
The first is this –

X X X X X
X X X X X

The second is this –

> The star in the sky
> The man on the earth

Now think, which one has the most potential to signify virtually anything?

Naturally it's the first one. Its ambiguity means it could signify pretty much anything; there are no restrictions on its imaginative potential. But as for the latter, even though it is easy to see that the literal meaning is meant to confuse, if you peel back the pretence then it wouldn't matter how much imagination might have been put into the cipher, it wouldn't matter if it was this or that, in the end the cipher has to be limited and restrained by the literal meaning of the words. But your father's efforts always had one particular purpose in mind, which was to arrive at the first type of cipher: to create a myriad of significatory possibilities – to be able to break away, intentionally or otherwise, from the common signifying chain – to abandon all limitations. The degree to which one is unconscious of things can be quite deep and the space of imagination can expand freely, but it demands limitations. In fact, whether or not a cryptographer possesses a certain excellence depends on whether or not they can increase the space between that which is part of the conscious world and that which is part of the unconscious world. Indeed, for a 'conscious' normal person it would be impossible to function in this 'unconscious' manner. At most they might be able to draw close to it. But drawing close to it cannot be considered the ultimate end – it is only one possible degree. The actual 'thread of consciousness' is fragile like gossamer: at any moment it can be torn, and if it is, then that's the end – you would go insane. So, decrypting is an absurd task. It's cruel, it constantly demands that you play the fool and feign madness, and you have to make the most supreme effort to reach the world of madness. At the same time, cryptography demands that you have the insight of the scientist; you must be able to accurately grasp the line between normality and insanity, but you mustn't cross over that line, for if you do all is lost – like burning out the tungsten filament of an old light bulb. A tungsten filament is brightest before it burns out. The best cryptographer is like the brightest tungsten filament . . . but at any moment, they can burn out.

Everyone recognized your father as being an amazingly accomplished cryptographer. He had a persistence seldom seen in normal people: years would seem like days to him, and he'd keep himself in the best of conditions for decrypting – the state of greatest brightness for a tungsten filament, itself a form of madness. Indeed, only a madman would dare do such a thing! One aspect of his character allowed your father to achieve great success and honour amongst us cryptographers. Another aspect of it, however, placed your father in great danger, on the edge of the abyss as it were – at the moment when that filament burns out. At any moment he could have fallen into madness. I think now, perhaps, you might understand why during those 800-odd days he spent outside the red walls, he suffered the problems he did – at the time, you thought it was a peculiar ailment, something unforeseen, but in truth it was destined to happen and so it wasn't strange at all. From my point of view, what should really be considered strange is the fact that your father didn't succumb to it, but that somehow he was still able to shine.

That was truly miraculous!

However, in the case of your father, his whole life marched from one miracle to another. One more certainly wasn't all that strange or unexpected, I suppose.

As for your father's 'go phenomenon', that wasn't as bizarre as you think. From a professional standpoint, there is a natural connection between cryptography and chess-like games because the techniques of both involve arithmetic: they are both mathematical games and thus very similar, like two fruits from the same vine. A cryptographer who has left the intelligence service needs something to occupy their mind, so it is entirely natural that they would be drawn to chess-like games. In a sense, these games are just another form of the same kind of work. You could say it was like . . . returning home, or like having never even left. Unquestionably, go had many points of comparison with the profound work of cryptography. But only to a certain degree. In another sense, the game of *go* was simple, basic even, compared to the work done behind those red walls. So it is not surprising that your father gave the impression of being a master at *go*. Other players might believe that his *dan* level was incredibly high – perhaps they'd think that he could see the game and work out his moves as easily as a computer makes calculations. Overkill, I suppose, like a chef who slaughters a chicken with a knife meant for a cow.

But in the end, it is just as you said: whether you put your father's problems down to eccentricity or to illness, they were directly related to the work he did behind those red walls – inseparable from it. In other words, the reason for his keen interest in the game of *go* was the result of the special profession he had been engaged in; it was his fate, unchangeable to the end. There are numerous professions in this world, but undoubtedly cryptography is the most mysterious, most absurd profession. It also causes the most misery. On the one hand it makes use of a person's very essence, and then it demands that that essence be used in the service of insane purposes. Every day and night to be immersed within that preposterous space of '*You certainly are not you, I certainly am not me.*' Meanwhile the answers that cryptographers rack their brains for are hidden away in the dark, always on the other side of the glass, in some far-off place, at the end of one's life . . .

To Chen Sibing

The letter I wrote for your sister is intended for you as well, since I know that even if I didn't write one to you, Sisi would show you the letter I sent to her. So, when I wrote that particular letter I deliberately used carbon paper. Hence there are three versions of it, one of which is yours (the third will be filed away by the work unit). You can read the letter I sent to your sister first: that way you will understand – you'll know why it is that you are receiving this letter today (though who knows when that 'today' will actually come). This letter is about your father, but I write it at a time when his file hasn't yet been declassified. Waiting for declassification to happen is the same as waiting for the unveiling of one's fate: we know that there will be one day in the future when everything is revealed, but we don't know when that day will come – only the heavens can know that.

Perhaps, as you read Sisi's letter, you discovered that I wrote it more than six months ago. And perhaps you're wondering why I waited so long before I wrote this for you? In fact, I know you're really hoping that I will tell you what 'that matter' was – the thing your father spoke of before he died – but at the same time I know that whatever I tell you will never satisfy you fully. So I kept thinking that I simply couldn't write this letter to you. However, I never thought that things would change so unexpectedly. I never imagined that these changes would give you the right to know about 'that matter'.

This is what happened. Two days ago Director Wang came to inspect our work, and of course we met. We talked about your father, about many things that I was not even aware of, and we talked about 'that matter'. At first, I was completely shocked because I had thought that this particular secret was between your father and myself. I couldn't imagine how Old Wang had come to know of it. As it turned out, the day after he had sent those dying words to me, just before death took him, he used his last strength to come clean, to tell the intelligence service about 'that matter'. Since the secret in question was directly connected to the cryptography division, no member of your family could possibly be allowed to be present when it was discussed, so you and your sister never learnt what it was. Only Director Wang was in the room at the time. According to him, after your father told him what 'that matter' was, it seemed as though he had done the last thing that was left for him to do in this life, and so he died almost immediately. There nearly wasn't even time for you to see him before he passed away.

Ah, *shifu*, you really shouldn't have. Why did you trouble yourself with revealing that secret? Why didn't you believe me? Oh, *shifu*, listen: what you thought it was, and what you said, neither is true. The only thing you've done is put me in a difficult spot, and this is so very painful . . . Ah-bing, contrary to what I promised, I want to tell you about 'that matter'. First, since your father has revealed it, those last dying words are not worth the paper they are written on. Second, what he said is untrue, and it is up to me to set the record straight.

Ah-bing, presumably you've already read the letter I have sent your sister, and so you know that your father's profession was cryptography. He was involved in decrypting ciphers, a mysterious, murky, shadowy job; a torturous line of work that can only ever drain one of life itself. But you could say that he was more than fortunate because in his dealings with ciphers, the only thing that was tortured to death was the cipher, not him. Over the course of his career, your father was responsible for decrypting seven mid-level ciphers and three high-level ciphers – his accomplishments were a rare feat. I think if there was a Nobel Prize for cryptography, surely your father would have won it – perhaps even more than once.

I arrived at Unit 701 in the summer of 1973. Already by that time your father had decrypted one high-level cipher and six mid-level ones. His stature was impressive. But all was not well. His current assignment, cracking DESERT 1, was causing him great difficulty and much stress. He was like a prisoner and hardly ever set foot outside his room. DESERT 1 had the code-name FIRE. It was a cipher used by all branches of the military in X Country towards the end of the 1960s. It was the most sophisticated cipher of the day. When it first went into use, numerous international military observers reckoned that it was safe for twenty years. It is normal to be unable to decrypt a cipher; it is decryption that is abnormal. For three years your father had been attempting to untangle its webs, unsuccessfully. This tells you what we were dealing with here. I still remember to this day what your father said to me on the first day we spoke. He told me he was engaged in an epic battle with an especially devilish cipher and that if I were afraid of such battles then I shouldn't be working with him. Ten years later, I regretted somewhat not having really believed his words, because the amount of time and energy we invested in trying to crack that cipher was uncountable. Even our dreams were tormented by it, but its inner secrets remained hidden – always over the next mountain ridge, just beyond the horizon. There were times I couldn't help but think that when all was said and done your father and I were not the same: he had already achieved so much success and honour for one lifetime, and even if he were to lose this particular battle, his career would still be considered an unbelievable success. But me? I had no name, no reputation and yet I had already spent ten years of my time battling FIRE. It all seemed so stupid and so arrogant. It was obvious that if I lost this battle, I'd lose my life. But thinking that way after ten years . . . it was already too late. I had little choice but to commit myself fully to the task at hand. With your father's encouragement, I transformed the concern I had over my fate into wolfish aggression. We had to succeed.

Then, one night, I silently packed away my bedding and headed off to the decryption room. Your father saw me and did the same. We were prepared to burn our boats, to stake everything on one final throw: to wage our last battle!

From then on we spent every minute together. We were inseparable. Your father superstitiously believed that in the middle of the night, man was part human, part devil; that the devil was at play in the deep hours of the night, and it was then that one could be inspired. Consequently, he had developed the habit of going to bed early and getting up early – normally he'd go to bed at 20:00 and get up at 02:00, then take a short walk and begin work. This is where your father's work habits and mine diverged, but it was because of this that I quickly discovered your father's secret: he often spoke in his sleep.

All told, not much faith can be placed in what a person says in their sleep. Most of it is incomprehensible – mumbling really, and like baby talk, very hard to make out. But occasionally things do make sense, and at those times I discovered that most of your father's dream-talk concerned FIRE. This meant that even in his dreams he was deep in thought trying to crack the cipher. There were even times when what he said was incredibly clear and easy

In the Dark

to understand – sometimes even clearer than what he said during the day. It was those queer and bizarre thoughts, however, that turned out to be most valuable. For instance, in the course of one evening I heard him call out my name whilst he was dreaming and then, as if he were awake, proceed to tell me the most extraordinarily odd idea he had concerning FIRE. What he said was well-structured, rational and logical; it was as though he were giving me a lecture. I thought his idea was more weird than I could say, but there was something captivating about it.

Let me put it like this: the answer to the riddle that was FIRE must be hidden in some far-off place, and so to get there we needed to first make a choice. Should we go by land, by sea, or by some other route? But the situation we were faced with was this: only stones and rubble lay in front of us; there was no horizon and neither was there a shore. In sum, the water option seemed to be excluded from the beginning. We had had to go by land, and we had already tried a couple of different directions that led nowhere. Consequently, we were at a loss as to which direction we should go in. This was the predicament we were in when your father spoke to me that night. He told me this: 'Underneath these stones and rubble there must be a hidden stream. We should try to take the water route and see what happens.'

I thought what he said was really strange and yet important; it was worth a try at least. It was also then that I committed myself to selfishness. On the following morning, in a roundabout way, I confirmed that your father remembered nothing of what he had told me from the night before, and then I raised his idea as my own idea. Almost immediately your father wholeheartedly agreed to follow this idea.

Please keep this in mind: this was the beginning of a series of bewildering and confusing events, and they all began with me 'stealing' your father's idea.

Impossible though it is to imagine, once we chose to follow this route, underneath our feet there did indeed turn out to be a barren and neglected stream capable of carrying us to that place of our imagination. We set off almost immediately. Ah, it's really quite unbelievable: we had expended over ten years of hard work, ten years of sweat and tears struggling to find something that seemed to be impossible to find, and then, finally, in a freak combination of events, we had made it!

This discovery was the key to cracking FIRE: we were halfway there. But there were still two important hurdles we had not yet overcome: the first concerned where to land, on what shore; the second concerned where to look, outside or inside. Of course, I'm using metaphors to describe this process. The only problem is even the best turn of phrase doesn't really describe it fully; it's inferior, even lame. But what else can I say? In truth, if I didn't use these metaphors, if I tried to explain things logically, not only would you not understand, but you'd never be able to – you'd never even have the opportunity to understand. I mean, if I tried to tell you exactly how we went about decrypting FIRE, you would probably go to your grave without ever grasping what it was I was talking about.

Anyhow, returning to my story: if we could resolve the two problems mentioned above, surely we'd be able to decrypt FIRE in a relatively short period of time – perhaps in the blink of an eye. The only issue was: how do we resolve these two problems? I placed my hopes on the ramblings of your father whilst he slept. Wasn't that absurd? No matter how stupid it seemed, I couldn't think of anything else to do. Hence, from then on I began to keep a record of everything your father said whilst sleeping. Everything I could make out I recorded, whether it dealt with FIRE or not. I put everything down on paper, and then I pored over it, looking for some form of inspiration. To be honest, deep in my heart, I didn't believe I would find what I was looking for; lightning rarely strikes twice in the same spot. It was already unbelievable that your father's ramblings had provided us with the starting point; surely it wouldn't happen again? Even in my fantasies I didn't dare believe it possible. And yet it was. Every time we ran into an impassable barrier, your father's midnight mumblings would provide me with inspiration, would show me the route to take and furnish me with the magic wand needed to overcome the obstacle. Miraculously we were drawing to the end; we were getting close to deciphering FIRE. In a certain sense, I began to feel that I was becoming increasingly like your father: I no longer spoke much, and my behaviour was becoming increasingly strange. At times, as I walked out of the cafeteria, I'd feel that the flies that had accompanied me, that buzzed back and forth in front of my face, were my confidants, that their buzzing noises were actually telling me secrets from beyond this world.

Two years passed in this manner and then finally, as if in a dream, we solved FIRE. We had written our names in the history of cryptography with one truly remarkable achievement. Thinking about it now, I can't help but wonder if we might not have solved FIRE that much quicker had I moved in sooner – if I had been able to understand clearly everything your father said whilst sleeping. I still think, even though deciphering FIRE was an incredibly difficult task, if someone had been able to decrypt your father's midnight ramblings, perhaps these types of tasks would have become quite easy. Everyone who works in this field knows that decrypting such sophisticated ciphers as FIRE never happens the way you expect it. It only ever happens inadvertently, by the combination of unanticipated factors, subtly, ineffably. This is the tragic nature of our work and the source of our triumphs. But like our almost 'magical' approach to decrypting FIRE, I'm afraid that in our world of mystery, in the history of cryptography, ours will become a buried and unseen record – a secret to the end.

Unfortunately, our triumph was short-lived.

Just as we extricated ourselves from the entanglements of FIRE, personal complications appeared between your father and me: just who would wear the champion's crown? Compared to FIRE this should have been a simple problem to resolve, but what confused matters first was the fact that both your father and I had an enormous amount of respect and gratitude towards each other. Consequently, he said that I should receive the accolades for decrypting FIRE, and at the same time I said that he should. Neither one of us wanted to fight over who had made the greatest contribution to cracking FIRE, nor did we wish to harm the other to benefit ourselves; we did not wish to seem disloyal and lacking in respect. On this I trusted your father completely, and I believed it true of myself. As I've told you, I never revealed to your father exactly where I got that first bit of inspiration. At first this was my own vanity, my desire to impress, but later as it happened again and again, I did begin to grow anxious. I feared if he learnt how things really were, mightn't it influence what I gleaned from his dreams? This was entirely possible, and it was something I was terribly afraid of. That's to say, originally things came to him quite unintentionally through his dreams, but if I were to expose this, to tell him the truth, then the 'unintentional' might become the 'intentional', the 'inadvertent' might become the 'deliberate'. Telling him the truth might have put certain demands on him, however unconsciously, and so, because of this concern, I dared not reveal to your father the source of my inspiration – I had to keep it secret. That said, I had already decided that if we eventually did succeed in deciphering FIRE, I would come clean and tell him the truth. And so, once we had cracked the cipher, as your father was in the midst of congratulating me, I told him everything. I had my reasons, but most importantly, I had hoped that by telling him the truth he'd be overjoyed and accept full credit for this victory. This also proved, to myself at least, that what I said above is true – I had no desire to claim victory for myself; no desire to take credit for something I did not do.

The problem was your father didn't believe me. Even after I showed him the records I had made whilst he slept he still didn't believe me; he said they proved nothing. In the end, it didn't matter what I said or what I showed him, he simply refused to believe me. He kept thinking I was trying to console him, playing modest. Of course, it was hard to believe. Thinking of it now, it seems more unreal than real, and to the layman it would certainly be unbelievable. But over those following days, I kept regretting that I had never made an actual recording of his sleep, or the mumbling he had done. If I had, perhaps I wouldn't have needed to say anything else. I kept thinking how making a recording would have been as easy as lifting a finger. The only problem was your father thought of this as well, and so for him, the fact that I didn't have a recording meant that my story was false. I just didn't really think of it at the time. That's often how things are. Who could have known that at that time, in order for your father to receive the proper honours, I would need to be pushed aside; that we couldn't both share the acclaim? And yet, I felt that yielding was much better than fighting over it. Wouldn't you agree?

No, things weren't that simple.

Once the leadership got involved, as well as the records office, things became even more confusing. During the first review of our report, your father noticed that my name was not there under key personnel, so he took the liberty of putting it there. In fact, he erased his own name and put mine in its place. Then the report passed to me. Upon seeing the changes he had made, I couldn't help but do the same as your father: I erased my own name and put his back in. During the second review, your father made a further adjustment: he placed his own name after mine, trying to indicate the order in which credit should be given. Once I saw the report, without hesitation, I scribbled out my name. Perhaps our more senior comrades who witnessed our repeated rewriting of names believed that your father's efforts to give me greater credit came from a pure and simple sense of friendship – love for one's disciple, as it were. In other words, even though we both kept trying to give the other person the lion's share of the credit for deciphering FIRE, the senior officials, perhaps not unexpectedly, felt that my efforts to put your father's name first were real and genuine whereas your father's weren't. They believed he was doing it for my benefit, to raise my standing, to help out his junior colleague. But can such honours be bandied back and forth? If so, wouldn't the senior comrades suspect that someone had neglected their duty? Unsurprisingly, in the end, the report ended up as it was at first: my name was not included.

This was the record required by the agency, and, to me, it was reasonable and fair. After all, how could someone such as me scale the heavens and seize the moon? I had stolen his ideas. The most I could have done was to assist *shifu* in his task, and so it was quite as expected that I should merit just a footnote in the official record.

How could I receive the same acclaim as him? At least, this was the perspective of those senior comrades, and in truth, I did feel the same way. To be honest, once the situation was sorted out, I felt no indignation whatsoever, nor was I resentful, nor did I complain. In fact, I thought that this was how it should be. But because of this, your father's heart became burdened. He couldn't shake the feeling that he had stolen the credit due me. He couldn't help but feel sorry, even though he had, in truth, no reason to be. At first, he had tried to get the official record changed. He had even gone to speak personally with several senior leaders, requesting them to make the change, to give us each an equal share of the credit. But was it as easy as that? Saying something that others do not want to hear usually doesn't work, and even if the senior officials had acknowledged that there was an error, it was just a mistake – it didn't mean necessarily that it would be changed. The thing was, they never believed that a mistake had been made. The fact that I never issued a complaint proved to them that no error had been committed. Of course, this train of thought was entirely correct. Correct situations must be adhered to, they must be propagandized, and they must be advertised. So much praise washed over your father, like a tidal wave; wave after wave, carrying him higher and higher. He was called a hero of the nation and wherever his accomplishment could be publicized, it was.

No one could have imagined it, but as the situation continued, your father's heart grew heavier and heavier, more and more anxious, more and more unsettled. At the beginning, you could say that the burden that tormented him was due in large part to the feelings he had for me, and so he spared no effort to protest against this injustice. Later on, however, things changed dramatically. The situation became much more serious, became something almost too embarrassing to talk about. He seemed to feel that he had done something wrong, that he had to make it up to me lest I plunge into depression. He had to disclose the whole story and make it known to everyone. It goes without saying that I objected to his feeling this way; objected to the fact that he wanted to tell everyone. I asked him if he was trying to make a fool of himself. In the end, the situation was completely impossible. He always felt he owed me a debt, and he had convinced himself that sooner or later our superiors would discover they were wrong and everyone would end up looking bad. I tried my hardest . . . I burned all the records I had made of what he had said in his dreams in front of him (and burning these was the best tactic I could use to bring him to his senses). But it all seemed to do little by way of curing him of his emotional anguish. Of course, destroying the originals didn't eliminate the possibility that I had taken copies, and no matter how much I swore I hadn't, how could I make him believe me? This situation didn't mean that your father had little trust in me. Instead, I believe he felt that this particular situation had tortured both of us to an unimaginable extent. Since he assumed that I was as agonized as he was, he supposed that my emotional state could have fractured at any minute. He thought I might even consider him an enemy, might feel as though I were a fish caught within a net struggling against an inevitable doom. Ever afterwards he had decided to do whatever he could to 'compensate' me, to console me, to remind me, to beseech me to swallow 'this matter', to bury it deep down, to keep it secret. And so, on his death bed, he had to counsel me on 'this matter' once more.

What else is there to say? We took our innocent consciences and ruined them. In this frame of mind, everything began to become complicated and confused. It all became a mess. I truly regret not having made a recording of what he had said while he was asleep. If I could have known what was going to happen, why would I have made all that fuss about not wanting to take credit? But that was then and this is now; what I did was out of a deep sense of the importance of the endeavour, out of respect and love for your father. Does that mean to suggest that I had no desire to be honoured? It was because I loved and respected him that I couldn't steal his glory. My heart just wouldn't let me do it. How could anyone know that things would turn out the way they did, that everything would become so terribly unbearable! But all of this – everything – none of it was created by us: the responsibility for that lies with those senior comrades who were too much concerned with appearances. At times, I can't help but feel that for your father ciphers weren't all that frightening. The things that scared him most were those things outside the world of cryptography, those things of the so-called real world. That was why life beyond those red walls was so difficult for him. He was unable to live the life of a normal man: such a life was a torture to him. Ciphers, on the other hand . . . I never once saw anything in them that caused him discomfort or concern. As you know, your father eventually returned behind those red walls, returned to the world of cryptography. This final time he was in charge of decrypting a new cipher called DESERT 2, also known as FLAME. It was the reserve cipher for FIRE.

FIRE had been in use for nearly twenty years by now, and had already begun to be phased out. Even if our adversaries had known we had broken the cipher, they still wouldn't have been using it because by that time they had already developed a new cipher know as SUNSHINE 111. Under these circumstances, they would never have used FLAME because it was too similar to FIRE. Once FIRE had been cracked, FLAME would have been compromised. Consequently, there was no real need to decipher it. So now you must be wondering why they asked your father to tackle this cipher. Well, to use Director Wang's words: they felt some loyalty to him; they wanted to give him something to do. You know what state of mind he was in – if things didn't change his problems would have become ever more intense, and eventually there'd have been no turning back. Director Wang told me that he was greatly worried about your father's condition; he would just get worse and worse if things carried on the way they were going. In order to prevent this, he arranged for your father to decipher FLAME. His purpose was clear: he wanted to immerse your father once more in the world of cryptography, to make him fight ciphers instead of that most devilish illness: senility. In other words, the organization decided to use ciphers to take care of him – to nip in the bud, as it were, the possibility of his illness becoming worse, to let him live out the last years of his life free of mental decrepitude. What man decides is not necessarily the same as heaven. Who could have guessed that his joy in being called back to work would be too hard on his heart; that being given this new cipher to solve would snatch his life away? From the day he re-entered that red-walled compound until he deciphered FLAME, your father needed only a little more than a hundred days. No doubt his quickness in cracking FLAME was due in large part to the experience gained in battling FIRE. It demonstrated once more your father's sublime ability in decrypting ciphers.

Ah, those of us who have been given to this profession live our life for ciphers, and we die for them as well. In your father's case, this is perhaps most accurate: the most perfect description for how he lived. The only thing denied to him was that until his death he was unable to decrypt his own cipher, the secret of 'that matter'. I have already told you the answer to this particular riddle; the only problem was that he refused to believe it. And so, at this very moment, I truly hope your father's spirit up in heaven can read the letter I have written to you. Perhaps in this way he will believe me, perhaps in this way he will be able to let go of the guilt and shame that followed him throughout those years. Whatever happens, you mustn't let Sisi read this letter. If she were to see it, she would feel that your father's last hundred days were yet another tragedy, which would only cause her even more grief . . .

Wind-Catchers

How wonderful it is to wake up in the morning and find out that one is still alive. Every operation could be our last. The work we do is the most secret and the cruellest there can be; an inopportune sneeze could mean our heads will roll. But death isn't frightening, since survival is not part of our calculations.

A Vietnamese Ghost Story

The second valley was divided into eastern and western court-yards. Walking into the eastern courtyard was like walking into a typical work unit: an administrative building stood to one side, a dormitory not too far off, an exercise yard to the other side, and everywhere there was the hustle and bustle of people. Once, this was Old Wang's realm, the training centre. The western courtyard, however, was nothing like that. There were only a few scattered buildings that seemed to be tucked away inside a lush green forest; there was little trace of human activity; all was silent and still. But it wasn't a peaceful silence; it was heavy, serious, almost smother-ing. The first time I found myself in there, the first time I felt this oppressive tranquillity, I had no idea that this was part of the centre for covert operations. I was under the impression it was used by Unit 701 for receiving and entertaining people from headquarters.

So I had to ask, 'How could this be part of the covert operations division?'

The answer was: 'If everyone just sat at home, how could they be conducting covert operations?'

You could say he hit the nail on the head.

The man who provided this answer was none other than Mr Lü, a senior intelligence officer – the one people called 'Old Potato'.

Mr Lü wasn't much of a talker, perhaps because of his long, soli-tary career in the underground. He didn't smoke either. Apparently during the 1970s, when China was engaged in the 'resist America, aid Vietnam' movement, Mr Lü was in Vietnam on active service, gathering intelligence. There was this one time, in the lobby of his hotel, that a young woman gave him a cigarette. Not long after-wards he collapsed and almost died . . . From that day on he swore off booze and cigarettes. Whenever he went out, he was always

In the Dark

smartly dressed, a camera hanging around his neck, a watch with a metal bracelet on his wrist, the appropriate hat for the season upon his head, two fountain pens in his chest pockets – he looked like a tourist. Were these things he carried with him weapons, tools of the trade . . . Well, I couldn't say. When I asked him, he said no, they weren't, but how could I believe him? He was an old hand at the spying game, Old Potato; you could believe what you saw, but not what came out of his mouth.

Mr Lü had a fascinating photo album. It was pretty old-fashioned; the cover was made from hand-woven coarse cloth, the pages were as yellow as could be and the binding was stitched together with hemp; the whole thing looked like something better off in the bin. When you looked through it, it was really odd. I say it was a photo album, but most of it wasn't actually photographs. Rather, it was overloaded with all manner of scraps of paper and clippings. The title page was adorned with half a cigarette paper with some handwritten notes on it. They read:

> How wonderful it is to wake up in the morning and find out that one is still alive. Every operation could be our last. The work we do is the most secret and the cruellest there can be; an inopportune sneeze could mean our heads will roll. But death isn't frightening, since survival is not part of our calculations. Hello there! I am fine right here.

Mr Lü told me that these lines were written by one of his superiors – a poet – not long after he had joined the underground. It was the very first time that they met. They were in a rickshaw when he wrote it; you could say it was like an old potato giving advice to a young one; it was also a souvenir of his first job. The year was 1947; he was a third-year student in Western Languages at the National Central University in Nanjing. Similar souvenirs would, without warning, present themselves over the years. Mr Lü said that since before liberation to after it, whether at home or abroad, from big events to small, from well-known operations to the anonymous ones, every job he undertook had this kind of 'testimony'. These were the things he kept in his photo album. In total, there were twenty-eight photos, eleven slips of paper, seven news-paper clippings and five pictures, as well as an assortment of odd objects such as an old steel coin with the centre drilled out, an envelope from a foreign country, and various receipts and busi-ness cards. Most items were accompanied by a word or two to explain them.

Out of all these bits and pieces, one photo piqued my curiosity. It was the picture of a dead man. There was an ugly hand that could be seen reaching into his breast pocket, as if about to steal his last possessions. Mr Lü explained that the hand hadn't 'stolen' anything; in fact, it was 'giving' something; the hand was giving a bank statement . . . and that the 'frightening-looking hand' was his own – he was giving the bank statement to a dead man . . . The whole thing is totally bizarre . . . Underneath the photo Mr Lü had written: 'My name is Vĩ Phu. Please don't call me Hồ Hải Dương.'

Mr Lü told me that the photo was of a young Vietnamese sol-dier, a man known to everyone as Hồ Hải Dương, even though his real name was Vĩ Phu. In life, the two were complete strangers, but in death they 'cooperated', in a manner of speaking, and per-formed a job that, to this day, Mr Lü considers a 'masterpiece'. However, he was quite prepared to admit that it was not his own idea; he based it on the famous Operation Mincemeat that was carried out during the Second World War. Operation Mincemeat was the work of two British intelligence officers: Ewen Montagu and Charles Cholmondeley. The main protagonist of this oper-ation was the corpse of a man named Glyndwr Michael, the time was the last day of April 1943, and the place was deep water off the coast of Huelva in Spain. On that day Michael's body was faked up to make it look like the corpse of Captain William Martin of the Royal Marines and from that moment it took on new life – it became Montagu and Cholmondeley's most important assistant. Indeed, this body accomplished its mission with a distinction that no living agent could have achieved. Mr Lü explained that he and this young Vietnamese man, Vĩ Phu, worked together in what was basically a replay of Operation Mincemeat. There was nothing new about it and even the 'surprise ending' was just the same.

There is a lot of documentation about Montagu and Cholmondeley's Operation Mincemeat, and about Mr Lü's re-creation of it,
probably because both of them were so remarkable and so successful. I have now accumulated several hundred thousand words
of testimony. In 1998, I accompanied a writer from the Ba Jin Lit-
erary Academy on a trip to Vietnam, where we visited the town Vĩ
Phu came from, a small place in the Lạc Sơn district of northwestern Vietnam. What we heard and what we saw would easily
amount to several hundred pages. It was after this field trip that I
felt I had finally gathered enough information, and knew how to
tell Vĩ Phu's story. I had the time period, the place, the background, the main characters, the supporting cast, the 'big' story
and the 'small' details. The only thing I had misgivings about was
that so many people had already told Vĩ Phu's story in so many
different ways. If I was unable to find my own path in telling this
tale – if I just regurgitated what had already been told – there
would be no point to it all. So I wanted to use a new method to tell
an old story. Eventually, I decided to tell it from the point of view
of Vĩ Phu's ghost. To tell the truth, the inspiration for approaching
the story in this manner owes much to what Mr Lü had written
beneath the photo of his corpse: 'My name is Vĩ Phu. Please don't
call me Hồ Hải Dương.'

Let the ghost speak from the other world. Listen, for it comes
from across the great divide . . .

1.

My name is Vĩ Phu.

Please let me say that again. My name is Vĩ Phu.

The reason I make such a point of my name being Vĩ Phu is that everyone's always calling me Hồ Hải Dương. Hồ Hải Dương isn't my real name – it's not even some nickname, or pseudonym, or pen name, or any such thing – it's actually the name of a complete stranger. I'd never even heard the name (let alone met the man) before, and I certainly never thought that the two of us would become so interconnected. But thirty years ago, for completely unforeseen reasons, I was mistaken for him. What's worse is that thirty years have passed and nothing has been done to correct this problem. It's an injustice that I can never be freed from; I have become Hồ Hải Dương for better or for worse. Quite honestly, I haven't stopped telling people that it's all a mistake; it's just that no one has listened. Relaying my plea from this world to the living isn't an easy thing to do . . . It's worse than fabricating a dream or using water to light a fire! Perhaps God has given me this seemingly insurmountable problem as a way to test my patience, or perhaps He is trying to explain something to me, I just don't know. Actually, come to think of it, understanding God's plan is something even more difficult. Oh yes, at times He seems to make His message plain, but more often than not He leaves us in a state of confusion, unsure as to what to do. *C'est la vie*, I suppose. Over here, we find God quite as puzzling as you do . . .

But I don't need to talk more about God. I need to talk about me.

I was born in 1946 in the northwestern part of Vietnam, in a small place called Lạc Sơn. My father was a tailor. He had a little wooden shack that hugged the side of one of the market streets; its walls were always adorned with all manner of clothes. A humid mist hung perpetually in the air, much like the entrance to a public bath-house. This was where I was born. This was my home. My very first memory was a 'zsst, zsst' sound. It was the ever-present sound of the steam iron being used on clothes. When I was ten, we moved house. We left our quiet two-room shack on North Street and moved to the hubbub of South Street; under a neon glare we rented a two-storey stone-built house, strong and sturdy. I think this demonstrates that Father attained certain advantages from being a tailor. But father didn't want us – me and my older sister, Vĩ Nạ – to follow in his footsteps – to spend our lives with a pair of scissors in one hand and a measuring tape in the other. He would always say, 'Given that I've made enough clothes for you, your children and grandchildren to wear, you two need to find your own path in life.'

Later on, Vĩ Nạ moved a bit further south to Cửu Long for work, and I entered the University of Hanoi. Before I left for university my father gave me a beautiful velvet-covered Chinese notebook, the size of a regular paperback, embroidered in gold with a four-clawed dragon. On the title page he inscribed: 'When the music and legends go silent, the architecture of a city still sings.'

I guess he wanted me to become an architect, or something along those lines. Unfortunately, in 1967, the final winter of my studies, while at home for the holidays, I contracted tuberculosis and never left my home town again. At that time, for someone to fall ill with tuberculosis was usually fatal. Whilst I didn't die, my life was completely turned upside down. For a good three years I couldn't lead a normal life: every day I'd be in hospital, then home; always taking medication, always worrying; I suffered a great deal over my own tragic fate. It goes without saying that with my waking hours consumed with worry over my disease I soon forgot all I had learnt at university. In actual fact, I only had one more semester to go to graduate with a degree in architecture. Later on, when it seemed as if I had got over the worst of it, my father advised me to return to Hanoi and spend another couple of months studying, but by then I simply had no interest in the subject. The tuberculosis had changed me. I began to think of his time spent within the vapours of steam irons in a new light. Further-more, given my father's age and experience, it seemed right that he should stand aside and give me pointers rather than having to exhaust himself. This is how I slowly became my father. The mem-ories of my illness faded, and I was content and happy with the 'zsst, zsst' sound of steam irons. This lasted right up until the day that American fighter jets tore through the sky, until the young people of the village rushed to the front lines, urged on by the call of the government and their relatives' tears. It was then that some-thing new called to me.

2

Là Kiệt had gone.

Lâm Quốc Tân had gone.

One day Mother told me that Tam from No. 32 had gone as well.

Then, from the southern front lines, a photo arrived of Vĩ Nạ in military uniform.

It was the summer of 1971. My friends and I, and other young people from the village, all wanted to enlist.

Ill as I had been for some years, I guess you could say I had reason not to enlist, and the military also had reason not to take me. In the spring of 1972, a naval unit arrived in the village looking again for new recruits. I tried once more to enlist, but the result was the same. A sympathetic officer looked at my health record, patted me on the shoulder and said, 'Next time. The war has just started; next time.'

To be honest, by that time I was fully recovered – I had even forgotten about the pain I had been through. I thought it was wrong that because I had been ill years earlier, this should determine my fate today . . . particularly since I had made a full recovery. I couldn't help but be furious: tuberculosis had already taken so much from me, I couldn't let it take more. Fortunately for me, the war had just started, and there was still a chance I could fight. In the autumn of the same year, three military divisions arrived in the village, again in search of recruits. One of the divisions was the same naval unit I had tried to enlist with in the spring. Without hesitating I went off to join up. Having learnt from previous experience, this time, on the enlistment card under the heading 'medical history', I didn't write anything. Leaving this blank, I thought they would accept me. However, the officer dealing with me (not the same man as before) saw me winded after only seven push-ups, so he politely declined my request to enlist. He told me, 'I think you'd be better suited to the army. They will want you.'

I had no choice. I went in search of the army recruiters. It turned out that the army didn't require all that much: they just spoke with me for a few minutes then handed me a uniform without any insignia. Of course, the fact that I wouldn't be wearing blue navy fatigues filled me with regret, but I really didn't have any other choice. The tuberculosis and the skilled nature of the tailoring business had conspired to make me frail, and the constant steam that billowed out from the irons had left my complexion pale and delicate. I must have appeared very feeble. I knew that if it weren't for the war, I'd never have been recruited. In a way, that I'd been accepted was just as Chairman Hồ Chí Minh had said in one of his broadcasts: war brings unexpected experiences to many men.

On 26 September in 1972, I and eight other young men hopped into an army transport and left the village of Lạc Sơn.

As the truck pulled away from the village I never once thought that this path I was now on would take me away from Lạc Sơn for ever.

3

I don't want to talk much about what it was like being in the army because on the one hand there just isn't much to talk about, and on the other, from my point of view, it would be completely pointless. What I mean is that, well, the whole experience just didn't match up to my expectations. I was unhappy most of the time, and it was incredibly gruelling, but not in a physical way. First, I should say that I wasn't accepted into the officer corps, but rather a 'special detachment'. As I understood things, at the time, graduates of Hanoi University were given the rank of executive officer, or company commander, or at worst, platoon leader. Even though I hadn't technically graduated, it was only the diploma that I didn't have, and I thought that compared to everyone else who had gone to university – well, I didn't think there was much of a difference between them and me; I thought I would be given the command of a platoon at least. But the army was a stickler for the rules and without a diploma – well, things didn't turn out as I had hoped. A farmer from just outside Hanoi – people said he was the grandson of some military commander – couldn't help but rub it in.

'Yes, it is true, but the problem is that you don't have a diploma, and you've no experience of working for the government. According to the rules, I can only assign you to a "special detachment", and that is really too good for the likes of you.'

Naturally, it being 'too good for the likes of me' didn't make me feel particularly pleased about this assignment.

Still, I resigned myself to the belief that being a soldier was the most important thing; after all I hadn't enlisted just to be an officer. I also didn't enlist because I felt inspired by Hồ Chí Minh's broadcasts. You could say that I was a lot more confused than most about my reasons for ending up in the army – in fact I could not have told you myself what I was doing there. Sometimes I think I enlisted because I just hated the American planes flying back and forth across the sky, terrifying those below. Then at other times, I think that this couldn't have been the reason, or at least that wasn't the only thing . . . there had to be something more, something I couldn't quite put my finger on, perhaps . . . maybe . . . I don't know. I really just don't know. But there was one thing I was sure about: right from the moment I joined the army, I was sure that there was no possible way I wouldn't make it to the front. In truth, such a wish was pretty dumb considering what was going on at the time, but the possibility of not being sent to the front lines just never occurred to me. Besides, I was quite convinced that wearing a uniform meant going to the front. It was only by going to the front, and taking part in battle, that wearing a uniform had any meaning. Therefore, when the crippled base commander À Ơn took me from the training grounds and sent me to a warehouse not far outside Hanoi, Uniform Warehouse No. 203 to be exact, and told me in no uncertain terms that from this day forward my sole military duty was to guard the front and rear gates of this warehouse, I was devastated and nearly cried!

Besides À Ơn, I had two other comrades. One was Old Đường, who had had the bottom half of his chin blown off by an artillery shell; the other was a noisy and mangy mutt. Could it be that I enlisted to prove that I wasn't a strong, strapping soldier, that I wasn't suited for the front, that perhaps I was only destined to spend the war with these people? I suddenly felt as humiliated as if someone had cheated me, as though the uniform I was wearing was not really my own, that I had stolen it from someone, that it was all some kind of trick.

Whilst I mightn't have been physically strong, I can say for certain that I didn't lack courage, if courage meant not being afraid. It's not that I wished to flaunt my bravery or the fact that I wasn't afraid to die, it's that just during my entire service I never once felt afraid. In boot camp, the sergeant who taught us to fire our rifles, a soldier who had been on the front lines and had returned, was a man we all called the 'One-Eyed Dragon'. That's because he had only one eye; apparently the other had been lost during a battle.

An explosion had ripped it free and hurled it into the Mekong, where it had been gobbled up by a giant thorn fish – perhaps a big male. He never once told us about his terrifying experiences. Once, when I asked him, he finally opened his mouth. But once he began speaking, he suddenly shut his one good eye and his whole body began to shake. It was obvious he had been traumatized by his experiences. But I never thought that it was frightening. From my point of view, what he experienced simply couldn't compare to the torture I had endured at the hands of tuberculosis. You could say that this disease had scarred my heart, but you could also say that my spirit had been forged by it. If there were any amongst us new recruits who were afraid of being sent to the front, I certainly wasn't one of them. I longed to be on the front lines, to be a part of this heroic conflict, to validate my bravery, my belief in myself. My only concern was that some unexpected horror on the field of battle would terrify me and that other people would despise me for it. That would have caused me pain, but I had never imagined that this – not being allowed to the front lines – would be the problem.

As the war expanded day by day, American bombers appeared with ever greater regularity in the skies above Hanoi, releasing their bombs. All too often we smelled the charred, heavy ash wafting through the air from the city. À Ơn worried that if things kept up in this fashion, it wouldn't be long before Hanoi would itself become the front line. I couldn't help but secretly long for that day to arrive. Because of this morbid yearning I knew that I had become a loathsome creature, that this was evil. But God knows that I never once cursed Hanoi, only my wasted life. As the workload increased, as the army quartermaster gave me more and more orders to fulfil, I realized that more and more men were hastening to the front. Everything that passed through my hands – each uniform, each helmet, each belt, each pair of gloves, each pair of shoelaces – was heading for the front line sooner or later; even if to begin with it went somewhere else, sooner or later it would be heading that way. From a certain point of view you could say that my sweat helped innumerable soldiers in countless battles, but could this prove anything? It only proved that I wasn't fighting myself. À Ơn often boasted to me, 'Ah, Vĩ Phu, you just don't understand – you're lucky you're here.'

Perhaps.

If it were up to me, I'd rather not have had this kind of good fortune. How could this be considered lucky? I spent my days with two cripples and one scruffy dog. Of course, what À Ơn said had some logic to it: the front certainly wasn't a fun place to be, and you wouldn't get anything out of it . . . in fact, it would have been stupid for anyone to go to the front longing for the fame and glory of war. As À Ơn warned me, 'With bullets flying this way and that . . . before you knew it you'd have something or other blown off, and you only have the one life to live.'

This I knew, of course.

But they just didn't understand. My desire to be on the front wasn't for fame and glory. Nor was it some kind of death wish. No. I just wanted to be with the boys, with the men I had come with. Assigning me to this hell hole – anyone would have thought that I was hiding out of sheer cowardice. God! Who could understand how lonely I was, how difficult everything was, how much I wanted to be as far away as possible from the crippled À Ơn and the pitiful Old Đường?

4.

I know, you humans are something else – or at least, you're cap-able of doing some astounding things. As for the things that haven't yet been done, you have faith that sooner or later you will do them. And those things that are not yet known, you have faith that you will, ultimately, know them. I lived for twenty-seven years: I know the greatness of humans, the confidence they have in themselves, but I also know that this greatness, this overconfi-dence can cause trouble, giving rise to bad habits – such as the penchant to procrastinate, to continually put things off. When I was alive, I was guilty of the same arrogance, perhaps even more so than most. Two instances will help to demonstrate this.

The first has to do with my marriage.

The second with the front.

I had so wanted to do these two things, but because . . . how to put this? I needed to first know that my life was not for ever; I needed to know that I would die. Perhaps then I would've been able to do both. But I didn't know. That is, I didn't know that my life would be so short, that I'd be so weak, so frail. Not long before I died, À Ơn, with tears streaming down his face, spoke these words to me, half crying, half cursing: 'Fuck! Every day, all day you'd keep on nagging and moaning about wanting to be on the front, and the first thing that goes wrong you die of it! You . . . Vĩ Phu, you're fucking useless . . . Vĩ Phu!'

To be honest, I had never seen a man cry like that. À Ơn . . . ah . . . you poor hopeless cripple, why'd you have to cry like that. Didn't you know? Those at death's door don't ever wish to see people cry like you did, it only makes their passing all the more painful. À Ơn, where are you now? I really miss you . . .

À Ơn wasn't the kind of person that people easily took to. He was a bit pompous, spoke too loudly, was too severe – his demeanour certainly didn't match his crippled body. But he was a good friend. I'd never betray him. Getting to know him – well, it was as though time patiently peeled back the layers. All those things that made him dislikeable were soon shorn away, and what was left – well, there was no way you could not like him. I became really quite fond of him. I still am, even though he should not have cried like that when I died. But I guess he didn't have much choice. Who told me to die next to him . . . I imagine if our situations had been reversed, I'd have cried like he did. I was very fond of him. I didn't know at the time that those dying didn't like to see those closest to them wail as À Ơn did: this was something I learnt after I died.

But what À Ơn said was right: it was the first little thing that killed me. It's been almost half a century now, but I still remember that day. It was winter – winter again! And you should appreciate this fact, for it was ten years before that, during winter, that I had first become ill, when I had first drawn close to death's door. That season, winter, seemed to toll the death knell for me . . .

That evening was the same as every other . . . With my radio in hand, I had gone to bed. The loneliness of this assignment had made me grow attached to listening to the radio – without it I'd have never been able to get to sleep. Because I always scanned the airwaves for a female voice, À Ơn had often made fun of me, saying that I wasn't holding onto a radio at all, but rather my ideal woman. Perhaps he was right . . . I just don't know. I didn't understand women; I still don't. I don't know what I think about them. I mean, there were times that I thought about them a lot, and then at other times I didn't think about them at all. Hmm . . . let's not talk about them right now, shall we? I'll have more to say later: let's concentrate on that night. Crawling into bed with my radio, I couldn't help but feel that something wasn't right. My head felt heavy, befuddled, and I was so cold. I told À Ơn about it, to which he replied, 'Hey, on such a cold wintry night, after a cold shower, who'd think it was warm? I'd find it chilly myself.'

'But I think I'm running a fever,' I said.

À Ơn came close and felt my forehead. 'Eh, you might be right.

In the Dark

Oh, but it's nothing: you're just tired, that's all. Turn off the radio and go to sleep. You'll feel right as rain after a good night's sleep.'

I couldn't help but think the same, and so I shut off the radio and settled down to sleep. It was already past four in the morning. We had been run ragged, me, À Ơn and Old Đường. The night before, Army Unit 179 had requisitioned winter blankets; they'd cleaned out nearly half of the warehouse, working us to exhaustion in the process. Later on, I thought that if I had just gone straight off to bed once our work had been done then I'd have been all right, but I was covered in sweat and reeking – I had to take a shower. It was Old Đường's turn to heat the water, but he couldn't. He was too tired, he said; so I decided to just quickly hop into a cold shower. We had just finished work and my body was boiling hot, so the idea of a cold shower didn't seem all that bad, and certainly not frightening. So I had my wash. Afterwards, I lay in my bed for a bit, listening to the radio, but unlike normally when my blanket would gradually fill with warmth, the opposite happened: it got colder and colder. I told À Ơn this, to which he replied, 'Hey, on such a cold wintry night, after a cold shower, who'd think it was warm? I'd find it chilly myself.'

'But I think I'm running a fever,' I said.

À Ơn replied, 'Turn off the radio and go to sleep. You'll feel right as rain after a good night's sleep.'

That's what I did.

The following afternoon when À Ơn woke up, he asked me how I was doing. My body felt as though it were on fire. I thought of telling him this, but my body just wouldn't listen. I couldn't open my mouth. A short while after, I heard À Ơn say, 'Fuck! How can you be burning up like this? Vĩ Phu? Wake up, Vĩ Phu! Open your eyes . . . it's me, À Ơn!'

Reality always repeats itself; change is temporary. When I finally opened my eyes, I saw what looked to be at least three blurred À Ơns frantically moving back and forth. I had the same feeling as I had had ten years before when tuberculosis first attacked my body – it was exactly the same . . .

5

When people are unconscious time has no meaning. When I finally awoke, I had no idea how much time had elapsed, nor did I know where I was. The brightness shining in through the windows and the trees standing tall outside made it clear that I was no longer at Warehouse No. 203. A young woman, mouth covered with a surgical mask, expressed surprise and happiness at my awakening; her accent made me think that I had returned home. She told me I hadn't, however. Rather, this was the military hospital near Hanoi; I had been here a couple of days already. She pulled down her surgical mask and spoke. 'I've seen your records. I know you're from Lạc Sơn; I'm from Duy Phổ.'

Her home town wasn't even ten kilometres from my own. It boasted a well-known zoo; every child in Lạc Sơn had visited it. Before the war, I actually had an older cousin who worked there. When I told her his name she broke down in tears. It goes without saying that she knew him, and that he had died in the fighting. Apparently he had fallen during what the Americans called the Easter Offensive. Two months earlier they had actually been part of the same convoy, and that was when they got to know each other a bit. War brings all kinds of people together and forges friendships; now I too had become her friend . . . her name was Ngọc.

Ngọc made sure that I was well looked after, that I received proper treatment for my illness. At her behest, a doctor by the name of Blanchet, the son of British parents, checked in on me every couple of days, repeatedly adjusting my treatment. Blanchet was the head doctor of the hospital and so he was responsible for looking after a great number of patients. More and more came every day, all returning from the front, all wearing uniforms adorned with various insignias of rank, all having served in the most difficult of circumstances . . . And then there was me, a regular tuberculosis case; no doubt Blanchet's concern for me was the result of Ngọc's efforts.

Besides ensuring that I was well looked after, Ngọc also made sure to combat my loneliness. Because I was suffering from tuberculosis, very few people wanted to be near me – in fact, they had placed me in an isolation ward. During the cold winter days, this particular ward was boiling hot, but even that couldn't drive away my dreary solitude. Only Ngọc could do that. She'd often come round to chat – day after day we'd talk of home.

Then one day Ngọc brought À Ơn along with her. Remarkably, À Ơn carried with him a letter from Vĩ Nạ, now based in Tháp Phước, near Huế. In her letter, Vĩ Nạ wrote that she had got married; her husband was a machine-gunner in the armed forces serving near Tháp Phước, hence her reason for being there. While she didn't give specifics, she did write, 'Compared to where I was stationed before, this is the real front line.'

Every day I listened to the radio. I knew that the fighting around Tháp Phước was particularly intense, but I couldn't criticize her decision. In war, what we hope to do and what we actually do are not often the same, and besides, she had a good reason for being there: she was with her husband.

Vĩ Nạ had also included a photo with her letter. It was of the two of them together, standing proudly alongside an awesome-looking machine-gun bunker; it seemed as though its guns were sighting an American plane somewhere out of camera range. When I showed Ngọc the photo she smiled and laughed, and then said, 'I thought it was a letter from your wife. Who is she?'

I told her.

'And your wife . . . ?' she asked impatiently.

In a highly affected manner, À Ơn answered for me. 'A wife? He's married? He should have a wife, but, in truth, he hasn't even got a girlfriend, let alone a wife – isn't that true, Vĩ Phu?'

I was too mortified to speak.

But À Ơn just wouldn't shut up. He turned round and in a voice that made my skin crawl, said, 'Ngọc, would you believe that poor old Vĩ Phu here is still a virgin?'

I had no one to blame but myself; I had told him this . . . and it was true. How could I have known that he wouldn't've believed me; that he thought I was joking? Fuck. À Ơn . . . he just couldn't keep a secret . . . worse than a bloody parrot.

At first, Ngọc seemed rather embarrassed by À Ơn's forthrightness, but as the moment passed, she drew close to À Ơn and spoke in a low voice. 'Ah . . . I understand your meaning; you mean to say that . . . Vĩ Phu still has much . . . ah . . . much that he needs to do . . . and so it's imperative that he recovers quickly . . .'

The next day, Ngọc came round and made sure to ask if what À Ơn had said was true.

I deflected her query by saying, 'Don't tell me that you think it might be true?'

6.

To be honest, my character and my body conspired against me; prevented me from knowing women. There was this one time, long ago, when a young woman seemed to be interested in me, but I can't even remember her name now. I don't mean to say that I was fickle or disinterested; it's just that there wasn't much between us, and even if there was, it was just the possibility of a relation-ship. I mean, something might have developed between us, but because of my timidity, nothing ever happened. I don't know what brought this young woman to Lạc Sơn, but I know she wasn't from around there. As my father said, there wasn't a young lady in their entire area he didn't know. Of course, what he meant was that he knew the clothes they wore; after all, he had stitched them.

The first time I saw her, she'd shown up at our shop, her eyes hid-den behind a pair of sunglasses. She chose some fabric and asked my father to make her a new blouse. He passed the order on to me – he knew straightaway that she wasn't from Lạc Sơn; he didn't recognize her clothes. Perhaps that's why he gave me the job; she wasn't from around there. At any rate, it was pretty much my first order. I am happy to say that both my father and the customer were satisfied. In fact, she was really pleased with it when she paid for it. As I watched her walk out with her parcel, as I stared at the figure she cut, I couldn't help but feel rather self-satisfied. The following day, however, she returned, her new blouse in her hand. Smiling softly she said there was a slight problem. I asked her what it was. She held up the blouse to show me, but I couldn't see anything wrong with it. She held up the arms and showed me the cuffs, laughing ever so slightly. 'I am sure this wasn't what you intended, but look: are you sure the cuffs should open this way?'

Then I saw what was wrong: I had sewn them on backwards. It

was really embarrassing. My father seemed even more humiliated than I was, and he laid into me. Fortunately, the one person who should've been upset wasn't. She seemed to think Father was over-reacting, and said with a smile, 'Hey, what's wrong with you? Is it something that can't be easily fixed? Just re-sew it; it's not a big deal.'

I don't know why she was so nice to me; perhaps it was just her nature. In any case, she was the best customer I ever had. As I re-stitched her blouse, I kept thinking about how I could make it up to her. Finally, I wrote a little note and tucked it away inside the pocket of her newly mended shirt. A few days later, she replied with a note of her own, asking me to meet her at the coffee shop near the village's south gate.

Meeting outside the café, we soon discovered that there was nowhere to sit, and so we decided to go for a stroll. I noticed she was wearing the blouse I had sewn for her. She told me she adored it; that looking at it made her think of me. I knew what she was getting at, but I couldn't figure out why. On our second date we went to the cinema; on the way there, in the quiet darkness of the early evening, she reached out her hand and took mine in hers. It was an evening like no other. I never would have thought that on my return home my father would see it fit to bombard me with questions, warning me: 'It doesn't matter who she is, or where she is from: it's over now. We have to think about your health.'

Father was right – at the time I still wasn't fully recovered. It wasn't the right time for a relationship. The problem was, if I waited until I was completely better, who'd be left? Would Father help me get in touch with her again? To be honest, before meeting Ngọc, this young girl was the only woman I had thought of, the only one who could stir such sweet emotions within me, such pleasant memories – but I never did find out what happened to her, where she went; even if she was still alive. She just disappeared into thin air. Although I could imagine her living somewhere out there, I had no idea how to find her.

I must have looked very upset when I spoke of this. To comfort me, for the first time Ngọc took my hand in hers and said, 'Vĩ Phu, I'm sure she must be somewhere waiting for you. Somewhere, I hope you will be able to find her, find your true love . . .'

Ngọc was overflowing with affection and kindness . . . thinking about her sympathy then is my most precious memory of being alive.

7

Losing loved ones during war is an all too common occurrence, but this doesn't mean that the pain is somehow lessened. It was on the 17th, 17 January 1973, that Vĩ Nạ's company, including her husband, was obliterated by an American B-52 bombing run, a final sortie of their Operation Linebacker II. I imagined what it must have been like: Vĩ Nạ, staring up into the sky as the bombers approached – a tiny, insignificant ant unable to escape.

The news of my sister's death did little to help my recovery: in fact, it made things worse. The fever took hold of me once again and seemed unwilling to let me go. A few days later, Blanchet came to see me, but he didn't say anything, he just stood at the foot of my bed, pondering something, and then left. I knew I was going to die.

That same day, as the sun set, Ngọc came round and gave me the same bit of news. I must say, however, that her method of relaying such bad news was entirely unexpected. That evening, as unconsciousness began to pull me under, I felt an icy draught pass across my face. I opened my eyes with difficulty and saw Ngọc standing alongside my bed gazing at me intently. I had never seen such intensity in her eyes. I had a premonition that she was about to tell me what Dr Blanchet had failed to that afternoon. With what little strength I could muster, I reached out and clutched her hand. 'Ngọc, you don't need to say anything. I know . . . Blanchet has already told me.'

'Eh? Dr Blanchet said that at this moment . . . your body is rallying all its energies to combat the illness, and that's a good thing.' She held onto my hand as tightly as possible. 'Fever is a good sign: it means your body is fighting the disease, it means you're strong, and getting stronger. It means you're going to be all right.'

I closed my eyes; there was nothing I could say. In the darkness, I felt Ngọc manoeuvre my hand onto something soft and warm. I heard her say, 'Vĩ Phu, this is yours. Do you like it?'

I struggled to open my eyes once again. Her white dress was pulled down past her shoulders, exposing her shimmering, silvery flesh. My hands had been placed upon her firm bosom – lost in the soft brightness of her skin. I thought I was dreaming, but Ngọc told me it was no dream.

'Vĩ Phu, I'm sure that once you're better we can get married, right? Please don't think I'm too forward, but I want to be with you . . . tonight . . .'

My eyes were fully open now.

Calmly she let her gown fall to the floor and gingerly climbed under the blankets.

The white gown was all she had been wearing.

God! Not in my wildest dreams could I have imagined her telling me I was going to die in such a fashion.

During that night – it wasn't all that long – I finally knew what it meant to be with a woman. Death ceased to matter. Three days later, with no regrets, only boundless joy, I happily departed your world.

Thank you, Ngọc. Goodbye!

8.

From here on, what I'll tell you about happened after I died.

It's often said that ill people – all ill people, regardless of what they may be suffering from – die at a certain time. Those with weak hearts tend to expire in the mornings, those with tuberculosis find the darkness of the night most amenable. I died in 1973, 28 January, at 2:38 in the morning right on schedule. Ngọc, À Ơn and Dr Blanchet were there to see me off. Compared to Ngọc, À Ơn lacked the proper preparation and so the shock of my death hit him hard. The last thing I saw were the tears flowing down his face, uninterrupted, mournful, devastated . . .

I used to believe that once a man died, there would be nothing he had left to say, but that's not how it is. In fact, my story, my brilliance all came after I died. Death is a passageway from one world unto the next; when death extinguished the light of my life, it also divested me of my sickly, weak, frail body. You could say that as a corpse I had nothing left to be ashamed of. After I entered the mortuary, I felt much better about myself. To be fair, in this place, one didn't really see whole undamaged bodies. Compared to those that I did see, mine was quite satisfactory: no scars or wounds of any kind; nor was it aged and decrepit. I am sure that when Bureau Chief Lü stood next to my body, he would have been struck by that point.

Bureau Chief Lü arrived in the afternoon of the day I died; Dr Blanchet accompanied him. I didn't know this man; nor would I have even known his name if it weren't for the fact that Blanchet mentioned it. I also found out that he was Chinese, one of those who had come to assist in our fight against the Americans. In military fashion they inspected each of the corpses in the morgue, exchanging words I couldn't understand. But I could tell they were looking for someone in particular. When they made their way to

stand in front of me, I could tell that Bureau Chief Lü had difficulty concealing his delight. 'Eh, who's this?'

Dr Blanchet quickly related my story, whereupon Bureau Chief
Lü replied, 'He's the one. He's what I've been looking for.'

A moment later an older man entered the room, pulled me off
the mortuary slab and lifted me onto a gurney so I could be
wheeled into an adjacent room. The orderly then bathed my body
and dressed me in a new, clean hospital gown. I knew then that
they were getting me ready for the crematorium. The only thing I
couldn't fathom was why they hadn't dressed me in my military
fatigues. Was I always going to be treated as a patient? I couldn't
help but feel miserable.

Upon leaving the mortuary I was transferred to Bureau Chief
Lü's jeep. The seats were packed with cases of medicine, so I was
laid on the floor. I guess they never realized that I wouldn't be able
to stay still. Needless to say, as the jeep bounced along the roads I
was tossed this way and that; eventually, a box of medicine fell
from its seat and pinned me to the floor. Bureau Chief Lü heard
the thump and peered behind him to see if anything was amiss,
but I guess he never noticed my unflattering position, or perhaps
he didn't care. This demonstrates, I believe, the differences between
the living and the dead: if you are alive, even if it is the last moment
of your life, no one would dare treat you like that. Conversely, if
you are dead, and even if you have only been dead an instant,
everyone treats you like dirt. Of course, the reason behind this
unconcerned treatment of the dead is plain: so-called 'humanity'
is only about protecting those like themselves; once they are dealing with a dead body 'humanity' is no longer an issue – they
abandon what makes them living persons. In a sense, the living in
this kind of situation are no better than the dead.

The jeep stopped and started, bouncing this way and that. Outside the window, the sky grew hazy. I had no idea where Bureau
Chief Lü was taking me, but I knew it must be somewhere rather
far away, definitely not in Hanoi. We passed by clamorous street
after clamorous street. Then we seemed to be on some larger

boulevard, speeding along as if we were the only vehicle on it. I was certain then that we had left Hanoi.

Could a city as large as Hanoi not have a crematorium?

Who was this Bureau Chief Lü?

Why had the hospital turned me over to him?

Where was he taking me?

For the whole journey, these questions plagued my mind.

When we finally stopped, I could smell the sea in the air and hear the sound of radio broadcasts. Even before the jeep had pulled to a stop, a young man wearing a Chinese navy uniform welcomed him and reached near to open his door. His manner was incredibly respectful and deferential, suggesting he wasn't an officer, or, at best, a navy ensign. I soon learnt that he was from Jiangsu Province, but I never learnt his name. I just took to calling him the man from Jiangsu, or 'Su', for short.

It was obvious that I wasn't at a crematorium, so I wondered where they had taken me. Later I discovered the answer: Harbour No. 201; a small port leased to the Chinese People's Liberation Army. Why had they brought me here? I was completely confused about the whole situation.

Once Bureau Chief Lü had stopped the jeep and got out, he came round to the back and opened the rear door. Gesturing to my feet, he said, 'This is him. I'm giving you an hour, and only an hour. I will be waiting for you on our submarine, the *Yangtze*.'

Su unloaded my corpse and carried me off to a brightly lit room. It was there that he attended to my entire body, being careful even to trim my nose hairs and clean the plaque from my teeth. All of this took the better part of half an hour, and I couldn't help but think that such delicate, circumspect treatment had to be reserved for officers of the highest rank, or at least those who had distinguished themselves in combat, rather than a corpse.

Things only got stranger.

In fact, the strangest was yet to come. Once Su had finished, he began to dress me: underpants, kneepads, undershirt, socks, shirt, trousers, overcoat – everything the same, layer upon layer, from inside to out: all of it was the uniform of a navy officer, of not insignificant rank, I must say. As you know, serving in the navy was my dream, but who could have known that it would come true in this fashion? Even more bizarre, once I was dressed, Su carefully strung a platinum cross and chain (no doubt a talisman of some sort) around my neck and then an incredibly fancy watch around my wrist (a French brand). I wondered why on earth, if my corpse was to be sent off to the crematorium, did they dress me so, especially with such expensive jewellery? If I weren't dead, such attire would surely be fit only for meeting senior officers.

Of course, I wasn't destined to attend such a meeting; I was destined to be loaded on board the submarine called the *Yangtze*. Upon seeing the work Su had done, Bureau Chief Lü was very pleased. He looked me up and down and affirmed, 'Not bad . . . not bad at all. It's just what I wanted; very good, he looks just like a professor's son.'

I knew my father was at most a moderately successful businessman: when on earth had he become a professor? Then it dawned on me. I knew why they had cleaned and dressed me in this uniform: they were going to pass off my corpse as that of the son of this professor. Maybe this professor's son had served on this sub (say as an interpreter) and unfortunately for him, he had been unluckier than I: he had died and they didn't even have a body to present to his father. How could a father say goodbye to his son without at least a body to grieve over? That was why they had brought me here. I guess I must have resembled him. Heh, heh, stranger things have happened, I suppose . . .

While I was mulling the situation over, Bureau Chief Lü and Su had quietly vacated the room. I assumed that the professor would be arriving at any moment; perhaps they had even gone off to meet him at the dock. I knew for certain that I wasn't anywhere near Hanoi. For this professor to come so far to see where his son had fought and died, to risk his own life in the process . . . It is the most pitiable duty for a parent: to bury their own child. Coming at night was a wise choice, since at that time the Americans rarely made bombing raids at night. How much I respected that professor!

Even though I wasn't his son, at that moment I felt the same filial love as his son must have done, and hoped that everything would go well for him.

Everything was quite different from what I had expected. Not long after Bureau Chief Lü departed, the sub began to pull away from the dock – swaying at first, before diving like some grand metallic fish. I began to wonder: if this professor wasn't in Hanoi, just where was he? Somewhere even further away? As you should all know, during wartime a submarine doesn't just nonchalantly steam out into the harbour and sail away. To arrange this whole charade, to give this professor a last chance to see his dead son – even if it wasn't his son he'd be actually seeing – to dispatch a submarine to carry out this dangerous mission; well, it became clear that this professor wasn't just anyone. He must've been someone of enormous prestige and importance.

As the submarine navigated out to sea, I could only wonder where they were taking me.

I'd never been on a submarine before, never realized how enjoyable being on one could be. To be honest, it was sort of like being rocked in a cradle, ever so gently. I felt as though I were young again, a babe in my mother's embrace. It was all like a dream, my first dream after dying. People who are still alive never remember their firsts – not the first colour they see, the first sound they hear, the first dream they have. But for those of us who are dead, all these firsts seem to be waiting for us, and so we remember them all. Not only do I remember this first death-sleep, I also remember when I awoke from it. This is how it was: someone had burst into the room, carelessly knocking over the hat stand that stood near the door, and let loose an unearthly sound that startled me awake. I didn't know who he was, but he had the look of a seaman. Without saying a word, he hauled me from the bed and dragged me out through the door before propping me up against a small airlock. A moment later I heard Bureau Chief Lü shout, 'Bring me the sea charts!'

I could now see Bureau Chief Lü. He had just emerged from the corridor.

Su, the same one who'd cleaned me up, appeared with sea charts in his hand. Perhaps it was because of the gentle swaying of the submarine, but the two of them knelt down beside me and spread the charts across my corpse.

'What is our position?' Bureau Chief Lü asked.

'Here,' Su indicated. 'Bạch Nhà Loãng beach. We're about ten nautical miles away from our objective.'

'What are the wind and wave conditions?' asked Bureau Chief Lü.

'Ideal. Under these conditions, by morning it'll wash ashore.'

Bureau Chief Lü considered the time, then turned to the seaman. 'Heave!'

The seaman opened the latch and flung me overboard.

I could never have imagined that this would be my fate.

9

My story and my unforgettable experiences advance step by step.

As I've said, thirty years ago, due to unforeseen circumstances, people mistook me for Hồ Hải Dương. More distressing, at least for me, is that for these past thirty years this mistake has remained unaddressed, and so I have remained Hồ Hải Dương, for better or worse. It goes without saying that this was not what I wanted and unfair, so I feel it's important to explain things. Finally, here and now, I wish to clarify my connection with this Hồ Hải Dương.

Things happened just as Bureau Chief Lü had hoped: the sea deposited my corpse on Bạch Nhà Loãng beach early in the morning, where I was soon discovered by two fishermen. I must say, I've always suspected that these two fishermen probably weren't fishermen at all, but rather Chinese operatives. Why, you may ask? Well, because upon discovering me they showed absolutely no concern for searching my corpse for valuable possessions; instead, they immediately reported their discovery to the US forces stationed nearby. All they got for me was a reward from the Americans.

My identity (a naval officer of the Vietnamese People's Army) immediately drew serious attention from the American military. Several of their operatives were dispatched to the scene in order to recover my body and return it to base. Once in their possession, I was given a thorough inspection. I knew they must be searching for classified documents or other military papers, but I was, after all, only an army orderly, charged with guarding a warehouse – how could I possibly be in possession of classified documents? But what they found proved that I had completely misunderstood the situation.

This is what they discovered:

1. A naval officer's ID and serial number identifying me as an operative of a special services division. My name: Hồ Hải Dương.
2. One photo of a beautiful woman, signed with the name Tuyết Nhi, together with two love letters from her.
3. A letter from home, identifying my father as someone of great political influence, a professor of something or other.
4. A bank statement, suggesting that I was the self-indulgent son of rich parents; a 'Little Prince'.
5. One top-secret document, written by the second-in-command of the Chinese forces sent to aid Vietnam. The document was addressed to the admiral of the VPA's naval forces. It seemed to divulge top-secret battle plans requesting naval support for an assault against the American forces stationed along the fourth defensive perimeter. It also revealed that at the time of the assault, decoy manoeuvres were planned along the seventh defensive perimeter.

I never suspected that I was in possession of such papers, especially such important top-secret documents. No one else knew, but I understood that this was all part of Bureau Chief Lü's plot. I may have been confused about what was going on before, but that was over now: I had completed the mission entrusted to me by Bureau Chief Lü. All that remained was to see whether the Americans believed it or not. Of course, I was hoping that they would. But what I wanted was of no account. Whether the curse I had brought upon them would come true, I would have to wait and see.

Compared to the secret documents I was carrying, my body itself was insignificant. However, it may have served its purpose in the grander scheme of things. I was expecting that they would simply throw my corpse back into the sea, but they didn't; they actually buried me. They put my grave next to the sea, and in doing so, the ebb and flow of the tide prevented me from resting peacefully. But at least the location allowed me to look into the distance towards home. Most people don't think much about their home when they're there, but when they're not, home is never really far from their minds. Whilst lying in my rather cold and cheerless grave, I often pondered the outcome of my 'mission' and wondered what the Americans did about it.

About two weeks later, the smell of flowers wafted through the air around my desolate grave, causing me to open my eyes. Standing in front of my rather dreary burial mound was a woman in a long windbreaker, her hands clasping a bouquet of roses. I didn't recognize her, and I couldn't imagine that anyone from this horrible place would have known me, and so I thought she must have come to the wrong grave. After all, since the war began, this whole area had begun to fill up with so many graves, many of them unmarked, that it would not be surprising if she had gone to the wrong one.

But when she opened her mouth and spoke I was amazed: she was telling me what I most wanted to know. She said that the Americans had fallen for it; they had had no reason to suspect the accuracy of the documents I had been carrying and so they hastily transferred their forces from the seventh perimeter to the fourth. Once the Americans had finished moving their troops, the VPA had launched its assault on the now weakened seventh line of defence and swarmed through the remaining American lines. It was a great victory. Finally, she said, 'Hồ Hải Dương, Bureau Chief Lü has sent me here to convey the gratitude of the Chinese army. You have made an outstanding contribution to your country and your people; you will be honoured for ever . . .'

I told her I wasn't Hồ Hải Dương. I told her I was Vĩ Phu. Vĩ Phu!

But did she hear me?

Will anyone ever hear me?

Such words are hard to convey across the boundary between life and death. I don't understand: did God burden me with this injustice as a test or is He trying to explain something? As I said before, trying to understand the plan God has in store for us is beyond difficult. At times He seems to make his message plain, but more often than not He leaves us in a state of confusion, unsure as to what to do. *C'est la vie*, I suppose. Over here, we find God quite as puzzling as you do . . .

God, when will I be heard?